First published 2023

First printed edition published 2024 by Drollery Ltd.

Copyright © Alice Coldbreath, 2023

ISBN 978-1-916736-11-5

I0564137

More books available by Alice Coldbreath:

The Vawdrey Brothers Series:

Book 1: Her Baseborn Bridegroom

Book 2: His Forsaken Bride

Book 3: An Ill-Made Match

The Brides of Karadok Series:

Book 1: Wed By Proxy

Book 2: The Unlovely Bride

Book 3: The Consolation Prize

Book 4: Her Bridegroom, Bought and Paid For

Book 5: An Inconvenient Vow

Book 6: The Favourite

The Victorian Prizefighter Series:

Book 1: A Bride for the Prizefighter

Book 2: A Substitute Wife for the Prizefighter

Book 3: A Contracted Spouse for the Prizefighter

I would like to dedicate this one to Angela Rogero, for pointing out an obvious truth that I was too blind to see!

~ Alice

Kinnerton

Jane trudged on, following her cloaked guide as they skirted the large gray stone house, keeping to the shelter of the shrubberies. The branches and leaves were wet and dripped water droplets onto her already-sodden cloak and hood.

She felt utterly wretched, and the cold, wet night in January accounted for only part of her misery. When she thought of how she had left things at the palace, she could not help but quake in her slightly damp boots. Her sister's letter had stressed the fact that time was of the essence and begged her not to delay.

As such, Jane had been forced to forgo the usual courtesies of requesting royal permission for her absence of leave. She had simply fled her post, and she knew exactly how Queen Armenal would view this abandonment despite the letter she had left explaining her behavior.

It was not as though there weren't plenty of other ladies at court vying to take Jane's place as royal favorite. An influx of northern ladies had captured the Queen's fancy of late. First, there had been Magnatrude Bartree, who was already encroaching on Jane's special duties, and then there was Lady Wymarka Kloch with her astrology and her predictions for the future, which the Queen seemed to find so amusing.

That was not even taking into account the usual courtiers hovering on the Queen's periphery. There were Constance Northcott and Margaret Pryor, both of whose ever-changing matrimonial prospects were a constant source of diversion to the Queen. Then there was the usual bevy of young lovelies the Queen kept on the outskirts until they did something she deemed worthy of notice, the likes of Osanna Spencer and her crowd.

Jane bit her lip. Seen in any light, the step she had taken was rash considering her precarious position at court. Then, of course, there was the fact her sister was the King's official mistress… This made an already-foolhardy course of action positively *disastrous*. The Queen would likely never forgive her for her betrayal.

Suddenly, the figure in front of Jane stopped and swept aside a curtain of vines, revealing a small arched doorway. The hooded figure turned back to face her. "'Tis this way, milady," she whispered, raising a finger to her lips.

Jane nodded and was glad they had reached the concealed entrance. She did not relish creeping around in the dark and cold, and their lantern had been extinguished as soon as they had reached the house. The estate the King had gifted her sister was a fine country property surrounded by thick woodland. Jane, however, had lived in cities since she turned thirteen, and a hooting owl nearby almost had her jumping out of her skin.

The young woman struck upon the door in a series of raps, and a moment later, Jane heard a key turn in the lock. The door opened silently, and to her relief, Jane recognized the face peering out of it, shrouded in a gigantic wimple. It was Ayleth, a servant who had originally been their mother's before she had accompanied both sisters to court.

Jane's shoulders relaxed just a tiny bit. It was not that she had suspected foul play, but she was just not used to all this subterfuge. She understood from her sister's letter that their uncle Phillip had joined her sister's household of late and she did not want him to know of Jane's visit. At least, not until she first had some private speech with her. *Why though?* Uncle Phillip and Helen had always been thick as thieves.

Ayleth skewered her with a faintly accusatory look—she had always favored Helen over Jane—and then ushered them inside, closing the door firmly behind them and turning the key. Jane walked past the old Cecil family servant without acknowledgment, following her silent guide up a set of winding steps.

At the top of the steps, Jane found herself in a large handsome bedchamber swathed with purple curtains and a lot of formal, dark-looking furniture. It looked nothing like a room her sister would have furnished, for Helen had always loved things uncluttered and airy, yet there, in the middle of a large square bed, lay the sister she had not seen in almost a year and a half.

"Helen!" she uttered, hurrying forward. When her sister lay pale and unresponsive, Jane whirled about to face the composed young woman who had led her here. "What ails her?"

"Let me take your cloak," the other said, holding out a hand.

Jane shrugged off her wet cloak and the young woman efficiently spread it before the fire. *What was her name?* Jane's mind turned momentarily blank, no doubt from the stress and strain of her two-day journey.

Helen must have written it in the letter Jane received three days ago, bidding her to travel at once to The Crooked Cross, meet her servant at midnight, and follow her to Kinnerton. *Beth, that was it.* Jane thought the name suited her well, for she had pleasant features and a neat, modest appearance.

Beth drew a chair for her up to the side of the bed. "Sit here, my lady, and speak soft and low. Ayleth will moisten my lady's lips with wine, and she will be roused presently."

Jane allowed herself to be ushered into the chair and then sat gazing in horror at her sister's waxen features. Helen's letter had not lied, or even exaggerated. She was grievously ill. It was the unnatural pallor to her sister's complexion that alarmed her the most. Helen had always been such a glowing picture of health.

Jane darted her eyes about the room but could see no crib. Had the babe died or had someone else taken charge of it? Helen's letter had been so disjointed, nothing more than a passionate plea to see her only sister, while she still had time.

"Has she seen a priest?" Jane asked, looking first at Beth and then at Ayleth, who was hovering close.

"She didn't want no priest," Ayleth responded fiercely. "Just you. Said she'll take you for her confessor."

"Ayleth!" Beth remonstrated, then paused a moment. "You will shock the Lady Jane," she added in a calmer tone.

"I am not so easily offended," Jane responded. "And besides, I know Ayleth of old." She wondered how long Beth had served her sister. It could not have been for more than eighteen months, as Jane had never heard of her. "It is not so many years since there were no secrets at all between us sisters," Jane continued, reaching out and taking Helen's hand in hers. It felt cool to the touch. She turned back to Beth. "You may leave us now."

Beth's eyes widened, and she looked for a moment as though she would argue, before lowering her gaze respectfully. "I will take myself off to a quiet corner," she murmured, "but I could

4

not stray far, in case my mistress should need me." She curtseyed and retreated to the far side of the room before quietly taking a seat and picking up some needlework.

Jane exchanged a glance with Ayleth, who bore a look of sulky resentment on her wrinkled face. "In whose employ is she?" Jane asked softly. "The King's or my uncle's?"

"She be warming your uncle's bed," Ayleth responded viciously. "Or so half the servants' hall reckons."

Jane dismissed this as mere gossip and spite. Beth looked nothing like the mistresses her uncle Phillip squired about town. He favored bold, forward women who commanded the eye. Beth was not that type, looking rather demure. She could, however, be in his employ.

"What became of the child my sister bore?" Jane asked quietly, turning her face aside so that Beth could not make out her words.

"'Tis in the west wing," Ayleth answered sourly. "There's a whole staff taken on for it, nursemaid, laundry maid, and wet nurse, fit for a King's son. Much good it will do anyone! 'Tis naught but a mewling girl, for all my lady's toil and careful planning!"

"Jane?" The husky whisper made both women start and turn their heads with one accord. Helen Cecil's dimmed blue gaze was trained on her sister. "You have come," she said with a sharp intake of breath.

"Of course I came," Jane responded. "I came at once."

Helen gestured that she would sit up, and Ayleth made haste to prop her with pillows. By the time it had been arranged to her satisfaction, Helen's face was flushed by the exertion and her breathing shallow. She held out an imperious hand, and Jane leaned forward in her seat to take it.

"I had hoped that the next time you saw me, I would be the triumphant mother of a son," Helen admitted shakily. "Then you would kneel once more at *my* feet instead of the Queen's."

Jane winced. "Your ambition was always monumental, sister."

Helen laughed with a painful catch in her breathing. "I vow you speak naught but the truth, and this time I hoped to o'erleap nothing less than a queen."

Jane stirred. "Did you really think—?" She broke off her words, sending a quick look first at Ayleth, who stood beside them like a grim statue, and then across the room at Mistress Beth, who was surely craning her ears to listen to their exchange.

"To supplant a queen?" Helen whispered with a flash of her old spirit. "Why not? If anyone could, it was me."

"A dangerous game to play," Jane murmured with a frown. She did not speak the word aloud that hovered on her lips. *Treasonous.*

Helen sighed. "Always so reticent, Jane. Wymer is our rightful King. Armenal is just his consort. Nothing more."

Her words immediately cut Jane to the quick, for they outraged her loyal service to the Queen. "On the contrary," she replied, "Queen Armenal is sister to one king and wife to another. She is a princess of the blood. *You*, sister, are the one he merely *consorts* with." Her lip curled; she could not help it. "Has the King even deigned to visit with you since your lying-in?"

As she knew full well the King had not left court this past month, her words were unkind, but the smile that curved Helen's pale lips was appreciative of her barbed words.

6

"Now *that* is a good deal more like it," Helen said approvingly. "*There* is the flash of Cecil spirit that Uncle always thought you lacked. But I know better. It was always there, buried under all your layers of respectability."

"Uncle can go hang," Jane responded angrily before she could stop herself, and Helen gave another of her attractive husky laughs, though she broke off midway to wince in pain.

"Yes, he can," she agreed after a moment. "He can go hang on a gibbet for all I care until the sun bleaches his every bone. May the gods rot him."

Jane's eyes widened at her sister's macabre words. "Relations have soured between the two of you it seems," she said slowly, "for you have always been his protégée."

Helen shook her head. "He saw me as a tool to secure a brighter future for himself, that is all. I should never have listened to him." She sounded bitter. "*You* never did."

Jane pulled a face. "I was never pretty or ingratiating enough to please Uncle Phillip."

"More fool me. See where being pretty and ingratiating gets you." Helen gestured to her body swathed in bedsheets. "These sheets will be my death shroud, Jane," she pronounced hollowly, "and I have neither title nor name to bestow upon my daughter for protection. I do not even have the time to warn her against the words of men…" Her words trailed off and she stared toward the foot of the bed, as though she could see someone hovering there.

Jane was unnerved enough to turn her head, though she knew there was no one. "At the end of the day," her sister started again jerkily, "I have nothing! Even this estate…" She gazed about at the room with dim, glazed eyes. "Who is to say the

7

King will not snatch it back and bestow it on some new favorite as soon as I am cold in my grave? I would not put it past him."

A shudder racked her body, and Jane panicked, quickly turning her head. "Ayleth—" she started to appeal, but Helen squeezed her hand tight.

"No!" she whispered hoarsely. "There is nothing she can do for me now. Nothing anyone can do, except you." Jane glanced at Ayleth, whose lips were pressed tightly closed. "Let us keep this between the two of us," Helen appealed, "like in the old days."

Jane hesitated but nodded. "What is it you would have me do, sister?"

"Ease my passing," Helen croaked. "For the sake of the love we bore each other, as girls."

"Right gladly, but how?"

"Give me your word that on my death, you will take my child as your own."

Jane's eyes nearly fell out of her head. "M-my own?" she muttered in shock. She saw a flaw in the plan at once. "But I am not married, sister, and am in no position to start a nursery!" Her mind worked quickly. The babe would naturally come under their uncle's protection as he was the official head of the Cecil family.

If Jane was to play any role in her upbringing, she would have to live in Sir Phillip's home once again and such a thing was *unthinkable*. "You surely do not expect me to live under my uncle's roof?" she asked hoarsely and began to shake her head. That was something she could not do. Give up her position at court and be subject to Uncle Phillip's strictures again? Not while there was breath in her body!

"No, I would never ask that of you." Helen's voice was low and urgent. "Besides, that way *both* you and Celestia would be at Uncle's mercy." She paused and seemed to brace herself for the next words. "There is another way that you can assume guardianship instead of him."

Jane's head spun. Try as she might, she could see no way clear to such an outcome. "How?"

"You must make a sacrifice for me now, Jane," her sister said grimly. "You must revise your plans for your future. I am asking you to marry at once and give my child a father." Jane's eyes widened as Helen began to pant between her words, trying to lift her head off the pillow.

"Marry?" Jane uttered with horror.

Helen clutched at her bedsheets, a fine sheen of sweat showing on her face. "You must give my baby a father that can stand up to Uncle Phillip. A father that can outshine even a King. That way she will never pine for one who does not care for her, and *no one* can deny the legitimacy of your claim upon her."

Jane was aghast. "But—but the King—" She faltered. "Will he not object?"

Helen made a noise of disgust. "He cares naught for daughters, Jane. If she had been a boy…" A wistful look entered her eye for a moment, but then it was gone. "But she is not a boy," she said harshly. "He will not care the snap of his fingers for a bastard girl, and neither will he raise one to prevent Uncle Phillip from turning her into a pawn in his play for power!"

"Uncle," Jane repeated hollowly. There was a horrible ring of truth to Helen's words.

"Now he *will* see a royal bastard as a means to an end, mark my words," her sister said fretfully. "No sooner am I lowered into

9

the ground than he will start his plotting and scheming. And how can I rest easy in my grave knowing my child is caught in his greedy grasp?"

Jane's stomach lurched. "I had not—I had not planned for marriage," she rasped desperately. "I had hoped—that is—I—"

"You intended to worship your Queen in faithful service until your end of days, I know," Helen said, unable to keep the mockery entirely from her words. Jane flushed. "You wish to live your days as a vestal virgin, yet the one you serve is not a deity, Jane."

"Neither is a husband a deity," Jane replied tartly. "Yet wives are expected to wait on them hand and foot and take their word as law."

"She's not wrong there," Ayleth chimed in dourly. "And you cannot deny it, my lady."

Helen hissed out her breath before nodding slowly. "You are not wrong," she conceded, "and I cannot say as I blame you, sister. We were very young when we formed our opinions about such things." She smiled bitterly, and Jane knew they both thought momentarily of their weak, irresolute mother. "I did not wish to subjugate myself either. I vowed to take direction from no man, save a king." She closed her eyes. "But even that did not serve in the end."

Helen tightened her weak clasp on Jane's fingers. "This will not be an easy path for you, Jane. I am selfish and self-serving, even in death," she murmured. "You will admit, I am at least consistent in this, if nothing else." A mirthless smile passed over her lips.

"You were not always thus," Jane said with quiet conviction. "Growing up, we were the closest and best of sisters. It was not until our uncle came between us—"

"I know," Helen interrupted her, closing her eyes as though against sudden pain. "Do I ask too much of you, Jane?" she asked raspily. "You see, you are the *only* one I trust, sister. I turn to you now, as I did in the old days."

Jane shut her own eyes a moment. Ah, Helen, *Helen*. "It is not too much," she heard herself say, though the words cost her dearly.

Her sister closed her eyes and drew in a long, ragged breath. "You will do it, then?" Her dull eyes turned keen for just the veriest instant. Jane nodded and Helen groped for her hand again. "Let me hear you vow it," she begged, "for I know you keep your word, Janey. You always did, no matter the consequences."

"No matter what happens," Jane promised, squeezing her sister's limp fingers, "I will keep my vow to you, sister. By hook or by crook." She swallowed. "I will make haste to marry and then petition the King to take your daughter for my own."

Her sister sighed and a pale smile touched her bloodless lips. "Then I can die at peace," she said, and the horror of it was that Jane believed she would.

2

The Winter Court at Aphrany

Alisander de Balon, Viscount Bardulf, frowned as he surveyed the Queen's chambers and found it decidedly lacking. *She* was not present. And by she, he did not mean the Queen. He masked his annoyance by adopting an even more exaggerated form of his habitual languor. "Good morning, Your Majesty," he greeted the Queen, executing an elegant bow before sauntering into the room.

"Ah, here you are, Bardulf," the Queen greeted him briskly. "You have kept us waiting for you an age this morning, and I am ill attended this day as it is." She waved away a page boy hovering with a bowl of honeyed nuts. "No, no, not now."

Alisander lifted a dark eyebrow and swung about to consider the gaggle of ladies in her midst. "Something *is* missing this morn," he agreed, turning around in an unhurried circle to take in the Queen's sitting room. "No, do not tell me what it is," he said, flinging himself down into a chair. "I will use my razor-sharp wits to deduce what it might be."

Several of the ladies in the Queen's privy chamber tittered, and the Queen tipped her head to one side, waiting to be amused.

"You have a new chair," he said, his eye falling on a handsome carved piece set next to the window overlooking the garden.

"No," the Queen answered promptly. "I have had that for a twelvemonth."

He turned instead to the waiting page boy and pointed a long finger his way. "This boy is a replacement to your usual attendant."

"Not at all. Arthur has waited on me for three months now," the Queen replied briskly. Arthur aimed a resentful glare in his direction.

"You have changed the way you arranged your hair this morning, my Queen."

"Nothing of the sort," Queen Armenal scoffed. "Your razor-sharp wits seem decidedly blunt this morn, Bardulf."

Alisander sighed and dropped his head against the back of his seat. "It is too early for observations in any case," he said, closing his eyes.

The Queen's most recently appointed lady-in-waiting, a tall northern woman by the name of Magnatrude Bartree, snorted loudly. "On the contrary, it is nearly midday, my lord," she said with heavy disapproval, lowering her embroidery.

"As I said, far too early." Alisander yawned by way of response, making the older woman's lips purse.

"You must not pay him any heed, Magnatrude," the Queen said, turning to her companion. "He is merely provoking us because his usual target is not here to receive his barbs."

Alisander's eyes sprang open. Did he detect an underlying sharpness to her tone? A somewhat soured note? It had him immediately intrigued. He had noticed Jane's absence the moment he had crossed the threshold, of course, but the fact that the paragon of virtue, Jane Cecil, was in the Queen's bad books was news to him.

"Of course," he said aloud, "that is it! Where *is* my sweet Lady Disapproval?"

Armenal's expression darkened. Now, this was *highly* unusual. Jane Cecil was devoted to the Queen and would never do anything to incur her disapproval. What could the little Cecil have possibly done to earn the Queen's displeasure? It would not be scandalous, of course; Jane was far too staid to do anything so interesting. Still…he wondered at the coldness in Armenal's manner.

"She has family troubles, it seems," the Queen answered curtly. "And has seen fit to prioritize those over her duties at court."

Alisander's interest abruptly dropped away. He knew it would be something dull. All the same, this did not suit him at all. How long would the Cecils' family problems take to resolve? Something about the Queen's brittle manner told him now was not a good time to ask. Jane's family, as far as he was aware, was not extensive. She had a mother, an inconsequential creature who lived somewhere in the country.

Then, there was her scheming uncle, Sir Phillip, but Jane seemed to avoid him at all costs. That left just her sister, of course, the most famous paramour in all the land, for she was the King's acknowledged mistress. These days, Jane seemed to avoid her sister too. Their loyalties were divided after all. It was odd how these things worked out. One sister, the Queen's favorite, and the other, the King's.

"You should be pleased, my lord," opined Lord Melvin's ward, Mistress Lucy Melvin, boldly. "For Lady Jane's looks and manner generally displease you, is that not so?"

Twelve elegantly veiled heads immediately turned in his direction to observe his response. Alisander regarded the speaker blankly for a moment. "Is this someone else new?" he

14

asked in complaining tones, half turning toward the Queen. "How can I be expected to remember all of these new faces? It is too much!"

Whispers and hushed giggles greeted these words as all twelve ladies noted his devastating snub. Mistress Lucy flushed bright red. "I have been at court some six months now, my lord," she said plaintively. "We have met at least a dozen times in this very room!"

"If you knew Lord Bardulf as well as I do, Mistress Melvin," the Queen said, regaining some of her usual spirit, "then you would know he has a very bad head for names and faces."

Alisander waved a hand which might be taken for either an apologetic or dismissive gesture, depending on your generosity of spirit. "What a dull, displeasing morn," he pronounced. And for once, he actually meant his words.

What had been the point in donning his new lavender tunic with its huge sleeves, if Jane was not there to shudder at its ostentation? His lime green hose was *wasted* on this lot, and the gold-fringed shoes were not even comfortable. They were pinching his toes damnably.

He had spent a good quarter of an hour last night memorizing a sonnet purely because he had known Jane would loathe it, and all that effort had been for naught. The morning crawled onward, and without Jane's disapproving eye on him, it felt interminable.

He made several observations and remarks which would have annoyed her a good deal and ruffled that milk and water composure of hers. Whenever he turned his head to note the spark of irritation in her eye, the rigidity about her shoulders, the flush of irritation to her cheek, she was not there.

15

It was disappointing, to say the least; indeed, it *almost* vexed him. When a troop of musicians arrived to entertain the Queen, Alisander could stand it no longer and made his escape. By the end of the week, Jane would doubtless be back where she belonged, sitting demurely at the Queen's side, and things could return to normal.

Without Jane there, it was a damnably dull business, and he found he had no taste for a lot of women prating and jostling for Armenal's good opinion. For now, he would quit the Queen's company for a few days, write his diplomatic reports and visit with some of his informants throughout the city. In a few days, things would be set once more to rights.

On the first day Jane Cecil had not attended the Queen, Alisander had felt mildly put out. When he returned some four days later and found her *still* absent, well, it was intolerable. It cast a pall on his entire day. Damn it! It was too much.

He wondered that the Queen would stand for it. *He* would not in her shoes, he thought as he surveyed the company scattered throughout the room: that monstrous Bartree woman with her sour face, the insipid Melvin girl, an ambassador from Samare who was depressingly loyal to his emperor, and the ruddy-faced Bishop of Hudde.

Gods, what a prospect. He did not even count the dozen young women fluttering about the place. In this, he was of the same opinion as the Queen. They were not even worthy of notice until they proved otherwise.

The only bright spot he espied was that little Lady Martindale was dancing attendance on the Queen for the first time in an age. She must have dragged her barbarous husband southward for one of their rare visits. He rather wondered that she was able to prize him from his cold, draughty halls at all.

16

Martindale was a dour, moody bastard who spent his time at court skulking and glowering and no doubt dreaming of a bygone time when they had their own court, and moreover their own king in the north. They were all the same, these northerners, Alisander reflected.

Karadok's civil war had been over for some years now, but the dust had taken a long time to settle, and resentments simmered, never too far from the surface. He heartily pitied Lady Martindale, forced to reside in the north, a ghastly place, where snow remained scattered on the mountains even in the height of summer.

Lady Martindale, seemingly oblivious of the need for condolence, looked cheerful as ever and threw him a dimpled smile. Though not remotely flirtatious, she was his best chance of diversion this morn, he decided, drifting in her direction. Alas, she was a devoted wife and mother these days and inclined to talk about these facts at length, if one gave her half the chance.

Still, before she had married, she had been a little mouse, terrified of her own shadow, so he supposed he should not complain. She was a good deal livelier these days, despite her lamentable marriage. No doubt his favorite quarry would be back soon and normal relations could, once more, be resumed.

However, on the following Monday, a full week later, when he entered the presence chamber, he was destined once more for disappointment. Resplendent in a purple cotehardie, embroidered down both sleeves with golden pomegranates, he was appalled to find Jane still absent. So appalled was he that he was moved to plain speech, something he usually abhorred.

"*Where* is the Lady Jane?" he asked loudly, perhaps not employing the tact and discretion he should have—but fuck it.

17

He wasn't in the mood. All heads turned in his direction, and he became aware of a curiously tense atmosphere in the room.

Alisander lifted a quizzical eyebrow as he scanned the various expressions of shock and disapproval or, at least, *pretended* shock and disapproval. These were courtiers after all, and appearances were everything. "You," he said, pointing at a relative newcomer to Armenal's retinue. "Speak."

Frances Lessimore cleared her throat and then turned quite puce. She sent an agonized look at Magnatrude Bartree, who seemed to have recently assumed a senior role in proceedings. Mistress Bartree unfroze her gaunt features sufficiently to turn her head and direct a stern look upon him. "Lady Jane is still attending to some family matter," she said haughtily, and Alisander deduced that there was rather more to this business than met the eye.

From The Bartree's manner, clearly, Jane was not dealing with something as mundane as an ailing aunt. He pondered a moment. *What else could it be?* His mind raced. It would not be the first time one of Armenal's favorites had fallen from grace. Eden Montmayne came to mind. Of course, she had run off and got herself married to a knight without the royal permission.

Had Jane left to pursue an unsanctioned offer of marriage? He felt a certain coldness sweep over him as if he had the ague. Maybe he was coming down with something? Once the giddy moment passed, he caught his breath. No, that was ridiculous. Jane would never do anything so audacious. She was a model of prudence and discretion.

He let his eye travel over Mistress Bartree as his thoughts raced. He marveled that the woman could look so severe, despite the richness of her burgundy gown. Likely that close-fitting black silk cap she favored did not help, for it made her look quite bald. He devoutly hoped it would not become a court fashion, for it was ugly as hell.

"Still attending to family business?" he drawled aloud. "How dull. I thought she had at least run off with one of the royal guards from the way you all reacted." His words did not make anyone start or exclaim, as though he had discovered some shameful secret.

Thus, reassured that Jane had not done anything so rash, he threw himself down onto the silk couch and lolled there for twenty minutes until Armenal finally made her appearance. As soon as all attention was on the Queen, he beckoned to one of her youthful male attendants.

The palace squires were regularly rotated to give them all an opportunity to serve Her Majesty, and Alisander was glad to see that today's official usher was one he recognized and had, moreover, generously tipped on several occasions. In fact, he'd always had an excellent memory for *useful* faces and names and Piers Winstanley *was* useful, for the Queen favored his willowy, handsome appearance.

Whenever it was Piers's turn to serve her, Armenal generously permitted him to accompany her, not only in the presence chamber and privy chamber but in her private quarters also. As such, he had access to the areas and conversations that Armenal shared with only her favored few.

"Piers," Alisander murmured, "justify my high opinion of you by telling me which family member the Lady Jane has been attending?"

Piers Winstanley's face broke into a grin. "The royal whore, milord," he answered in hushed tones, surprising Alisander a good deal.

"The royal—?" He sent a quizzical look in Piers's direction. "Are you *sure*?"

The youth nodded, lifting a hand to shield his mouth from anyone who might be observing them. "Oh aye. It's not widely known," he added in hushed tones. "But the Queen's spitting mad about it."

"I'll just bet she is." Alisander pulled a face, making the lad chuckle before he returned dutifully to the Queen's side.

The royal whore? Alisander pondered. What the fuck was Jane doing, jeopardizing her position at court to visit with her sister? Everyone knew the King's interest had waned in that quarter. Since he had pensioned Helen Cecil off to his late mother's estate, Wymer had scarcely even visited the mistress he had once showered with lavish attention.

Indeed, most whispers around court agreed that this final gift was nothing more than a payoff and an excuse to send her away. Of course, there *had* been some rumor a few months ago, he recalled dimly, of a possible child resulting from the union… He considered this a moment before dismissing it. Even so, what of it?

It would not be Wymer's first bastard, and likely not his last. The boys he tended to provide with minor titles and the girls were generously dowered. If their mothers were noble and unwed, they were provided with advantageous marriages. If they were already married, then their husbands received additional lands and fortunes.

If they were *not* wellborn, such women were given generous allowances and sent off into rural obscurity. To give him his due, Wymer did not expect his Queen to suffer the indignity of a pregnant mistress flouted before her nose.

King Wymer was also notoriously fickle when it came to the objects of his affection. None of them ever lasted long, and as such, the Queen was usually indifferent to his fancies. The fact this liaison had lasted twice, if not three times as long as was customary, had meant the Queen *had* sat up and taken note.

For a time, some had wondered if Helen Cecil would prove the exception to the rule and a permanent fixture where the King was concerned. Alisander found himself wondering if the Queen, too, had harbored such thoughts before it had become apparent that Helen was nothing more than the latest in a long line.

Perhaps that was why Armenal was prickly now that her own favorite, the quieter Cecil sister, had defected to her sister's side. "Foolish Jane," Alisander tutted under his breath. Why had she chosen to endanger her position at court now? It was inconvenient. It also did not make sense. She just wasn't the reckless type. Try as he might, he could not dismiss the niggling suspicion he was missing something here.

He could see no reason for Jane's loyalties to suddenly switch sides. Even if Helen Cecil had been delivered of a healthy son, what did it matter? King Wymer had at least two acknowledged bastard sons and, moreover, a legitimate one stashed somewhere in the kingdom. Jane served the Queen. More than that, she hung off her every word. He could see no reason why some niece or nephew from the wrong side of the blanket should steal her loyalty away from Queen Armenal.

He stuck it out for another hour or so, begrudging every minute, and then made his way toward the palace's west wing. He had several sources he could approach, but he felt in this instance, instead of wasting hours approaching multiple people, he would much rather take the easiest approach. This meant bearding the lion in the den, and by the lion, he meant the King's spymaster, Earl Vawdrey.

Oswald Vawdrey had an extensive spy network at his fingertips. The trouble was, he was not in the habit of sharing his resources with others. Alisander sighed. Still, in the past, despite serving different interests, they had managed, if not to collaborate, perhaps, *cooperate* with one another on several occasions.

In fact, once, Alisander had even gone out of his way to perform Vawdrey a rather sizeable favor… Funnily enough, that had been a tip-off about Lady Helen Cecil, he recalled now with an ironic smile to himself. Vawdrey was honorable enough to consider this a debt of sorts.

It would be stupid to use this favor up on an insignificant thing like this, he reflected as he drew nearer to the large spacious rooms that Vawdrey occupied during his working hours. It was hardly a matter of life or death.

Alisander slowed his steps once he reached the west wing of the castle. He had a suspicion, after all, of what must have occurred. Her sister must have borne a child. Before long, it would doubtless be whispered in the palace corridors that the King's current mistress had been delivered of a royal bastard. What was the point in his asking Vawdrey now for more information?

Still, if that was all it was, then why would Jane have flown thence? As the Queen's favorite, Jane's place should have been at Armenal's side, supporting her through this latest indignity, not celebrating her sister's triumph. It did not make sense, unless…unless something had gone amiss. And rather badly amiss, for it to have driven Jane from the Queen's side of the chessboard.

He hesitated when Vawdrey's door came into view. He needed to make up his mind. Only one outcome he fancied would have wrought such an effect on steadfast Jane's loyalties. Her sister's life must be in peril. On such occasions, family grievances and disputes could be swept aside. Was that it? And if so, what did this mean for Jane's court position?

And more importantly, what affair was it of his?

He did not care so much for that last sneaking thought. It put him out of countenance. Ignoring it, he sailed into the antechamber where Vawdrey's assistant sat plying his pen.

The industrious Bryce's face fell. "Oh—er—Lord Bardulf!" he exclaimed, clambering hastily to his feet. He knew Alisander's habits of old and was determined to get between him and the door to the main chamber.

"Good morning, good Master Price," Alisander greeted him, deliberately misnaming the fellow. "Your master awaits within?"

Bryce flattened himself against Oswald's door and gestured urgently toward a neat row of seats. "If you would—sit yourself down, my lord," he panted, "then I will enquire if Earl Vawdrey is at liberty to receive you."

Bryce was rather out of puff, for he was a plump young man with what Alisander could only consider an execrable taste in clothes. He looked more like a friar than a clerk. With a last affronted glance at Alisander, who was now lolling in a chair, Bryce knocked smartly at the door and whisked around it, shutting it firmly behind him.

Luckily, Alisander did not have to wait long before he was ushered into Vawdrey's office. As usual, Oswald Vawdrey sat behind his desk, dressed head to toe in his customary black. It was a credit to the presence of the man that he did not seem remotely dwarfed by either the hugeness of his desk or by the piles of paper sat awaiting his attention.

"Viscount Bardulf," he said pleasantly. "You honor me. I do not think you have visited me anytime this past month. To what do I owe the pleasure?"

Alisander ignored the chair that had been set down for his use and instead walked over to the large window, where he stood looking down at the courtyard below. "Has it really been so long?" he asked absently.

He knew, of course, exactly what he was supposed to say and do for the next quarter of an hour. They were supposed to verbally spar. He was supposed to dance around the subject, throw a few feints in Vawdrey's direction, a bunch of misdirection here, a lot of hoodwink there, while his opponent parried and deflected.

Then, when the King's chief advisor was least expecting it, he should deliver his real attack. Casually throw in *Oh yes, has the royal whore been delivered of her bastard yet?* in the hopes it would catch a cool devil like Vawdrey off guard. Whether to make it look like mere impudence or as though the Queen had sent him, should be Alisander's only dilemma.

Strange to say, he just was not in the humor for it this morning. Instead, he wheeled about and gazed at Vawdrey rather hard before asking directly, "How long do you think the Lady Jane will tarry at Kinnerton?"

A look of brief surprise flickered over Vawdrey's face. He opened his mouth as though to reply he knew nothing of the matter, then seemed to think better of it. Also breaking with convention completely, he asked curiously, "Why do you ask?"

It was his own damned fault, but he was a little jarred by Vawdrey's directness. It was bad form. He wanted to say as much, but then the tricky bastard would retreat behind his mask again. Instead, he gave an unconvincing shrug. "She's been gone over a week now," he replied lamely, fiddling with the sash at Vawdrey's curtains. He had a horrible suspicion that a little color was creeping into his cheeks. He *must* be feverish.

"The Queen is no doubt feeling the loss of her favorite," Vawdrey ventured, giving him a convenient out.

He wasn't even tempted to take it. "Armenal has plenty of substitutes for the likes of Lady Jane," he pointed out, thinking of the awful Bartree woman.

"But you do not?" Vawdrey asked silkily. *Damn him.* Alisander dropped the curtain sash and glared at his opponent. Vawdrey smiled. "Dear me, this *is* an interesting development," he pondered.

"Has something delayed her?" Alisander pressed on.

Vawdrey settled back in his chair and steepled his fingers. "I'm afraid it looks unlikely that her sister, the Lady Helen, will ever rise from her lying-in," he said gravely. Alisander started. It was no more than a confirmation of his own suspicions, yet for some reason, he was still surprised by it. Helen Cecil had always been such a vibrant creature. "Lady Jane attends her now at the last," Vawdrey concluded with gentle finality.

Alisander swore under his breath. He had been so secure in his conviction that Jane's loyalties would never be swayed, but he had not considered such a thing as a family death. If ever there was a thing that could wipe the slate clean of resentment and estrangement, it was that. Especially with a creature as conventional as Jane. *Fuck.* She would be singing hymns to her martyred sister's sainthood before the week was out!

25

Looking up, he found Vawdrey regarding him with a gleam of speculation in his eye. Alisander scowled. "What?" he demanded sulkily.

"Oh, nothing," Vawdrey answered airily. "Just rearranging the pieces on my board, in the light of your clearly vested interest."

Alisander had to bite back his instinctive retort that he had no such thing. Any vehemence at this point would be a mistake. What he should do was laugh and lament that without Jane there to torment, he was merely bored. It was the truth after all, wasn't it? Instead, he walked over to the waiting chair and dropped into it, attempting to assume something in the line of his usual manner.

When Lord Vawdrey rose from his seat, Alisander half expected him to utter some words of dismissal, claiming he had a meeting to attend or some such, however, he merely headed for a side table and poured them both some refreshment. As usual, Oswald Vawdrey's glass contained more water than wine. Alisander accepted his own goblet from him wordlessly.

"You do not ask about the King's issue," Vawdrey prompted him after rounding the desk and returning to his seat.

"What?"

"The child."

Oh. That. "It survived?"

Vawdrey nodded. "A girl."

Alisander pulled a face. "I'll warrant the mother was *sorely* disappointed with that outcome." He took a swig of wine. "Does the King know?"

"He does." Vawdrey sent him a level look. "He was not overly enthusiastic about the news, though he sent a fine present.

26

His—er—*predilection*, shall we say, had cooled in recent months. He has not seen the Lady Helen in person, since—oh, let me think—it must have been the feast of St. Danicus."

Alisander snorted. He could imagine nothing less likely than Wymer dancing attendance on his heavily pregnant mistress.

"To speak frankly," Vawdrey continued, "I thought back as far as last September, that little business had run its course."

Alisander plunked down his glass. If the King *had* tired of Helen Cecil, as indeed popular gossip concurred, then there had been no rumors yet of a replacement that would confirm the fact. "If it was a congé, then it was a handsome payoff he gave her," he commented. "Nothing less than a royal estate."

Vawdrey gave his wintry smile. "It is hardly that. Kinnerton formed a minor part of his mother Queen Etheldreda's dowry. It was the original seat of the Barons of Kinnerton, a now-defunct title. The male line died out over a hundred years ago."

"You Karadokians and your primogeniture," Bardulf murmured. "It is always a mistake to put all your eggs in one basket."

"As you say," Vawdrey concurred, "it has its drawbacks. Not a mistake your own family made, as I understand it." He turned his enigmatic gaze on Alisander, who felt an uncomfortable prickle up his spine.

"I am flattered you deign my own family history worthy of note," he said, lifting his glass again to hide his surprise.

"You are the last of your line, is that not so?"

"Quite so."

"You have never felt any compulsion to remedy that?"

Now that did bring a laugh to Alisander's lips. "Never," he clarified.

Oswald Vawdrey nodded slowly. "Perhaps you should reconsider, in light of recent events."

Alisander's mirth died an abrupt death. "And why would I do that?"

"Merely because, in some obscure corner of this kingdom, a certain lady has made a most imprudent promise. One she will find extremely hard to fulfill." When Alisander refused to be drawn, Vawdrey continued softly. "A young woman, you have recently become aware is…how shall I put this…indispensable to your comfort?"

That was putting things a bit strongly in Alisander's opinion. Words of denial hovered on his lips but remained unspoken. He eyed Vawdrey suspiciously. "Imprudent promises? Doesn't sound like the Jane Cecil I know. She's cautious and careful to a fault."

"A dying sister might be considered extenuating circumstances," Vawdrey suggested.

Alisander's mind whirled. He did not ask how Oswald Vawdrey could know such things. He had eyes and ears everywhere that might be considered the King's business. Even in the household of a discarded paramour. "She *can't* be promising to raise her sister's bastard," he protested aloud. "Such a notion is absurd. The Queen would never forgive her, and she lives for the Queen's approval."

He glanced at Earl Vawdrey, who was pursing his lips. "You're forgetting the deathbed setting," Vawdrey chided him. "The moment is a powerful one. Do you really imagine the Lady Jane could deny the last request of her only sister?"

Alisander cursed softly again. No, damn her, she would not. *Jane, what the fuck are you doing?* Throwing away her court career, that was what. He groaned. "Stupid, so stupid." And for what? A mewling infant who would keep her from the life at court she truly enjoyed?

"Not only stupid," Vawdrey continued, "but also one that is bound to bring her into contention with certain…factions."

Alisander's eyebrows rose. "Aren't you being rather dramatic? Armenal would no doubt cut her off, but she is not so vengeful as to hound her husband's illegitimate offspring."

Vawdrey shook his head. "I would never malign the Queen in such a manner. No, I speak of your lady's uncle, Sir Phillip Cecil. A man of singular ambition. It was he who brought the sisters to court in the first place if memory serves." He shot an enigmatic look at Alisander. "I believe it was you who first brought that fact to my attention."

Alisander paused to remember that particular interview in this same office many moons ago. "Ah yes," he reminisced, stalling for time. What the fuck was Vawdrey driving at? His usually keen mind felt dulled and weighed down with trivial cares. Absently, he picked up one of the many-colored inkwells and felt its comforting weight in his hand. "How is your charming countess?" he asked aloud. "She has not graced us with her presence at court these past few weeks."

Instead of tensing, as Alisander had anticipated, Vawdrey's features relaxed into a genuine smile for once. "She thrives," he said simply. It was a curious fact and much remarked at court that the Vawdreys all made peculiarly devoted husbands.

Alisander gave his head a slight shake to try to clear it. "Sir Phillip," he stated heavily. "What has he to do with it? You

29

think he means to use this child," he said slowly, "to further his own ends?"

"He will certainly wish to keep it under his wing in case it may become useful to him later. Which would mean his niece, the Lady Jane, would also be drawn once more under his control." Vawdrey looked thoughtful. "I do not think she would enjoy that."

Alisander replaced the inkwell with a thud. "She's a little fool," he said abruptly. "If she made such an idiotic promise then she deserves everything that befalls her."

Vawdrey smiled a damn knowing smile and Alisander leaped out of his chair like a scalded cat. Only by the greatest effort did he manage to perform his elegant bow and make his way out of the office with some decorum. Never before in his life had he been so tempted to slam a door.

Beneath his urbanity, he was seething at this unexpected development. *Fucking Vawdrey. Stupid Jane.* It was none of his damned business and he would not be drawn into it.

3

It was three nights later that Alisander's resolve snapped, and he found himself once more approaching Lord Vawdrey. This time, during a feast in the Great Chamber. It was no easy feat to sidle up to anyone when one was dressed as extravagantly as Alisander, but he fancied he had made an art of it by this point.

Still, he did not flatter himself that Oswald Vawdrey was unaware he was being stalked. Not by so much as a raised eyebrow did he express surprise when Alisander addressed him. Indeed, he might even have moved to the shadowy far side of the hall in order to give him that very opportunity. Alisander would not put it past him.

"That matter of which we spoke the other day," Alisander said softly.

"Yes?" Vawdrey did not turn his head, and it was possible their fellow revelers did not even realize they were conversing.

"Have matters progressed?"

"Oh, indeed. Time marches ever on and awaits no man's pleasure."

"Has the lady in question…?"

Vawdrey bowed his head. "She is past mortal cares by this point."

Alisander sent a quick look at the King, who had been moody and fretful all night. "I *thought* he seemed a little off his oats tonight."

"Oh, the King's distraction has quite another source, I assure you." At Alisander's vague noise of query, Vawdrey looked grave. "The good Bathilde is failing, and the King is taking it hard."

"Bathilde?"

"The King's nurse."

Alisander pulled a face. They were sentimental, these Karadokians, with their childhood bonds. He doubted his own sovereign, Wilhelm, even acknowledged he'd once been a puling infant. Yet here was the mighty Argent Lion, the king who had united all of Karadok, sniveling over his aged nurse.

"Whoever will tuck him in at night when she is gone?" Alisander murmured facetiously.

Instead of bridling at this slight to his monarch's manhood, Earl Vawdrey looked suddenly thoughtful. "I don't suppose the Queen could be persuaded to step up into the role?" he remarked. "Perhaps you could suggest it to her? Sadly, she is not at all amenable to my influence."

That was putting it mildly, Alisander thought, examining his nails. Armenal bitterly resented the fact the King could barely blow his nose without Oswald Vawdrey first flourishing a handkerchief in his face. A musician approached, strumming his lute, and a pair of lovers dodged behind one of the columns. They fell into a mutually agreed silence until all three interlopers had moved away.

"You want me to suggest to Queen Armenal that she takes over Bathilde's duties," Alisander murmured, "folding his stockings and fetching his milk?" He could not keep the skepticism from his voice and, indeed, made very little effort to even try.

Oswald Vawdrey nodded, refusing to be drawn. "In a manner of speaking," he agreed mildly. "After all, there is no denying that the King is susceptible when it comes to feminine charm.

32

Bathilde provides him with familiarity and comfort; she always has. Oh, his mistresses have warmed his bed throughout the years, it is true, but they have *never* commanded his loyalty or true affection as she does. Imagine, if a woman were only able to take on the *combined* function of both roles. What sway would such a woman hold at court!"

Alisander narrowed his eyes. "I doubt very much that this idea has only just occurred to you," he commented dryly. "Do you expect me to believe you have not been raising stables full of beautiful women to capture his attention over the years?"

Vawdrey snorted. "My dear Bardulf, *many* have tried over the years to produce such a paragon. Do you imagine Lady Helen appeared at court fully formed and armed with every artifice to tempt a king without the tutelage of an ambitious man?"

That gave Alisander pause. "Her uncle groomed her to snare a king?"

"Of course he did." Vawdrey nodded and exchanged a few pleasantries with a passing noble. Alisander accepted a goblet of wine from a servant.

"And now that lady is gone," Vawdrey continued seamlessly as soon as the coast was clear, "I fear there will be the usual undignified scramble to thrust some new fancy under his nose." A look of distaste passed over his handsome features. "Then we shall have the whole tiresome process of vetting whose pocket they are in and just whose words they are whispering in his ear."

Alisander was amused. "You sound so suddenly weary of intrigue, my dear Vawdrey."

"Intrigue, never, but I confess the matter of the King's peccadilloes is tiresome to me. It would be so much *neater* if he would simply fall in love with his own wife."

Alisander choked on his wine. "After twelve years?" he spluttered as soon as he had swallowed the offending mouthful. "They have been at odds ever since she stepped off her ship!"

Vawdrey shrugged, looking entirely unabashed. "Why should he not? The Queen is a handsome and resourceful woman. You simply need to put the notion into her head so that she makes the requisite effort to snare him."

"Why should I?"

Vawdrey directed a surprised look his way. "My dear Bardulf," he said reproachfully. "Is it possible that you have forgotten your role as ambassador in this country? Surely, your duty to the Western Isles dictates you should wish its favorite daughter to be the most powerful woman in Karadok?"

Alisander stifled a yawn. Loyalty to his homeland was rarely uppermost in his thoughts, and he suspected Vawdrey knew this well enough. "She is already Queen of this land."

"Indeed, she is, due to the fact she wears His Majesty's ring. Only imagine, for one moment, if she also held his *heart*."

Alisander was frankly unconvinced. "I never imagined, for one moment, you were such a romantic, Vawdrey."

"You should ask my wife." Vawdrey smirked. "You might be surprised."

Alisander had pushed his shoulders away from the wall and was all set to leave when Vawdrey added casually, "By the way, you might like to know that Lady Jane left Kinnerton yesterday morn bound for the Dowager Viscountess of Morpington's

34

townhouse in Aphrany. She should have reached there by nightfall."

Alisander's ears pricked up. "She's back in the winter capital?" He should be more concerned at how the news made his heart race, but he would examine that later.

"You are focusing on the *wrong* part of my news." Vawdrey's tone was gently reproachful.

"The dowager viscountess?" Alisander said slowly. It was true, he had seen Jane in the woman's presence some few times over the past couple of years. "You attach some import to that fact?" he asked.

"It is known, is it not, that the dowager has long been in search of a *calming* presence for her son, the wayward Viscount Morpington?"

"*Morpington?*" Alisander swung around to stare Lord Vawdrey directly in the face. "You are not serious? Jane would never countenance joining her lot in life to the likes of him!"

Vawdrey coughed and darted his eyes to the left and right. Reluctantly, Alisander leaned back against the wall and relaxed his stance. He cleared his throat. "You're surely mistaken about the intent of their meeting."

"I have seen copies of letters exchanged betwixt the two of them," Vawdrey said with damning frankness.

"Jane and Morpington?" He felt that strange swooping sensation once again. It was singularly unpleasant.

"Jane and the dowager viscountess," Vawdrey corrected him.

"And these letters mentioned the possibility of *marriage*?" Alisander said incredulously. "I do not believe it!"

35

"There were tentative forays into that very subject on both sides."

Gods. The thought of prim little Jane and the dissolute Viscount Morpington disturbed him more than he could admit. His every instinct rebelled. Not while he lived.

"Perhaps you are unaware," Vawdrey continued unhurriedly, "that their childhood homes neighbored one another at one point? Lady Jane doubtless harbors the illusion that her playmate lurks somewhere beneath that dissipated exterior."

"He has drunk and gambled and whored his father's fortune away in less than three years," Alisander said bluntly. "He would turn her hair quite gray within a twelvemonth."

To his annoyance, he thought Vawdrey looked amused by the strength of his reaction. "No doubt," he murmured in agreement, "but the lady finds herself backed into rather a corner at the moment, does she not? From her position, he might not look like her worst prospect."

"Gods, I would hate to think, then, what did!"

"Perhaps life under her uncle's yoke?" Vawdrey suggested. "You have met Sir Phillip, have you not?"

Alisander made a quick gesture of annoyance, dismissing Phillip Cecil with the contempt he deserved. Vawdrey lifted his hand to cover his mouth, and Alisander had the distinct impression he was smiling behind it. "Something amuses you, Vawdrey?" he asked coldly.

"Not at all, my dear Bardulf, I assure you."

Alisander continued a moment in resentful silence. "And what conclusion does the most brilliant mind at the Argent court come to?" he asked tauntingly. The fact there was a hint of

36

hopefulness in his voice irritated him, but he had tried his best to disguise it.

"Another match could be suggested," Vawdrey ventured tentatively. "A more palatable one to rescue the lady from such an odious fate."

"Such as?" Alisander flung at him in clipped tones.

Vawdrey's eyelids flickered. "Lord Andarl?" he offered blandly.

"He's fifty if he's a day!"

"A very good age for marriage, or so I've heard."

"Nonsense!"

Vawdrey's lips twitched again, damn him. "Havering?" he proposed.

"He's on the lookout for a rich wife," Alisander pointed out scathingly.

Oswald Vawdrey hesitated. "If the King could be persuaded to endow the child with the estate at Kinnerton," he said slowly, "then the Lady Jane might be considered well-dowered indeed."

Alisander felt himself turn cold. "Who would persuade the King to do such a generous thing as all that?" he asked, already knowing the answer.

"Me," answered Vawdrey mildly. "If the mood took me."

"Well, then don't! She'd have every fortune hunter and opportunist in the country after her!"

Vawdrey spread his hands. "At least that way, she could have her pick of the bunch. Come now, you must admit that broadening her current prospects would be the kindest thing I could do for her. Already my wife is lamenting poor Jane's fate and hinting at my intercession. I do not think I can hold out for much longer without tarnishing my image in Fenella's eyes, something I never do, if I can help it."

Alisander frowned furiously but could think of no reply. Even his wits were failing him now.

Lord Vawdey settled back once more against the tapestried wall behind them. He tipped his head to one side. "Why don't you simply marry the lady yourself, Alisander?" he asked. "Put yourself out of your misery."

Alisander choked on his reply. *Ridiculous*, he wanted to object. *Unthinkable, absurd!*

"Why don't you look at it as a challenge?" Vawdrey suggested. "See how many months it would take for *you* to turn her hair gray."

Alisander eyed him accusingly. The bastard was definitely smiling now.

*

Long after he had left the reception, Alisander could hear the words of the King's chief advisor rattling around his head. *Why don't you simply marry the lady yourself?* Why could he not dismiss that troublesome advice? Why, oh why, did the proposition keep reverberating through his head?

Marry her. As if that was even on the table. Jane Cecil would no more accept his suit than she would a brimming cup of poison. He knew full well Jane was not as in tune with her feelings as he. She thought the antagonism that crackled in the air between them was purely caused by dislike.

Maybe, on her part, it was, he conceded, but he had always known deep down that the reason he liked to tease Jane was not due to dislike. Far from it. And now Vawdrey was going to hang a fortune over her head, plague take him. It would act as a target for every fortune hunter to take a shot at.

He braced himself and brought Sir Richard Havering to mind. In truth, he had nothing against the fellow. He was on the right side of forty and had a pleasant, if slightly bovine, appearance. It wasn't even his fault that he stood in dire need of funds. Havering had inherited most of his struggles from his debt-ridden sire.

Alisander rubbed his eyes. No, it was no good trying to be generous. He detested the thought of that clod Havering getting his meaty paws on Jane. There was no point in lying to himself. The mere thought of Jane becoming Lady Havering made his gorge rise. The gall of the man, thinking he was fit to touch even her feet!

"My lord?" quavered his aged manservant, Robert, who was haphazardly piling logs next to the fireplace. "Have you been taken ill?"

Alisander looked up from the goblet he was white-knuckling. "What was that, Robert?" He forced a smile to his face and his fingers to unclench from the stem. "Nothing ails me, nothing at all," he assured the worried-looking man. "I am merely contemplating my future."

A faintly anxious look returned to Robert's countenance. "The future, milord?" He faltered. One of the logs slipped out of his gnarled grasp and rolled across the rug. Instead of scooping it up, the old man simply stared at it. His lips quivered. "Will we be returning to the old country?" he asked in a choked voice.

"Never. Put that out of your head," Alisander responded quickly. "Set those down and come sit here with me awhile. Wat can sort those. He has a stacking technique that pleases my eye."

The old man clambered to his feet and shuffled over to the chair. "I'm old now and useless," he mumbled. "Wat can manage better without me muddling everything." His rheumy eyes filled with tears as he lowered himself into a chair.

Alisander poured him a cup of wine and passed it to him. "Nonsense. Wat is all very well, but he has not known me since I was a babe in arms. He is not Lasconian, like we. He does not *remember*." Precisely what they were supposed to remember, he was not sure. He profoundly hoped that Robert's memories were nothing like his own. "Drink," he prompted after a moment.

Robert lifted the goblet and took a sip. "This is your good stuff, milord. You should not waste it on an old servant like me."

Alisander rolled his eyes. "You are my oldest friend as well you know, you cozening rogue. I would no sooner part with you than I would my ruby necklace," he added flippantly. "Now quit your mopes, for your master has need of you."

Robert's face brightened, and he sat up in his seat. "Yes, milord?"

"I am thinking of taking a wife," Alisander hedged. "What say you to that?"

Robert nodded slowly. "'Tis high time, Master Sander," he said gravely, and apparently without noticing, he had fallen back on a manner of address not used for many years. He hesitated. "What's the young lady like, if I might take the liberty?" he asked, looking hopeful.

40

Alisander tipped his head to one side. "How to answer, that is the question," he said slowly.

Robert looked unimpressed. "How, but truthfully?" he said with the familiarity of a very old family servant. His bluntness brought a smile to Alisander's lips.

"Very well, I shall try. She's very...*punctilious*," he started slowly. "She believes in all the virtues and attempts to demonstrate them daily. She gives alms to the poor, attends chapel, and her manners are impeccable. She never has so much as a hair out of place. She is assiduous in her duties, would *never* permit herself to show up late to supper, to turn her back on her host, or neglect any of the social niceties. She is highly discreet, and I doubt so much as a morsel of gossip has ever passed her lips. As a consequence, she has no particular friends, for no one likes a paragon."

Alisander refilled his cup as Robert's eyes grew rounder. "Her manner of dress is conservative, with no particular flair for individuality. She dances passably well while possessing no great talent. She is pretty in a pale, insipid sort of way. Her mouth is too small, but very neat. Her figure is good, but nothing special. Her carriage and deportment are pleasing, without possessing any true distinction.

"Her waist is trim, her bosom nothing to boast of, her skin, a little on the washed-out side. The habitual expression upon her face is meek and downcast like that of a virtuous statue. She is entirely colorless, except for when she grows annoyed, and then, though she tries to hide it, a most unbecoming rash will spread across her neck and décolletage, betraying her, and her eyes flash like twin topazes in the perfect oval of her face."

Robert picked up his cup and took a swig. "So, she has eyes like jewels and you're in love with her," he said contentedly.

41

"That's good." Alisander gave a crack of laughter. Well, if that was what Robert took away from his list of attributes, so be it. "She sounds like a good girl," Robert continued, nodding his gray head. "And has the makings of a good wife to ye, milord."

"Well, now I have your approval, my good Robert, I shall proceed apace," he assured his servant. "Let us drink to success in my wooing." He lifted his own cup aloft and Robert joined him in the toast.

It was not until two days later that Alisander received sudden word that Jane had left the Dowager Viscountess Morpington's abode and was on her way to the Queen's chambers. He did not precisely hurry his way there—hurrying was something Alisander seldom did, if possible, and *never* in public. Still, he was forced to slip through the neglected inner maze of the castle without so much as donning a concealing cloak along the way.

He made a startled maid squeak on emerging into a servants' staircase. Her attack of nerves was mercifully allayed when he swiftly produced a coin to quell her exclamations. He reached the Queen's rooms without further event and swiftly passed through her presence chamber and into the privy chamber, unchallenged by the ushers who stood guarding the doorway. Disappointingly, the room was empty. Armenal must have Jane closeted in her bedchamber, he realized with a twist of his lips.

He stood hesitating only a moment before moving to the window seat. He tossed a cushion into one corner and then stretched out, letting the curtain down to conceal him. Then he waited, his eyes closed, for the drama to unfold. He did not have to wait long.

4

Jane had approached the Queen's chambers in a positive quake
of nerves. No sooner had she arrived back in her rooms at the
palace, tired and disillusioned, than a royal summons had been
delivered. It was decidedly formal in tone and nothing like the
usual relaxed communication she enjoyed with the Queen.

If she had not just suffered through a frankly nightmarish two-
day visit with the Dowager Viscountess Morpington then she
was sure she would feel even more anxious. As it was, she
scarcely felt like things could get much worse. It was
consequently with a strangely fatalistic mindset that Jane bent
her steps now toward the Queen's private apartments.

She could not marry Rodrey, she knew that much. Even
thinking now of his bloodshot eyes and bilious countenance
made her give an involuntary shudder. His conversation, or
wanton lack of it, his shifty eye, and general twitchiness, all of
it combined to convey the worst possible impression of his
potential as a husband. She did not even want to contemplate
what kind of father he would make.

And that had been before he had tried to corner her in his
mother's sitting room. Jane had not hesitated to drive her elbow
as hard as she could into his soft stomach. Mercifully, his
mother, on reentering the room, attributed the overturned table
and the fact her son was doubled over and retching in the corner
to the aftereffects of an evening's overindulgence, and scolded
him roundly, ushering Jane from the room.

Jane had heard, of course, vague rumors that Rodrey was sadly
intemperate these days, but she had been unaware of the extent
of his excesses. Even her short visit was sufficient to see why
the dowager was so anxious to marry him off. She remembered

the quiet, rather nervous boy he had been and felt more bewildered than bereft at how he had turned out. There could be no solution there to her problems.

No, there was nothing for it now, but to throw herself on the Queen's mercy and hope for the best. In happier times, Queen Armenal had alluded to a respectable match which could eventually be made for a favorite lady-in-waiting. Jane had always passionately denied any interest in a husband. Instead, she had assured the Queen of her devoted service to the end of her days.

How bitterly did Jane now regret her vehemence on that score! If only she had been more moderate in her plans for the future, she would not appear so ridiculous now, turning around and begging the Queen to find her a husband!

Then, too, could she even rely on the Queen's goodwill, with a child in tow, whose mere existence was an insult to her? Jane's heart quailed. She was not looking forward to this interview. The Queen was not in her presence chamber, and the attendants waved her through to the privy chamber, which again, was empty.

Hoping her inner turmoil was not too evident, Jane approached the double doors to the Queen's bedchamber. She had paused a moment to compose herself before giving a discreet knock upon the door. A page opened it, but instead of stepping back to make way, he uttered her name over his shoulder and seemingly received a reply that she was to be kept waiting.

With a stony face, the young lad closed the door in her face, and Jane felt herself flush at the slight. Glancing around, she saw the ushers from the previous doors observing her reception with interest. Jane stiffened her spine and pressed her lips together. How many courtiers had she refused admittance to in the past?

She had done so without compunction, trusting they deserved such treatment, every one.

Well, maybe they had, and maybe she did now. Armenal had every reason to be angry, Jane reminded herself. She vowed to withstand the Queen's subsequent displeasure with grace. This vow was put under immediate strain when Mistress Bartree finally opened the door and looked Jane over with haughty disdain. "Her Majesty will see you now," she intoned, making it clear she thought Jane undeserving of the honor.

Despite her intention to bear herself contritely, Jane found herself giving a barely there curtsey, and instead of bowing her head and following humbly in her wake, she aimed her look of smoldering resentment between Mistress Bartree's shoulder blades. Well, the Queen had not waited long before finding a new favorite, it seemed.

Was this how Eden Montmayne had felt when returning to court after her unsanctioned marriage? She had found herself supplanted, and Jane the new favorite. The thought made her uneasy. For the first time, it occurred to her to wonder: who had come before Eden? Was Jane simply the latest in a long line of usurped favorites?

The Queen was sat upon a low couch with an arm extended regarding a bracelet of delicate filigree about her wrist. She did not turn her head at their approach, but instead stood up and moved to survey herself in a long looking glass. "The emeralds, I think, Magnatrude," she uttered, ignoring Jane's deep curtsey.

Magnatrude Bartree hastened to the open jewelry box and extracted a necklet of surpassing beauty which she approached the Queen with reverently. "You may place it about my throat," Queen Armenal said graciously, in the manner of one

45

bestowing a great favor. Jane felt a pang. That used to be her, performing such duties.

The Queen took her time surveying the results before she turned to Jane. "Well, Jane," she said coolly. "You are returned to us, I see."

"I am, Your Majesty."

"Your outside business presumably concluded; I trust you can now devote yourself to your duties here at court."

Jane hesitated. "Unfortunately not, Your Majesty."

"No?" The Queen raised an eyebrow and glanced toward Magnatrude Bartree. "How extraordinary."

Jane's cheeks burned. She took a deep breath. This was going to be harder than she had envisaged.

*

The door was flung open and Alisander heard the Queen's voice sailing through long before her footsteps.

"You had no right to make such a promise, Jane! How can you take the child? It must go to a foster family. This is absurd!"

Alisander's ears pricked up, but he could not make out Jane's subdued reply. Again, the Queen's plaintive tones. "She surely meant for you to take an interest as its aunt. A kindly, benevolent, yet removed interest," the Queen insisted. Then, in a more conciliatory tone, "Only consider, Jane…"

He could not make out the words, but their intonation was cajoling. Jane's voice again. Her words were not distinct, but he could hear the note of stubbornness, loud and clear.

"This is intolerable!" the Queen burst forth, and footsteps heralded the arrival of three pairs of feet into the Queen's privy chamber. "It is an insult to me! Can you not see that, Jane?"

"I can," Jane sobbed. "I do and I can only beg that you show me clemency, my Queen."

Armenal let out an explosive noise of disagreement. "If you do this thing," she said warningly, "if you commit to this cause, you will have to leave court. To live in seclusion with no company to speak of, just a handful of stupid yokel servants. *No one* will see you." Her words were brittle and cold. "You will have no society, no intelligent conversation. You will be all alone, with naught but a mewling babe for company."

"I cannot break my word." Jane was openly weeping now.

"I gave you too much credit, it seems," the Queen concluded dispassionately. "I thought you were more sensible than this. I thought you were like me. One who does not allow emotion to rule you."

Bardulf swung his legs over the side of the window seat and swept the curtain aside. He affected to yawn and stretch. Three surprised faces turned in his direction. "Dear me," he murmured, letting his eyes travel over the tableau they presented. Jane had sunk to the floor and looked a pitiable sight in her position as supplicant. After a moment, his eye dismissed the Queen and Mistress Bartree altogether.

To his surprise, he found he was not repulsed one bit by this glimpse of Jane's heightened emotion. Her trembling mouth looked swollen and kissable. He rather liked how abandoned she was to grief. Would she be abandoned in other places? he found himself wondering. Like his bed.

47

When the Queen spoke, he had to tear his gaze away from Jane's kneeling figure. "We had no idea you were there, Bardulf." She was clearly displeased.

Alisander shrugged and stifled another yawn. "As you see, Your Majesty."

"Shall I show the viscount out, Your Highness?" the Bartree fright suggested. Alisander inspected his nails but did not fail to see the speculative gleam in the Queen's eye. She knew full well how much Jane would dislike him seeing her in such a state.

"We are all old friends here," the Queen answered after a heartbeat, "and need not stand on ceremony. Magnatrude," she said warmly, "perhaps you could have refreshment sent for?"

"Certainly, my Queen." The older lady-in-waiting hurried away, leaving the three of them listening to her hasty footsteps fading into the corridor outside.

"Tell me, have you heard the misfortune that has befallen the Cecil family?" the Queen asked without more ado. "Answering truthfully will spare Jane the necessity of hearing me tell the dismal tale."

"I have," Alisander admitted lightly.

The Queen gave a hollow laugh. "Of course you have," she muttered. "Jane, you will do me the courtesy of rising now from your heap."

Jane rose unsteadily to her feet, and Alisander could not help but shoot out a hand to catch her elbow when she stumbled. Seeing the Queen's eyes narrow with displeasure, he retracted it as soon as she was steadied.

"You are clumsy today, Jane, and most unlike yourself," the Queen said with an edge to her voice.

Jane made no answer, just looked tired and resigned. Alisander did not think she even cared by this point that he was witnessing her at her lowest ebb. She had not flinched at his touch, and had barely seemed to register it. This would never do.

"If you ask my opinion," he drawled, "there is no need for all these theatrics." He turned to the Queen. "You must simply find her a husband who will not keep her from court."

The Queen uttered a short laugh. "Does such a husband exist? Not in my experience," she added bitterly.

"Is it such an impossible task?" He allowed a note of faint incredulity to enter his voice.

"You know nothing of such matters, my dear Bardulf. Only consider, I scarcely see my dearest Eden nowadays. The King's Champion, that boorish Sir Roland, keeps her buried in darkest Vawdreyshire, producing his heirs."

"No one would ever claim the Vawdreys made reasonable husbands," he pointed out.

"Given a choice, I would not have picked one for her," Armenal admitted discontentedly. "The matter was taken entirely out of my hands."

"That is too bad, but Lady Jane has not committed herself so rashly. She will put herself wholly in your hands, I am sure." Armenal shrugged pettishly. "I suggest you choose for her more wisely than your previous favorite did for herself." They both turned to look at Jane's unhappy face.

49

Armenal huffed out a sigh. "Sir Reginald Stimson?" she suggested without enthusiasm.

"Who?"

A look of irritation passed over the Queen's face. "Sir Reginald is a doorward for the King," she answered testily, "and not without distinction."

Alisander flicked an invisible speck from his sleeve. "Would it not be wiser to choose a courtier of your own rather than one of Wymer's hangers-on?"

"There *are* no eligible bachelors attached to my own retinue," Armenal retorted sharply, "save for"—he saw the moment the idea occurred to Armenal—"yourself," she breathed. A gleam entered her gaze as it darted from him to Jane and back again.

"*That*, of course, is out of the question," he said smoothly. "But I am persuaded you are now on the right track, Your Majesty."

"Let us not be so hasty," the Queen replied, slipping an arm through his. "Instead, let us take a turn about the room together, my dear Bardulf, while Jane recovers her composure." This critical comment seemed finally to penetrate the fog of misery surrounding Jane, for she averted her tearstained face and moved quickly aside for them.

Alisander allowed the Queen to tow him in the opposite direction. He dragged his heels a little. It would not do for the Queen to guess she was being maneuvered into this decision.

"Only consider how convenient all round," she was now rattling away brightly. "Really, I wonder that it has never occurred to me before!" Alisander demurred but without quite as much conviction as the first time. "No, it is true," Queen Armenal insisted. "And would really work out most conveniently for everyone involved. Do you not think so?"

"Thus far, I have never found it remotely convenient to be saddled with a wife."

"But really, I do not know how you have avoided it for so long. It is high time you took on some responsibilities." Alisander gave a murmur of mild disagreement, which the Queen ignored. "Then, too, this could be an admirable solution to—er—your own problems," she said, waving a vague hand.

"What problems?" Alisander asked in some surprise.

"Your lack of an estate, of course," the Queen answered promptly. "Or heir for your title."

"Oh, that." He pulled a face. "It is not likely that a refugee from Lascony, such as my poor self, should hold lands in fair Karadok," he pointed out.

"Your Lasconian lands were confiscated, were they not? On behalf of my brother," the Queen asked with an almost breathtaking lack of tact.

Idly, Alisander wondered if the circumstances of his family's fall from grace had slipped her mind for the moment. "They were," he agreed affably. "And my entire family put to the sword."

Armenal did gasp slightly at his reminder. "Er—yes," she agreed with a faint wince. "I remember now. Wilhelm has always been very thorough and his trust in Sir Reginald's judgment was absolute. I rather wonder *you* did not share their fate."

Seeing that she did look genuinely curious on this score, Alisander enlightened her. "I was but twelve at the time," he explained without rancor. "His gracious Majesty, King Wilhelm, spared me of any complicity in the conspiracy against him."

"Hmmm." Armenal slowly nodded. "You must have caught him on a good day."

Alisander's answering smile did not touch his eyes. "As you say," he replied smoothly.

"It is likely," the Queen said, briskly dismissing this distasteful topic, "that Wymer could be brought to entail some property on this unfortunate child Jane now finds herself burdened with." Alisander almost checked his step and Armenal's eyebrows rose. "Why, Bardulf, I do believe this notion displeases you."

The Queen's flashes of insight could be discomposing at times. "I do not know that I care to be burdened with the responsibilities of an estate," he admitted carefully. "Especially one that I would only serve as caretaker."

The Queen gave a short laugh. "All landowners are merely caretakers, my dear Bardulf. It is entrusted only for a short time, and you cannot take it with you. Besides, to all intents and purposes, it might as well be yours. Us poor women are powerless before the role of father and husband that you would occupy."

"You envisage me in such a role?" he drawled. "You flatter me."

"Why not?" Armenal answered coolly. "There are as many disinterested husbands and fathers in noble houses as there are elsewhere."

"I wonder if I would be..." he mused aloud, casting a glance over his shoulder at Jane, who was now sat hunched in a window seat looking utterly dejected.

"Would be what?" the Queen asked in bewildered accents.

"Disinterested."

She gave a rippling laugh and patted his arm. "My dear Bardulf, there can be no doubt on that score. And that would suit Jane's purpose admirably, let me assure you. She would not want a devoted spouse dictating her every move. She belongs here at court, by my side," the Queen continued ruminatively. "It is true that I am most annoyed with her at present, but even I will admit that she has been my most devoted lady-in-waiting up to this point. It would vex me greatly to be without her."

Alisander nodded. They had reached the other end of the room and turned about. "Still," he said thoughtfully, "I am not convinced that my own lot in life would be so improved by such a move."

"Well, then, you must allow me to convince you," the Queen rallied, "for I am quite persuaded that this would solve all of our problems in one fell swoop!"

5

Jane was not sure at which point during the afternoon that the meaning of the Queen's cryptic comments swam into horribly clear focus for her. By the time the prickle of alarm shot up her spine and made her eyes widen and the breath catch in her throat, it was all too late to cry *Halt!* or to protest she could not possibly consent to such a match.

She had spent the past two hours wallowing in a hopeless and wretched misery, and by the time the Queen unbent enough to address her with any kindness again, she felt like a complete lackwit. So grateful was she to receive Armenal's smile, however cool, that she had already agreed to the Queen's proposal before she even knew what she was agreeing to.

"V-Viscount Bardulf?" she repeated now with sudden panic. Surely, she had misheard Her Majesty? She shot a terrified look in his direction and found he was smothering a yawn. Had he not heard what the Queen had suggested? Jane felt her heart lurch with alarm.

"The viscount is in wholehearted agreement with me on the matter. Is that not so, Bardulf?" the Queen said, turning smugly to him.

"Of course, Your Majesty," he replied, looking entirely bored by the topic of conversation. In Jane's opinion, he seemed to be contemplating his tasseled shoes with more concentration than the matter of impending marriage between them. He had not heard the Queen's outrageous proposal, Jane thought anxiously. He could *not* have heard her, or he would hardly be so sanguine in his manner.

"You see, Jane," the Queen said with satisfaction. "It is all settled nicely between us."

"But—"

"I shall speak to Wymer about it directly," the Queen added, her pleasure at the match seeming to fade at this thought. A rather grim expression settled over her features, and Jane's heart quailed. That would not be an easy conversation for the Queen, she thought with a pang. Securing the future of her late rival's child.

Seeing her expression, Queen Armenal nodded. "I am glad to see you are conscious of the indignity this will cause me, Jane," she said with quiet gravity.

Jane swallowed and bowed her head. "Yes, Your Majesty," she whispered, feeling mortified.

The Queen nodded. "And now you will all leave me," she announced, "with the exception of my faithful Magnatrude." The older woman hurried forward. She was flushed with pleasure at being so singled out. "I am exhausted," the Queen continued, "by all of this planning and pother. Over *such* a topic too," she complained. "It is too much!"

"Your Majesty should not be bothered with such things that are wholly beneath her," Magnatrude uttered, sending an angry look in Jane's direction.

"You are right, of course," the Queen sighed in agreement as Jane performed a wobbly curtsey. "But I have always felt entirely too responsible for the fate of others. Once my good opinion is bestowed, I find it so hard to retract it even in the face of errant unworthiness."

"You are too good, too kind," Magnatrude Bartree agreed fiercely. "And others take advantage of that fact!"

Receiving a wave of dismissal from the Queen, Jane turned at once and headed for the door, her face aflame. She was scarcely even aware of Viscount Bardulf's unhurried step behind her until he prevented her from blundering into a closed door by extending an arm to push it open for her.

"Oh! My lord, I had n-not realized you were there," Jane stammered as he fell in step beside her.

"Well," he said with a quirk of his lips, "let us hope that we can continue in such blissful ignorance of one another for the next fifty years or so." At her blank look, he elaborated, "Your years, I believe, are five and twenty, and mine number only three more than that. Fifty years might be a little optimistic but not outlandishly so for the sum of our married life together."

Jane's step faltered and she swung about to face him. "So you *did* hear it?" she exclaimed in a choked voice. "The Queen's plan, I mean."

"Of course," he agreed, his eyebrows shooting up. "A lack of hearing has never been one of my failings."

"I—but—" Jane floundered hopelessly. "I thought you weren't paying attention!"

"You would not be the first to make that mistake," he admitted, and if Jane was not so badly rattled, she would doubtless have been annoyed by such flippancy.

"You are agreeable to the Queen's scheme, then?" she asked incredulously.

Again, he shrugged an elegant shoulder. "These disagreeable duties come to us all eventually. At least this way I shall not be expected to beget an heir, for you will come with one ready-made, is that not so?" Jane gaped at him. "Then, too, I will be spared the necessity of performing some elaborate courtship."

When she continued silent, he quirked an eyebrow in her direction. "Or am I wrong in that supposition?"

Jane practically shuddered at the idea of being wooed by Viscount Bardulf. "No, I should not expect that," she agreed fervently, and she thought he smirked, though the corridor was rather shadowy at this point, so she could have been mistaken.

"Then, of course," he mused, "there is the matter of your dowry. Wymer will doubtless dower you handsomely in the hopes of getting the wretched brat off his hands."

Jane felt herself bristle at this unflattering allusion to her niece. "That *wretched brat* would be your legal ward if you agree to these terms," she pointed out, her voice shaking with indignation.

"Of course," he agreed offhandedly. "But what's a daughter, here or there? Hardly worth quibbling over, are they?"

Jane came to an abrupt halt, regarding him with a sudden, awful suspicion. "You do not…have some already, do you?" she asked faintly.

"Daughters?" He burst out laughing. "Jane, are you envisaging yourself raising a houseful of bastards now?" She felt herself turn hot all over. Of course, part of it was outrage he was addressing her with such familiarity. "No, Jane, you are the only one of us entering our marriage with an illegitimate child in tow," he assured her mockingly.

"Do not—!" She glanced around. "Do not say things like that! This topic of conversation is hardly proper!" she hissed, forcing herself to put one foot in front of the other. He quickly caught up with her again.

"Dear me, I did not mean to offend your sensibilities," he muttered, "and I hate to point this out, Jane, but 'twas you raised the matter of bastards in the first place."

If she was not better raised, Jane would have been tempted to stamp her foot. She *detested* the man. How in the world did the Queen expect her to take him for a husband? Pulling herself up to her greatest height, she turned her most severe look upon him. Annoyingly, she still had to tip her head back to do it.

"Jane," he commented softly. "When you are Mistress Bartree's age, that frosty expression may stand you in good stead. For now, however, you are far too young and pretty to pull it off with any measure of success."

So surprised was she, by his calling her pretty, that she continued tongue-tied until the next turn in the corridor where they were to part ways. "Good evening to you, Lord Bardulf," she managed to voice in freezing accents.

"And to you, my good Jane." His voice floated back over his shoulder as he turned to the left. "May you dream sweetly of me."

She very nearly tripped over an uneven flagstone. By the time she reached the modest rooms she shared as part of the Queen's entourage, Jane was all of a quiver. She shut the door behind her as though pursued by a pack of hounds and leaned back against it, catching her breath. *This was not happening to her…it could not!*

A tinkling laugh from the adjoining room startled her. She had thought to have the place to herself since Magnatrude Bartree remained with the Queen. She had thought the other two ladies she shared with, Osanna and Patience, away from court at present.

Hearing excited accents, Jane realized her assumptions were quite wrong. "I assure you, Patience, 'tis entirely true, for I heard it from Lord Morgan himself and *he* heard it from…"

Jane did not tarry to hear anymore, instead fleeing to the privacy of her bedchamber. Even in there, she could not breathe easy, for disquieting thoughts crowded her head giving her no peace. Clapping her cold hands to her hot cheeks, she paced from one wall to the other, muttering under her breath. What was she going to do?

"Jane?" A hesitant knock at her door had her gasping. "Is that you?"

Jane closed her eyes a moment before making for the door. She opened it a crack and found Osanna Spencer's concerned face peering in at her. "Yes, it is I," Jane responded after a heartbeat.

"I thought I heard your step in the corridor. I hope we did not—that is—we did not realize you had returned already from the country," Osanna said. "Patience and I were just discussing the sad estrangement of Lord and Lady Beswick." As she said this, Osanna's cheeks turned bright red. Jane realized with surprise that she was lying through her teeth.

Why was she bothering to lie? Jane wondered. Gossip was always rife at court and… *Oh.* Seeing the expression of guilt on Osanna's face, the truth finally dawned. They had been discussing Helen. Or rather, Helen's untimely death. Silly of her, she should have expected that the news would not take long to reach the palace.

An image flashed into her mind. A freshly dug grave. That cold, chilly morn a week ago. Her uncle's speculative expression and the terrible numbness of it all. How could her lovely, lively sister now lie under that dark earth?

"—were wondering if you would like to accompany us down to supper?" Osanna was babbling, twisting her hands together. Jane gazed back at her blankly. Then she realized an offer had been extended for her to accompany Osanna and her friends down to the Great Hall.

Generally, Jane did not sup or mingle much with the other ladies-in-waiting. She opened her mouth now on an instinctive refusal, but then found herself hesitating. After all, cowering here in her room like a frightened child was not going to help matters. She needed to maintain appearances and look at least as though her whole life was not falling apart.

Jane nodded. "That would be most agreeable, thank you," she murmured and saw the flash of surprise on Osanna's face. She, too, had been expecting Jane to decline.

"Oh good!" she responded swiftly, though Jane did not know how sincere her words were. She knew the others thought her sadly standoffish and had never really cared. Secure in her position as the Queen's favorite, she had not needed anyone else's good opinion.

Osanna talked brightly as they went to meet her friends who loitered still in the sitting room. On reaching the sitting room, all three seemed similarly astonished at Jane's joining them. Still, after a moment's awkwardness, they greeted her politely enough. Patience Stanhope hesitantly offered her condolences on Jane's recent loss and the others quickly followed suit.

Jane had responded with courtesy and her habitual reserve. Mercifully, they seemed content with this and soon became their usual chattering selves. Together they had gone down to supper, and Jane had managed to get through the ordeal without showing herself up too badly.

It was true that Osanna had been forced to slyly nudge her a couple of times to prompt her participation, and there was one course she simply could not bring herself to touch. Helen had always favored roast beef and mustard above all dishes.

She fancied there were more whispers and glances her way than usual, but she found these easy enough to rise above. On the whole, she thought she managed tolerably well. Neither the King nor the Queen made an appearance in the banqueting hall that eve, and Jane wondered if they were, even now, in the midst of a heated argument about the King's latest bastard. A morsel of food stuck in her throat, and Jane was forced to take a swig of wine to wash it down.

Taking a deep breath, Jane considered matters calmly. If the King agreed to the wild scheme, then her niece could be freed from their uncle's clutches. That was her primary objective after all. Other considerations, such as choice of bridegroom, could be swept aside in the urgency of securing the child's future, she told herself, gripping her goblet stem for dear life.

Whether Viscount Bardulf was any better than Viscount Morpington she had no notion. At least he was not a drunkard unless he hid it considerably better than Rodrey. Did he gamble? That, too, she did not know, and if he was a lecher, then she had never heard 'twas so.

Of course, it was an accepted fact that men played at the dice cup and consorted with mistresses. Their reputations did not suffer for such things, so long as they kept them in their rightful place. In truth, such behaviors were expected of them. Then again, Viscount Bardulf was not the typical Karadokian male, maybe because he was not one.

Jane knew nothing of the Western Isles, but as the Queen's countryman, she supposed she could not hold that against him.

He must have been an established part of Wymer's court for several years now, she thought. He had certainly been a staple ever since she had arrived.

She gave her head a quick shake. She had just decided that her bridegroom was not the most important consideration, had she not? Instead, she must concentrate on the child. At present, her niece was safe enough, surrounded by the staff her sister had engaged to provide for her every need.

Uncle Phillip could exert no malign influence while she was a mere babe in arms. Indeed, it was highly unlikely he had gone anywhere near the infant since its birth. He had no interest in children. Instead, he was likely contenting himself with ruling the roost at Kinnerton and devoutly hoping the King did not kick him out in light of Helen's death.

"Jane," Osanna murmured in her ear.

Jane gave a start. "Yes?"

"We are leaving."

"Ah, yes, of course." She rose hastily from the bench and filed out after the others. As she passed through the hall, the murmured conversations grew considerably in volume.

Osanna slipped an arm through hers. "Pay them no heed," she recommended.

"They could at least have waited until Jane had left the hall," Lady Millicent Everidge commented loudly in a carrying voice. She glanced about the hall, seemingly enjoying the moral high ground.

"So ill-bred," Patience Stanhope agreed loftily, conveniently forgetting that Jane had overheard her gossiping on the subject only two hours previously.

Strangely, the show of solidarity from her fellow ladies-in-waiting *did* comfort Jane a little. Once they returned to the east wing, the other ladies tentatively suggested Jane join them awhile, but they quickly accepted when she demurred, pleading tiredness. Jane tried not to think they likely had much to discuss in her absence.

Osanna sent their shared servant in to attend to Jane first. The fire was speedily lit in her room and water fetched for her to wash. She was helped out of her court dress and trappings and soon Jane was lying in bed, staring up at the ceiling, exhausted yet unable to find sleep. Something nagging at her mind prevented it.

With a sigh, she let herself admit just what it was. *Viscount Bardulf.* She needed to face up to cold, hard facts. Unless she did something drastic, then in the not-too-distant future, she would end up his wife. The breath froze in her throat. She simply could not imagine it. Wife to the *one* man at court in whose presence she *always* felt gauche, however much she strove to hide it.

She did not care how attractive he was and, in any case, his looks were not the kind Jane admired. If pressed on this point, she would say a man who was modest and neat in manner was superior in every way to an ostentatious peacock such as Viscount Bardulf.

His height was generally admired, but Jane did not care for it. It made her feel at a disadvantage when addressing him. She did not like men with imposing physiques, and while it was true, Viscount Bardulf was not bursting out all over with muscles like some of the knights she could mention, he was not a slight man. No, she thought, frowning, he was not slight. He was *lean*. There was a difference.

63

When he wore hose, especially with a short doublet, Jane had often thought he looked more than a little indecent. His thighs were not those of a boyish squire but of a man. Displaying muscular thighs even in a discreet black velvet did not seem like nice behavior to Jane, let alone maroon or crimson.

Moreover, she felt sure somehow that he practiced deceptive arts when it came to his appearance. He was always lounging on seats and leaning against pillars, so you did not notice the true strength and stature of his build. She had often reflected on it.

His hair for instance. He wore it far too long and it curled, making him appear prettier than he really was. When you took a good look at him, his eyes, which so often gleamed with irreverent mirth, were merely an indeterminate shade of hazel. His smile, which she had heard called charming, was more often than not cruel.

He drew your eye, quite deliberately in her opinion, to his pretty rings and beaded sleeves, so that you almost failed to notice the bejeweled dagger at his hip. When he laughed, if the jest was not directed at her, she could admit he was *almost* handsome. Oh, very well, he was handsome.

He was extremely handsome. She could admit it when alone in the quiet of her room. It was just not the sort of handsome she personally cared for. Once she had noticed with surprise that he had quite extraordinarily beautiful hands. Then he had teased her mercilessly for a half hour, speculating that she must covet his ruby ring.

If Jane could cross a room to avoid him, she would, but as he was so frequently found in the Queen's presence, she had come to view him almost as a necessary evil. A man of whom she had always heartily disapproved. A frivolous, insincere, and vain man, who cared only for his own hedonistic pursuits.

Of course, she had only the vaguest ideas of what those pursuits might be, and perhaps that was just as well. She did not approve of the ones she *was* aware of. She knew he must spend inordinate amounts on his jewels and apparel and his showy horses. He was probably the most elegant man in Aphrany; he was certainly the most fashionable.

None of these things were particularly heinous vices, she told herself bracingly. Many of her fellow nobles were vain spendthrifts. It was his own money he frittered away after all. It was just that Viscount Bardulf's manner could be so devastating when it suited him.

She thought of all the times he had casually insulted her, his eyes dancing with malice. That time he had told her that she should never be permitted to read poetry aloud, for she made it sound like a laundry list. How the Queen's other ladies had tittered. She smarted now even to think of it.

She thought fleetingly of Osanna and Patience, who had flanked her at supper. If she was no longer the Queen's favorite, then she should probably cultivate their friendship. Maybe she should have all along. Perhaps then they would not have laughed to see her mortified.

Then again, her fellow courtiers did seem to find Viscount Bardulf's barbed tongue amusing. He was considered quite the wit at court, though Jane did not think the King liked him much. Not that she cared about *his* opinion. In her present frame of mind, the fact King Wymer disliked him was a point in Bardulf's favor.

Then, of course, there was the fact that he had just now told her that he had no desire to beget an heir... That was certainly worthy of note. She had not been entirely surprised, for she knew he did not admire her remotely. This would be a marriage of convenience, nothing more. A marriage to retain position and status at court.

Jane sighed and rolled onto her side. Even so, was she really going to join her lot in life to his, even if it was in name only? It would mean spending a good deal more time in his appalling company. Shying away from the thought of his handsome, mocking face, she thought instead of Helen, not as she'd been on that awful night, but as she had been throughout their childhood together.

Yes, she realized. She would do whatever it took to keep her promise to her sister. Resigned to her fate, she closed her tired eyes at last and finally found sleep.

6

The next morning, Jane had discreetly joined the other ladies-in-waiting in the presence chamber and did not so much as approach the inner sanctum of the Queen's privy chamber, as was her custom. Quite frankly, she was uncertain of her welcome there these days.

Instead, she settled herself on an available seat and concentrated on her needlework, affecting not to notice the speculative whispers all around her. A swift glance told her that Osanna was nowhere to be seen, and without her presence, she felt unsure of the friendliness of the others.

Finally, a discreet cough notified her to the fact Estrilda Rheinholdt was stood directly in front of her. "You honor us with your presence this morning, Jane," she said, rather too loudly.

Jane's heart sank. Clearly, Estrilda was acting as the spokesperson here. Everyone else had fallen silent and was listening avidly. "Not at all," she responded after a moment too long. "Is there some matter I can help you with?"

"Well, as a matter of fact," Estrilda started importantly but was cut off by the loud ringing of approaching footsteps. She turned her head, as indeed did everyone to see who it was. To Jane's surprise, it was none other than Lord Bardulf, whom she had never thought of as particularly heavy-footed before, but this morning, his every step was echoing off the walls.

Jane's mouth practically fell open as she watched him saunter into the room. He was dressed this morning in a close-fitting maroon tunic, with a large hawk embroidered elaborately on both shoulders. There were long strategic slits to his pearl-encrusted sleeves which revealed an undershirt made of cloth of gold. Slung about his hips was a jeweled belt that glittered with gold and flashed with precious gemstones.

What was it her sister had said? she wondered dazedly. That she must provide her baby with "a father who would outshine even a king." Viscount Bardulf certainly did that. Who would even spare the likes of Wymer a glance when this vision was in the vicinity? In the privacy of her own thoughts, Jane could admit he cut a striking, even dazzling figure. Of course, he should look ridiculous, she told herself hastily. The fact he did not must have more to do with the sheer assurance with which he carried himself. The man was monstrously arrogant.

Quite unabashed by the staring courtiers, Bardulf continued his progress at a leisurely, if noisy pace, until Jane started to get anxious that *she* might be his intended quarry. *Surely not.* Her mouth turned dry. He would not address her in front of everyone, would he? Not about…

"My dear," he said, coming to a halt smartly before her. "The Queen wishes to speak to us both about that *little matter* of ours."

To her chagrin, Jane found herself flushing up to her roots. "Now?" she asked, shooting out of her seat with unbecoming speed. She wanted to forestall any further indiscretion, if at all possible.

He inclined his head, then appeared to finally notice Estrilda stood there. He looked her up and down with surprise as though she had only just appeared. "Does this little bird desire speech with you?" he asked Jane offhandedly.

Estrilda gave a choked splutter and beat a hasty retreat to where her sistren awaited her with wide eyes and small cries of sympathy. Belatedly, it occurred to Jane that perhaps she was not the only one who feared his mocking slights. Bardulf turned back to Jane with a shrug. "Her flock awaits, it seems." He offered his arm. "Shall we?" Jane took his arm.

They found Queen Armenal in a strange mood within her private chambers. On their entrance, she whirled about from where she was contemplating her reflection, crying out, "There you are at last!" Which seemed a strange thing to say, when Jane had received no summons.

Mercifully, the Queen gave her no chance to reply, seizing her hands and holding them out to her sides. "Well, Jane, is this to be your wedding gown?" she asked critically. "I prefer you in your houppelande, but I daresay it is of no very great matter."

Jane caught her breath and turned her head to cast a panicked look at Lord Bardulf. Were they to be wed this very day? She could not catch his eye, however, for he had replaced the Queen at the looking glass and appeared to be examining the cut of his sleeves.

"I am not sure they should not be a little fuller," he murmured to himself.

Jane turned back to the Queen. "The King has agreed to—?"

"He has!" Armenal interrupted her swiftly, and something about the look in her eye urged Jane to drop the subject. She needed to obtain clarification about her niece though. She could not leave that to chance. She drew a fortifying breath. "And the child?" she asked boldly.

Mistress Bartree, who was lurking in the background, gave a hiss of disapproval as the Queen's eyes flashed with momentary ire. "Did I not say that I had arranged it all, Jane?" she asked testily.

"My apologies, Your Majesty, but if you did, then I, too, must have missed that part," Lord Bardulf said, finally turning away from the mirror. "When can we expect to receive the…er…bundle of joy?"

The Queen gave a tight laugh. "The two of you will journey to Kinnerton directly after the ceremony today to collect *your daughter* and acquaint yourselves with your new estate. There! Satisfied?"

"Yes, Your Majesty," Jane answered, abashed.

"On your return, you will have it known far and wide that your union has been blessed with a daughter and henceforth she will be known as such."

Jane nodded, unable to speak past the lump in her throat. She did not care what the courtiers would make of that turn of events. The truth would trickle out, but she doubted any would dare to speak of it to her face. Helen's child would be safe in her keeping. That was all that mattered.

The next hour passed in a blur. The Queen made the announcement of the marriage in her presence chamber to great excitement and consternation. "Rally around, ladies," she announced, clapping her hands, "this wedding is to take place within the hour in the palace chapel!"

Jane was surprised to find herself immediately surrounded by a flurry of ladies, vying to chafe her cold hands or pinch her pale cheeks.

"Has he a ring, I wonder?" Lady Millicent whispered excitedly. "If so, I am sure it must be a very elaborate affair!" Jane was relieved to find the question was not aimed at her but rather at Frances Lessimore, who agreed breathlessly that Lord Bardulf's jewels were always a sight to behold.

70

Feeling the hem of her brocade gown being lifted, Jane looked down in alarm. "Your pardon, Jane," Emma Thackeray said, peering at her ankles. "Will you take one stocking off now?" Jane gazed down at her blankly. "To gift your bridegroom," Emma explained patiently. "Or mayhap you just give him your garter?"

Jane opened her mouth to deny the need, but Estrilda interrupted them at this point. "Oh, Emma," she said with a superior air. "No one bothers with the giving of such trifles these days."

"Really?" Emma, who had not long come to court, frowned. "What about chasing the bride afterward to tear off a scrap of lucky cloth from her gown?"

"Goodness, what backwater province do you hail from, Emma?" Lucy Melvin snorted, and a chorus of giggles greeted her words. Poor Emma dropped Jane's hem looking quite crushed.

"Where is Osanna?" Jane asked on impulse. "And Patience?"

"Shall I run and fetch them?" offered Frances. "I believe they are in the east wing working on a tapestry."

"Yes, please, Frances. If you would be so kind." Jane suspected that her roommates would be most put out if they missed her hasty marriage altogether. Frances sprang up and darted from the room as the others started to herd her in the direction of the chapel. Though Jane turned her head, she could not spot the Queen.

"He went ahead," Lady Millicent said, guessing incorrectly that Jane was searching for her groom. "With the Queen."

They had reached the chapel doors before Jane heard hasty footsteps and Osanna's upraised voice. "Jane!" she cried,

71

elbowing her way to the front. Patience was close on her heels. Jane forced a smile of welcome to her lips. "But why are you not wearing your houppelande?" Osanna protested.

"And your opal brooch?" Patience added, sounding disappointed. "The one the Queen gave you."

Jane could hardly confess she had not known today would be her wedding day. "Well…" She trailed off. "I thought this one better suited for the occasion."

Osanna looked her over frowningly, and Jane felt a twinge of annoyance. She certainly thought her court gown of moss green brocade was sufficiently grand.

"Perhaps she hopes the Queen will gift her another, as 'tis her wedding day," said Lucy Melvin sotto voce. There were a few titters at that, but Jane ignored them. She suspected the days of the Queen singling her out with such attentions were well and truly over.

Estrilda sprang forward to rap on the chapel door. "The bride approaches!" she cried, and Jane flinched. Estrilda had such a shrill voice. They could likely hear her in the courtyard below. The doors were flung back by two palace pages, and Jane straightened her spine as the ladies fell into single file behind her.

"Approach now," summoned a calm, authoritative voice, and Jane was surprised to see it was none other than the King's chief advisor, Earl Vawdrey. Was he standing up as groomsman to Lord Bardulf? For some reason, Jane was a little surprised at that. They usually stood on opposing sides of the court after all, with the earl ranged firmly in the King's corner and the viscount in the Queen's.

Lord Vawdrey beckoned them in. "Welcome one and all," he greeted the bridal party pleasantly. "Come in, come in. You are among friends."

Jane could not help but give one fleeting glance over her shoulder as the pages closed the doors behind them, cutting off her retreat. Seeing there was no chance of escape now, she squared her shoulders and sailed into the fray.

7

The deed was done, Alisander told himself with satisfaction. The various legal documents signed by the King, the deeds made over, and the royal seal imprinted into the dark red wax. True, he was not sure where precisely his bride was at this moment, for they had been swept into an impromptu celebratory reception directly after the ceremony, but she was his, alright, and he could rest easy.

He did a discreet sweep of the room, receiving felicitations from the random assortment of guests that the Queen's ladies had managed to round up after a hurried scouring of the palace. Mostly their well-wishers consisted of errant clerks, curious pageboys, and bewildered-looking visitors to the palace who clearly had not been expecting to attend a wedding that day.

He finally spied Jane, sat between Patience Stanhope and Emma Thackeray. Both seemed to be talking her ear off while Jane sat looking dazed. *She should wear peridots about her throat with that gown*, he thought critically.

Here in Karadok, they ignorantly considered any green stone an emerald, but he was more discerning. The yellow-green shade of the gemstones would perfectly offset the green and gold of her gown.

"Congratulations, Lord Bardulf," a diplomat from the more obscure provinces intoned, interrupting his thoughts. Bardulf returned his bow, and he scuttled off looking relieved.

"Er—congratulations, my lord," a bearded man of middle-age said uncertainly. Behind him stood three more of his fellows hurriedly echoing the sentiment. They were dressed in sober dark robes with guild badges pinned to their breasts.

"Your name, sir?" Alisander asked, glancing at the tools depicted on their badge. He thought at first they must be stonemasons. Then he realized the tools depicted were those of glaziers. One of them clutched a large sheaf of papers in his hand. Alisander deduced they were, in fact, petitioners at court that morn and, in all probability, ignorant even of his name.

"My name is Arnold, my lord, Edmund Arnold," the man responded unhappily, as though their presence in the room had been brought into question. "We—er—apologize if we are not supposed—"

"You are very welcome, good master Arnold." Alisander gave them all his most charming smile. "Gentlemen, you are very good to interrupt your business to attend my nuptials. We appreciate your well wishes. Please, partake of the refreshments and take your ease."

Their expressions brightened at once from awkwardness to gratification. "Your servant, sir!" they assured him before heading for the nearest servant passing out goblets.

"Your bride looks a little fatigued," Vawdrey's voice commented to the left of him. "Perhaps you should not delay setting forth for your estate, Lord Bardulf."

Alisander turned to face him. "Why? Is it in poor repair?" he asked, immediately suspecting the other's words of holding more weight than first appeared.

"Not at all," Vawdrey assured him. "In fact, it is very well maintained, for its late occupant employed an extensive staff when first she moved in." He hesitated. "Some might even say she took on rather too many."

Alisander's eyes narrowed. "Indeed? You interest me."

By mutual accord they began to walk slowly along the length of the hall, side by side. "Alas, the old caretakers soon found themselves out on their ear," Lord Vawdrey said. "It caused quite a stir among the local populace."

"The lady considered herself a new broom that sweeps clean?" Alisander ventured.

"Indeed. She wished for staff whose first loyalty would be to her, rather than the status quo."

"There is something to be said for that philosophy," Alisander reflected after a slight pause.

"Oh, I quite agree, however it is not one that will endear you to the locals."

"No, I do not imagine it would."

"Congratulations, milord!" A red-faced man in a mustard tunic interrupted them with a clumsy bow.

"You are too kind," Alisander responded, and the other hurried off, looking relieved to have done his duty.

"I believe it is considered lucky to be congratulated by a Wheelwright on your wedding day," Vawdrey mused.

"Is that what he is?"

"He is at the palace pricing some repairs to the royal conveyances this morn."

"I see, and why is that considered lucky? I am not yet fully acquainted with all your quaint customs in this land."

Vawdrey gave a slight smile at the faint contempt in his voice. "I believe it is something to do with moving ever forward like a wheel in your lives together."

76

Alisander turned as a particularly violent gust of wind rattled the nearest window. Raindrops next battered the murky glass with force. "And what of rain on a wedding day?" he asked. "Is that also an omen of good fortune?"

Lord Vawdrey looked amused. "You make your own fortune when it comes to marriage, my good Bardulf, as you have already demonstrated admirably."

"Hmmm." Seeing that a gaggle of pageboys was approaching, Alisander reached for the purse of coins suspended from his belt. "It seems I must now pay off the lucky pageboys before they run riot," he commented dryly.

Vawdrey laughed, clapped him on the shoulder, and melted away into the crowd. On emerging from the group of excitable youngsters, his purse considerably lighter, Alisander made his way back around the room toward his bride. His progress was slow, for he was scrupulously polite to all who offered him congratulation, but as soon as he saw a space appear on the bench beside her, he was quick to secure it for his own.

"Wife," he greeted her with a nod. Disappointingly, this did not make her start or color as it should.

Instead, she said in a low voice, "Did you mark the Queen's withdrawal?"

"No, has she gone?" he answered, unconcerned.

Jane bit her lip and nodded. "She took no leave of you?"

"None. Did she of you?"

"No."

"Well, well, she has been busy this day and is likely worn out from all her exertions," he answered flippantly. This did make her flush, likely with annoyance, but he found he derived no pleasure from this.

It seemed to him, suddenly, that this wife of his ought to be more concerned with his frame of mind than the Queen's. Wanting suddenly to needle her, he asked, "By the by, whatever happened to Viscount Morpington? Was he not in the running at one point?"

Jane's goblet nearly slipped through her fingers. "In the running for what?" she replied tensely.

"Your hand, my dear. Was he not your most prominent suitor? I think the tale I heard was one of childhood sweethearts."

Jane's color rose. "We were no such thing!" she said indignantly, and seeing a few heads turn in their direction, she lowered her voice. "And I don't believe for one minute that anyone ever described us as such! You are merely trying to torment me."

"No? Mayhap I had the tale confused with another in my head," he replied carelessly. "I could have sworn 'twas you and Morpington."

"Stop linking our names together like that!" Jane hissed. "You will start a ridiculous rumor all by yourself!"

"So, a young Morpington did not chase you around the mulberry bush in the idyllic days of youth?" Jane pressed her lips together and shook her head. "He ne'er attempted to kiss you 'neath a mistle bough, not even one time?" he continued whimsically.

For the veriest instant, a look of guilt and panic flitted across Jane's face. He should have found it funny, but for some reason, he did not. "No." She gulped. "Of *c-course* not."

Alisander narrowed his eyes. "Never?" he asked softly. "Viscount Morpington ne'er tried to steal a kiss from you. Not even once?"

"Not then," she prevaricated, trying to avoid his eye.

"When, then?" he pressed, and a sudden suspicion dawned. "While you were under his mother's roof on your recent visit?" *Of course he would, the young degenerate.*

Jane gave a violent start, her head whipping round to look at him. "How did you—?"

"Aha! An intrigue," he said calmly, though he felt anything but. "Did he kiss you, or did you—?"

Jane was halfway off the bench, and he had to catch hold of her elbow to draw her back down. He'd pushed her too far. "Shhh now, Jane, calm yourself, everyone will think we are having a quarrel. We would not want to set tongues wagging so soon after making our vows."

She tried to wrench her arm free of him, and he saw her eyes go wide when she realized she could not. "I'm a lot stronger than I look," he commented dryly.

"Sir! You are ungallant—and—and—incorrigible!" Jane whispered in a furious undertone, abruptly giving up her struggle.

"I know," he admitted. "I am fully aware of my faults, but you must not be cross. Surely it is perfectly natural for me to wonder about rivals?"

"Rivals?" Jane repeated in horror. "Rodrey—I mean, Viscount Morpington and I were *never*—!"

"And now, I am starting to think it is deliberate. You are trying to make me jealous," he complained. "Am I not your husband?

And all you have ever addressed me as is Lord Bardulf. Yet here you are, bandying around the first names of some *other* viscount as though you were on terms of perfect intimacy."

"I assure you; we are no such thing!"

"It is too bad of you, Jane. You play fast and loose with me."

She cast a quick desperate look about them. "People *are* starting to stare," she finally noticed.

"People are starting to stare, *Alisander*," he corrected her.

Jane gave a small gasp. "Alisander?" she repeated.

"Yes?"

"That is your given name?"

"It is."

"Oh."

"An observant woman would have noticed as much when we recited our names to the priest. For my part, I made particular note your middle name is Margaret." Before she could make a reply he carried on steadily. "When you say, 'we are no such thing,' do you mean with Morpington, or did you mean that you and I are not on terms of intimacy?" he asked.

"I meant…that Viscount Morpington and I are nothing to one another," she replied in strangled tones.

He felt his shoulders relax. "I still want to know about that kiss," he said and was surprised to hear he almost sounded apologetic.

Jane glared at him. "It scarcely even qualifies as such," she said in a furious undertone.

"What happened?" He gestured to a passing server and took a cup of wine from the tray. "And don't skimp on the detail. I'll know if you try," he warned her.

Jane huffed. "Oh, very well!" She took a deep breath. "The dowager asked me to await her while she fetched a skein of the finest yarn to show me. In her absence, Rodrey pounced on me, and we struggled. We overturned a table; I got a pair of horridly wet lips glued to my brow and he got my elbow buried in his stomach. By the time his mother returned, he was retching in the corner as though he was about to lose the contents of his stomach."

"Dear me!" Alisander's shoulders shook. "Poor Rodrey!"

"He is an odious wretch!" Jane shuddered. "Fortunately, the dowager assumed he was suffering the aftereffects of too much drink."

She looked primly disapproving at this, and once again, Alisander wondered that he did not find her priggishness a stumbling block. "I see you are not to be underestimated when it comes to defending your honor."

She looked at him a little askance. "I would hope such a necessity would not arise with my own husband."

"You would not expect your husband to kiss you?" he asked with a lift of his brow.

Jane turned an interesting shade of puce. "Well, I—" She regarded him helplessly a moment. "Not like that, no!"

"Tell me, was it the pouncing or the sloppy nature of the kiss that so repelled you?"

Jane made a choked noise in her throat. "I—well, I hardly—"

Disappointingly, they were interrupted at this point. A momentary lull at this moment facilitated a voice drifting over from a nearby crowd. "—a positive crowd of *nobodies*!" Lucy Melvin's well-bred tones pronounced damningly. "I declare, I would be ashamed to have such shabby company celebrating *my* wedding day!"

Alisander watched the color climb into Jane's cheeks and felt strangely compelled to come to her rescue. He examined the sensation for a moment in some surprise, for he was not sure he had ever felt such a compulsion before, but even under scrutiny, the strange impulse did not dissipate.

Coming to his feet, he clapped his hands together for attention, and the hum of conversation in the room hushed. "Friends, honored guests, I bid you welcome all on this my wedding day. I thank your indulgence in adhering to the customs of my own land, which must seem strange to you all, where 'chance' must play the ultimate role in determining the wedding party." He paused to let this sink in and heard a few excited whispers.

"I think by now, you must have all realized that in fair Lascony, or 'the Western Isles' as you Karadokians refer to it, we hold some very curious traditions. My own family, the de Balons, have always held that it is fortune alone that must determine the day, the hour, and the party that assembles to celebrate the marriage."

He let his eyes travel benevolently over the assembled crowd. Lucy Melvin was now looking extremely red-faced. "Fortune's finger pointed at every single one of you this day, and marked you out as witnesses of our union," he concluded. "We must keep things brief because my wife and I must travel shortly to our estate; however, I must now make some toasts." He lifted his goblet. "I must make first mention of Master Arnold and his guild of glaziers." He turned to face the group of sober-looking gentlemen whose eyes now stood out on stalks.

"In my homelands, a newlywed must espouse the cause of the first man of business he comes across as a married man. If I am not mistaken, Master Arnold, you and your associates have come to the palace today to plead some cause."

Master Arnold's mouth dropped open. "My lord, that is remarkable," he said in all amazement. "We are come this very day to obtain royal permission to expand our premises on Jarman Street…"

"Say no more," Alisander said with a wave of his hand. "I henceforth vow your cause is my own, and I will add my voice to yours as petitioner here at the palace."

"My lord! You are graciousness itself!" Master Arnold said, quite choked by this promise. "We—well, actually we have been in search of a patron for several months without much—"

"I accept," Alisander told them glibly. The guildsmen went from gasps of disbelief to dazed gratification in the blink of an eye. They jostled one another trying to hang on to their composure as they whispered joyfully to each other.

"Which brings me to the next custom. This one I take from my bride's people." He nodded to the crowd. "So, I am sure I do not have to explain this one to you. Where is the royal wheelwright?"

Everyone started looking about in consternation before the red-faced man elbowed his way to the front. "I am he, milord," he said, looking rather ill at ease.

"Ah, good sir, you have congratulated me and thus bestowed a lucky greeting upon the groom. I ask that now you likewise bid my wife happy in her marriage." He extended his hand to Jane and pulled her to her feet.

The wheelwright made haste to greet her and kiss her hand and Alisander tipped him handsomely for the privilege. When Jane would have sat back down, he hung on to her. "Nay, wife," he said. "The customs are not yet done with. Stand still." Jane's eyes widened but she stood obediently beside him for the next part.

With great ceremony, Alisander reached for the back of his neck and unclasped his gold collar set all about with amethysts. Ignoring the tremor which ran through his wife at his touch, he fastened it about her lovely throat. She blinked at him as he next removed his elaborately jeweled belt and clasped it around her hips.

"You see now why I wear such an elaborate tunic," he murmured. "As I must end this day without adornment." He did not remove the ruby which dangled from his ear, for no one in Karadok pierced their ears except sailors, and he had already given her the gold ring from his finger during the priest's blessing. Still, he removed both his bracelets, one diamond and one pearl, and fastened them about her wrists.

"And now, wife, you must give me your garter," he said, holding out a hand expectantly.

"You see!" one of the ladies-in-waiting huffed nearby. "I *told* you so!"

Jane tried and failed not to look horrified. After a moment's speechless indecision, she turned toward the group of ladies and said faintly, "Emma, would you help me?"

The girl darted forward at once. "There, now, didn't I say?" she gabbled as she knelt and lifted Jane's hem. "And no one listened!" She sprang up triumphantly moments later and handed a plain scarlet band to Jane.

"Thank you," Jane said gratefully. Alisander tipped the girl, and she bustled back to her friends looking well pleased with herself.

Jane held out her hand and Alisander received the garter, closing his fingers around it, for it was still pleasingly warm to the touch. With his other hand, he reached out and gently took her chin, turning her face toward his. "Jane," he murmured, "I am going to kiss you now. It is a wedding custom in Lascony, so you must try and bear with it."

Surprise flitted over her face, but she offered no resistance, and he cupped her face and went for her lips. It should be a peck, really, he told himself as he pressed his lips firmly to hers. If anyone asked, he would simply tell them that in his country a lingering kiss was customary.

Jane's lips were slight and sweet and trembling beneath his own. Her cheek was soft under his hand. He let his eyes shut for an instant and savored the moment. Someone started clapping and the rest followed suit. Reluctantly, he drew back, though he was not remotely inclined to.

Afterward he spoke some other words, bidding their guests be merry on his purse and in no hurry to disperse, despite the fact bride and groom must soon depart. The rain continued to lash against the windows, and he summoned his efficient servant Wat and bade him to go and check that the conveyance would be ready in the hour.

"I am not packed!" Jane whispered frantically. "I had no notion—"

"Wat will carry word to your servant," he assured her smoothly.

85

"I have none! Rather, I share a maid with two other ladies, and Marta may not be at liberty to devote herself to my—"

"No maid? My dear, this must be remedied at once."

"It is hardly my most pressing need," she argued.

"I disagree; we leave within the hour. Look to the skies, Lady Bardulf. The roads will be quite washed away if we do not make haste." He was exaggerating, of course, but Jane's eyes flew wide with alarm.

Wat coughed. "Shall I go and see if I can rouse this Marta, my lady? Where might I find her?"

Jane's expression wavered. "Well, if you would, that would be very kind."

In all, the packing took closer to two hours, but as he kept remembering things essential to his comfort and sending Wat back with instructions to Robert, the blame for this did not rest solely on Jane's shoulders. By the time they assembled in stable courtyard, cloaked, and hooded against the driving rain, and surrounded by their various trunks, Jane was pale-faced and anxious.

"Allow me to help you up, my dear," Alisander said, "and we will shelter within." She took his hand, and he guided her up the steps into the elaborate wooden conveyance which mercifully included a substantial covered roof. "Wat!" he shouted over his shoulder, and his servant darted over from where he was instructing the packing of a second wagon. "Blankets?"

"Of course, my lord." Wat hurried away as Alisander climbed in after her. The servant was soon back with a pile of blankets and cushions for their comfort.

"Take off your wet things," Alisander said, removing his own. "Or they will soak you through."

"This is a very grand carriage," Jane commented nervously as he flung her cloak over the back of the seat and wrapped a blanket about her. "The one I rode in previously was not painted or tooled in leather as this one."

"Well, only the very best will do for the Bardulfs," he replied, sitting down beside her. "We can share this one," he said, enveloping her skirts with his own blanket and tucking it about her waist.

"That is very generous, my lord," she said faintly, and he had to hide his smile.

"It will be damnably cold and damp after we have been sat in this box for over an hour," he reflected. "How long did this journey take you previously?"

"Five hours, my lord, or thereabouts," she admitted, and he winced.

"I recommend we try and sleep for the most part."

"Sleep?" Jane sounded startled.

"Why not? We can't exactly enjoy the views," he pointed out, for the window openings were covered in oil cloths to keep out the rain.

"My lord?" Wat called. "All is ready to depart."

"Then let us do so with all haste!" he shouted by way of reply and stretched out in the seat, wedging a cushion behind his neck. At Jane, he directed a fleeting "Good night," and closed his eyes.

8

The carriage jolted again, quite violently this time, and Lord Bardulf moved his arm across to prevent Jane from lurching out of the seat. So discomposed was she that she clutched at his sleeve a moment before releasing him. Thankfully, he did not open his eyes, so mayhap he had not noticed what a nervous traveler she was.

"The road is getting a good deal rougher here," she commented nervously. "I think we may have to stop soon." He frowned, still maintaining the pretense he was asleep. Though he had not opened his eyes once for the past three hours, he had prevented her from falling from the seat several times, and even spoken the odd word if she addressed him directly.

"Do you not agree?" She faltered, for Jane was sure at this point that they would end up in a muddy heap or else sliding into a flooded ditch.

"It is not so very late," he pointed out mildly. "And did you not say you made this same journey in five hours?"

"Yes, but it did not rain with such violence as this the whole time," she answered through chattering teeth. "All this rain may have damaged some of the lane's surfaces. It could be dangerous."

"No, no," he assured her. "Wat has a steady hand at the reins." When she did not look convinced, he added, "If we stop now, 'twill be at a common hostelry. I am convinced you should not wish to spend our wedding night in such a place." Jane opened her mouth, then closed it again. He opened one eye to look at her. "Am I wrong?"

"I would rather spend it in an inn than a ditch, my lord," she answered with some asperity.

His lips curved into a smile, and he shut his eyes again. "Very practical. I believe you will make me an admirable wife."

"Is practicality what you always sought in a spouse?" she asked, though in truth, she could not say why she was so desperate to keep him talking. When first he had feigned sleep, she had been grateful, for it would rule out any awkward conversation. Three hours later, she was desperate to fill the wretched silence.

"I am not sure I have ever sought one out," he admitted after a moment's consideration. "In truth, I have very little notion of how to treat a wife. I think the easiest thing will be if I simply treat you as my latest mistress." Jane was so astonished by this reasoning that she simply stared at him. "Does that offend you?"

"I am not sure," she admitted. "The only thing I know about mistresses is that they are left to die alone."

He opened both eyes at that. "She was not alone if you were there at the end," he said finally.

"Maybe so, but I have no sisters left to attend my deathbed," she answered quietly.

"Perhaps not, but you have a daughter now, according to royal proclamation. I believe daughters are usually dutifully present at such events."

"Celestia," Jane said aloud.

"I beg your pardon?"

"That is…our daughter's name," she finished awkwardly. She ought to get used to addressing her as such, she supposed.

"Celestia?" He pulled a face. "Celestia de Balon. Well, maybe she will grow into the name. Have you seen her?"

Jane shook her head. "Helen was so perilously ill… It did not seem a good time."

"Are you cold, Jane?" he asked suddenly. "Come over here and I will warm you up."

Jane glanced at him doubtfully. There was not much room left on the bench with the way he was sprawled out. "The only way I could get closer would be if I crawled into your lap."

"I have no objection."

Jane flushed. Perhaps he was starting now to treat her as a common doxy. "You are pleased to jest, my lord," she said stiffly.

"Certainly not. I never jest about my own comfort. Perhaps I should have phrased it this way. I am devilishly cold. Please bring your delectable self over here."

Jane huffed but inched a little closer. "There is not much room to maneuver—" she started and promptly found herself seized and rearranged so that she was practically draped atop him. Once she could breathe again, she blinked down at him in astonishment. He had lifted her with such ease that she felt almost winded. "My lord—" she protested feebly.

"Alisander," he corrected her. "Now pull up the blankets to trap in the heat generated by our bodies." Unsure what else to do, Jane reached out and started bundling the blankets around them. "That is better," he sighed and closed his eyes again.

"Are you really managing to sleep?" she asked after a moment's disbelief.

"Yes, now lower your head and you may indulge in the luxury also."

Jane gazed down at him a moment, conflicted. But after all, if she stayed like this for the rest of the journey, she would get a very stiff neck. Given little choice, she lowered her head to his chest and shut her eyes tight.

When next she woke, it was with a gasp, for the carriage had come to a stop and she could hear shouting outside. "Wha—?"

"What is it?" Alisander called out from underneath her. "Why have we stopped?"

"A wagon across the road, my lord," the servant called back. "They are asking for our aid."

Alisander's reply was swift. "Do not stir a step till I am there! Let me out." This was addressed to Jane, even though he had already set her body aside and was hastily retucking the blankets about her. "Do not move from this carriage," he added, drawing on his cloak. "Unless I say so."

Jane nodded and he disappeared out into the night. For the next few minutes, Jane listened to the muffled shouts and groans and guessed that all must be putting their shoulder to the wrecked wagon. She was glad there was another stout servant in the wagon behind them to lend a hand. She did not think her husband would be much use when it came to brute strength, for all she had realized his slim frame was deceptive.

When the minutes dragged on, Jane found herself growing restless. She drew the curtain aside to peer out at the murky woodland scene. Her startled eyes made out the shape of a man laid on the ground in a heap and another man holding a bloodied cloth to his head.

"Help me drag him to the side," her husband said, casually addressing his servant, and Jane watched Wat help him heft the fallen man and prop him against a nearby tree trunk.

His servant turned to him, as though asking him something, and Jane surmised the fallen man must be insensible. She saw her husband shake his head but could not make out his reply. Instead, he turned and spoke to the fellow with the bleeding pate, and the three of them returned to the wagon and set about removing it from the road. By the time he returned to the carriage, Jane's curiosity was burning. She waited only while he removed his sodden cloak.

"What about that poor man?" she asked. He paused and shot her a keen look. "I saw you drag him from the wreck."

"His friends will soon be back for him; I have no doubt."

"Did they run to fetch help?"

"Most assuredly."

"Should we not wait for their return?" Jane asked. "He looked grievously injured."

"I think that would be most imprudent." Seeing her frown, he added dismissively, "All will be well, Jane. You must not squander your concern on him."

"Well, what about the man with the bloodied head cloth?" Jane persisted as he settled in the seat beside her.

"That was Davis, the driver from our second wagon," he explained. "He—er—got injured moving their conveyance."

"Oh, I see." She frowned. "Well, what about their horses?"

"There weren't any."

"But—"

"They must have broken loose before we reached them." He yawned. "Can we drop the subject now? It grows tedious. Give me a share of your blanket, wife," he added before she could grow affronted. "I shall catch a chill and be laid up at this rate."

His hair *was* wet, she noticed, and curling at his neck, for he wore it rather long. She was just reaching for the blanket when she noticed a smear of blood across his knuckles. "My lord!" she said, snatching up his hand. "You are injured!"

"Most likely just a splinter." He shrugged, wiping it away with a handkerchief. "I'm more cold than injured." Picking up on his hint, Jane shifted closer and started unwrapping herself to share the blankets. He set an arm about her shoulders as she tucked him in and sighed. "That's nice."

"I hope you have not actually taken ill," she muttered, trying not to focus on the fact Viscount Bardulf was cuddling with her in a carriage.

"So do I," he murmured. "For I make a devilishly bad patient. Complaining and feeling sorry for myself and the like."

She ignored this, staring down at his hand. There was no splinter. Indeed, she could not even see a graze. "How far do you suppose we are now from Kinnerton?" she asked and thought her voice sounded unnaturally high and thin. Why did he make her so nervous? she wondered for the hundredth time.

"No more than an hour now, hopefully rather less."

In all, Jane was pathetically relieved when Bardulf's manservant shouted back at them that they had turned off the road for the Kinnerton estate. She had no idea what kind of welcome they would receive there, for no one was expecting

93

them, and likely her uncle had been quick to step into the master's shoes.

She felt in no mood to tackle him this evening about rightful ownership, for she was tired and sure the damp cold had seeped into her very bones. There had been a persistent drip from the roof of the carriage for the past half hour that she could not dodge however much she squirmed about on the seat.

It was twenty minutes later that they finally came to a halt. Her new husband handed her down the steps, and she heard the door being pounded by Davis, the driver from the second carriage. He now had a bloodied bandage wrapped about his head and looked more than a little disreputable in the evening light. "Open up within!" he bawled, and Jane surmised he had sustained no serious injury.

A window opened somewhere above them. "Who's there?" quavered a suspicious voice.

"Your new master and mistress!" Viscount Bardulf answered in cool tones. "We bring orders from the King. Make haste, if you please."

The window slammed shut again, and Jane found her cloak being bundled around her shoulders by a solicitous Wat. "Lest you take cold, my lady," he said. She thanked him and they heard the sound of a bolt being drawn back.

"Mercy!" was the exclamation on first sight of the looming wagon driver, who was now leaning against the door frame. "'Tis brigands!"

"We certainly met with some on the road!" Wat explained, hurrying forward. "But we are not thieves. We have journeyed here on orders from the King himself." He started exchanging hurried words on the steps as Bardulf yawned beside her.

94

"A tiresome business," he murmured. "I hope they will not keep us waiting out here half the night."

"What did Wat mean, we met brigands on the road?" Jane asked him accusingly, for suspicions were now forming in her mind.

"Well, those tolls we paid coming out of Aphrany were nothing short of daylight robbery," he replied.

Then suddenly, Davis seemed to stagger, and Lord Bardulf darted forward so quickly, Jane was startled. He caught the man, even as he started to fall. "Wat!" he shouted, and his servant left his spot arguing on the step and came to his master's aid.

To Jane's surprise, no sooner had Wat helped lower the fallen man to the ground than Alisander sprang up, marching for the door. "Move aside," he said in an upraised voice. "This man needs urgent attention. He has suffered a blow with a cudgel."

He did not wait for them to change their mind; he simply shoved his way in to protesting cries on the other side of the door. "That's enough!" he said crisply. "We have shown patience and you are now denying your rightful lord admittance!"

Jane hurried forward, pulling back her hood. "Perhaps you recognize me!" she said quickly. "I attended my sister's burial not two weeks ago." By this point, however, the servants had fallen back and were all standing about in various states of nervous resentment.

"You!" Alisander said, pointing to the burliest. "Go out and help carry him in."

95

The man looked as though he would like to refuse but did not quite dare. Sullenly, grumbling under his breath, he made his way outside.

"Will someone kindly go and fetch Mistress Beth," Jane asked. "Tell her that Lady Helen's sister is below." A pinched-faced woman hesitated, then turned on her heel and marched off, presumably to do her bidding.

"Go and fetch Sir Phillip Cecil from his bed," Alisander said, turning to the most senior-looking servant. "Or should I say, from *our* bed," he amended thoughtfully. "For I make no doubt he has helped himself to the grandest chamber."

Jane felt her color rise but said nothing as the servant slunk away. "Have him laid down," she said urgently as Wat and the other man carried in the fallen driver. "His wound must be dressed, for I can see it has broken out with bleeding again."

"Where is the Great Hall?" her husband demanded. "Through here?" No one answered, so Jane nodded, and he gestured to Wat and his helper, who bore Davis off in that direction. "You!" he said, pointing to another skulking servant. "Have our horses attended to. They need stabling." The man mumbled something, but when Bardulf turned to face him, he quickly hurried outside.

"What a curious bunch," he commented laconically. "Come, my dear." He offered his arm, and Jane took it and found herself escorted into the Great Hall.

Wat, having arranged Davis onto a wooden bench, was now poking out the fireplace and coaxing the remains of a blaze back into life. "The house cannot long have been abed," he commented, glancing up. "You there, go and bid someone bring my lord and lady refreshment from the kitchen."

96

The burly man who had helped carry Davis in started mumbling something about waiting to hear "what the master would say about this."

"I *am* your master," Bardulf replied, sounding bored. "At least until I decide to have you replaced, that is." A hurried footfall in the doorway had them all turning their heads.

"What is this? What is all this sound and fury?" Sir Phillip Cecil demanded tetchily. He looked ill-put-together, as though he had dressed in a great hurry. "Pounding at a man's door at this hour of night! It is outrageous!"

"My dear sir, the hour is not much past ten. You are keeping country hours indeed if you imagine the hour an advanced one."

Sir Phillip froze, staring at him in horror. "Viscount Bardulf?" he said hoarsely and gave a stiff bow. Jane noticed the servants stirring.

"Yes, it is I. My wife I think you know already," Alisander said, turning toward Jane and holding out his hand.

Jane took it and gave a brief dip for her curtsey. "Uncle," she said briefly.

Her uncle stared at her accusingly. *What have you done?* his narrowed gaze seemed to say. "This is a house in mourning," he said coldly. "I apologize if your welcome was lacking; however, we are ill-equipped for visitors at present—"

"You quite mistake the matter, my dear sir. We are not visiting," Alisander replied lazily. "We are taking possession."

"I beg your pardon?"

"By royal command, no less."

97

"Taking possession?" Sir Phillip echoed, plainly horrified by this news.

"Indeed. I have papers here, proving that Lady Bardulf and I are the new possessors of this estate and legal guardians of the child, Celestia."

Sir Phillip's face turned a mottled color. It was dark in the Great Hall with none of the candles lit, but even in the gloom, Jane could see he had turned quite purple. "I don't believe it!" he flung back at them, collapsing into a seat. "This is preposterous!"

The murmuring from the servants who had crept into the hall showed he was not the only one.

"Naturally, I do not expect you to take my word on the matter," her husband responded mildly. "As I said, I bring papers with official seals." He glanced about. "Wat?"

His servant was already unbuckling a pack to retrieve said papers. "My lord, I have them here," he said, ignoring Sir Phillip's outstretched hand and taking them instead to his master.

"Thank you." Bardulf unfurled the papers and started to read the King's edict in a monotone voice. Jane paid no attention to this, for she already knew the substance of it. Instead, she drifted over to the bench where the injured man lay outstretched. A groom was dabbing at his head with a cloth.

"Is he conscious?" she asked in a low voice.

"Aye, though someone tried to dash his brains out, alright," the man answered, his eyes flickering nervously to Lord Bardulf and back again.

"Well, it was not my husband," Jane corrected him shortly. "There was a wagon lying in the road. At our approach, they pretended distress and asked for assistance." That must have been when they attacked Davis, she supposed.

The groom nodded. "A robber's ruse," he said glumly, "to take folk unawares."

"Will he live?"

"I expect so, milady. His constitution don't look delicate to me." Privately, Jane agreed with him, for Davis looked a roughhewn type. "A good thing them robbers attacked him and not your lord and master," he added, and Jane wondered about that for a moment.

In the flickering light of the fire, Viscount Bardulf did not quite cut the figure of fashion he did at the palace. He was wearing traveling clothes, of course, though they were nearly as gorgeous as his court garb. Still, they somehow invested him with a different air than that of frivolous courtier.

He looked tall and more than a little sardonic as he watched her uncle's discomfiture, a smile curving his lips. It was not a nice smile, and he did not look like a nice man. She wondered about those robbers who had faced him in the rainy forest. Did they count themselves fortunate to have met him this dark night?

Remembering the blood on his hand, she doubted it somehow. *Was that man dead?* she found herself wondering, remembering the figure she had seen them prop up against that tree trunk. Jane shivered. Suddenly, she was not so sure she wanted the answer.

"My lady?" It was Wat. "Take this chair beside the fire," he urged. "You are cold, and little wonder. I will see to Davis."

99

Jane allowed herself to be ushered to the seat before the fire. Moments later, she saw Mistress Beth flit discreetly into the room and glance about in some surprise. She was as neat and presentable as the previous occasion Jane had seen her. As soon as she caught sight of Jane, she hurried to her side. "Lady Jane!" she exclaimed. "I little expected to see you back at Kinnerton so soon."

"No? But you must have heard my promise to my sister?" Jane was not really sure why she said it, for she was not usually so confrontational, but the girl flushed guiltily and lowered her eyes.

"I—that is, yes," she answered. "But I did not think—"

"You did not think that I would keep my word?"

She hesitated. "It was a tall order," Beth admitted, "and no small thing your sister asked."

Well, that was true enough. "The child is well?" Jane asked, changing the subject.

"She has everything a baby can require and more."

"Do you see much of her?"

Mistress Beth shook her head. "Your sister, the Lady Helen, enlisted the very best and most experienced nurses to care for your niece. They keep mostly to themselves and their own company."

"I see."

"Sir Phillip does not think it beneficial that the child should mix much with the rest of the household."

"Because of the risk of disease?"

"Sir Phillip never explained his reasoning to me."

Suddenly, unwelcomely, Jane remembered Ayleth's words, that Beth was her uncle's lover. "Where is Ayleth?" she asked. "Does she take an interest in the child?"

"Ayleth?" Beth looked pained. "Alas, Ayleth has not left her room once since the Lady Helen was laid to rest. She has been wholly abandoned to her grief."

Jane nodded slowly. Ayleth had always been devoted to Helen. She remembered the old servant's red-rimmed eyes at Helen's graveside. She had not come to bid Jane farewell when she had left the next afternoon, and Jane had not blamed her. Still, that had been over a week ago.

Her uncle's sudden upraised voice distracted her from pondering Ayleth's fate, and she found him stood aggressively in front of her husband with his hands on his hips. Viscount Bardulf flicked something off his sleeve and looked vaguely embarrassed at Sir Phillip's excess of emotion.

"You roll up here at some ungodly hour—"

"A little after ten," Alisander corrected him mildly.

"And have the unmitigated gall to have me thrown out of my own bedchamber!"

"There are plenty of guest chambers, I am sure."

"Then why can't you use one of them? Answer me that!" her uncle demanded.

"Because, my good sir, *we* are not guests here." Alisander shot him a pitying look as though her uncle's wits had gone begging.

"I will complain to the palace itself about my shocking treatment—"

101

"Feel free, my good sir. The King himself endorsed it."

This last seemed to strike a blow. Sir Phillip opened and closed his mouth before saying feebly, "The King must be ill-informed indeed if—"

"I would caution you against voicing that opinion. King Wymer does not take kindly to such insinuations."

"His daughter—"

"Ah, now there you are quite in the wrong," Alisander said in a voice that brooked no argument. "For Celestia is *not* his daughter. Neither is she the Lady Helen's, not anymore." He lifted his voice to the rafters. "She is mine, and this lady here is her mother. Your King has made it so. Anyone who disputes that is, in fact, committing treason."

Several simultaneous gasps went through the hall, and the wind went out of Sir Phillip's sails as his whole body seemed to sag. He stared in stupefaction, first at Alisander and then Jane. "The King—?" he said hoarsely and shook his head. "No. He would not. Not deny his own flesh and blood!"

Her husband merely looked amused at this assertion. "I assure you he has, and not for the first time. I have it in his own hand here, if you would care to peruse the document." He laid the rolled-up scroll on the table as Sir Phillip shook his head and slumped back into his seat. "However, that must be the last time you mention flesh and blood when it comes to my daughter if you prize your own neck. Now," he finished, swinging around and glancing at the stunned servants who had gathered in the hall. "Who is preparing our bedchamber? My lady and I have traveled many hours and I find our welcome *distinctly* lacking. We seem to have so many servants and yet so few of them seem able to follow even the simplest of orders."

102

Beth stepped forward from beside Jane's chair. "My lord, I will have the maids change the bed forthwith."

"Please do so," he said, barely affording her a glance, and Jane was annoyed at herself for being glad of the fact. There was something about Beth she just could not warm to, and she felt a little ashamed about it. The young woman curtseyed deeply and then backed out of the room.

"Perhaps she thinks me a duke," Alisander pondered. "My dear," he said, turning to Jane, "you must explain the distinction of my rank to her on the morrow."

Once Beth had capably taken charge of proceedings, things moved at a more efficient pace, and within the next half hour, they were led up the main staircase to the bedchamber that Jane remembered so well. She marveled that her uncle had moved so swiftly into the room where her sister had breathed her last. He must scarcely have waited for her burial, she reflected with distaste.

"This room does not please you?" Alisander asked, catching sight of her expression.

"It has certain unfortunate associations," Jane admitted.

Enlightenment dawned on his face. "I see," he said quietly. "But after all, likely many of the past masters and mistresses of Kinnerton have died within these walls. Death is an ever-present part of life, is it not?"

"It is. Sometimes prematurely." He nodded in dismissal of the servant who set down the candles and quietly closed the door after himself.

"Did you kill that man today?" she asked before she could stop herself.

He paused in the act of unlacing his cuffs. "Why do you ask?" He sounded merely curious, not remotely offended or cross.

Somehow, Jane thought it would have been better if he had been. She shook her head. "I'm not sure," she admitted. "It's just that—all day, really—I have been having the oddest feeling as if I scarcely know you at all. Which is *so* strange…"

"Do I frighten you, Jane?" he asked with a directness that was almost shocking.

"No, you don't," she answered after a heartbeat, "but I am starting to wonder if you should."

A smile touched his lips and was gone again just as quickly. "You, *never*. Others…perhaps."

She held her breath a moment. "You would never hurt me?" she clarified. He shook his head. "Or Celestia?" His eyebrows rose, but he shook his head again. "Even if I enraged you somehow?"

"Enraged?" He seemed to consider this. "I don't know that I have ever been *enraged* by another person, precisely. I do not kill from rage, Jane, you need have no fears on that score. Now, shall we for bed? I am so fatigued that I shall not even object to sharing with you." Jane gave an involuntary start. "It is not my habit to share a bed," he explained solemnly, and Jane gazed at him. "You seem surprised."

"Well, it is just that you said earlier that you would treat me as though I was one of your mistresses, and so I thought you must be used to—to, well, *sharing a bed*," she concluded, red-faced.

His puzzled expression cleared. "Oh, I *see*. Well, Jane, the truth is, I have never invited a woman into my own quarters, let alone to share them. I have so many lovely things I like to have about me: my shoes, my clothing, my jewels," he said, waving a hand. "I simply cannot spare the room. When I take up with a mistress, I will simply visit with them for an hour or so. That is generally sufficient for my needs."

Jane blinked. "I see." She turned uncertainly toward the bedroom door. "Should I—?"

"No, no." He waved a hand. "Do not trouble about it tonight. Besides, it is our wedding night, is it not? We can certainly share the covers for one night at least."

Jane eyed him uncertainly. "If you say so."

"Certainly, I do. My trunks will likely not even be brought up before tomorrow." He returned to his shirt lacings. "It is possible I was a little precipitous earlier when I said I would treat you as a mistress," he said with a shrug. "There are likely some distinctions between the roles of mistress and wife." At a loss for how else to respond, Jane had to be content with nodding uncertainly. "Come," he said. "Let us undress and wash and get a good night's sleep."

"Sleep?" Jane echoed hopefully.

"Sleep," he repeated. "We are both tired, and besides, I can wait."

"You can?"

He nodded and gave her a slow smile. "Until you, Jane, can tell me you are not afraid of me, and be remotely convincing about it."

9

Despite the fact she was worn out, Jane slept poorly. If she had not been so conscious of the man lying in the dark beside her, she would certainly have been tossing and turning all night. With Viscount Bardulf so close at hand, she did not dare. What if he woke up and changed his mind about sparing her? He had said he would treat her as his mistress, had he not?

Then again, apparently, he did not actually *sleep* with them. Jane frowned over this in the dark. He would rather have his "lovely things" around him than his kept women. She supposed that made sense when you thought about the gorgeous things he paraded about in at court. It would be difficult, indeed, to find a mortal woman as lovely as that precious jeweled belt he had fastened about her hips earlier that day.

She would have to hand that back to him in the morn. In the haste of packing, she had been forced to pack it with her own things. She was quite sure he had not meant to gift his jewels to her permanently. After all, the ring he had placed on her finger had been markedly plain and lacking in gemstones. She felt for it now under the covers and traced the image on the plain gold signet ring. A two-headed serpent.

'Twas strange, now she came to think of it, for she had never seen him wear that particular emblem, though his tunics were always elaborately emblazoned with hawks and horses and other decoration. She had even seen his sleeves decorated with beaded pomegranates before now.

The ring, she thought, had the appearance of a family heirloom, but if the emblem of the Bardulfs was a two-headed serpent, then why had she not ever seen him wear such a device? It was a mystery. Like so many other things about the man.

She turned her head to try to make out his profile, but the darkness under the purple canopy obscured everything. What if he was looking back at her now, and she did not even know it? Jane's breath caught in her throat. He was right; she was a little afraid of him, and it galled her that he was aware of that fact.

She wanted to be the sophisticated courtier around him as she had been back at the palace. There, she had not been scared of Viscount Bardulf. She had heartily disliked the man, but at least she had been unafraid. Then again, she had not known he had it in him to kill a man, and then complain he wanted a share of her blanket.

Of course, the man *had* been a bad man. Perhaps he was the one who had attacked poor Davis. She hoped Davis would not also die. It seemed most unpropitious to have *two* men die upon her wedding day. She sighed and started to roll onto her side, only to feel an arm reach around her and haul her firmly back against him.

Jane froze, but other than breathe out noisily against the back of her neck, he did nothing else, and after a moment she dared draw breath again. After all, she supposed it was no worse than what they had done in the carriage on the way there. She was still in disbelief about all that.

By some miracle, shortly after, she fell into a deep slumber and knew no more until morning when a knock at the door had her eyes springing open. "Make it stop!" groaned a voice behind her, and Jane sat up with a gasp, dislodging his arm from about her waist. "Ugh," he complained and rolled over, turning his back to her and the door and lifting the covers up over his head.

Hastily, Jane tugged at the neckline of her shift as a maid entered with a basin of steaming water and placed it on the side. Another had entered close on her heels and started piling logs

107

into the fireplace. Jane cleared her throat. "It is water for us to wash," she said, glancing over her shoulder at him, or rather at the lump he made under the blankets.

He made a noise low in his throat which seemed indicative of displeasure. Guessing he was a late riser, Jane gave up on him. After asking the servants for news of Davis, who apparently had survived the night, and requesting her trunk was fetched up, she had her wash and set about freeing her hair from its braid.

Looking around, she found a fine carved ivory hair comb which must have been her sister's. After she had retrieved her own, she would put it up for Celestia. No doubt, when she was older, the child would want some personal keepsakes of her mother's.

Another knock on the door, far more discreet this time, proved to be Beth, who was as neat and meek-faced as always. "I thought you might need help to dress, my lady, as you brought no personal maid with you," she murmured, glancing curiously toward the bed.

"Thank you," Jane said, rising from her seat, "however, my trunk has not yet appeared, and I would rather not wear my travel-stained clothes from yester'een."

Beth perked up. "I shall have them sent up immediately, my lady," she said, hurrying from the room. Jane crossed to sit in the chair in front of the fire for a moment to warm herself, for there was a decided nip in the air.

"There's something distinctly irritating about that girl," Viscount Bardulf sighed, flinging an arm out of the covers.

"Stop being horrible," Jane said virtuously. "She is a very obliging and neat young woman."

"Maybe that's what's so annoying," he mused aloud. "She reminds me a little of you, whenever you're around Queen

Armenal. Oh, *so* obliging and dutiful." Jane flushed, but before she could reply, he added thoughtfully, "She also seems to me as though she's putting on an act."

"Perhaps that's why she irritates *me*," Jane retorted in a flash. "For in that, she reminds me of *you*!"

He smirked, but answered innocently, "Oh, so she annoys you too, Jane? Great minds seldom differ in thought."

Jane bit her lip. She had not meant to admit to her irrational dislike of Mistress Beth. "What makes you think she is putting on an act?" she asked, unable to prevent herself from curiosity.

He propped himself up on his elbows and shrugged. "Just a feeling." His hair was in disarray, flopping all over the place. He was also bare-chested, and was that an emerald dangling from one of his earlobes?

"We are probably doing her a great disservice," she said aloud to distract herself from her disquieting observations.

"Now, don't start mouthing platitudes at me this morning, Jane," he begged, collapsing back onto the bed with disgust. "I cannot stand a proper woman in the bedchamber."

Jane felt herself bristling up but managed to swallow the words that sprang to her lips. She had already displayed a shocking want of manners that morning by implying she found her newly wedded husband irritating. She was quite horrified with herself. The arrival of her trunk gave her an excuse to disappear into the adjoining room to dress, and in this, also, Beth proved herself to be extremely capable of aiding her.

"Shall I dress your hair, my lady?" she offered.

"Did you dress my sister's hair?" Jane asked.

"On occasion."

"Very well." She watched the girl's face in the mirror as she pinned her tresses into place. "I do not wear my hair as high as Helen did."

Beth paused and duly adjusted the height of Jane's arrangement. "How is this, my lady?"

"Much better, thank you." Jane selected a small pearl brooch to pin to her bodice as Beth deftly worked on her hair.

"Will you wear a veil today, or your velvet hood?" Beth asked, glancing down at Jane's accessories.

Jane turned her head to look out of the window at the bare trees and gray morning light. "The hood, I think," she answered after deliberation, for it would keep her neck warmer.

Her toilette was completed, and she made her way out of the dressing room without returning to the bedchamber where she was sure Viscount Bardulf stilled lolled abed. She wondered if she would ever find it easy to think of him simply as *Alisander*, which still seemed shockingly informal. Even the thought of it caused her cheeks to redden now as she crossed the landing, striving for composure.

Jane paused at the head of the staircase, swallowing hard and smoothing her russet brown skirts. *I must be calm*, she told herself firmly. She must start as she meant to go on, and no one here at Kinnerton must ever realize how sadly rattled the events of the past few weeks had left her. Helen would never have paled and quaked at facing down a hall full of curious stares.

Starting a slow and stately descent, she realized that several heads were turning to watch her progress and marveled at the sheer number of servants about the place. Was it because they were all hoping for a glimpse of the new master and mistress that they now found an excuse to loiter in the Great Hall? she wondered.

As she reached the bottom step, they seemed to quickly disperse and melt away, and Jane glanced around at the large, cavernous room. The high table at the dais was not laid, but there were some plates set out at the table nearest to the fireplace. Without anyone to direct her, she simply made for that and sat herself down with her back to the blaze of the fire.

Someone would appear to wait on her presently, no doubt. For the moment, she would simply appreciate the warmth at her back. Jane let her eyes travel over the high vaulted ceiling with its many beams, the handsome arched and mullioned windows, and the sumptuous tapestries which adorned the walls.

Over the fireplace was an elaborate overmantel with scrolling plasterwork depicting three red chalices surrounding a white glove. *Now whose coat of arms would that be?* She leaned back on the bench to try to make out the scrolling motto beneath it. The writing was in a faded red paint, and she was just narrowing her gaze in concentration when a ringing voice proclaimed, "In Life, fail not the Friend."

Jane started and righted herself, throwing an accusatory look over her shoulder at her husband.

"Curious is it not?" he mused, descending the last few steps of the staircase and strolling across the hall. "I noticed it last night. It must be the motif of the fallen Barons of Kinnerton."

"The Barons of Kinnerton?" Jane repeated, eyeing him warily as he joined her at the table, sitting directly across from her.

"They were once masters here, by all accounts," he continued airily. "Their line died out, sometime in the last century. Wymer's mother, Etheldreda, was apparently some distant

111

connection of the family, and thus the property became part of her bride settlement."

"I see." Jane glanced back at the overmantel. "It is a nice motto," she ventured.

"*Nice*," her husband repeated with distaste. "Heavens preserve me from such a dull epitaph. One can see why they failed to thrive."

"I should not worry if I were you," Jane replied with asperity. "I doubt very much anyone would ever ascribe *you* with such a virtue." He smiled so widely that Jane was forced to look away. Why, oh, why did her tongue keep running away with her like this? She could not remotely understand it, for she had never suffered such an affliction before.

"Well, this is all very informal," he drawled after a moment of Jane staring fixedly at the opposite wall. "Are we expected to toast our own breakfast on the hearth?"

Jane pursed her lips, but as they had been supplied with neither bread nor meat, let alone a toasting fork, she knew he was being facetious. He leaned back in his seat, glancing to the left and right of him. "How long have you sat here unattended?"

Jane flushed. "Not above a couple of minutes, I assure you."

He pulled a face and swiftly rose from his seat. "I will return. Do not move."

Jane turned her head and watched him as he made for the screen beneath the gallery and ducked around it. She felt a moment's panic, but after all, what was the worst he could do? Doubtless, the kitchen deserved a scolding, though strange to say, she could not imagine Viscount Bardulf delivering one.

No, he was more likely to be scathing in the extreme, his words dripping with sarcasm. She only hoped he would not put too many backs up. Not until they had found their bearings at least! He reappeared only a few minutes later, and Jane felt herself relax when she saw his unruffled expression. He could not have done anything too dreadful, she told herself as he approached, his step unhurried.

Before she could prevent them, her thoughts returned to the murky wood last night and the body slumped against the tree trunk. Jane drew in a sharp breath before reproaching herself fiercely. She was being quite ridiculous. He would hardly assassinate the kitchen staff for mere tardiness!

"Why, Jane," he said, resuming his seat opposite her, "I believe you are sat too close to the fire; you look quite flushed."

"No, no, I am fine," she replied quickly, and luckily at this point, two manservants appeared bearing bread and butter and a pitcher of ale.

"Apparently, *Uncle* Phillip does not rise until noon," her husband commented loudly, "whereupon he falls upon three courses with a monstrous appetite. Doubtless to dispel his morning fog."

"Morning fog?" Jane enquired, accepting a cup of ale.

"He retires every evening with a full wineskin, by all accounts," he replied, lifting his own cup. "It is fully depleted on the morn."

Jane tried not to look disapproving but likely failed in the endeavor. She did not believe her uncle had always overindulged in such a manner, but perhaps she had been too young when she lived in his household to recognize the symptoms?

"I have told the cook that instead of roasted mutton and venison, Sir Phillip should be served on rising with raw eel and ground almonds. That is a most efficacious remedy, or so I have heard," he continued thoughtfully.

Jane almost choked on her drink. "Indeed?" she asked as soon as she was able. "And have you ever tried this remedy yourself?"

"Certainly not," he answered piously. "I have never suffered from morning fog above twice in my life."

Jane regarded him doubtfully, but after all, she did not think she had ever heard it whispered that Viscount Bardulf was a drunkard. Then again, she had always prided herself on never encouraging scurrilous gossip.

Now she found herself wishing that she *had* paid more attention to his reputation. She had always felt so secure in her conviction that Viscount Bardulf was naught but a frippery, vapid courtier. Now she had a terrible suspicion that something much darker lurked beneath his glittering facade.

"You look troubled, Jane," he commented, setting down his ale. "Come tell me, what vexes you?"

"Nothing, my lord," she assured him hastily as a dish of stewed herrings appeared at her elbow, followed by a platter of what looked like smoked lampreys. She regarded both queasily before looking back at her husband.

"Have some bread and butter," he suggested instead. "Have you any fruit syrups or honey?" he asked, raising his voice for their server. "If so, bring them out. If not, have the cook procure some."

"Aye, milord," the fellow muttered before retreating. When he reappeared, he bore a look of long-suffering and a bowl of apricots preserved in a sweet syrup of dates.

Alisander spooned half of them onto her plate and then half onto his own. "Remove the fish," he requested when the servant started to withdraw. "We'll have none of them."

The servant snatched them up and Alisander started buttering some bread. "You have a fondness for sweet things, I find," he commented thoughtfully as Jane tucked into her apricots. "I had not heard that about you."

Jane lowered her spoon. "Well, why should you?" she asked. "It is hardly a point of interest after all."

"I disagree, though I do not know if that is simply because I find the subject singularly intriguing," he debated, tipping his head to one side.

Jane swallowed her apricot with effort. "You are pleased to amuse yourself," she said after clearing her throat.

He shrugged and leaned forward to place a slice of buttered bread beside her. "I think I want to know *everything* about you, Jane," he said slowly. "Tell me honestly, will you find it taxing to indulge me in this?"

Jane cut the large piece of bread in half. "I think you would soon tire of the subject."

"Let us find out," he suggested bracingly. "Till then, you can answer three questions about yourself at breakfast, and another three before bed, until my curiosity wanes. What say you?"

Jane's eyes widened with alarm. "That I would prefer to simply present the facts, rather than be interrogated."

He clicked his tongue with disapproval. "Very well, you will have the chance to do so, but if you fail to think of three, then I can question you instead."

Jane lowered her knife. "If you insist," she conceded grimly, "but in return, I must beg the same favor."

His eyes gleamed. "Well, this is encouraging," he said, smiling as he buttered himself some bread. "I had no idea you were similarly afflicted."

Instead of letting his words ruffle her, Jane took a deep breath. "I only ever had one sibling; I was born at my grandmother's house in Fulford, and my father died when I numbered some two years of age."

He paused with his cup halfway to his mouth. "So frank in the matter of your origins, Jane," he said sarcastically. "I will respond in kind. I, too, only ever had one sibling. I was born at my father's house in the province of Gerlaise, and he died before I reached my fifth year. Now why do you look so startled?"

"One sibling?"

"This surprises you?"

Jane poked her apricots with a spoon. They were, in fact, far too sweet for her taste. "No, I suppose not," she said slowly. To her surprise, she found she wanted to ask him where his sibling was now and if they were close. Shooting a look at him, she found him watching her, a knowing smile playing about his lips. "You had prior awareness of my sister," she said defensively.

"Yes, I suppose that is true. Very well, you can ask me one further question"—he held up a finger—"about said sibling. Choose wisely."

"Brother or sister?" Jane asked promptly.

"Brother. *Older* brother," he added. "You see how generous I am, to volunteer two facts?"

Jane pushed away her apricots to concentrate instead on her bread and butter. "You are generosity itself, my lord."

"It is heartening to learn we have so much in common, is it not?"

Jane's eyebrows rose. She could only suppose he meant the fact they both possessed only one sibling and had dead fathers. "I do not really have a sweet tooth," she admitted when he commandeered her bowl of abandoned apricots and started tucking into them. "I simply do not care for fish when breaking a fast."

"Well, as you are being so open with me, I will confess I am not considered remotely generous," he replied with a shrug. "In fact, quite the opposite. I am usually considered quite selfish."

Jane frowned. *By whom? His mistresses?* Her thoughts startled her, but at least she had not spoken them aloud. "Speaking of generosity," she said, "I have your jewels with me. I did not like to leave them unattended at the palace, although that seems rather foolish in light of the attack upon our wagons last night. They are packed in my trunk."

"Mine?" he murmured, lifting his eyebrows. "I think not, and if you imagine I will be returning your garter, you are destined for disappointment."

Jane hesitated. "Was the exchange not simply ceremonial?"

He shrugged. "I will take my bracelets back from you, for they were hanging off your wrists in an ungainly fashion, but you may keep the collar and belt for bride gifts." Jane flushed and

117

opened her mouth. "No, do not argue, for I grow bored of the subject already," he begged with a wave of his hand.

Jane huffed. "If you are trying to convince me you are not generous, then you are doing a very poor job of it." He lifted his eyebrows but made no reply. "Alisander." To her annoyance, she felt her cheeks warm at her use of his given name. "*Were* those men going to rob us last night?"

"Doubtless, but do not let it concern you. It was nothing."

Nothing? One man was dead and another was badly injured. Was life so cheap, then, to this husband of hers? When he looked up, she lowered her own gaze.

"My dear, make sure you run up and put on your jewels before your uncle rises," he said. "I would not want *him* to think your husband was cheap as well as self-absorbed."

Instead of asking why he cared what Sir Phillip thought, Jane nodded. After the meal, such as it was, was finished, she made her way up the staircase and, on impulse, asked a passing servant to direct her to the nursery. The young woman led her in that direction, before scurrying off and abandoning her at the door. Jane knocked and walked in and was immediately confronted by three middle-aged women in wimples so wide they seemed almost to span the entire room.

"Can we help you?" one asked forebodingly, stepping forward. "Are you lost?"

Jane bristled at the woman's tone. "I am not lost, no. I have come to visit with the child," she finished, loath to use the word *niece* or *daughter* in connection with the infant. The whole business was so very awkward, and she was not at all sure that the events of last night would have reached the nursery staff. It certainly did not appear so.

118

"I am afraid," the woman said with a chilly smile, "that our charge is sleeping presently and cannot be disturbed."

Jane paused. "Is it possible that you are in ignorance of my standing in this house?" she asked with quiet dignity.

The woman colored faintly but stood her ground. "I am aware of your connection with both house and child, my lady," she said with a shade more politeness in her tone, "but from the moment of my employ, I was made aware of the importance of this child's standing. In short, that it is connected with the highest personage in this land and, as such, its safeguarding cannot be taken too lightly."

Jane blinked. Clearly, Helen had not exaggerated when she had told her that at one time she had thought to fit to rival the Queen herself. "Might I ask, at the moment of your employment, whether my sister was aware she had delivered a girl child?" she asked, her tone dry.

The woman pressed her lips together. "I was employed a month before the Lady Helen was delivered," she admitted stiffly.

Well, there you had it. At that point, Helen must still have been fervently hoping for a boy. "What is your name?" Jane asked after a heavy pause so that her pointed words might sink in.

"It is Lingard. Mistress Lingard."

"Well, Mistress Lingard, the King himself has sanctioned my visit. Do you mean to tell me you will try and turn me away?"

The woman hesitated, as though she would like to do just that, but did not quite have the nerve. Reluctantly, she moved aside, leaving just enough room for Jane to pass her into the next room where the door stood ajar.

119

Jane walked through and made her way quietly toward the large wooden cradle in the center of the room. It was a grandiose affair of carved dark wood with embroidered sheets. Even in the dim light of the room, she could make out both her family's coat of arms and those of the house of Argent.

To her shock, the Cecil family crest, that of an ash tree, was crowned with the coronet of an earl, something it had not had the right to display for many a day. Well, those would have to be burned. What had her sister been thinking? Had she anticipated the King would reward her son with the restoral of their late father's title?

After all, if the babe had been a boy... It would not be the first time Wymer had rewarded a male bastard with a title. Perhaps Helen had been right, and the King might well have made this child the second Earl of Cecil. Jane gazed down at the sleeping baby, whose birth had been such a bitter disappointment to her sister.

The vastness of the crib doubtless made the slumbering child look even smaller than it already was. *Celestia*, Jane thought. Such a little girl, for such a grand name. All she could see of the babe was its little pink face amid a nest of sheets.

Its diminutive size was disconcerting. Certainly, she looked smaller than any other baby Jane had come across. Then again, maybe she had never encountered a newborn before? She could see no trace of Helen in the baby's tiny features. The shock of hair on its head was dark, and she could not determine the eye color, for Celestia's eyes were shut fast.

Jane was not sure how long she spent gazing down at the sleeping child, but when she stirred from her quiet reflection and turned toward the door, she found Mistress Lingard standing there, watching her in stony disapproval.

Jane walked toward the doorway and the woman once more fell back to make way. Jane kept on walking until she reached her own room. Once there, she turned the key in the lock and sat on the bed, her thoughts in turmoil. She could not disappoint her sister or fail this child. She *could* do this. She would do all that was required of her. She would be a fit mother to her niece, and all would be well.

Jane sat quietly until she began to feel like a coward, hiding away like this. Then she stood and went to retrieve Viscount Bardulf's jewels from her chest. He might insist they were now hers, but as Jane fastened the small fortune in jewels about her person, she knew she would never really believe they belonged to her. Any more than she would ever believe herself a mother and a wife.

10

After breaking his fast, Alisander summoned the household steward, who turned out to be a churlish-looking individual by the name of Simpkin. On informing Simpkin that he required a tour of the house and lands, he was confronted with a bunch of humming and hawing and "Sir Phillip"–ing which soon grew so tiresome, he was forced to be frank with the fellow.

Given no other choice in the matter, Simpkin performed the tour with an offended, yet nervous air, and Alisander spent a dull day, indeed, surveying the Kinnerton estate. Even he, who had no appreciation for such things, could recognize it was a handsome property, but he took no pride or pleasure in riding around its boundaries and surveying its many features.

It had a pretty wood, a handsome lodge, some pretty tenant cottages, and a babbling brook; but none of them raised any pride in his breast or gave him the remotest pleasure. As far as he was concerned, he was burdened with holding the place in trust for the child Celestia, in whose blood there was at least a faint trace of the ancient baronial line that had built it.

He would fulfill his responsibilities, ensuring the place was well maintained, but nothing more. He had no intention of becoming tied to such a place. Why should he? He knew only too well the perils of believing you belonged somewhere, that your fate was somehow intertwined with that of a few acres and the people who lived on it.

Such thinking was a mistake. There was a spot in Gerlais, for instance, that housed the bones of his own forefathers. It now stood lush and green, with precious little remaining of the soaring towers of Castle Bardulf. All that remained of the once-fabulous edifice was a single solitary tower, standing incongruously amid a green meadow.

And on this hauntingly peaceful spot, a great tragedy had once occurred, within living memory, though it was hardly spoken of and scarcely even remembered these days. The truth was that the land did not mourn his brother. It had started to heal as soon as the smoldering piles were put out. It had grown over the footings in a riotous jumble of green roots and climbers. The nearby villagers and the tenants had mourned, maybe a sennight, for the lordling who had tried to stand firm in their interests, against the edicts of a grasping government.

Then they had shaken their heads and agreed he was a bonny lad and good, too good mayhap for the likes of this world, and they had turned their hand once more to the plow and their thoughts had returned to the daily grind of their own lives.

The less scrupulous among them, or maybe the most in need, had even looted the remains of the castle under cover of darkness, scavenging for anything they could repurpose to their own ends. More than one cottage was fortified with stone that had once shored up a far grander residence.

And why should they not? Life was a struggle, particularly for the peasant. Alisander did not resent the fact they had neither inclination nor time to grieve his family's loss, any more than he begrudged the brambles and moss that had swarmed to obscure the bones of the old castle.

He braced himself now, as the gallows loomed starkly in his mind, and Henri mounting its steps. Gods, but he had been young. Five years younger than he was now. He made a sound, an involuntary noise in his throat, and Simpkin halted, looking to him for instruction. "I will make my own way back to the house," Alisander said shortly. "You go on ahead."

123

"Aye, milord."

Alisander took a deep breath and expelled the air from his lungs, along with the lingering memory. Gods, he was growing positively melancholy. This would not do. It was the country air that did it. He vastly preferred the fetid, teeming air of a town. He would turn his mind to pleasanter things. Namely, his bride and how he would go about her seduction.

That alone brought a slow smile to his lips as he began his own circuitous route back to the house. He still needed to show much patience, of course. Jane was so damnably reserved; it was no wonder she found it so hard to make friendships with others. She was something of a loner among the Queen's ladies.

He could not even flatter or cajole her presently, for she took compliments so ill. Perhaps it was somewhat his fault; his trifling manner meant she would never accept his words at face value. Still, he was inclined to think she would react poorly to *anyone's* addresses, for she always suspected the worst, namely that she was being teased.

No, that was not entirely true, he reflected with a faint frown, for she accepted the Queen's praise with every evidence of pleasure. His steps slowed as he remembered the first time Jane had really captured his attention.

He could see it now, though he could not recall the precise gown she wore that day, or what jewels she wore about her neck, details he usually noted assiduously. Doubtless, neither had been worthy of attention, for Jane always dressed to fit in rather than to stand out. A mistake, he always thought.

Her face, though, he could remember that, alright, and the overwhelming gratification she had shown when the Queen had sought *her* out for particular praise and named her the worthiest of commendation that day, above even one so elegant and accomplished as Eden Montmayne, and despite the presence of her far more striking sister.

The dazed joy that had dawned on Jane's face when the Queen had praised her and bestowed a jewel of her own upon her had been a revelation, for suddenly, right in front of his eyes, the rather bland and dull Lady Jane had burst into the most vivid of color. *Emotion* quite transformed her.

Suddenly, Jane was so flushed and bright that it had almost hurt his eyes to behold the adoration blazing from her own as she beheld the Queen. Was it the first time anyone had ever deemed her praiseworthy? He wondered now, as he had wondered then. What would it feel like to have someone look at you in such a way? Armenal barely seemed to notice. She took it as her due.

Jane, of course, had never realized what the Queen had been about that day, despite how glaringly obvious it had seemed to Alisander. Armenal had used her as an instrument to score off the King and defeat his machinations to advance his new favorite at court. By deeming Jane the pick of the current crop of ladies, she had relegated the King's choice into the shade.

He wondered, not for the first time, how Jane would feel if she ever discovered the truth, that the Queen had been making a power move that day on the chessboard, using her as a pawn, before checking the King. Ever since that moment, Jane had viewed Armenal through the eyes of a devotee, never resenting her for being selfish or thoughtless. In her eyes, the Queen could do no wrong.

Alisander could read Jane with such ease that he rather wondered at his fascination with her. There was no mystery to Jane. She had been overlooked her whole life, outshone by a more beauteous sister, and likely starved of praise and affection at home. Likely she had always felt guilty about any twinges of jealousy or resentment she must have felt and ruthlessly suppressed them in the name of duty.

He rather wondered where her distrust of men had come from. She was no flirt and had never shown the remotest interest in being courted that he had ever seen. Could it have been that nonentity Viscount Morpington who had broken her heart at a formative age? he mused. But no, he simply could not see it. Not after her account of the attempted kiss.

No, it must have been something else. At some point, Jane had simply decided never to trust the capricious whims of men and had instead foolishly devoted herself in service of the Queen like some holy vocation. He supposed she had known a happiness of sorts or the closest approximation that one with an existence like Jane's could feel.

She had no close friends or confidantes, and after close observation, he could see the poets and artists that so delighted the Queen left her quite cold. Jane had no appreciation of the arts. For all her decorum, she was a practical creature. She had carved out a life for herself that was quiet and dignified and gave her independent standing at court. That had been all she desired, not truth nor beauty nor love.

Then something horrible and unexpected had happened, calling all her loyalties into question. Her sister had died, but not before wringing from her a promise which had turned her life completely upside down. Jane had gone against the Queen, had lost her favor, and found herself stood at the altar with the person at court she disliked most.

Alisander smiled broadly. *Enter Bardulf.* His good humor restored, he pursed his lips and started to whistle a tune whose name eluded him. He whistled it all the way back to the house, thrice over, and he was just approaching the east side of the house via a raised terrace when a wooden shutter was flung wide.

Sir Phillip Cecil's head appeared at the opening, and he regarded Alisander balefully. "Ah, there you are, Bardulf," he said coldly. "Wondered who the devil that was. 'The Merry Husband of Narrimoor,' if I'm not mistaken. Curious choice of tune for one in your shoes."

"Do you think so? I thought it rather apt." Sir Phillip's eyebrows rose but Alisander did not elaborate.

"I would like a word with you, if I may," the other continued after an awkward pause. "Man to man."

Alisander stifled a sigh. *What a bore.* "But of course," he answered smoothly. "Where might I find you within?"

"My st—I mean, er, *the* study." Sir Phillip amended himself quickly and cleared his throat. He cast a quick, furtive look at someone stood by the door, but Alisander had already seen Mistress Beth hovering there. Alisander gave him a nod and continued unhurriedly on his way. He had known, of course, that such a confrontation was inevitable. Best they got it over with at once, but what a perfectly dreary ending to an already ghastly day.

*

Alisander could only be grateful that Sir Phillip possessed the presence of mind to not appear at dinner that evening. He credited him with neither tact nor finer feeling on the subject, instead suspecting the older man was still sulking after their interview that afternoon.

In the end, he had rather enjoyed himself, making the wicked uncle's nostrils flare with anger as he had to bite back hasty words. Alisander had been all disinterested politeness as he had

127

let Sir Phillip know that he had no intention of letting him hold any position of influence over "his little family" as he had so touchingly phrased it.

"You mean to reap the reward, then, of my labor!" the old man had exploded, thumping a fist down on the desk.

"*Your* labor?" He had quirked a brow. "My good sir, the result of your labor lies in a grave in the nearby churchyard."

"The child still lives; that is the important thing!" Sir Phillip had replied hoarsely. "I have a vested interest in it, and I will not be cheated of my due!"

Alisander had inspected the braiding at his cuffs. "My daughter, you mean?" he'd asked softly. "By royal decree."

Sir Phillip's face had turned a mottled purple in color. "This will not stand! This is a travesty of the natural order! I will not abide by such arbitrary—!"

"If you will not abide by your King's pronouncement, then you must take that up with him," Alisander had interrupted the fuming man. "For my part, I recommend you seek an audience with him at once. Why delay? In any case, there is no place for you here." Sir Phillip's mouth had opened and closed, for he had seemingly been struck speechless.

"We shall be vastly reducing the staff here," Alisander continued, "and putting the house on half board while the family winters at court." Sir Phillip's jaw had dropped. "My wife and I have positions to maintain," he concluded blandly. "And cannot tarry in the country until the summer months." *And not then for too long, if he could help it.*

After supper, he followed Jane up the staircase to the solar, which was a good deal cozier than the draughty Great Hall.

"We ought to have supped in here," he commented, throwing himself down onto a cushioned bench next to the flickering fire.

"We had not known then that my uncle would not be joining us," she said, glancing over at the small table with only four chairs.

"Ah yes, I should not wish to be cloistered with him in such a cozy setting," he agreed, pulling a face. "But as a matter of fact, I had a suspicion he might not join us tonight."

Jane, who was selecting a book, looked over her shoulder at him. "You did?" she asked.

"I let it be known we expected him to take leave of us very soon," he admitted, draping an arm along the back of the settle. "I trust I did right?"

She turned from the bookcase and gave him a solemn nod. "Quite right, but tell me, how did he make reply?"

"With lots of bluster and hot air," he admitted. "And avowals to take up his cause with the King."

Jane's eyes widened as she took a seat opposite him. "Do you suppose he will actually do so?"

"Not if he has any sense. Does he?"

"Some," she admitted cautiously, "along with a good deal of self-interest."

"Both of which ought to prevent him from making a fool of himself in front of Wymer."

Jane bit her lip. "One would hope so."

"For his own sake," Alisander added. She looked rather pale, even in the golden candlelight. "You should not look so

129

worried. It mars your expression. What have you been about this afternoon?"

She clutched her book. "I paid some visits," she said hollowly. At his querying look, she added, "To Celestia and to my sister's servant, Ayleth, and…and to my sister's grave."

"Very dutiful," he responded. "How did you find them? Well, I trust."

"Ayleth is still plunged in deepest mourning," Jane said quietly. "She barely leaves her room, and I could scarce draw above ten words from her, though I tried."

"And the child?"

She did not answer for a few moments. "She—she looked small and terribly vulnerable to me," she confided in a rush, and he saw some color mount her cheeks.

"Is that not customary for the young? I understand kittens cannot even open their eyes for over a sennight after they are born." She stared at him. "I forget who told me that," he said with a wave of his hand, though that was a lie. He knew full well who had told him. It was funny how much Henri had been on his mind all day.

Jane lowered her gaze and made a great show of opening her book. "I suppose," she said after a moment staring at the title page, "that it's just the fact…well, she will be depending on *us* to protect her."

"Again, quite customary, as I understand it." She looked up quickly at that. "Children usually look to their parents for such things, do they not?"

Jane swallowed audibly. "Do you really not find such a thing daunting at all?" she asked in a hushed voice.

130

"What thing? Babies?"

"Parenthood," she corrected him firmly.

He tipped his head to consider this. "I think it is just that you take your duties very seriously, Jane, whereas I choose to take mine lightly."

Instead of replying, she turned her face aside and stared at the fireplace. "Perhaps so," she whispered.

He should let it drop. Clearly something was troubling her, but that did not mean there was an obligation on him to pry for its source. "Something weighs heavy on your mind?" he heard himself say.

"I am troubled," she admitted. He lifted his brows but waited for her to continue instead of dismissing her fears. "My uncle, he is a consummate schemer," she continued haltingly. "That is why I agreed to the Queen's proposal. I do not want my niece to be used as a means to further his own ends."

"Your daughter, you mean," he interrupted. The gods knew why, but it was galling that she believed his offer of marriage originated with the Queen. She would never know how he had pulled the strings, but even so.

"Yes, that was what I meant," she said, flushing. "My daughter." Even the way she said it was awkward and unconvincing.

Alisander gazed at her. "Why do you struggle so with this?" he asked curiously. "You simply need to state something with confidence and then it is simply so. It is not hard."

Jane stiffened. "Merely saying something out loud does not make it so."

131

"It is the first step in doing so." He shrugged. "At least, I have always found it to be."

Jane regarded him indignantly. "When?" she asked suddenly. "When have you ever found that to be the case? Can you cite me even one example from your own life?"

Alisander considered this a moment. "An example? Let me see… Ah yes, after my brother's execution," he replied, snapping his fingers.

Jane gasped. "What?" she asked faintly.

"King Wilhelm asked me if I bore him any grudge for the execution of my family in front of me and the razing of our ancestral home to the ground. I answered him promptly, 'Of course not, Your Majesty. As a loyal subject, I know it was your perfect right.'"

"King Wilhelm of the Western Isles executed your family in front of you?"

"Oh yes," he agreed evenly. "Or rather, he invested one Sir Reginald Hervey with the authority to do so. Sir Reginald was the King's highest representative in our region at the time. I really don't know why you Karadokians persist in calling it 'the Western Isles' though. Its true name is Lascony." He pulled a face. "Actually, I might have a small suspicion why."

"Why?" Jane faltered.

"Well, personally, I think it is because none of you wish to acknowledge it is an independent nation of its own ruling. Instead, you persist in some ancient myth that it was once some outlying part of Karadok—"

"I *meant* why was your family executed?" she interrupted him pointedly.

"I just told you, Jane." When she continued to gaze at him in bewilderment, he added, "My older brother, Henri, went against the authorities. He committed an act of treason by withholding our estate's tribute that year. There had been a drought, and there were various other contributing factors locally that I will not bore you with. He thought his duty lay not in paying the King's taxation, but in protecting the interests of our land and our dependents. Two of my cousins were also implicated in the insurrection, and an uncle on my mother's side."

"Were they also—?"

"Oh yes. All four of them were hanged that day. Along with my brother's steward, a capable man named John Tunney, the only one who was entirely blameless in the debacle." An expression of regret flickered over his face. "John, I was really fond of. He used to carve me wooden birds to play with."

Jane was silent a moment. "How old were you?"

"Hmmm?"

"How old were you?" she persisted. "When this…this terrible thing happened?"

He screwed up his eyes. "Some twelve years."

Jane swallowed. "And what happened to you afterward? I mean, with your home destroyed and your family all dead?"

"I was made a ward of the Crown, of course."

If anything, she turned rather paler. "Was that as bad as it sounds?" she asked, sounding dismayed.

He opened his mouth, intending to say something entirely flippant, when her expression stopped him. Was she feeling sorry for him? It gave him the strangest feeling in his chest and changed his mind about how he would answer. Instead of being glib, he decided to stick with the truth, well, the bare bones of it, in any case.

"Wilhelm had me placed in the home of one of his most rabid supporters," he replied in measured tones, "where I spent the next ten years of my life learning my trade."

Jane still looked troubled. "Your trade?" she repeated. "Diplomacy, you mean?"

He shrugged, dropping his gaze. "What else?"

Jane did not answer, and when he did venture to look her way again, she seemed to be frowning furiously. Was she trying to make sense of him? And why did he like that idea so much? "What are you thinking about, Jane?" he asked softly.

She opened her mouth, then closed it again. "Why—why did you say that, about liking your brother's steward, John Tunney?" she asked abruptly. "Did you not like your older brother, then?"

He paused a moment. It was sort of shocking to hear a name from his past on her lips. He was not sure if he liked it or not. He never spoke of the past. Why was he doing it now?

"I did not *dislike* my brother," he admitted slowly, "but we were not close. Not in age and not in sympathy. When I was twelve, he was twenty-three. My parents lost several children between the two of us, and besides, Henri was…something of a paragon. I've always thought he would have made a very good saint."

"You were not much alike in temperament, then."

"Decidedly not." He grinned. She gazed back at him, and he thought anyone but this woman would smile back at him, even if it was only out of politeness. But Jane looked so serious in the flickering light. Why was he so drawn to her? It baffled him

134

still. On impulse, he sat up in his seat, wanting to be closer to her. "The fire in here is dying down," he said. "Shall we repair to our bedchamber before it grows colder still?"

*

Jane was already tucked up in bed by the time he had undressed and seen to his ablutions. The two of them, by unspoken agreement, moved between the bedchamber and dressing room, giving one another privacy in these moments.

He had half expected her to have extinguished the candles on her side of the bed and be feigning sleep by the time he joined her but found he was not destined for such disappointment. Jane was propped up on her pillows with the same book from earlier open in her lap.

She wore an unbecoming white cap over her braided hair and had a mantle thrown about her shoulders, obscuring any glimpse of her shift from him. He smiled to himself as he added a few more logs on the fire before climbing into the bed.

Taking her example for his own, he threw a couple of pillows behind his back and turned his head to look at her. "What is that book that so fascinates you?" he asked, glancing down at it. It seemed to him she had not turned a single page.

"Is that the first of your three questions?"

He smirked at her hopeful tone. "Ah, so that is why you are sat so quietly and expectantly. You remembered our agreement. What an honorable creature you are."

She narrowed her eyes at him. "You say that as though it were more insult than compliment."

"Believe me, insulting you is not uppermost in my mind right now. If it were…" He let his eyes travel over the linen cap fitted tightly over her head and winced.

"It seems our taste in bedtime attire does not correspond," she observed, her eyes glancing at his bare chest and head before veering away. "I would have thought Viscount Bardulf's nightly apparel would have been a good deal more elaborate. Instead, you go to bed practically naked, I find."

The way her pale skin turned pink even at the word *naked* should not delight him like this. He should tell her that he did not usually even sleep in braies, but instead, he reined himself in. "Pray tell, what did Lady Jane imagine clothed my body while I slept?" he asked with interest, rolling onto his side toward her and tucking a pillow against his shoulder.

"If I am to answer this, then I am taking this as the first of your questions," she warned him.

He nodded. "Please do, for I am strangely intrigued."

A wrinkle of concentration appeared on her forehead. "I would have expected a nightcap of towering proportions, with a very long tail and…and many pleats and ribbons all about."

He nodded. "Anything else, or was I quite naked apart from the elaborate headwear?"

"Certainly not! I imagined your body was decked for sleep in the very finest of linens," she said promptly. "It would be a lot of voluminous fabric with cunning tucks and ruffles to give it shape and…and very large sleeves."

He hid his smile. "Perhaps I should have you speak to my tailor and make this stunning creation a reality. Is that the lot?"

She shook her head. "On your feet, you would also wear stockings with very long pointed toes."

"How *disappointing* the reality must be!" he exclaimed, "but the fact of the matter is, Jane, that there is no bed robe so decadent as nudity. You should try it sometime."

She reddened and faced forward. "I would be far too cold for that, I fear."

"I can assure you, you would not be. Not if I was there."

"But you said—" She stopped abruptly.

"What, Jane?" He propped his head up with his hand. "What did I say?"

"You said you do not care for a bedpartner," she pointed out.

"Ah, but I was not talking about sleeping."

She cleared her throat. "Oh, I see. This would be one of those sporadic visits. The kind you pay your mistresses," she added, sending him a fleeting glance.

He frowned. "The thought displeases you?"

"I know nothing about such things."

"When do you think you would like to learn?" he asked with a directness he did not usually employ.

She was silent a moment. The gods alone knew why he was holding his breath. "Is this your third and final question?" she asked.

He paused. "My third? You are being generous this evening. In truth, I thought I had used up all my questions already."

She plucked at the bedsheets. "Well, it seems only fair. I have already asked *you* more than three this evening." She threw a quick look at him. "Earlier, in the solar."

"I answered them." He shrugged. "Besides, they were…interesting questions. Not what I would have expected from you."

"You expected me to ask dull ones?" she said with a challenging lift of her brows, which should *not* have sent his pulse racing. It was doubtless the setting, lying in a bed with her like this. It felt intimate, even though they were not on such terms.

"I have never found you dull precisely," he admitted lightly. "Instead, let us say, excessively polite."

"Perhaps it occurred to me you might not care for polite women in the bedchamber," Jane said, and he almost gasped.

"Jane," he whispered. "What a very bold thing to say."

She was bright red by this point, but she kept her voice steady. "Perhaps you have underestimated me, Lord Bardulf," she said, sounding so correct and prim that he wanted to roll right on top of her, drag that ugly cap off her hair, and kiss that prim mouth until it forgot to be polite.

Instead, he eased himself onto his back, breathing hard until he had the impulse under control. It took embarrassingly longer than it should have. "You did not answer my final question," he pointed out in a gravelly voice.

"Whenever you see fit, my lord," she answered like the dutiful wife she was. Sadly, being dutiful was the last thing he wanted from her in this respect. *Damn it.*

Breathing out heavily, he shifted away from her to blow out his candles. "Good night, Jane," he said, and even to his own ears, his tone sounded off. It was far too rough and husky; she must have noticed.

"Good night, my lord," she answered, and he listened to her rustling around in her starchy linens as she extinguished her own light.

11

Jane lay awake longer than she had the previous night. She did not know if Alisander slept or not, but the thought of him lying there beside her, wide awake and conscious of her every move, made her feel even less inclined to sleep. Maybe this was why he did not like his mistresses to share his bed? It was a wholly unnatural thing, to sleep beside someone you knew so little.

Then again, he did keep giving her the strangest glimpses into his private life. Why was he doing that, if not to foster some spirit of understanding between them? She could not help her thoughts from turning toward that extraordinary conversation in the solar earlier.

Jane had foolishly assumed diplomats were chosen for the love they bore for their country. But how could Alisander possibly love the Western Isles when such a tragic incident had marred his childhood? Such a thing seemed well-nigh impossible to her.

Then, too, there had been that business of him being raised by someone fanatically loyal to King Wilhelm. The King who had so cruelly allowed the execution of his entire family over what, it seemed to Jane, was a wholly petty matter, the collection of tithes. There was something decidedly jarring about that, and something else was bothering her too, that she could not quite put her finger on.

She turned the conversation over in her mind until she discovered the source of her unease. It had been the part where he had said he had learned his trade as a ward of the Crown. Something about his tone told her he had *not* meant diplomacy; she was sure of that much.

Sir Reginald Hervey. She filed away the name for future reference. Something suggested to her it was important. A clue to this strange man lying beside her. She felt profoundly shaken by the peek he had given her into his childhood. No wonder he thought lying over her niece's parentage the merest trifle, after the lies he had been forced to voice, merely to stay alive.

At some point, she must have fallen asleep, for the next thing she knew she was being shaken awake and a sharp voice said "Jane? What is it?" in her ear.

She gasped and sat up. "Naught," she mumbled. "It was naught, just a bad dream." His hand fell away from her shoulder, and she hugged her knees a moment, squeezing her eyes shut against the fading images. Her heart was still pounding, and she had a horrible feeling she had cried out in her sleep. *How humiliating.*

"Care to tell me what it was about?" he asked casually out of the darkness.

So shaken was she that refusal did not even occur to her. "I was…trying to…hold the baby, but it turned to brittle twigs in my arms and fell apart. I could not keep it in one piece." Spoken aloud, the dream lost a good deal of its horror for her. "Quite ridiculous, of course," she choked out.

"Dreams often are, in my experience." He paused. "However, yours sounds disturbing."

"I am not usually so nonsensical, I assure you."

"Dreams are frequently that way, you should not be ashamed of it."

She turned her face toward him, though she could see only his outline in the dark of the room. "Did you ever have nightmares? As a boy, I mean. After—well—after all you endured."

The silence stretched, and when he finally spoke, she had almost given up on receiving an answer. "At first," he admitted. "Every time it happened, it was duly reported, and I was summoned to Lady Hervey to explain myself."

Jane's mouth felt dry. *Lady Hervey?* Was Hervey not the name of the man who had executed his family? That would mean that on his family's death, they became his guardians. *How cruel.* He had not told her that before, she thought slowly. At least not explicitly. Somehow, she had received the impression he had been brought up elsewhere. "What did you tell her?"

"I made no mention of their true substance. Instead, like a loyal subject, I claimed my sleep was disturbed by fears something might befall the King. Of course, she told me this was treasonous and had her steward whip me soundly for it." At her appalled gasp, he explained, "Because Wilhelm was King by divine right and the gods would never allow him to be displaced."

Jane shook her head. "What *was* their true substance?" she asked with some trepidation.

He sighed, "Jane."

"Tell me," she uttered, though she did not know why.

"I was very young."

"Tell me," she repeated with uncharacteristic insistence.

"Stretched necks," he admitted bluntly. Jane made a choked sound as she tried to hold back a startled sob. "Are you on the verge of laughter or tears?" he asked, sounding alarmed.

"Laughter?" Jane repeated with horror. "How could you think—?"

"Tears, then," he said swiftly. "You must not cry for that boy, for he is long gone. He was not a nice child in any case. My brother Henri was the nice one. Little Jane would not have liked Little Alisander."

"Yes, I would have!" she vowed recklessly.

He chuckled. "Well, I suppose if you could be fond of Lord Morpington as a child, you could like anyone."

"Rodrey was not so very bad as a boy," she protested.

"I was."

"I don't know that I believe you."

"Really?" He sounded thoughtful. "What if I told you my fondest fantasy was tampering with the parapet, so that one day, when taking her morning constitutional, Lady Hervey would plummet to her death into the filthy moat water below?"

"I would not be shocked," Jane insisted after a momentary pause. "Children often fantasize about such things. As a child, I myself frequently thirsted for revenge."

"You did?" He sounded startled. "Upon whom?"

"Lots of people, both my uncles in particular. I felt powerless and thwarted in life and my only ally was a beautiful and clever younger sister, who outshone me in every way."

He was quiet a moment. "*Both* your uncles? I did not know you had more than one."

"I have a maternal uncle as well as Sir Phillip," she answered with a shrug. "He joined my mother's household when she became a widow."

"And what did he do to earn Little Jane's enmity, this uncle of yours?" he asked softly.

"Silly things, petty things, hardly worth mentioning," she admitted.

"Such as?"

She would never repeat any of these things in the cold light of day, Jane realized. Was it wise to speak of it now? Somehow, it seemed to relieve her feelings. "My uncle Humphrey told me many times over the years that I would ne'er make the match my mother did before me, that my manner was too stiff and unyielding for a woman, that I needed to learn to smile more and be more amenable. I used to…imagine confronting him with a dazzling match and crowing about it." She cleared her throat. "I told you it was foolish."

"Uncle Humphrey lives still?" Alisander asked casually.

"No, he died some five years ago."

"A pity."

"Yes, my mother was always very fond of his companionship."

"What about your other uncle?"

"You know he still lives," she pointed out in surprise.

"No, I mean…what did *he* do to earn your wrath?"

"Oh, he was also dismissive of my abilities," she said lightly. "He, too, contrasted my prospects unfavorably to Helen's. He was a good deal more objectionable about it too. Uncle Humphrey was just a buffoon at the end of the day, whereas Uncle Phillip…" She trailed off her words. She did not really want to dwell on her unpleasant, bullying uncle.

144

"What sort of revenge did you imagine yourself enacting on Sir Phillip?" Alisander asked. When Jane hesitated, she felt his fingers close about her own, where her hand lay on the bed. "Tell me."

The warmth of his hand on hers made her heart thud. "I—one time, after he was particularly scathing about my performance on the psaltery, I walked behind him the entire length of the long gallery pretending that, when we reached the staircase, I would shove him violently from the top step," she admitted.

Part of her could not believe she was admitting to such a thing. It was one thing to want to rub one uncle's nose in a personal triumph, quite another to want to shove one to his death! "Unfortunately, another party was climbing the stairs at the time. My mother, observing my expression, screamed out loud with horror." Alisander gave a low chuckle. "My ill intent must have plainly shown on my face. Indeed, my sister said afterward that I looked quite murderous."

"You would make a very poor assassin," he observed lightly.

"No doubt." She gave a weak laugh. "Though I never intended to act on it, of course. It was just to relieve my feelings at the time. Afterward, Helen laughed so much over it that she was almost sick. Do you know," she said slowly, "she never blamed me once for loathing Uncle Phillip, even though she was his favorite?"

"Why should she?"

"I don't know. My mother always said we should be grateful for all he did for us, taking us under his wing."

"What did your sister say?" His tone was low and soothing; she did not hesitate to answer.

145

"She advised me to direct my anger into more useful channels, such as my studies, in order to prove him wrong."

"That was good advice."

"Yes, it was." Though, sadly, her diligent practice had never resulted in a proficiency that could approach Helen's natural talent. For some reason, her thoughts turned toward Alisander's relationship with his brother. She could not stop imagining him bereft of his family and delivered into the keeping of a hostile family.

Alisander's voice broke into her thoughts. "What are you thinking about?" he asked.

"You and your brother," she confessed.

"Ah. You are drawing parallels betwixt us?"

"Yes. I don't know that I could have done without my sister at that age. You must have felt"—she hesitated—"terribly alone."

He gave a short laugh. "At thirteen or thereabouts, most people would agree I was, to all intents and purposes, already a man. What were you doing at thirteen?" he asked curiously.

"At thirteen?" She considered this a moment in silence. It was at that point when their uncle had sown the seeds of dissent between herself and her sister. "At thirteen I left my childhood home behind me. My sister and I were sent to my uncle's house in Aphrany to begin our training for court. Uncle Phillip said it was what my late father would have wanted."

"Your mother let you go with him unattended?"

Jane nodded. "Why should she not? I was thirteen and my sister some twelve years of age. Most folk would have considered us almost full grown." He gave a huff of laughter, and Jane knew he appreciated that she had turned the tables on him.

"Besides," she continued, "my mother was always rather intimidated by my father's family and made a point of never disagreeing with them." Why was she telling him all this? It was foolish and would only serve to give him further material to tease her with later, but now she had started, she could not seem to stop. "Her father was a country squire who had never ventured outside of his native county of Mertford. Even when my father married her, he never brought her to court or even to the capital."

"His brother's argument, then, seems rather weak." She turned an enquiring look on him, not that he could see it in the dark. "That your father would insist his daughters were exposed to such things," he explained.

"Yes," she agreed, "but my mother was not the kind to put up a fight."

"Not like you, then."

"Me? I am not remotely contentious!"

He ignored this. "Tell me about your time at your uncle's house."

"I'd rather not," Jane admitted uncomfortably. It was a period in her life she did not care to dwell upon.

His eyes narrowed. "You disliked your aunt as much as your uncle, then?" he asked.

"My aunt? Why would you think that?"

"Surely you would have learned the ways of a fine lady under the aegis of your aunt, rather than your uncle."

"You would think so, would you not?"

"Now Jane, you are being evasive," Alisander said sternly. "And you were being so delightfully confiding earlier. Do you not realize how much more it intrigues me when you act so tight-lipped?" When Jane remained stubbornly silent, she could hear the smile in his voice.

"Did I so much as ask you in what direction Mertford lay? Or press you for the name of your maternal grandfather? I did not, because you were artless and open about that part of your life." He let his point sink in.

Jane plucked at the blankets. "My uncle's wife was an invalid, and we did not see her much," she admitted.

"Ah," he said, and she heard him rustle the blankets as though settling more comfortably for the story. "Go on."

"What do you want me to say?"

"You surely do not expect me to believe your uncle taught you how to curtsey and dance the galliard."

"I—no, of course not!" She was getting flustered. "My uncle hired...various tutors and experts for that purpose."

"Yes?" he murmured. "And it was this point at which he singled out your sister as his better bet?" he prompted when she fell silent. Jane made a noise of agreement. "He informed you both of this fact?"

She nodded again, even though he could not see it. "Yes," she added softly.

"Of course he did. Tell me, what did he say to you, this uncle of yours?"

Jane took a deep breath. "Merely that having observed us both and consulted with his instructors, he had determined Helen held all the promise for a glittering match." She was pleased to

148

hear her voice was steady, not showing any foolish hurt after all this time. "It was hardly a surprise," she added frankly. "My sister was always more beauteous and clever than I. I knew that long before I reached the age of thirteen. Neither of us was shocked by his words."

"Now that is more like it," he uttered approvingly. "Such composure and *sense*. Truly, womanly virtues to aspire to." He lapsed into silence for a moment. "For all that, I expect your aunt preferred you."

Jane huffed with irritation. "Well, you suppose wrong," she said roundly. "My sister was perfectly charming to a miserable invalid. She brought laughter and amusement to her sickroom while I stood awkwardly by and bleated platitudes."

He laughed at that. "I have never met a charming thirteen-year-old, and if I did, I would be extremely wary of them."

"My sister was twelve at the time."

"I was not talking of your sister."

Jane sighed. "You are so—"

"What? Tell me."

"Maddening!" she burst out, turning on him. "Why are you always thus with me? Why must you poke and prod at me until I am ready to *burst*?"

He laughed. "Do you really want to know?" he asked, the laughter suddenly gone from his voice. There was a challenge there that made her instantly breathless. "Because I don't know if you're ready for it, Jane." Something about his tone made the words stick in her throat. Finding her quiet and still, he leaned in close. "I have a confession to make," he whispered, his words tickling her ear. "It matters not one bit how open you are with me, Jane, it is not enough."

"What does that mean?" she asked, resisting the impulse to scratch her ear.

"It means that everything you do and say intrigues me, and my appetite for all things Jane grows at a *monstrous* pace."

She had to bite back a gasp. "I don't know what you—?"

"On the morrow," he continued coolly, ignoring her interruption, "I shall look up Mertford on a map, just so I can better picture youthful Jane in her original setting."

"What?" she gasped. "Why on earth—?"

"Then I shall send out enquiries," he continued thoughtfully, "for anyone who can give me a firsthand account of your time there."

"No one in the vicinity would even remember me!" she burst out, appalled. "I was entirely forgettable as a child. You surely do not mean to bother my mother and her household?" She quavered as the horrible thought occurred to her. Oh gods, what would everyone at Mertford make of this husband of hers?

He laughed under his breath. "What a charming notion. Is it possible you have not yet informed your mother of our recent union? How unfilial of you! Or…" he said, drawing out the word, "is it possible you would be ashamed of me, Jane?"

"Of course not! It's not that! I wrote her a very brief note before we left the palace." She really did not know why she was so vehement in her denial, but hearing his chuckle relieved her. She huffed out an indignant breath. "But you knew that already. Sometimes…"

"Sometimes, what?" he asked, sounding intrigued. "Tell me."

150

"Sometimes, I feel exactly like a struggling mouse under your cat's paw!"

"Ah, but the truth is, you hold all the power in this little game of ours," he murmured. "You are just too blinkered to notice the fact." Jane caught her breath. "Though you were right about one thing," he said thoughtfully. "I *do* want to poke and prod you until you burst. I have a notion; the view will be spectacular."

"View? What view?" She felt completely at sea by this point.

He reached out and patted her knee, making her jump. "Rest assured; I will wait for the right time. Lie back for now and breathe easy."

She would never sleep after all that stimulation, Jane was sure. Still, following his directions, she lowered herself onto the mattress and, after a while, sleep did come. When next she woke, it was to find she had overslept and the hour much later than customary. Moreover, she was lay in the bed alone.

12

Jane spent the next hour scrambling to catch up on the time she had lost. The house was strangely quiet. It took her a while even to summon a servant to fetch her water to wash and dress. When she asked for Beth, the maid looked uncomfortable and said she knew not where to find her at this hour, for the house was "quite turned upside down with all the doings."

Jane gave up and made do with the girl's offices, though she needed a good deal of instruction, and at the end of it, Jane had to pin her own veil over her hair which was far from its usual standard. By the time she ventured belowstairs, it was surely after eleven.

The whole household should have been up and about; however, the place seemed practically deserted. Jane took a seat near the fire and reflected on how dissatisfactory everything at Kinnerton was. Hearing a footfall, she turned her head and found Alisander gliding into the Great Hall from the opposite direction.

"Ah, there you are," he hailed her. He was as beautifully turned out as ever in a forest green tunic, trimmed with gold braid, though he wore no jewels this morning.

"Where did you spring from?" Jane blurted in surprise.

"The kitchens," he said, waving a vague hand in that direction. "Wat will bring your food out shortly."

"Wat?" Jane was astonished. "But why would your servant—?" At that moment, Wat entered, forestalling her. He was carrying a salver piled with bread, butter, and honey.

"Where is everyone?" Jane asked in puzzlement. "And why is it that Wat is serving us at table?"

"Hmmm?" Alisander looked from her to Wat and then back again. "Oh, I dismissed them all."

"Dismissed them?" Jane turned to stare at him.

"Yes," he said, sitting down opposite her. "You must agree, my dear, that they were hardly worth retaining."

Jane's mouth fell open. "All of them?" she squeaked.

"Well, maybe not *every single* one," he extemporized. "There was still some old crone turning the spit when I left the kitchens. Oh, and a young lad mucking out the stables."

Jane looked around a little wildly as Wat set the food down before her. "I scarcely know what to say," she started.

"Oh, and the nursery staff, of course," he added thoughtfully. "I have not approached them. Yet."

Well, thank heavens for small mercies! "Who is tending to Davis?" she asked after taking a deep breath.

"Who?"

"The injured—you know full well who I mean," she broke out with exasperation.

"*The injured*—?" A look of comprehension dawned on his face. "Oh, *him*. Well, between the spit-turner and the mucker out, I am sure they can see adequately to his needs."

Jane paused in the act of selecting a piece of bread. "This is a huge house, Alisander," she pointed out rather tartly. "It cannot run with a staff of only two servants."

153

"I feel sure there must be more than two left," he said, frowning. "Wait, there is another locked in the attics upstairs, I believe."

"Ayleth?" Jane asked, wide-eyed. "Have you seen her, then?"

He shook his head. "I have heard of her by reputation alone. And then, of course, there is—" At this moment, Beth slipped discreetly into the room. "—*this* young woman." Beth looked more startled than Jane. "Tell me, Mistress Bess—"

"It's Beth," Jane muttered through clenched teeth.

"How liked you serving in Sir Phillip's employ?"

Jane's eyes flew to Beth's face which seemed for a moment to grow rather tight. The girl recovered quickly. "Why, as to that, my lord, I scarcely know the gentleman. Sir Phillip has not resided in this house above a few weeks."

"Ah, but I have heard you knew him long before that," Alisander said critically. "Come, you must not be reticent with us."

Jane held her breath. How had he known that? A clever guess? Beth's composure slipped and she looked almost afraid. "Yes, my lord." She gulped. Rather than press the girl, Alisander held his tongue, reaching for some bread which he started unhurriedly to butter.

Beth smoothed her hands down her skirts and cleared her throat. "My mother served in his late wife's employ," she answered, her expression a strange mixture of defiant and mortified. Jane rather wondered at it.

"Your mother is yet living?" Alisander asked, idly glancing up as Wat reentered bearing a jug of ale.

"Yes, my lord, only she's respectably married now." These last few words were choked, and the significance of them took Jane a moment to catch. *Oh.* The implication was clear enough. Beth's mother had no room at her table for her illegitimate daughter.

"So, you must fend for yourself, Beth?" Jane asked quietly as Wat passed her a foaming cup of ale.

Beth lifted her chin. "Sir Phillip, he found me this position and the two I held before it."

"I see," Alisander commented, looking directly at Jane. There seemed to be the light of query in his eyes, though she had no notion what he could be asking her.

Well, there could be no question where Beth's loyalties lay, Jane thought. It was strange to think that Beth was, in all probability, a blood cousin of hers, and a first one at that for all it was the wrong side of the blanket. Not that such a thing would ever be acknowledged.

Still, if her uncle troubled himself to lift a finger for her, he must believe Beth was his natural daughter. He just was not the philanthropic kind. Jane could not help but feel it was a little ominous that he had placed his daughter in Helen's household, but after all, *was* it so very odd? Men seemed to have decidedly odd views concerning the provision for their bastard, only consider the King.

"How is it that Sir Phillip did not inherit your father's title on his death?" Alisander asked lazily as he spooned honey onto his piece of bread.

It took Jane a moment to realize he was now addressing her, not Beth. "My father?"

"Your father was an earl, was he not?"

155

"I—yes he was," she agreed slowly, "but it was not a long-held family title. He was awarded the honor after the late war when he retrieved the King's standard at the Battle of Hollingbrook. He only held it for five years before his death. He was the first Earl Cecil, and on his death, the King repealed the title."

Beth gave a little cry, and they both turned to look at her. Her face flamed. "That—is that true, my lady?" she stammered, looking intently at Jane.

"Yes," Jane replied, feeling rather surprised by such a strong reaction. Beth was usually so discreet and did not usually thrust herself into a conversation like that. "The King allowed that my sister and I could continue to be styled as ladies, but as my father had no son…" She shrugged. "There was no grand estate attached to the title, after all, and no lands. Uncle Phillip took no part in the war, and apparently, the King did not see why the title should fall to him."

Beth looked stunned and stared down at her hands a moment before mumbling, "He always made out he was cheated of his birthright! Sir Phillip, I mean."

"Oh, I am sure he did," Alisander drawled. "That will be all for now, Beth." The girl nodded and tottered from the room, looking a shadow of her usual efficient self.

"Is it not a strange thing for my uncle to do?" Jane asked. "Setting his own illegitimate child, brought up a servant, to watch his niece's child, also born out of wedlock, raised with every luxury?"

Alisander did not seem unduly perturbed at the notion. Maybe it was just she who thought it more than just a little cruel. "Sir Phillip does not seem to me a sensitive man," he said mildly, placing the bread he had prepared onto her own plate. He sat back, sucking the honey from his fingertips.

156

"Er, no, he is not," Jane agreed, trying not to stare. So unnerved was she that she picked up the bread without arguing. "My mother never said anything about him resenting the fact he never inherited my father's title though."

"Would you say your mother was a perceptive woman?"

Jane thought of her mother's admittedly narrow outlook on life. "No," she answered hollowly.

Alisander shrugged. "Well, there you are, then." Jane lowered her eyes and sat a moment in silence while her thoughts raced. "Eat your bread and honey," he prompted.

Unsure what else to do, Jane did so. When she had finished it, he leaned forward.

"I have been thinking. We should go together to greet our daughter before we return."

"Return?"

"To court, I mean."

"Return to court?" Jane repeated, sitting up in her seat. "But my lord! We—we have scarce arrived!"

He looked bewildered. "Jane, surely you cannot want to remain *here*, languishing so far from Aphrany. Now we have ousted your wicked uncle—"

"Ousted?"

"Oh, have you not heard? He left in the night."

"He left?" Jane was astonished. She had expected Sir Phillip to put up more of a fight than that.

"He did. And, as I say, now he is gone, there seems precious little reason for us to tarry. I do not hunt. I do not hawk. I do not even ride, without a specific destination in mind. I have never seen the point of riding hither and thither about the place. Therefore, I can see no appeal in the country." He rose from his seat. "Why should we not return?" he persisted, making for the fireplace and standing there with one hand against the mantel. "There is nothing left for us to do now we have set things to rights here."

"Set things to rights?" Jane echoed incredulously, standing from her bench and regarding him with open amazement. "You have dismissed almost all the staff!"

"None that will be missed," he claimed airily. "In any case, my dear, they were hardly old retainers. The place can run just as well without them. Now we are rid of the usurper, I say we can leave with clear consciences." Jane hesitated and he crossed his arms over his chest. "What?" he asked mockingly. "Come, let me hear your list of objections."

"Celestia," she said, lifting her chin.

"What of her? By the way, I looked in on her last night at one point. I could not sleep," he said, noticing her start of surprise. "She is a puny thing and unlikely to cause much bother. If you will not leave her, then you must simply bring her with us." At her astonished reaction, he added, "I do not mean to tear her from your arms if that was what you were thinking. I'm not a *monster*. Now that you have explained your maternal feelings on the matter, I am quite willing to compromise."

"Well, but..." Jane sat back down again, feeling quite flummoxed. For some reason, she *had* been expecting an argument on this score. She knew the courtiers' rooms at the palace were poky and small. Was there really room enough in his quarters for Celestia's attendants? She regarded him uneasily. Besides, he must be aware that there was no question

158

of wresting the child from her arms. Jane had not even summoned the nerve to hold her yet. She swallowed. "I do not yet feel quite sure of myself—"

"You are the child's mother and naturally know what is best for her," he interrupted in bored tones. Jane's face flamed. He was right, of course; that was the line she ought to take, but she felt so hopelessly out of her own depth. "Come!" He held out his hand to her. "Let us go and visit now with our tiny, red-faced daughter."

"My lord…" Jane murmured reproachfully, but she stood up and rounded the table all the same, taking his hand. As he dragged her toward the staircase, she noticed, here in the country, he did not bother so much with his affectations. His stride was firm and brisk as he towed her along the passageway.

"And while we walk," he said firmly, "I will convince you of our need to return forthwith to court. Firstly, there is your somewhat tenuous position to take into account, my dear."

"My position?"

"While it's true, the Queen made great concessions to secure your role as wife and mother, we should not ignore the fact you have several rivals vying for her favor. Mistress Bartree was quick to pick up your offices and take them for her own," he pointed out, and Jane stiffened. "I cannot fathom her appeal, personally," he mused aloud, "but perhaps she fills the gap left lately by Lady Doverdale." He glanced at Jane, clearly looking for corroboration.

She cleared her throat. "Lady Doverdale was forced to retire as Mistress of the Robes due to the increasing stiffness of her joints," she murmured.

159

"Ah yes. I expect her son-in-law is quaking in his boots, that she might now expect to occupy a place at his table."

Jane thought fleetingly of Lady Martindale's big, brutish-looking husband. She could not imagine the Marquess of Martindale being scared of anyone, even Lady Doverdale.

"Lucky for you," Alisander continued conversationally, "Magnatrude Bartree is a sour-faced old bitch and Queen Armenal likes a pretty face or two around her."

"Lucky for you, you mean!" Jane retorted, feeling needled by the coarseness of his language.

He stopped on the stair above her. "Why Jane," he said, turning toward her with a lazy smile, "are you flattering me?"

Jane glared at him. "I'm sure you are well aware of your own appeal, my lord!"

"Why, so I am," he conceded, "but I was not at all sure that you had fallen victim to my charms." His eyes roamed over hers and he tutted. "You are so lamentably reserved, wife."

"In any case, you have told me I am pretty, and now I have told you the same," Jane said, scrabbling for composure. She was sure she was beet red by this point.

"Quite right," he agreed. "It is good to know one's own worth. Armenal would be foolish indeed to lose such a pretty pair of courtiers as we."

His eyes were still alight in that strange manner that made Jane nervous around him. She bit her lip and nodded in agreement, though that was not what she had meant precisely.

"I like the way you do this," he said, lifting a hand to her bosom, but hovering it above rather than touching the prickly rash that had sprung up on her décolletage. Jane gaped at him.

160

He liked her dreadful, unsightly red blotches? "I can feel such heat from you, Jane; it radiates out like a furnace."

"It—it happens when I grow agitated," she told him defensively.

He nodded. "I know. Shall I tell you a secret?" Jane stared at him, quite tongue-tied by this claim to like the thing about her that vexed her the most. "I should like to feel you all hot and flushed beneath me, giving me all that heat. I feel sure you would warm my *whole body* with it."

Jane was not sure at this point if what she felt was disbelief, horror, fascination, or a strange mixture of all three. The look in his eye was *so...* She made a strangled noise and it seemed to snap Alisander out of his strange trance. "Well, another time perhaps," he said and seized her hand once again, sweeping her along in his wake as they climbed the flight of stairs.

On reaching Celestia's rooms they found her three attendants sat in a huddle in front of the fire, folding linens. The oldest, and presumably the most senior, immediately sprang to her feet and started toward them, a forbidding expression on her face. "The child is currently sleeping, my lord, my lady," she started dismissively. "I do not think—"

"Yes, they do that a lot, don't they?" Alisander said agreeably enough, but something about his tone had Jane turning her head sharply to look at him. "What is your name?"

"It is Lingard," she said stiffly. "Mistress Lingard."

"Well, you are standing in our way, Lingard," he said briskly, brushing past her. The woman stepped smartly aside, her face like thunder, and they walked through to the next room where the baby lay sleeping.

How could she be trusted to take care of something so little and defenseless? Jane stopped before the crib, looking down at the tiny figure swathed in white. In sleep, Celestia's little face was relaxed, and she looked almost…

"Thank the gods, she looks a little less froglike in slumber," Alisander said, interrupting her thoughts. "Last night she displayed at a singular disadvantage. Her wailing mouth seemed larger than her whole face."

"She looks nothing like a frog!"

"Funny how her hair is so dark," he continued ruminatively, "when your sister's was golden and Wymer's the color of rotting straw." Jane shot him a furious look. "Very well, I should say, is it not strange, my dear, when your own hair is so golden—"

"My hair is not golden," Jane corrected him stiffly.

"No, you are quite right," he agreed after a moment. "I have wronged you. Your hair is a good deal paler than gold. Very well, is it not strange that our daughter's hair is so dark when your own hair is as pale as—"

"What color was your hair as a child?" Jane said, interrupting his nonsense. She found she actually wanted to know.

"Strange to say, as a child, my hair was white blond. As I grew older it darkened considerably."

Jane glanced at him. "I suppose that accounts for it…" She trailed off thoughtfully.

"For what?"

"Well, it's just…your hair. It's dark but contains no reddish hue to justify calling it brown, and neither is it pigmented enough to call it black. I suppose 'tis almost ashen, like…an absence of

162

color." A slow smile curved his lips. "Why do you smile?" she asked defensively.

"No reason, Jane. I just like that you've dwelt on the matter." She opened her mouth to deny it, but he lifted a hand. "No, do not shatter my illusions, I beg of you. You are giving me precious little by way of encouragement. Let me have this."

The baby let out a whimper, and they both turned to look down at it. To Jane's surprise, Alisander reached down to touch the child's hand which immediately wrapped around one of his fingers. "She's got quite a grip," he commented. "It's curious to think—" he started absently, then broke off his words.

"What is curious?" Jane asked after a slight pause.

"Well, that four days ago, I was the last of the de Balons," he said softly, "and now there are three of us that bear my father's name. Did I ever mention that the Bardulf title can pass down the female line?" he added. "It is much more common in Lascony than here in Karadok," he commented as Jane drew in a sharp breath. "Celestia may someday inherit my title too, if we don't have any more children."

"What?" She was aghast. "I had no idea!" He looked untroubled, but it was hard to believe he would happily bestow both name and title on her niece. "Is that—? I mean, does that not bother you?" Jane asked carefully. She lowered her gaze and forced the words past her lips. "That Celestia is not actually a de Balon?" she practically whispered. "Not by blood, I mean."

"No," he admitted. "It doesn't bother me at all." He watched the swift play of emotions on her face: doubt, confusion, surprise. "Do you find that strange?"

"A—a little, yes!"

He shrugged. "Perhaps I do not set such store by blood as you."

163

Jane could think of no reply to this, so she simply turned back to contemplate the small child. "I was born with a full head of black hair myself," she remembered suddenly.

"Really?"

"Yes." She nodded. "I heard the tale many times as a child. My mother was terribly put out, and there were whispers in the servants' hall that I might be a changeling. Yet, by the age of two years, my hair was lighter even than Helen's."

"Perhaps they swapped you back," Alisander suggested, turning his hand to contemplate the tiny fingers.

"Who?" Jane asked in confusion.

"The faeries. I hear the thing to do is brew beer in an eggshell, then the changeling will leap up and reveal itself, and the true child will be returned." Jane considered him frowningly. "According to the folklore," he added.

"Oh. Well, what I am trying to say is that perhaps Celestia will take after me."

"I certainly hope so."

A cough in the doorway announced the head nurse's presence. "If the child could just be left to sleep now, I feel sure she would feel the benefit," she began officiously.

"Ah, Mistress Lingard. A timely interruption this time, for I have something to tell you. Now let me see, what was it?" He frowned. "Ah yes, that was it, to inform you that your services are no longer required," Alisander announced.

"My lord?" she gasped incredulously.

"You and the rest of your coven will oblige me by packing up and leaving the premises by nightfall."

164

"Nightfall?" Mistress Lingard looked outraged. "Sir Phillip will have plenty to say about this, I assure you!"

"Nothing worth listening to," Alisander replied calmly. "Besides, he has left and holds no sway over what happens in this house. The King has granted Kinnerton and all its contents to my wife here, and she, in turn, has conferred them on me, her lawfully wedded spouse."

The older woman's face froze. "The King—?" she said hoarsely. "But surely—"

"You have been laboring under a sad misapprehension, Mistress Lingard. I have papers in my possession that show this child's lineage. Our marriage has legitimized her. She is our legal daughter. The King has made it so, and as a loyal subject of the Crown, I am sure you will not wish to oppose that view. You may leave now."

Mistress Lingard turned a waxy color and looked frozen to the spot. Stiffly, she inclined her head and turned on her heel, exiting the room. Jane was reeling; she plucked at his sleeve. "Who will take care of the child?" she whispered, aghast.

"Someone less objectionable, I would hope." He glanced at her worried face. "Fear not, we could scarcely hit on anyone worse."

"Yes, but—" She heard the sound of hastily exiting footsteps from the room next door. "Alisander! The wet nurse!" She started forward, but he caught her arm, preventing her from giving chase.

"We will employ a new one," he told her calmly.

"The need is pressing! The baby's health will fail without nourishment!"

"I am aware of how it works," he replied unruffled. "Fret not, they will most likely have filled her belly before placing her in her crib. I will send Wat into the village to find a new one. Some local woman, who either lacks a husband or despises him, so she will be grateful to escape this hole and give us her undivided loyalty."

"No husband?" Jane sounded startled. "But..."

"You think only nobly born women bear bastards, Jane?"

She colored hotly. "No, of course not," she said in a stifled voice, "but..."

"But what?" He gazed at her conflicted expression. "Perhaps you are of the belief that virtues and vices can flow from a mother's milk, as well as sustenance?"

"I—I barely know anything about such things!" she burst out. "But should we be subjecting Celestia to—to questionable influences at such a tender age?"

Alisander paused and watched while the hypocrisy of Jane's words dawned on her. "Do you really want me to answer that?"

She swallowed and shook her head. "No," she muttered, glancing away.

"We will do much better without the staff your late sister hired. They have strange ideas and likely a fair few of them are in your uncle's pocket too," he added with a sly look, likely guessing that would get her on board with his plans if nothing else.

Jane considered this awhile. "How will we know which are in his employ?" she asked slowly.

"We can take an educated guess. I have been doing so all morning. Hence the fact the spit turner remains and the stable lad." He extended an arm to her, in order to escort her from the sleeping baby's room.

"I don't like to leave her unattended."

He tutted. "What an anxious mother you are! She is asleep. We have the final details of our departure to discuss."

"Final details!" Jane burst out a little wildly. Her eye fell back on Celestia. "Any one of the disgruntled staff could come in and snatch her!"

He rolled his eyes, then leaned over the side and lifted the sleeping child out. Not by even a bat of his eyelid did he acknowledge Jane's alarmed step back. He simply held the baby against his chest and then turned back to Jane. "Come on, then."

She fell hastily into step beside him, staring at the odd picture he made cradling a child as he walked along. "My suggestion is this," he continued smoothly, "that we dismiss everyone that was not already here in situ when your sister took possession of the place. That way, we keep a skeleton staff who are familiar with the running of the estate, while we, the family, are away."

Jane regarded him helplessly. "Oh really? It's as simple as all that, is it?"

"Why not? There is hardly any point in us keeping on a full staff here. *We* are not in exile."

"Maybe not," Jane conceded after a moment. "Not yet anyway."

He tipped his head to one side. "You take a bleak view in life, Lady Bardulf, though I will admit, it is true that your good standing with the Queen has been rocked. You have some ground to make up. If you are not careful, you will be slipping down the ranks."

Jane flushed and he smirked. "You do not like that I am frank with you?" Jane pressed her lips together and he laughed. "You know as well as I that the Queen will usually present a favorite of good standing with some piece of bridal finery, but you, she did not gift even so much as a button."

"Yes, yes," Jane said testily, thinking of Lucy Melvin's words. *Perhaps she hopes the Queen will gift her another, as 'tis her wedding day.* "Let us not dwell on such things."

"Alas, Jane," he murmured. "It is just as well that you have a husband now to supply that need."

"What need?" she grumbled as they rounded the corner to come face-to-face with another frosty-faced servant. "Ayleth!" The old servant glared at them.

"And who is this?" Alisander asked gently, turning toward Jane.

"This is an old servant of my mother's," Jane answered after a heartbeat. "Her name is Ayleth, and she has served my sister these past ten years."

"Where are you going with that baby?" Ayleth asked fiercely, but Jane noticed she could not look fully at the child.

"We are taking our daughter belowstairs," Alisander answered coolly. "Perhaps you should tell Ayleth about the royal edict, my dear?"

Jane turned to face the squinting servant. "I am lately married, Ayleth. This is Viscount Bardulf, my husband. The King has decreed that Celestia is our daughter." Only by the tiniest flicker of her eyes did Ayleth react to this startling news.

"Well," Alisander murmured, "now everyone must know. Let us proceed, for I must send Wat on his mission into the village."

Ayleth followed them after some hesitation. "Where's that old sow, Lingard? I'm surprised she allowed you within a country mile of the child."

"Mistress Lingard has been sent packing," Alisander informed her, and to Jane's eye, Ayleth seemed to perk up considerably at this news. She cheered right up once she heard that the entire nursery staff had been dismissed. "Humph! Good riddance!" she pronounced with satisfaction.

Once they reached the Great Hall, Jane watched anxiously as Alisander gave Wat his instructions for finding a new wet nurse in the village. Her husband seemed entirely nonchalant about the child sleeping on him. *What if no one was suitable?* It was all very well, Alisander being so insouciant, but without milk, the baby would surely perish.

13

Jane could not rest easy until Wat returned an hour and a half later with a well-favored woman with a round plump face and a lustrous head of brown hair. She also held a bouncing baby boy in her arms. Wat brought her into their presence and stopped before Jane as though she was the proper person, despite the fact Alisander still had the babe sleeping on his shoulder. Jane stood up, determined to rise to the occasion.

"My lady, may I present Mistress Anne Lee," Wat pronounced.

"I am very pleased to meet you," Jane said as the girl dipped into a perfunctory curtsey.

"Lower than that," Wat growled at her out of the corner of his mouth. "I told you, she's a viscountess."

Anne's eyes opened wide. "Beggin' your pardon, milady, but it's difficult to curtsey, what with Bertrand here being so heavy," she said, bobbing awkwardly once more.

"He's a beautiful child," Jane commented. "Your own?"

"That he is," Anne replied with evident pride. "And only ten months old. Even Mother, who says he has brought mortal shame on our family, will own that he is the handsomest babe she ever clapped eyes on."

Jane felt her color rise. "A handsome name also," she said, in lieu of anything else springing to mind.

Anne nodded enthusiastically. "Picked it meself, I did. I once heard tell of a man called that, from over Wycherton way, and always liked the sound of it."

Bertrand bestowed a gummy smile on the room at large. He certainly looked well-fed. She glanced toward Alisander, but he was gazing off into the distance, seemingly wholly uninterested in proceedings.

"Do you have any ties in the village?" Jane ventured. "Perhaps the boy's father…?"

"Oh no, milady. A traveling peddler he were, what seduced me with his lovely face and honeyed words." Anne sighed. "He was long gone by the time Bertrand here was letting his presence be known."

Jane cleared her throat. "If he is only ten months then you must still be feeding him yourself?" she said, not quite meeting those round brown eyes.

"Oh yes," Anne said cheerfully. "But I got plenty to spare for your little one. Master Watkin here said as she's a poor little thing, failing to thrive." Jane's face must have reflected her anxiety, for Anne started forward. "Nay, do not look like that, milady. I'll soon have her putting on flesh. Only look at Bertrand here. He started out a slip of thing too, though it's hard now to believe it."

"Yes." Jane nodded, feeling quite choked. "Thank you." She took a moment to pull herself together. "Would you, well, like to take a look at her?" she asked.

"Right willingly, milady."

Jane gestured toward Alisander, who now held a book in one hand and was absently patting the baby's back with the other. At Anne's approach, he lifted Celestia away from his chest and wordlessly handed her over to the newcomer. Anne turned back and passed Bertrand on to a surprised Jane.

Anne cooed and clucked over the tiny perfection of her limbs as Jane hefted Bertrand, who was indeed a fine big lad. "You can see she's a dainty little thing, like her mother," Anne said artlessly. Jane bowed her head and did not dare look at Ayleth, who was eyeing the girl with disparagement. "Will I try feeding her now, milady? She's awake."

"Er, yes, if you are content to try, that is, Anne. Let me lead you to this quiet corner," Jane said, ushering her away from the others, though Anne seemed cheerful enough about the task and not remotely awkward. "Shall I leave you in peace while you—?"

"Oh, no need, milady. And if you step too far, Bertrand will likely set up a great wailing. He don't like his mum venturing far away from 'im."

Jane glanced down at Bertrand in some trepidation, but he looked placid enough. As she watched, he placed one chubby fist in his own mouth and started noisily sucking on it. Was he supposed to do that? Jane was not sure. Anne was otherwise occupied, unlacing her neckline, so she hoped it was not particularly hazardous to his health.

"Is it possible Bertrand might be hungry?" Jane ventured nervously.

"Oh, 'im! He's got a full belly, don't you worry," Anne said with a gurgle of laughter. She cradled Celestia to her ample bosom and then smiled at Jane. "She's latched right on."

Jane breathed a sigh of relief. "Oh, that's wonderful. Thank goodness."

When Anne saw her expression, her own turned curious. "You couldn't feed her, then? I thought—well, it was on account of you being a fine lady."

"No, I could not feed her," Jane confirmed awkwardly. "Are you certain that you will be happy to leave the village behind you? Only my husband is anxious to return to Aphrany."

Anne nodded enthusiastically. "It's like I told Master Watkin, I got nothing keeping me here nowadays. My mum will be glad, too, of the room, for my brother's lately married and, as some might say, three women under one tiny roof is two too many." Anne laughed heartily at her own joke, and Jane forced a polite smile in return. "Why don't you sit down, milady?" Anne asked comfortably, "My Bertrand is a heavy weight and you're looking wearied already."

Jane sank down onto the bench beside her. "I am not usually such a poor creature," she said apologetically. "But we made the five-hour journey from Aphrany only two days ago and now my husband tells me he means to drag us all the way back there. I feel exhausted just thinking about it."

Anne tutted in sympathy. "And you so lately with child too!" she murmured reproachfully. "It's no wonder you're a tired thing." Her shining eyes told a different tale, however. She clearly could not wait to see the winter capital.

"Have you been to Aphrany before, Anne?" Jane asked, keen to change the subject.

"Never!" the other replied. "I'm that excited, milady! I could hug meself! Is it really everything they say?" When Jane hesitated, she elaborated, "The palace, the cathedral, the city walls?" Jane nodded solemnly. "Fancy!" breathed Anne. "Me and Bertrand won't know where to put ourselves!"

After Celestia was fed, Jane led her upstairs and showed her where to put the baby down. Bertrand was more vocal by this point, and Jane was glad to hand him back to his mother. "If you would not mind, er, packing up the baby things as best you can, Anne, I would be very grateful. I will send word when I know what hour we depart. Did Wat bring your own things with you?"

"He did, milady," Anne assured her. "Not that we has much."

On returning to the ground floor, Jane found Alisander gazing out of the window, having cast aside his book. "Ah, here you are," he said. "How dare you leave me so long. I have been unutterably bored. Come and sit down here beside me."

She could hardly avoid so direct a request, so Jane sat down on the window seat beside him. "Were you indeed serious about our returning so soon to Aphrany?" she asked, turning toward him.

"Of course I am serious. Never more so. Only consider, Jane, what the hells would we do with ourselves otherwise?"

"Familiarize ourselves with the estate," she answered promptly.

He blanched. "I am as familiar with it as I wish to be." He shuddered faintly. "Moreover, wife, you do not fool me. The prospect of staying here another week does not fill your heart with joy any more than it does my own."

Jane cleared her throat. "It is not a matter of joy, but of duty." He snorted. "Very well," she conceded, "I will own that I prefer life at court—"

"You see."

"But we have *obligations* here."

Alisander rolled his eyes. "Ah yes, obligations," he murmured. "Perhaps my own diplomatic duties have momentarily slipped your mind, wife?"

Jane gave a guilty start, for she had somehow forgotten his official capacity at court. "I—you are right," she admitted stiffly. "I beg your pardon."

He made that airy gesture that he was so fond of, the dismissive wave of his hand. "Pray do not give another thought."

Jane's heart sank as she realized she ought to suggest he returned to court without her. The thought of being left here alone with Helen's household filled her with dread and misery. She opened her mouth to speak the words of dutiful obligation, but her tongue refused to utter them.

She remembered the Queen's cruel words: *You will live in seclusion with no company to speak of... No one will see you. You will have no society, no intelligent conversation. You will be all alone, with naught but a mewling babe for company.*

She would molder here in this perfectly pleasant country house. The child would offer nothing by way of companionship for at least two or three years, she was sure. She would be horribly alone.

"I wish you would tell me what is running through that torturous mind of yours," Alisander commented mildly. "You look terrified."

"Should you wish to return to court without me?" Jane asked hollowly and then stared down at her hands, too afraid to meet his eyes when he answered.

"No," he replied after the shortest of pauses. "*So* sorry to shatter your hopes for quiet tranquility, Jane, but I am deriving far too much entertainment from your society to part with you just yet."

Jane was so relieved she slumped in her seat. "Are your mistresses usually such a source of diversion?" she asked

175

without thinking. He made a choking sound, and Jane fought down her rising blush.

"Not really," he said after appearing to consider the matter. "I usually pick them on looks, not personality."

"Men typically do, or so I've heard," she responded before biting her lip. She ought not to have said that, of course. Sneaking another glance at him, she found he was giving her a long considering look. *Oh gods.*

"You are certainly growing a good deal bolder in the conversational arena," he commented. "Not that I'm complaining. May I take this as a sign your fear of me is dissipating, wife?"

"I was never actually afraid of you," she replied quickly. "It was simply a fear of the unknown." He inclined his head, as though acknowledging this was perfectly natural. Suddenly, Jane knew she had to change the subject and quickly. "Anne seems a caring sort of girl," she said hurriedly.

For a moment, he looked thrown by the change in subject, then he shrugged. "Ah, yes? That is good." He looked from Jane to Wat, who was piling more logs on the fire. "Though, I do wonder if it is customary for a wet nurse to bring her own infant along with her?"

Jane shook her head. "I hardly know," she said. "But what could it possibly signify? If Anne is happy to tend to both, then mayhap it will benefit Celestia. Anne assures me that she— well—that she would not struggle to provide nourishment for both babies," she finished awkwardly.

"She would not leave her own child, milord," Wat put in apologetically. "I offered her plenty of coin to foster it out with a local family, but no amount would budge her."

"I think that does her maternal feelings credit," Jane said firmly. "If she had so readily abandoned her own child, how could we depend upon her nurturing instincts?"

Alisander shrugged. "It makes no odds to me, so long as her methods prove efficacious."

"Very well, then, Anne and Bertrand shall accompany us back to Aphrany," Jane pronounced.

"Bertrand?"

"That is her child's name."

He considered this a moment. "She does not affect to shorten it in any way?"

Jane regarded him with some exasperation. "Not that I am aware. Has that question some relevance?"

"But of course it has, my dear Jane. For example, I could not countenance harboring a child called Bertie under my roof, not even for an instant."

Her brows snapped together. "Upon my word, for a heretofore bachelor, you have decided views upon the naming of children!"

"Certainly, I do," he agreed. "It is as well to know such things about oneself from the outset. If you assure me that she will never address the infant thus, then I agree to appointing her."

"Very well," Jane answered sarcastically. "You have my assurance on that score."

Wat coughed and straightened up from before the hearth. He gave them a quick bow and hurried out of the room about his thousand and one duties.

"I can never tell when you are teasing me," Jane admitted. "Tell me, how much of your manner is affectation and how much in earnest?"

"Out of one hundred? The proportions would be seventy-thirty," he replied promptly.

"At all times, or merely on this particular occasion?"

"Seventy-thirty or thirty-seventy, depending on the circumstance." Jane suppressed her sigh. She ought to have expected nothing less, she supposed.

"By the by," he asked casually, "which are you leaving in charge of the house: Beth or Ayleth? Please bear in mind that the other must accompany you back to Aphrany, at least temporarily, as your maid."

Jane blinked. Ayleth had trailed upstairs behind her and Anne and the children earlier but had not accompanied them into the nursery. Instead, she had drifted off back to her attic room. "I do not think Ayleth is in the right frame of mind to run a house. She is…still mourning the loss of my sister. She has taken it hard. Beth seems the better choice."

"Does she?" He looked surprised by her conclusion.

"Well, I think so, but if you disagree…?"

"No, I am perfectly willing to concede to your superior opinion. Mistress Beth seems capable enough to keep house, though she would likely have made you a better maid than Ayleth. Still, you can always replace her once we reach the capital." Jane opened her mouth but did not get the chance to argue the point for he was already carrying on. "Wat has reappointed a few former post-holders from the village. They were let go when your sister assumed the reins to the estate."

178

Jane was startled. "He has been busy."

Alisander nodded. "Beth should be ably assisted in keeping the house running."

Jane frowned, remembering something. "I did not realize that Wat's name was Watkin. I thought it must be Walter," she said faintly accusingly.

"Did you?"

"I feel a little rude I have been using it so freely. What *is* his first name?"

Alisander cast his eyes up at the ceiling as though in contemplation. "I don't think I have ever known," he concluded finally.

Jane clicked her tongue; she could not help herself. He was exasperating! "When exactly do you envisage us setting out for Aphrany?"

"If I had my way, we would set out directly," he answered, glancing out of the window behind them. "But it seems Wat still has much to arrange, and besides, you still have that little matter to deal with."

"I?" She frowned at him. "What little matter?"

"Appointing Beth to take charge of the place in our absence."

She gave a start. "You have dismissed the steward already?"

"Simpkin." He nodded. "Yes, believe me, he was most dissatisfactory all round."

Jane stood up. "Then I had better speak with her sooner rather than later."

179

He did not argue, and after making an enquiry, Jane found that Mistress Beth had taken to the small bedchamber she shared with two other servants. The door was ajar, but Jane knocked first before entering. Inside, she found Beth packing her things. Her eyes were almost as red as Ayleth's. "I'll soon be gone," she assured Jane. "I won't stay somewhere I'm no longer welcome."

Jane shut the door behind her. "But we do not want you to leave, Beth. Far from it. In fact, I was wondering if you would assume the housekeeper's role here."

Beth's mouth fell open. "Housekeeper?" She sat down abruptly on the narrow bed.

"I am sure there must be nicer quarters than these attached to the role," Jane commented, gazing about the poky room.

Beth stared. "Are you in earnest? I would have Master Simpkin's quarters?"

"Yes, my husband has already dismissed him."

"*Why?*" Beth asked, then when Jane opened her mouth, she clarified, "I mean, why, in the name of all that is holy, would you give me the position? When you have all but driven Sir Phillip from your doors."

Jane pondered a moment how to answer, then went with brutal honesty. "I am afraid I do not like Sir Phillip, for all that he is my uncle," she began. "Think carefully, if that will prevent you from taking the post, then please say so now from the outset." When the woman continued speechless, Jane added, "I ask you purely on your own merit and capabilities, Beth. Not because of any other reason."

Beth seemed to waver for a moment before averting her face. "The truth is," she whispered, "that I do not like Sir Phillip much either."

"Well, I cannot say as I blame you, and you always seemed a very sensible woman," Jane answered with unaccustomed frankness. "Will you take the position, Beth?" Beth hesitated, then, as though words were beyond her, she nodded dumbly.

Jane felt instantly relieved. "I apologize for the disarray we will leave you in, but my husband is determined we leave for Aphrany without delay. He has instigated many changes without the smallest regard for how they will affect the running of the place." She shook her head. "You will surely have disgruntled servants on your hands for weeks."

Beth gave a tight smile. "Yes, so I've heard. Truth be told, I can see his reasoning. Your sister had rather grand ideas," she added, "the servants' hall *was* overfilled."

"Well, if you should require more help, my husband wishes you to appoint from previous staff hired here, before my sister's day. Will that be difficult?"

Beth shook her head. "Most of the old staff were from the village. I can easily make an enquiry."

Jane nodded. "You must write to me by direction of the palace at Aphrany and keep me apprised of events. I will expect you to keep me posted."

"Of course, my lady." Beth stood up and bobbed a determined curtsy.

Jane nodded in reply. "Good, I'm glad."

"My lady," Beth started awkwardly. "I just want to say that, well, you can count on me. And that—that you need not worry about my having conflicted loyalties." She turned bright red.

"It is good of you to give me such assurances," Jane said after a momentary pause. "And I appreciate it. I will, of course, be taking the—I mean, my child with me to the winter capital…" She faltered slightly. "Ayleth also."

Beth had looked startled at the mention of Celestia, but she seemed relieved to hear Ayleth's presence would soon be removed. Happily abandoning her own packing, she assured Jane she would start on hers.

As for Jane, she squared her shoulders and continued along the narrow passage to inform Ayleth of the change in her circumstances. To her surprise, the old servant took the news without protest. "After all, what difference does it make? There is nothing here for me now," she muttered bleakly. "How long do I have before we leave?"

"Not more than above a couple of hours," Jane replied, thinking of how fast things were progressing.

"I will spend that time at my lady's graveside," Ayleth pronounced, lifting her chin.

"You may spend it however you see fit, so long as you are ready for departure by three o'clock."

The servant nodded and stood, and Jane turned on her heel to start her own preparations for departure.

*

Jane's head was still in a spin when she joined the others in the courtyard a couple of hours later. Their packing had been rushed and she felt rather flustered. Davis was loading her trunk

182

into the second wagon. "Your man Davis is fully recovered, then?" she asked, turning toward Alisander.

"Oh yes; he is a stout, dependable fellow. He will drive Anne, Ayleth, and the children to Aphrany in the second carriage."

Jane shot a look at Ayleth, who was glowering at this news. "Perhaps—"

"I would caution you," he said, catching her elbow and whisking her a few steps away, "to think before you give utterance to that thought, Jane."

She looked up at him in surprise. "It is only that Ayleth will not be merry company for Anne, and she is so very excited for the journey," she hissed.

"Well, neither would Ayleth be merry company for us," he pronounced, "and I for one have no intention of sacrificing my own comfort for your sour-faced maid."

Jane eyed him impatiently. He did not even trouble to lower his voice. Then again, he was at least honest about his selfishness. She glanced over at Anne, who was watching proceedings with interest, Celestia cradled in her arms, while Beth stood beside her with Bertrand. Both babies were bundled up warmly and seemed to be currently sleeping.

"Well, in that case," she began, "perhaps—"

"If you are fondly imagining those infants will continue in such seraphic silence for the five-hour journey, you are much mistaken," he warned her, a note of finality in his voice.

"It is just that, well, we will be passing through that wooded area again on our way back, and—"

"My dear Jane, it is broad daylight. We will hardly be set upon by villains at this hour."

183

"Oh, very well!" Jane gave up. "Seeing as you are determined to think only of yourself, my lord!"

"I am," he agreed. "It is my habit and an excellent one. You should try it."

"Women are not raised to think thus. Such thought is discouraged in our sex as unnatural."

He cast her a surprised look. "Yes, I suppose that is true," he remarked, ushering her toward their own carriage. "However, as my wife, I would encourage you to break with such conventional thinking. I will certainly not encourage it in our daughter. Climb aboard, Lady Bardulf," he recommended as Jane halted on the step, quite astonished by his words.

"You seem stunned," he commented as she clambered into the carriage.

Jane lowered herself onto the seat. "I never supposed that you— well, that you—"

"Would have views on how my daughter should be raised?" he asked, climbing in behind her. He reached for the blankets at once. "But of course I do," he asserted coolly. "She will bear my name, and possibly even my title in the future. I will have the liveliest interest in her upbringing."

Jane sat in silence as he tucked the blanket about her legs and waist. "I see," she said, rousing herself at last.

"I am sure between us that we will do a tolerable job of raising her," he said blandly.

"It is a shame she will have no cousins, aunts, or uncles," Jane commented as the carriage gave a jolt and they started forward, "due to our own lack of siblings."

"That might be a blessing in disguise," he retorted. "At least she will not be burdened with the likes of Uncle Humphrey."

"He was not *all* bad," Jane insisted, feeling uneasy now that she had maligned her departed kinsman to him.

"Now, do not lie, Jane," he said, leaning his head back against the seat and closing his eyes. "Not for conventionality's sake. You described your uncle as a buffoon who made your childhood miserable."

"I was overly sensitive as a child," she insisted, turning her gaze toward the window. "My mother always valued him highly."

"Yes, but your mother sounds a stupid, shallow sort of woman."

Jane gasped, whipping her head around. "I never described her in such terms, and I never would!"

"I made no such claim." He shrugged. "I reached that conclusion by my own deduction."

"You are offensive, my lord!"

"Frequently," he agreed, turning his head to look at her. "Tell me," he asked softly, "did you write to her? On the occasion of your sister's death?"

"Of course I did," she answered stiffly. "I would hardly leave her in ignorance of such a fact."

"And her response?" Jane pressed her lips together before turning her head away to look once more out of the window. The oil cloth there flapped about, but at least it was not raining today.

To her surprise, she felt her hand lifted from the blanket and pressed to warm lips. "Don't be cross with me, Jane," he murmured. "I'll behave." Her hand tingled. He did not release it but carried it to his chest, where he pressed his palm to hers, interlacing their fingers. "Tell me, how much *do* you know about child-rearing?"

"Next to nothing," Jane admitted.

"Excellent. We can make up our own rules as we go along. We have already made a most satisfactory start."

"Have we?" Jane asked.

"When it comes to balking tradition, certainly. Everyone knows children thrive in the country, not the town."

Jane regarded him skeptically. "*Is* that an acknowledged fact?" she asked.

He shrugged. "How many courtiers do you see dragging their offspring to court?"

"There are some," she insisted. "Besides, I am not so sure that it is always for the child's benefit that the parents leave them behind."

He smirked. "So critical, Jane. A mother for all of three days and already you think yourself far superior to the other mothers at court." Jane felt her face turn bright red, her words lodging in her throat. Was that how she appeared? She stared down at her lap, suddenly mortified. "Now don't turn tongue-tied," he sighed. "I'd rather have you arrogant than dull."

"I am not remotely arrogant!"

"My dear Jane, you are objecting to entirely the wrong insult," he murmured.

Jane ground her teeth. "I meant no criticism of our fellow courtiers—" she started doggedly.

186

"I should not care if you did," he interjected smoothly.

Jane glared at him. "Are all our journeys together to be like this?" she demanded. "With you endlessly *needling* me?"

"*That*, my sweet wife, is entirely up to you," he answered.

That brought her up short, and she regarded him suspiciously. "How is it up to me?"

"You have only to stop reacting in such a delightful manner, and I will stop at once."

"Delightful?" She regarded him a moment with frustration. What was he saying? Essentially, that he liked annoying her. "You are so childish!" she flung at him. "I can't understand how you ever became a diplomat!"

"Now, as I recall, our last journey passed most amicably. Let us emulate those circumstances." He tugged on her hand, and Jane found herself being gathered into his arms and hauled across the seat. "Let us while away the time by having a nice nap together," he suggested. "Lift up your feet and set your head down here." He patted his shoulder.

Jane complied but eyed him suspiciously all the while. "I am starting to think this is why you did not wish to share a carriage with anyone else," she said darkly as he settled an arm about her waist.

"Ah," he answered with a smirk. "You are beginning to understand me at last, wife."

14

For all his assurances, Jane was tense as they passed along the woodland track. Alisander supposed he would have to distract her somehow. Sadly, they were not at the point where he could do so with kisses. He was just casting about for some topic of conversation when she spoke up of her own accord.

"Is this how you would usually conduct yourself with your mistress?" she asked in a stifled voice. "Only, I am not sure this stratagem of yours will prove at all effective with a wife."

He was silent a moment. "Why not?"

"The trouble, my lord, is that I know *nothing* about mistresses. I would not know how to respond in kind."

Well, this was worth pursuing. He decided to give her a verbal shove and see how she responded. "That seems strange," he replied, "considering the role your own sister played as likely the most foremost paramour in all the land."

Jane's cheeks flamed red, and he thought for a moment she would spring from the seat. A smile curved his lips. She was ridiculously sensitive about her sister being the King's mistress. It was absurd. Most noble families boasted of such things almost as a badge of honor.

"You imagine that she was taught the craft from an early age?" Jane asked instead with a dangerous sort of calm which intrigued him greatly. "Perhaps at our mother's knee?"

"Your mother's? No, by all accounts your uncle, Sir Phillip Cecil, who had her tutored for the role."

He watched the red trickle from Jane's face until she looked entirely pale. "Is that—?" She broke off, looking stricken.

"Common knowledge?" he supplied. She gave a jerky nod, her eyes fixed on his face. "In court circles, yes," he admitted. "Was it meant to be a secret?"

Her eyes flashed a moment, and he caught his breath. Was Jane about to lose her famous composure? Then her eyelids dropped, hiding her expression, and she gave a tight smile. "Well," she said shortly, "if that *was* the case, then he soon realized that *I* was ill-suited for such purposes and so should you!"

Alisander snorted. "What nonsense! You rose through the ranks as swiftly as your sister after all. If she was the King's favorite, then were you not the Queen's?"

"You are also a favorite of the Queen's," she responded shortly. "She has many, I find, these days."

He had to suppress his smile. Another sore spot. He already knew that Jane was jealous of others encroaching on her spot, but this was practically an outright admission of the fact. "And do you imagine that your sister had a monopoly on Wymer's attentions?" he asked softly.

Jane shook her head. "I know nothing of the King's love affairs," she answered with a curl of her lip, "and care even less."

"And therein lies the reason your uncle focused on your sister's success," Alisander concluded swiftly. "You simply would not apply yourself."

Jane opened her mouth on a retort she disappointingly did not voice. Instead, those little white teeth of hers clicked together as she averted her face. It did not really matter, for he already knew what she had been about to say.

Instead of letting the matter drop, Alisander stretched out further on the seat, taking up even more of her space. Jane

189

pressed her lips together but declined to comment. "But what other reason could there be?" He paused as though to consider and thought she gritted her teeth slightly. "You are very good at pandering to the royal ego, so that would not be a barrier to success."

Jane let out a little gasp. "What do you mean by that?" she demanded, turning her head sharply.

Ah, now he had her again. "Why merely that you flatter and abet the Queen to a degree that most monarchs would find agreeable," he answered innocently, "and practically all men would enjoy."

"I do not—" She broke off a moment to catch her breath. "I do not *flatter* the Queen to curry favor with her," Jane protested hotly. "I merely let my actions show how greatly I esteem and admire Her Majesty!"

He did not trouble to hide the smile that curved his lips. "So sincere," he murmured. "I meant no insult. I was merely observing that you possess precisely the instrument to please most men. Namely a pretty tongue. Now, why don't you try turning it on me? I assure you I will be most receptive to it."

Jane looked frankly astonished by his words. She blinked at him before rallying. "It is not a pretty tongue that most men appreciate," she argued feebly, "but a pretty face!"

"That goes without saying," he agreed with another of his shrugs. "But as you are in possession of both, I fail to see why you should cavil at this point." Jane's mouth dropped open. "Now, where's my compliment? The longer you make me wait, the more extravagant I shall expect it to be."

"C-compliment?"

He nodded and cast her a sly look. "Of course, if you cannot think of one, I can find another way for you to employ that pretty tongue of yours. One I should like just as well."

Jane blushed a deeper red. "I don't—that is, you are vastly elegant, my lord," she blurted, clearly making a great effort.

"Why, so I am," he agreed. "Was that not easy? Mayhap we should pay one another three compliments at breakfast, instead of plain statement of facts."

"We did not actually do that this morning," she pointed out.

"No, not formally," he agreed. "But we have been blabbing our life stories to one another with such distressing frankness that it hardly seemed necessary."

She peeped up at him. "You do not usually exchange confidences?" she asked.

"With my mistresses? Gods no!"

"Oh." She reached out and pushed the curtain aside. They had cleared the wood by that point and feeling the rigidity of her body relax against his own, just a little, he smiled. She just had to accustom herself to him, that was all.

The bells of St. Danita's church were striking eight by the time they reached the city walls of Aphrany. Night had fallen some two hours, so poor Anne would not have had much of a view for her first glimpse of the royal city.

They had entered the southern gate before Jane stirred, and Alisander glanced down to find her rubbing her eyes. "We've arrived," he told her. When she struggled to sit up, he let her, though he felt a surprising reluctance about it. Jane fussed with her cloak fastenings while he pushed aside the curtain and spoke to the guards.

It was not until they had all climbed the three flights of steps to the courtiers' housing and he started towing her in the direction of the west wing that she dug her heels in. Behind her, Ayleth and Anne, carrying the children, and Wat and Davis, carrying their trunks, all came to a halt. "But where are we—?"

He halted. "To my quarters," he responded.

"*Your* quarters?" She looked at him blankly before gazing away to the left.

"Married couples are not permitted in the east wing," he pointed out. "Only single ladies reside there."

"But all my things…"

"Your possessions were removed to my rooms after we left. My servant Robert saw to it."

"Oh." She still sounded uncertain, but noticing the others all patiently waiting, she cleared her throat and inclined her head. "Lead on."

Old Robert answered the door at his knock and peered out at them in confusion. "Milord!" He faltered, his face falling. "I had not prepared for your return so soon!" He looked down at his stockinged feet in mortification. "If I had but known…!"

"It is of no matter, Robert," Alisander assured him, squeezing his shoulder as he walked past him. "So long as you have a merry fire burning in the grate, we will forgive you all. Now make way, there's a good fellow, for our household has increased apace and there are many introductions to be performed."

Robert peered shortsightedly out into the corridor and gave a start at the number of people gathered there. "Of course, milord, of course." The old man fell back at once. Alisander drew Jane immediately inside.

"Jane," Alisander said, "this is my faithful Robert, who I trust above all others. Robert, this is your new mistress, the Lady Jane. I have told you much of her already."

"Milady," Robert cried, looking as though he wanted to burst into tears. "Forgive me, naught is made ready for you. I had your trunks brought down but—"

"Please do not fret yourself, Robert," Jane responded kindly. "You could not possibly have anticipated our arrival."

"Everyone come inside," Alisander beckoned. "Jane, you sit here," he said, leading her to the table where Robert's supper was laid, half-eaten. "We have interrupted your meal, Robert," he observed. "Apologies."

The poor old man looked much stricken, as everyone gazed down at the white loaf, buttered capons, and the bottle of red wine he had been enjoying.

Anne's stomach rumbled. "Beggin' your pardon, Master Robert," she said, "but is there any chance you have any more of that stowed away, only I'm powerful famished, not having eaten since noon."

It took Robert a split second to realize she was referring to him. "Of course, dear lady," he said, taking a hurried step toward the door. "Let me just repair to the kitchens, and—"

"No, Robert," Alisander said gently, taking his arm and leading him back to his seat. "You do not have any shoes on. Finish your meal. Wat can go."

"Yes, my lord," said Wat, looking up from dragging his master's trunk inside the door.

193

"I couldn't eat another morsel," Robert protested faintly, "not when there is so much to be done." He attempted to get up from his seat, but Alisander prevented him by pressing down on his shoulder. "You are not to stir a step," he said sternly. "Now eat your supper."

Feeling Jane's gaze on him, he could only hope she would ascribe his solicitude to eccentricity. "Make sure you bring plenty for everyone, Wat," he added as the servant disappeared out of the door. "Davis, collect the rest of our things and then join us for supper." Davis nodded and followed after Wat. "Now, Robert, you must attend carefully to everyone's names. First, I think, you must meet my daughter, Celestia."

Anne stepped forward and deftly twitched back the blanket covering the child. Robert gaped down at the sleeping face. "Daughter, you say?" he quavered, blinking. "That were quick work, Master Sander."

"Yes, wasn't it?" he agreed. "And this is Anne, her nurse," he said, gesturing to the beaming young woman.

"Pleased to meet you, Master Robert," she said, bobbing a curtsey.

"And this is Ayleth, Lady Bardulf's maid," Alisander continued calmly, turning to where Ayleth stood scowling. She looked the old man up and down, her eyes dwelling on the spot where his toes poked through his stockings. "Humph!" she pronounced. Bertrand chose that moment to open his mouth and let out a loud wail. Ayleth, who was holding him, jumped as though scalded.

"Oh, *Bertrand*!" Anne tutted, turning to Jane and passing Celestia into her lap before hurrying to comfort her son.

"Oh, er—" Given little choice in the matter, Jane passed her arms about the baby, an almost fearful look on her face. Celestia squinted up at her a moment, before closing her eyes and dozing off again.

"Well," said Alisander as Anne bounced Bertrand on her hip, "is this not merry?"

"I'll—er—pour the wine, milord," Robert quavered. "If you will permit me to fetch more goblets."

Goblets were fetched, wine was poured, and by the time Wat reappeared bearing trays full of cold fowl, bread, and cheeses, everyone was seated and had removed their cloaks and hoods. It was true, the reception room was looking decidedly cluttered, and Ayleth still looked sour as vinegar, but Anne and Davis seemed to be on the best of good terms, and Jane looked vastly relieved as Celestia continued to sleep on her lap.

It was not until the conversation turned to sleeping arrangements that a discordant note was once again struck. "My lord," Robert whispered, leaning forward. "Where are you going to put 'em?"

"Put what?" Alisander asked, lowering his chicken leg.

"All these people," Robert hissed. "Only, we ain't got the room, milord!"

A quiet fell across the table. "Nonsense! We can put the baby in the guest bedchamber. Anne and Bertrand will also have to sleep in there," he added. "My apologies, Anne."

"It would be for the best, milord," Anne hastened to assure him. "That way, I can tend to her in the night, and Bertrand too."

Robert cleared his throat. "But what about her ladyship?" he persisted with an agonized expression on his face.

195

"Hmmm?" Alisander frowned, for he was fully occupied in peeling a quail's egg.

"Your good lady wife?"

"Oh." Alisander turned to Jane, who was still sat stiffly upright in her seat so as not to disturb the sleeping child. He shrugged. "My wife will just have to sleep in with me until I can arrange for larger quarters. It is a barbarous practice but will have to suffice for the short term."

"And what about me?" piped up Ayleth grimly. "I trust *I* am not expected to share with babes or these three rogues," she said, turning to look disapprovingly at Wat, Davis, and Robert. Alisander nearly choked on his pickled egg.

"No indeed, dear lady," Robert hastened to assure her. "I can easily vacate my room and sleep in a truckle bed in your dressing room, Master Sander."

"You will do no such thing, Robert," Alisander interrupted him. "Your room remains your room. Wat, however, must move his bedding in with you. Ayleth can have his old room." A spasm of irritation showed on Wat's face, and Alisander wryly acknowledged the change in circumstances would cause him some inconvenience.

Robert looked doubtful. "Wat's old room is naught but a cupboard, my lord," he protested in an urgent whisper, which Alisander ignored, turning back to the table at large. "Davis does not live in with us in any case. He bunks down in a shared room above the kitchens."

Davis nodded, for his mouth was currently occupied chewing his third plate of food.

"You've a fine appetite, Master Davis," Anne marveled, just before Bertrand set up a loud and furious wail at being neglected for so long while his mother ate. Anne stood up hastily and started to energetically pace about the room, jiggling the child in her arms. "There now, Bertrand, look at the fine pictures and candlesticks," she encouraged him. "Is this not quality living?"

After supper was finished, Wat and Davis were dispatched to fetch hot water for baths. The trunks were thrown open, and Robert and Ayleth started unpacking them. Anne disappeared into the guest bedroom with both babies to arrange things to her satisfaction.

Alisander took the opportunity to show Jane into his bedchamber. It was a large handsome room with a huge stone hearth, a large canopied bed in black and gold, and vibrant tapestries depicting unicorns and dancing beasts which practically covered three of the four walls.

"None of my things have been placed in here," she commented, glancing about.

"No," he agreed. "I will have them brought in. Robert would not have anticipated we would have to share." He crossed the room. "Through here," he said, flinging open another door, "is my dressing room."

Jane looked surprised that he expected her to take a look, but she dutifully followed and peered around the door. "Alisander, this room is huge!" she gasped, turning back to look at him. "It must be the biggest room in the entire apartment!"

"Of course." He shrugged.

"But...for *dressing*? You could fit three beds in here!"

"Why should I? This is where I house my clothes."

Jane gazed about open-mouthed at the trunks full of clothes, the cabinets stuffed full of pearl-studded hats and dyed leather shoes, the studded strong-boxes wherein he housed his jewels, and the full-length mirror propped against the far wall. "Do you really wear *all* of these things?" she asked, clearing her throat at last.

"At one time or another," he confirmed.

She gave her head a little shake. "I think it will be a difficult task to find you a larger suite than this. I know whole families of noble birth housed in smaller rooms than yours." Her tone was faintly accusatory.

"You seem to forget my position as an important foreign ambassador at court. Besides, it is a question of priorities," he said firmly. "I am simply not willing to compromise when it comes to such things, and neither should you. Which brings me to my next point. I have ordered an urgent fitting with my tailor."

"Oh yes," Jane replied without interest. She appeared transfixed by his shoe collection. "You must own close to a *dozen* pairs," she muttered, sounding quite scandalized.

"I own at least two dozen," he corrected her before clarifying, "and the tailor's appointment is for you."

That caught her attention. "For *me*?" She wheeled about. He nodded. "But I have no need of a new gown."

He winced. "My dear Jane, you have a most pressing need for an entirely new wardrobe."

"I? But I assure you—?"

"*None* of your gowns were selected with the diligence that ought to be employed in such matters."

"Diligence?" she repeated blankly. "Alisander, I assure you the tailors I employ are always prominent ones at court. In any case, I do not believe that anyone has ever accused me of being a poor dresser."

"You are not a *poor* dresser; you are merely an adequate one. You dress simply to fit the occasion. All of your court gowns could have been designed with *any* prominent noblewoman in mind."

Jane looked bewildered, actually bewildered. "Well, what is wrong with that?"

"*What is wrong with that?*" He felt winded. "They were constructed without any consideration for your complexion, figure, and the shade of your hair," he explained carefully. "And I find that *unforgivable*."

She looked taken aback. "If I had some stand-out attribute, such as extraordinary height, then I could understand your reasoning, but there is nothing remarkable about any of my features." She broke off, seeing him clutch his brow and sink onto a velvet-topped trunk. "What is wrong?" she asked in alarm.

"Jane, stop, I beg of you! Not in this sacred place. I cannot listen to such heresy. It pains me beyond belief."

"Are you teasing me right now, my lord?" she asked, sitting down heavily on the trunk next to his. "Because I warn you, I am tired and I am weary and I am starting to suspect I am no fit sparring partner for you, even on a good day."

He turned and looked at her consideringly. "You are my sparring partner of choice, Jane," he replied, "but rest assured on this subject, I am not remotely teasing. Now that you bear my name, I cannot countenance you drifting about the place dressed as you do." He eyed her sternly. "We de Balons do *not* fade into the background, not at any cost. Even the saintliest of our number," he added thoughtfully, "dared defy a king."

"Is it your custom, then, to dress your mistresses?" she asked, and something about her tone had him narrowing his eyes at her.

"No," he answered truthfully. "And I am starting to think that notion of mine was hardly helpful where you are concerned." He eyed her frowning. "Henceforth, we will forego all talk of mistresses, agreed?"

He thought she gave a faint snort, or something as close to a snort as someone with impeccable manners could approach. "You are my viscountess, Jane, and a reflection of me, whether you like it or not. In this matter, I want you to put yourself in my hands, both figuratively and literally. Do you think you can bring yourself to do that for me?"

She sighed and closed her eyes. "I am willing to concede; I am no expert in matters of fashion. If you can procure me some privacy and a bath for the next hour, then I promise, I will not object to some new court gowns."

Victory secured, he stood up at once. "But of course, nothing could be easier. I think I hear Davis's clumsy tread upon the floorboards even now. I will see the tub is brought into the bedchamber for you to bathe."

15

Jane felt a lot better after her bath. Alisander was as good as his word, and she was left entirely in peace to wallow in the large round wooden tub. Not only was it filled with hot water and herbs, but a chain was suspended from the ceiling with tented curtains, ensuring her privacy throughout, even while she could hear people hurrying in and out of the room, unpacking and lighting a fire in the hearth.

"Is that you, Ayleth?" she called out when she thought it finally time to emerge.

"Aye, it's me," the servant replied dourly. "I'm putting away the last of your possessions. His lordship said you're to have this walnut chest given over for your own usage."

Jane swept a curtain aside. "That was good of him," she murmured, eyeing the handsome piece of furniture which was both carved and inlaid.

"You've got doubles of your vanity items." Ayleth said, avoiding looking at her, and Jane knew she must have recognized the pieces.

"Those are to be wrapped in cloth and put away in a bottom drawer. I packed Helen's comb and mirror to put up for Celestia when she is older."

Ayleth's rigid stance relaxed. "Oh," she said, picking up the ivory comb and running a thumb along the carving. Then, quietly, "That were a good thought."

"Well, I thought so. Could you pass me a drying cloth?"

Ayleth attended her in silence, helping her into her shift and wringing out her wet hair. "Seems a funny thing," she said, picking up a comb and running it through Jane's hair, "that your husband took such issue with the overstaffing at Kinnerton. When he has a whole fleet of his own, I mean."

Jane considered this. On the whole, she thought it a positive thing that Ayleth was taking an interest in the world around her once more. "I suppose," she said slowly, "that before our marriage, he only had Robert, Wat, and Davis." Even to her own ear that sounded like a lot for a bachelor. "He is an ambassador, do not forget, and has official duties to discharge."

"That old one is less than useless, and long passed his best," Ayleth said with a curl of her lip. "Did you mark those holes in his stockings? Shocking."

"I do not think Lord Bardulf would require his servant proficient in darning and mending," Jane answered lightly. "I imagine he relishes any excuse to buy new. You should see his dressing room."

Ayleth sniffed. "Did you see the wine the old rogue was quaffing when we surprised him? You could tell from the bottle it was good stuff. And the fine pandemain bread? That weren't meant for a servant's mouth! The scoundrel clearly helps himself to the best of things while his master's away. I wonder that his lordship would allow such liberties. Why, at Kinnerton, they went in holy dread of him!"

They did? "Pass me my mantle," Jane said aloud. She wanted to encourage Ayleth out of her mopes, but she should probably quell any attempts to sow discord among her husband's servants. "We should not rush to judgment here, Ayleth," she advised as the maid draped her mantle over her shoulders. "Robert seems to be his countryman and likely accompanied him from the Western Isles. In any case, he introduced him as his oldest and most trusted servant, do not forget. That counts for a lot."

Ayleth pursed her lips but made no comment as she braided Jane's damp hair. Once it was done, she pulled back the heavy covers for her to climb into the bed. "Will that be all, my lady?" she asked formally.

"Thank you," Jane said, glancing at the bed, "but I want to check in on Anne and the children first." Ayleth looked even more disapproving if that was possible. "Have you had the opportunity to inspect your own quarters?"

"Such as they are," Ayleth answered with asperity. "At least that Wat is a neat and orderly fellow." She fetched Jane's embroidered slippers and set them in front of her.

"Thank you, Ayleth. You are now at your leisure for the evening."

"I'll go and unpack," Ayleth responded promptly and showed a clean pair of heels.

Jane found Anne gazing out of her window as she rocked Celestia in her arms. Bertrand was sat in the middle of the bed, kicking his legs and gurgling. He was clearly fresh out of the tub and looked very cherubic.

"Do you suppose that spire is the cathedral, milady?" Anne asked excitedly, turning from the window.

Jane glanced out at the view. "Yes, undoubtedly." She hesitated. "You are interested in ecclesiastical architecture, Anne?"

Anne looked puzzled. "Well, I likes to see the grand buildings, if that's what you mean," she said cautiously. "And to light a candle or two for prayer on occasion."

Jane nodded. "Well, there are churches, chapels, and shrines aplenty here in Aphrany. I am sure you will find one suited for your worship." She glanced about the bedchamber, which was a decent size, though nothing like as big as Alisander's two dedicated rooms.

In one corner of the room stood what appeared to be a large wooden box, though it looked wider at the top than the bottom. It had already been dressed with blankets, and Jane was relieved to see Anne had not used the ones with the Earl of Cecil crest.

"That crib at Kinnerton was too big and fancy to bring with us," Anne explained. "Wat found this one. There's a family two doors down that don't need it anymore. I reckon it's big enough for the two of them to go either end." She glanced uncertainly at Jane. "Course," she said hastily, "Bertrand usually sleeps in with me. It's just that he's started rolling over recently, and I do worry about him tumbling out the bed when I'm asleep."

Jane waved this aside. "I am sure that will be fine, Anne," she said and saw the maid was relieved.

"Only I don't want you to think I'm forgetting me and Bertrand's place."

"Not at all. There is no question of that."

Anne hesitated, seeing the direction of Jane's gaze. "Do you want a hold of her before bed, milady?" she suggested. Jane wavered. It would be awful if Celestia went from contented to miserable just because she interfered in proceedings. "She's a full belly," Anne added encouragingly. "And if you sit here in this chair by the fire, I think you will both be comfortable."

"Then, yes," Jane blurted, "for a moment." Anne beamed as Jane lowered herself into the chair and passed the baby to her. Jane felt a thrill when Celestia settled in comfortably in her arms. "She does not open her eyes much," she observed anxiously. "Is that…normal?"

"Oh yes, milady. She'll open 'em more and more over the next few weeks. You'll see."

Jane recalled Alisander's nonsensical words about kittens, or was it puppies? She was not sure, though she remembered him comparing Celestia to one. She did not know how long she sat there, cradling the baby in her arms, but when the door opened and her husband looked in, she found her face was wet.

"Here you are," he said, affecting not to notice her tears. "I was wondering where you had hidden yourself. Shall we to bed?"

Jane wiped her eyes and looked to Anne, who was hurrying over to take the baby. "Yes, I'll come now." She stood up, bade Anne good night, and followed him out into the corridor and then to his bedchamber.

"I hope you have your questions ready, wife," Alisander said with relish, whipping his shirt up and over his head as she slipped under the covers.

Jane's mind turned blank. Dragging up the blankets, she noticed the gold ring he had given her on their wedding day. "This ring," she said on impulse, "is it a family heirloom?"

His brows snapped together. "You're surely not squandering a question on *that*," he said, pulling a face. "Some ring I picked up off a tavern floor years ago."

"A tavern floor?" She was startled.

"It is gold, however," he added, "and as they say, 'finder's keepers.' Before you take offence, recall I did gift you my jeweled belt to make up for it."

Jane narrowed her eyes, for something about his words did not ring true to her ear. She did not think he would give her such a ring on their wedding day. "A serious answer, if you please," she insisted. "And yes, this is my first question."

Her words were met for a moment with heavy silence. "I can see you are determined to be tiresome tonight, wife," he commented dryly, not troubling to hide his displeasure. "Very well, if you are determined to ask only *dull* questions, so be it." He flung back the covers on his side of the bed and climbed in beside her.

Jane gazed up at the beams on the ceiling. Suddenly, she felt entirely certain of herself. "It is a family piece, isn't it?" she asked with quiet conviction.

"Yes," he replied shortly, and Jane realized he was not going to volunteer anything further.

"Second question." She snuck a look at him. "Why was it on a tavern floor?"

He closed his eyes. "Jane," he groaned. "This really *isn't* what I had in mind with this game."

"I want to know."

"You really don't."

She rolled onto her side toward him. "You won't tell me?"

He breathed out noisily. "It was on a tavern floor because the man I stabbed to retrieve it dropped it there. Satisfied?"

Jane swallowed. Well, she had asked. "Third and final question. Is the crest engraved on it that of the de Balons?"

"Yes," he said through gritted teeth.

"It was your brother's, wasn't it?"

"You're all out of questions, wife, but I would think any fool knows that heirlooms pass down through several people's hands."

"That's a yes, then," Jane said calmly.

"I retire from the field," he said, throwing back the covers again and climbing back out of the bed.

"Where are you going?" She sat up in surprise.

"Somewhere I won't face a constant barrage of tiresome questions," he answered, slipping his shirt back over his head.

"Well, you won't face any more here, for it is your turn now," she pointed out, though why she was so offended at the idea of his leaving, she could not possibly say.

He pulled a face. "If I stay, you won't like my questions. My mood has soured."

Jane pressed her lips together and lay back down. "I see," she said in mounting ire. She ought to leave it at that. To roll over and turn her back to him and let the promptings of his own conscience show him the error of his ways.

The only problem was…she was not precisely sure that Alisander *had* a fully working conscience. Or if he did possess one, it possibly did not work in the same manner that other peoples' did. The words flew from her lips before she could check them. "I see that it is only *you* who may ask uncomfortable questions while I am not permitted the same freedom."

He huffed and pulled up his breeches. "I was not going to pry tonight," he responded in clipped tones. "I merely wanted to flirt with you. A practice you are *lamentably* unfamiliar with."

207

Jane stared up at the ceiling. *Oh.* "I did warn you of that. My lack of experience, I mean. It was never going to work, treating me as you would one of your mistresses."

"And *I* told *you* that we would dispense with that strategy altogether! My gods, I never even started! Do you really think I usually sit around playing three questions with a woman before I bed her? We had better ways to employ our time, I assure you!"

Jane stiffened. Now he was being deliberately offensive. "Well, why don't you go a find yourself a strumpet now if you find their company so agreeable in comparison to mine? You can go and find one with my blessing!" she responded hotly. "I also have better things to do in bed than bandy words with you, my lord! Namely sleep!" A stunned silence greeted her words.

Jane rolled away, so her back faced him, and squeezed her eyes shut. Her face was blazing hot, and she felt utterly appalled with herself. How *could* she have said anything so awful? Now her outburst was spent, she felt herself to be on the brink of tears. What in heavens was *wrong* with her lately? She felt all over the place.

"Jane," said an unsteady voice after a few heartbeats. "Tell me, my darling, did you really just utter those outrageous words or are my ears deceiving me?"

Her eyes flew open. "Are you *laughing*?" she asked incredulously. The bed dipped and she realized he was climbing back onto the mattress beside her.

"Jane, did you just lose your temper with me?" he asked, sounding utterly delighted. He seized her upper arm, rolling her onto her back so he could see her face.

"I—what are you—?"

208

"Oh my gods," he murmured, his eyes roaming over her face and neck. "You're *so* flushed. And your eyes…they're so bright." The way he said it astounded her. His voice was sort of warm and velvety. "I love it when your composure slips, Jane," he added appreciatively. "I always have."

Jane's mouth fell open in astonishment. "You——?"

"I did tell you once before," he reminded her, easing his body to lie flush against hers. "Remember?"

Jane gazed up at him. How could he possibly be so entranced by such a thing? Suddenly, she realized he was waiting for her to answer. "Um," she swallowed. "Was it at Kinnerton? At the foot of the staircase?"

"Yes," he replied, still looking extremely distracted. He could not seem to tear his eyes away from her. "Do you remember what I told you?"

Jane's mind reeled. "Something … about liking my rash?"

"I can see it now, peeping out of the top of your shift," he admitted roughly. "I wish I could see more of it." He caught her gaze. "May I, Jane?"

Jane struggled a moment with her response. "More?" she asked breathlessly.

He nodded. "I want to see … how far down it extends."

If she was not mistaken, he was actually holding his breath for her response. He was not teasing for once, not about this. Something about that made her feel very strange. He was putting her in a position where she did not feel foolish, wooden, or lacking in any way. Despite the fact that he had all the experience here and she none, he was making her feel as though she had the upper hand.

When she reached up hesitantly for her neckline, his gaze seemed to ignite. "Wait!" he said quickly, reaching behind them for some pillows. "Let me just prop us up." He piled some pillows behind them both, "Comfortable?" he asked, and Jane nodded, though she was not sure that was precisely the word.

Then he settled again expectantly beside her. "I'm ready," he said, and his obvious eagerness dispelled the remainder of Jane's doubts. He *was* in earnest about this, she realized, despite the fact she still felt stupefied that he could be so keen to see her unsightly mottled skin. Strange to say, his keenness for this gave her a spurt of confidence. He wanted to see it? Very well, she would show him! Then see what he had to say.

Her chemise was a loose-fitted one, gathered at the neckline with a pull-string, so she simply untied this and loosened the short bodice, drawing down the thin linen to expose her skin to him. His sharply indrawn breath gave her all the encouragement she needed. She halted for modesty's sake at the tops of her breasts and snuck a look at his face. His gaze was riveted to her décolletage.

Doubtless, he was disappointed at her timidity, she thought, her throat dry. He had wanted to see how far down it went, after all. Still, she could not do it. Her every impulse rebelled, telling her to cover back up instead of revealing further.

"Ah Jane," he breathed, his voice raspy. "It's even more beautiful than I imagined."

Her eyes flew to meet his own. He was not disappointed, even remotely. His eyes, usually so cold and shrewd, blazed with some emotion Jane could not identify. Finally, his words registered with her. "You've imagined it?" she squeaked, turning even redder.

"So many times," he groaned. "Does it … feel hot to the touch?"

"Yes," she replied and saw him hesitate, words trembling on his lips. He wanted to touch it, she realized incredulously. *What was it he had said before?* Something about wanting to feel her, all hot and flushed. She was blazing like a furnace by this point. Taking a deep breath, she reached out tentatively toward him and saw his eyes widen.

"Give me your hand," she said before she could lose her nerve. When he did so, she drew his hand toward her breast and placed it gently against her skin. He made a noise in his throat, but Jane could not look at his face. "Can you feel it?" she asked after a pause.

"Yes," he whispered.

"Is it …how you imagined?"

"No." He swallowed. "It's one hundred times better." Jane dragged in a breath of air, and he made that noise again at the rise and fall of her chest, as if he could not help himself.

"Jane," he said almost reverently. His hand felt cool against her heated skin. How could he be so enraptured by it? she wondered. His every reaction told her he was not dissembling.

Then again, this was probably the most flesh she had exposed in her life. Not for her, the low-cut bodices that exposed your bosoms to all and sundry, however fashionable they might be at court. Closing her eyes briefly, Jane released his hand, and before she could change her mind, tugged down on the loosened neckline till it pooled at her waist. He actually gasped.

She opened her eyes. "You said you wanted to see how far down it went," she said quickly, but he was not attending to her

211

words. Instead, he was staring at her with the strangest expression dawning on his face.

"Gods, you're beautiful," he said thickly, which Jane knew was not true, but strangely did not feel like protesting in the moment. "No wonder you cover yourself up. They'd all lie at your feet. The whole pack of them."

Jane blinked. *That was a bit much.* She glanced down uncertainly at her pale, bare torso. No, nothing had changed. Her breasts had not magically transformed into anything remotely impressive. She had seen far larger ones about court, even when only the top halves had been showing above a low-cut gown.

The only remarkable thing about them was possibly the unsightly blotches of red that were dotted about her skin. Still, Alisander's fingers trembled where they lay against her sensitive skin. His breathing seemed almost labored at this point, as though he was struggling with something.

"Jane," he said harshly. "Can I move my hand?"

"Of course," Jane said, thinking he must have tired of it and meant to remove it. To her shock, he slid it down and cupped her right breast. "Oh!"

"Is this permitted?" he asked swiftly.

"I—yes," she said, feeling a fresh surge of embarrassment.

"The red does not go down beyond your bosom," he commented lightly.

"Er, no," she agreed, staring past his shoulder.

"Your breasts are so soft." Again his words were hushed and almost awed. He stroked a thumb across her nipple, and Jane nearly jumped out of her skin. "Except for these impudent nipples," he murmured.

"That…that sometimes happens when it is cold," Jane whispered, feeling mortified.

"They're so pretty."

Her nipples? Jane ventured another look at his face, but no, he was not looking at all sardonic. He was in deadly earnest. She could not help it, she had to take another look, but she did not expect the jolt that ran through her, seeing his hand curved about her breast. It affected her powerfully and made her feel peculiar all over.

"Jane, can I kiss you?"

"Kiss me?"

"You sound so astounded," he replied with a short laugh, and to Jane's surprise, she felt herself relax a little to hear that hint of teasing in his voice once more.

"Well, yes." She gulped.

"Yes, you're astounded, or yes, I can kiss you?"

"Well—both," she conceded, and no sooner were the words out of her mouth than he was lowering his mouth to hers. She thought she knew what was coming from a kiss, at least, but this kiss was different to the one he had bestowed upon her on their marriage.

After a moment of hot breath and the brushing of their mouths together, it dawned on her that he wanted something more than just the sealing of their lips. *What though?* Her mind turned blank as he dragged his lips across hers more roughly this time, more insistently.

Something else too… Had he moistened his lips with his tongue? The kiss felt wetter. His hand closed about her breast and squeezed. Jane jolted against the mattress, and he rolled more firmly atop her to anchor her in place. He was all around her; he *surrounded* her.

His cool skin was pressed against hers. She could feel the light scattering of his chest hair rub against her sensitive breasts. She should feel overwhelmed by him, but the strange thing was that she did not. She could not possibly like this, could she?

His other hand had slipped between the pillows at her back, and was caressing her there, urging her closer still. She closed her eyes and whimpered. He drew back. "Put your arms around me, Jane. I need to feel your embrace."

Strangely, the thought of that still managed to fluster her. Her arms were clumsy as they closed about his back. He shivered slightly. "Yes," he groaned. "Like that. But tighter. And open your mouth, I'm begging you."

Open her mouth? His lips were on hers again, insistent, and almost desperate. He tore his mouth from hers again. "Please?" he asked roughly. Jane found herself nodding at the appeal in his eyes. He groaned as he crushed his lips to hers once more, and when Jane parted her own, she felt the dart of his tongue dipping inside. She froze, but almost immediately, it was withdrawn with a flicker against her lips, like that of a snake.

Jane gasped, and his tongue was back again, bolder this time, sweeping her mouth, but withdrawn by the time she had stiffened once more with shock. This time, he caught her bottom lip between his teeth and gently nibbled her there. "Fuck, Jane," he groaned. "Tell me you like this. Tell me you like kissing me."

"I don't know," she gasped. He tried to draw back, and she tightened her arms about him at once to prevent him.

"About which part?" he asked gruffly.

"The tongue," she admitted. "It feels…oh, I don't know."

"Hmmm." To her relief, he did not look disappointed in her. "Mayhap you should let me ply it elsewhere," he suggested, pressing light kisses along her jaw.

"Where?" Jane found herself asking foolishly.

"Your heated skin," he murmured against her ear. "Let me bathe it with my tongue. I've imagined that before too," he admitted silkily. "Many, many times." Jane clutched at his back as he traced the shell of her ear with the tip of his wicked tongue. "Yes?" he asked.

She gave a whimper, then the faintest "Yes." Fortunately, he had good hearing, for she could not have repeated it, even to save her life. He did not need encouragement in any case, for no sooner had she uttered her assent than he was kissing down her neck.

"Let me see, the skin is reddened here. Let me see if it is hot." He ran the slope of his nose against her throat. "Oh yes," he whispered. "So hot, however shall I stand it?"

Jane swallowed and had only just started to wonder what, pray, he had to withstand, when he ran his tongue hither and thither up her throat, making her squirm.

"Does that give you relief?" he asked huskily against her skin.

"No, it is even more of a torment!"

He laughed softly. "Poor Jane." He was inspecting her décolletage now, and leaning in to bestow slow licks on patches of skin which Jane could only suppose were blotchy. She huffed, blowing out her cheeks. Suddenly, his fingers pinched at her nipple, making her cry out in surprise.

"I want it to stay nice and hard," he explained, seeing her look of outrage.

"My nipple?"

He smirked. "Yes."

Jane was speechless while he continued his way leisurely across the tops of her breasts. "Next time," he said thoughtfully, "I want you to wear jewels."

"Next—? What do you mean?"

"Next time I get you naked," he elaborated. "Don't you think the cold stones would feel good against your flushed skin?"

Naked, but wearing jewels? Jane had no words. Even if she had, they would have fled as soon as he opened his mouth over her nipple. "Alisander!" His tongue lapped her there, and she squawked and made a grab at his head, catching his hair to drag it back. "Wh-what are you *doing*?"

"I'm worshipping your bosom, Jane," he answered, completely unabashed.

"But *why*?"

"Because it is, undoubtedly, the most splendid bosom in the known world. And also, because I want you to feel good. Does it?"

"Does it what?" Jane's brain was too befuddled to follow the thread of conversation by this point. *Splendid?* She glanced down uncertainly once more at her wholly mediocre breasts. They were no such thing! He must be teasing her again.

"How about you let me pay my respects to its fellow? Hmmm?" He lightly cupped her left breast. "May I?"

Instead of answering, she released his hair from her clutches and gave a nod. The instant look of gratified pleasure on his face *seemed* sincere enough. She did not know what to think. Jane drew in a sharp breath as he sucked her other nipple into his mouth and made a sound of rumbling pleasure that set Jane all of a quiver. She seemed to feel it in some very peculiar places.

"Gods, Jane," he whispered and just dropped his head so it rested between her breasts. His breathing was ragged, and he mouthed her tender flesh there, rubbing his face against her skin and whispering words that she could not catch. They sounded almost tortured, yet also somehow, *blissful*.

Suddenly, she was desperate to know what they were. "What did you say?"

"Nothing of import," he said huskily, lifting his head to look at her. "I want to put my hand between your legs," he said with sudden crushing bluntness. "May I?"

Jane felt her flutterings come to a screeching halt. "Your hand?" she replied faintly.

"Yes, just my hand." Something else seemed to occur to him. "Actually, maybe also…my mouth?" he mused. "How should you feel about that?"

His mouth? Between her legs? Jane opened her mouth and closed it again. Suddenly, she felt panicked he would turn amused at her prudishness. She could not *bear* it if he laughed at her at this moment. Not when she had heard him sound so tormented with pleasure.

"Yes," she said quickly. Giving permission was far easier than admitting how she felt about it, which was flabbergasted.

His expression turned heavy-lidded. "Ah, Jane," he murmured, and she felt his hands dragging her nightgown up her legs. "Please be"—he paused as his hand slid shockingly between her thighs—"wet," he said thickly. They both gasped as his finger slid into her cleft. "*Jane*," he groaned. "Oh, my darling." And her shocked ears could even hear her wetness. His eyes gleamed. "You are…deliciously wet."

It facilitated the slide of his wicked fingers. There was no resistance *at all*. She made a strange noise that would have been mortifying under normal circumstances, half strangled cry, half moan. What was happening? "Alisander!" His name burst from her in panicked tones.

"Shhh, my darling, just let me…" His fingers played over her, teasing and toying with her trembling flesh. Jane was reeling. He was taking *outrageous* liberties with her. She ought to be protesting, not whatever it was she was doing right now. Sort of shifting against his fingers, her face hot with effort and terribly out of breath.

This was dreadful. It was indecent. His finger just slid up right inside her! She started to shake her head when his thumb pushed up firmly against something that caused pleasure to zip right through her loins, robbing her of breath altogether.

"Thought you might like that," he murmured. "What do you think?" Jane beheld him speechlessly. "Shall I do it again?" Without waiting for her reply, which was just as well, his thumb pressed down again and Jane's whole body jolted. She managed a shaken exclamation this time, squeezing her eyes shut against the overwhelming sensation. "*Oh!*" She tried to turn her hot face away from his.

218

"Now, now," he tutted, "you must not try to prevent my view." Her eyes sprang open. Of her face? Her gaze sought his. He was staring down at her intently, a smile playing about his lips. "Very nice, Jane," he said approvingly. "But this time you have to ask for it."

Every pass of his fingers seemed to turn her hotter and wetter. Jane sobbed and twisted against them. She did not know how or what to ask for. She just *needed*.

"Such a good girl," Alisander practically purred. "*That's* it, you can do it."

Every time she tried to catch her breath, he sent shocks of pleasure streaking through her body that robbed it from her lungs again. Her whole body was shaking. She felt like she was coming apart at the seams. "Please!" she burst out.

"So impatient," he chided in a whisper, "but you should know by now how much I like teasing you, Jane. Don't you know, it just tempts me to draw it out even longer?"

Her eyes flew open. She was aghast. He was laughing! No, that wasn't right. His eyes were alight with something, but it wasn't quite laughter. "I did tell you, did I not, that I wanted to see you burst?" he said, his voice somehow tender and rough at the same time. "Open your legs wider."

She was beyond hesitation by this point. He shifted down the bed as she struggled to free herself of the nightgown, tangled around her legs and impeding her efforts. Suddenly, he was helping her, shoving the skirts up around her waist as she let her legs fall apart.

He drew in a deep breath, gazing between them, his eyes gleaming. "Jane, I have done you a grave disservice," he said thickly. "You, my darling, are absolutely breathtaking."

Jane only had the chance to glance uncertainly down at the wet blond curls between her legs before he had lowered his face between them. Feeling his breath against her most private of places, Jane sucked in a breath, and her mind turned mercifully blank.

Then he applied himself with an utter abandon that had her covering her mouth with her hand to muffle her sobs. By the time he lifted his face to rest his cheek against her stomach, he was panting, and she had completely collapsed.

"*Fuck*, Jane," he groaned, his chest heaving. "That was too good." With part of her mind, she marveled that she was just lying on her back, legs spread while he breathed heavily against her most private of places. He sighed. "I need to put a clean sheet on the bed."

She swiped at her embarrassingly teary eyes, struggling up onto her elbows. "What? Why?" She surely had not been *that* wet.

He levered himself off the bed gingerly. "Because you, my dear, are far too exciting," he said casting a rueful look down at the bed. He crossed the room to the basin and splashed around in it awhile as Jane struggled back into her shift.

By the time she was sat up, looking rumpled, but hopefully decently covered, he had donned a clean pair of braies and collected some clean bedding from one of the trunks. "Hop down and I'll put the bed to rights," he recommended. "I've poured clean water for you."

Jane slipped out of the bed and across the room to the ewer and basin. She hoped to goodness she had not been too loud. What if she had roused anyone else from sleep? Her face burned as she took a hurried wash, and by the time she had finished, he had efficiently stripped the sheet off the bed and replaced it with a clean one. "Come back under the covers," he recommended, glancing at the dwindling fire.

Jane scurried back into the bed, drawing the covers up to her chin before she dared to venture a glance in his direction. He was now climbing into the bed, looking completely at his ease. "Oh my gods, that was so"—he settled down beside her, his gaze lingering on her face—"lovely," he concluded with a faint air of bafflement. "I can think of no other word."

Jane cleared her throat. "Well…good," she said lamely, unsure what else she could say.

"I can't believe I spilled all over the sheets," he added without shame. "Remarkable really. *This* was something like what I wanted with you," he continued conversationally, "on our wedding night, but it was too soon. I did not want you to be afraid of me, as you were that first night in Kinnerton." When she made no response, he carried on apologetically. "After you realized what had happened in the wood, I mean. The timing was…unfortunate to say the least."

"That dead robber, you mean," she answered, feeling some reluctance for speech, especially on that topic. Why was he so keen to talk right now? She felt languorous and falling asleep seemed a far more sensible course of action. "In any case, I was not afraid," she felt compelled to add for the hundredth time.

He sent her a dry look. "We both know if I had indulged myself in your charms that night, you would have gone into a state of shock."

Well, that was probably true. "I'm still a little shocked," she admitted, darting a glance at his face and then away again.

"I know." She could hear the smile in his voice, but it was not remotely mocking this time. He was pleased with her, she thought, because she had given him free rein over her body.

"I've never actually done that before, you know," he said conversationally, turning his head on the pillow toward her.

"Done what?" Jane was startled.

"With my tongue," he admitted. Seeing her expression, he elaborated, "Between a woman's legs, I mean." At her obvious shock, he shrugged. "I've just never cared enough about a partner's enjoyment before, I suppose. I did tell you; I was selfish."

"Why did you do it to me, then?" Jane asked in failing tones.

"I couldn't resist."

"You...you enjoyed it?" Jane asked and was promptly appalled at herself.

"Oh yes." He licked his lips and glanced down fleetingly at her body which was now covered in bedsheets. Jane felt her cheeks turn red. There were times, she reflected, when he was entirely lacking in subtlety. "I will happily repeat the experience, any time you should be agreeable, wife."

Fortunately, he did not seem to expect a verbal answer, so Jane just lay there, feeling shaken.

"Tired?" he asked sympathetically, inching closer to her in the bed until the lengths of their bodies aligned and even touched at certain points. It seemed to Jane an odd thing for someone to do who did not relish having a bedfellow, but after all, he *was* quite strange.

"Yes," she answered briefly. He nodded and smothered a yawn. Just then, one of his feet slid across and nudged against her own. Jane shot a quick look at him, but his eyes had drifted shut. Perhaps it had been by accident, rather than design. Her own eyelids were so heavy that before long she obeyed their promptings and drifted off to sleep.

16

Alisander woke to the sound of a kitten mewling in the early hours. Then he realized it was not mewling, it was wailing. Then he realized it was not a kitten at all. He groaned, remembering that the second bedchamber had been appropriated for a nursery, and groped above his head until he found a spare pillow and slammed it over his head.

Mercifully, the horrible sound abated after a couple of minutes, so he cautiously lifted the pillow and turned his head to look at Jane, who was still lying peacefully on her back, oblivious. Faint light was breaking through the window, so he could make out her sleeping features.

He propped himself up on his elbow to better appreciate the view. She looked serene and unworn by cares. Most likely this was the face she would like to present to the world, he thought wryly. She was wholly unconvinced that her flustered state had a charm all of its own.

Gods, he loved it when she was undone. She was even more spectacular than he had always suspected she would be. Before he even realized what he was doing, he was moving closer to her, crowding himself around her. Curious, this inclination for closeness. Doubtless, it was the novelty, and he would soon tire of it.

Or would he? A slither of doubt crept into his mind as he slipped an arm about her waist. She did not stir in the slightest, and he marveled that Jane should be a heavy sleeper. He slept like a cat and the smallest sound would wake him. Maybe she was just worn out from all that coming? He smiled to himself. Oh, she had been enchanting. The sounds erupting from staid Jane's lips had been…extremely invigorating.

On the morrow, he would set out his plans for her court return. She would likely put up some resistance, of course, but he was already looking forward to convincing her. Settling his head back on the pillow, he lay still with his eyes closed for another hour or so, savoring the warmth generated between them, his thoughts flitting hither and thither while his body lay still and snug, curled about his sleeping wife.

Of course, it was not all amusing diversion. He needed to set up several meetings now he was back in the capital, not least with that tiresome fellow Alphonse Hubair, the ambassador for Kloberg, who was creating quite a fuss about some betrothal of an archduke. He would have to appease the fellow somehow and prevent him from stirring up a hornet's nest by firing off dozens of hysterical letters to Lascony on the subject.

Alisander suppressed a groan. Usually he enjoyed the twisted machinations of his official role. A whisper here, an allusion there, then it was just a case of sitting back and waiting for the fish to bite. More often than not, he ended up being told a rumor that had originated with himself, as though it were plain matter of fact. He usually derived a good deal of satisfaction from his contributions.

Now, though, he could not help but feel he had better things to be about than such intrigue. He had a wife to seduce. His eyes roamed once more over Jane's sleeping profile. Strange, that up until recently, he had thought her features without particular distinction. How had he neglected to notice the charming proportion of brow to nose, and nose to jaw?

It must have been a form of self-preservation, he supposed, for he had already been far too preoccupied with her, even then. He resisted a surprisingly strong impulse to reach out and trace the bridge of her nose. In vain, he told himself there was nothing noteworthy about Jane's nose. It was neither large nor small. It

225

was not straight or pointed, or pleasingly tip-tilted, or even impudently snubbed. In short, there was nothing about it to draw his eye. Why, then, did he feel so preoccupied with it?

Dimly, he remembered the description he had once given of her to Robert. Her figure is good, but nothing special, and he almost squirmed. At the time, in his defense, he had thought he was speaking plain matter of fact. Or, something approaching it, he amended conscientiously. He had not realized that Prim Jane had it in her to make him come like that.

He had been perilously close to it from the moment she had exposed that pretty bosom of hers to him. Even the memory had his cock stirring. He had known he had a strong inclination for her company, of course, but he had not anticipated just how perfect her hot flushed body would be bared to his touch. He shivered. Well, maybe he had had some dim idea, but *nothing* that had stood up to the reality.

He had come perilously close to spilling, just from the feel of her soft breasts beneath his tongue, he remembered incredulously. And he had made a complete mess of himself once he had slid his tongue between her pretty drenched curls. Unbidden, the image rose in his mind's eye of her slick pussy, and he groaned. He had come hard and fast, and who could blame him in the face of such provocation?

Jane had been a delight in the sheets. Thank gods, he had succumbed to temptation and married her. He might never have known, he marveled. He might have spent the next twenty years thinking how amusing it was to tease her, and never knowing what a sweet, slick pussy she hid between her thighs, and the desperate sounds she made when he touched her there.

He could not wait to actually fuck her. He *would* wait because he did not want her to shrink from him. That meant he had to

226

continue taking his time with her. He smiled, remembering how she had lost all patience with him when he had vowed to leave their bed. She was certainly growing a good deal bolder with him, and he liked that. He liked a lot of things, he thought contentedly, when it came to Jane.

His eyes dwelt fondly on her profile. It was no good. He was going to have to do it, he realized. No matter how strange and foolish the impulse. He could deny it no longer. Reaching across he lightly touched the tip of his finger to the end of her nose. There, it was done. A strange impulse, but he had discharged it without incident. No one need ever know he had ever indulged it.

Alisander rose just before dawn and breezed through the palace in a suit of plain black, leaving a concealed note here, a coded message there. He slipped through the servants' stairs and the concealed passages with long accustomed ease, collecting missives that had been left for him at various pickup points as he went. He would pick up his official letters later, with great ceremony, but they were a different matter altogether.

He had returned to his rooms and his bed long before the first stirrings of their household, which predictably was Wat, lighting the fires and quietly moving around before he descended to the palace kitchens. Alisander lay in bed, mentally composing a prosy note to the Kloberg ambassador, who was a great stickler for decorum.

He heard the quiet scratch on his door, and after glancing once more at Jane, who slumbered on, he called softly, "Enter," and Wat crept in with his pile of logs and saw to their fire. The servant kept his eyes discreetly averted, and Alisander made a great show of yawning and rolling over as though he fully intended to sleep on.

227

Once Wat had departed, however, he quietly slid from the bed and donned a flamboyant robe of emerald green. Catching hold of a chair, he carried it to the fire, where he plunked himself down to read his clandestine communications. Efficiently, he scanned through them, consigning most of them to the flames. The palace, as ever, was rife with speculation and gossip. Some of it had political undertones, but nothing that leaped out at him with particular interest.

His own marriage, unsurprisingly, had raised certain brows in Lascony. His unofficial contact in Aphrany wanted him to make a full account for it. It seemed there were a few ruffled feathers back home, but he already had his excuse ready. The Queen, Wilhelm's own sister, had demanded it. He was not unduly concerned about reprisals, though it might look to an outsider as though he was currying favor with the Karadokian King.

He kept back a few of the more harmless missives to strew carelessly about his room. He stuffed one deep in the pocket of his dressing robe, another he dropped down between the legs of a small decorative table, and a third he threw just wide of the fire so that at least a portion of it would be preserved for Wat to fish back out again later, perhaps a little artistically charred.

After all, he had to leave something for Wat to report back to Lord Vawdrey. Couldn't have the poor fellow being denied his second income. That would never do.

The whole time, he was very aware of the still figure lying in the bed. His eyes strayed to her constantly. It was fascinating how little she moved around in her sleep. Once he was done, he was tempted to clamber back under the covers with her, but perhaps that would be unwise. He had much to do today, and besides, he had resolved to take things slowly, had he not?

He disappeared into the dressing room for a half hour and dressed at a leisurely pace, choosing his outfit with great deliberation. On emerging, he found Jane's eyes open, though she did not appear to have moved an inch. "Ah, awake at last," he commented, sauntering in the direction of the bed. He sat down on her side, directly next to her. "And how are we?" he asked, lifting her hand from where it rested and casually kissing her wrist.

Jane blinked up at him. "Morning," she mumbled and glanced across at the window before her eyes came to rest back on him in faint confusion. It seemed that Jane did not wake of a morn with her wits altogether intact. For some reason, he found his lips quirking up at this discovery. Really, hc should release her hand at this point, but finding her so passive, he kept hold of it.

"It would please me greatly if you would confine yourself to our rooms for the next few days," he remarked, playing absently with her fingers.

Her brow puckered. "Why?"

"Because, I have a fantastic debut planned for my viscountess, and it involves your new wardrobe. Besides," he said, shrugging, "we need to build the mystery and anticipation of the moment. Court has been very dull without us, and we need to capitalize on the opportunity. Everyone will be positively agog to see how we deal together."

At this, she looked unenthusiastic, so he decided to try a different tack. "It will also be an opportunity for you to accustom yourself to motherhood," he said slyly, "and to keep a close eye as our household adjusts. I do not want anyone upsetting Robert, and by anyone, I mean, of course, that barbed-tongued servant of yours."

She colored slightly at this. "Ayleth," she muttered.

229

"Precisely." Jane started fidgeting, so he released her fingers.

"What of you?" she asked, her gaze flickering over his apparel. "You are going about, it seems."

"Yes," he admitted, holding out his arms so she could appreciate his embroidered sleeves. "This tunic demands an audience; you must agree." Seeing her pinched look, he relented. "I also have some official duties to discharge."

"Oh."

"You slept well," he remarked. He should likely leave it at that, but he could not resist following it up. "Is your sleep always so unbroken, or did I wear you out with my attentions?"

Jane cleared her throat. "I am usually a sound sleeper," she answered matter-of-factly. "The nightmare I suffered at Kinnerton was not typical for me. I suppose I have simply grown used to you being there."

"And what of the excessive clinging?" he added, straight-faced. "Is that something I must accustom myself to?"

"I beg your pardon?" she asked with dawning horror. "Did I—?"

He shrugged. "I will own, it was a little constricting, but mayhap with time I will grow accustomed to it."

Jane colored vividly. "I—I hardly know what to say, my lord," she stammered, looking appalled.

He had to work hard to keep the laughter at bay, but he just about managed it. "Pray do not trouble yourself on my account."

Her hand flew to her throat, and he wondered if she was covering up her flush there. He had to squash the impulse to move her hand away and take a look for himself. If he did so, he would never make his first appointment of the day. "I take my leave of you, then, my lady," he said instead with exaggerated civility.

"Er, yes," Jane responded, clearly thrown by his formal manners when she remained abed in her shift. "I trust your day goes well, my lord," she managed.

This time, his wayward smile would not be quelled. He nodded. "I will send Ayleth in to attend you" was his parting shot, and with that he quit their rooms and sallied forth on official business.

It was not until four hours later that he returned to their apartment. He had not actually intended to return until late afternoon, then he had started making excuses for himself. Hubair had been tiresome and difficult to appease. He deserved some respite after such a trying time.

He found Jane sat before the fire with Bertrand in her lap. Anne was sat in a nearby chair with Celestia and Robert hovering in attendance.

"My lord!" Robert was startled. "I did not expect you back until suppertime."

"'Tis of no great matter," he assured his manservant. It was not typically his habit to return at midday, though he would rather this was not brought to Jane's attention. Luckily, she was preoccupied, wiping some dribble from Bertrand's chin.

"Oh, you are returned, my lord," she said on catching sight of him. "Can you pass me that square of linen?" He turned and passed her the item, and she mopped up Bertrand's drool. "Apparently, he has teeth emerging from his gums," she confided, looking slightly queasy.

231

"Oh, really?" he responded politely, perching on the arm of her seat.

Jane shot a look at their nursemaid. "Is that not so, Anne?" she appealed.

"That's right, milady. You just prize his mouth open; you'll soon see."

He and Jane exchanged glances, clearly communicating that neither of them desired to stick their fingers in Bertrand's mouth. Mercifully, Anne did not seem offended they did not take up her offer. "Me old mum said as how I should ease them through with the application of butter." She continued comfortably, "But *'er* mum always said as it should be dog's milk, by rights."

"Dog's milk?" Alisander repeated, lifting his brows. "How positively barbaric. For the dog, I mean." Jane sent him a disapproving look.

Anne laughed merrily. "If you fink that's bad, milord, you should hear what the wise woman used to tell 'em to use in olden times. Rabbit's brains," she said with glee, and Jane blanched.

"I think butter must suffice for now," Alisander said smoothly. He turned to Robert. "Remind Wat to bring back extra from the kitchens this evening." Turning back, he cocked his head. "How long before our own progeny starts sprouting teeth, do you suppose?" Anne gazed back at him blankly.

"He means Celestia," Jane explained.

"Ohhh, not for a while yet, bless 'er 'eart. Do you want a hold of her, milord?"

232

Nothing loath, he came to his feet and wandered over. Anne passed the small bundle over and straightened up. "You content with Bertrand, milady? Only"—she looked wistful—"I was wondering if I could nip and get a bite to eat from the kitchens."

"If you needed victuals, then I would happily procure them, Mistress Anne." Robert started forward anxiously. "I have been most remiss in my duties, letting a nursing mother go hungry."

"Not at all, Master Robert," Anne hurried to assure him. "I don't want to send you down all them steps. In any case," she said, nudging him in the side, "I wanted the chance to stretch me legs, truth be told."

"I will be here for the next hour or so," Alisander said, looking up. "So, by all means, Anne, take yourself off." Anne sent him a grateful look and made a hasty exit, and Robert disappeared into the adjoining room. Jane sent a wide-eyed look in his direction. "What?" he murmured.

"What if one of them gets hungry?"

"They can certainly wait until her return, I am sure."

"*You* have not heard Bertrand's roar of discontent."

"I hate to correct you, Jane, but I most certainly have." At her querying look, he elaborated, "In the early hours of this morning, while you were hanging around my neck, wholly oblivious."

Jane colored but refused to rise to the bait. Instead, she stood up with Bertrand and walked toward the window where she proceeded to point out several scenic features to him.

Alisander glanced down at Celestia, who, as was her custom, was fast asleep. It seemed to him that Bertrand was far more

233

demanding a charge, but he suspected Jane felt comfortable holding him, as he was the more robust of the two.

On reflection, he fancied it was likely Celestia's wail he had heard, for Bertrand looked as though his lung capacity would be far greater than that wavering cry that had broken his sleep. Slyly, he watched Jane out of the corner of his eye as she paced about the room with her charge.

All was well for the first few minutes, and then Bertrand started to get discontented. Tentatively, Jane jiggled him in her arms, first gently, and then with more vigor.

"Shall we do a trade?" he suggested when her efforts became increasingly desperate. She cast a quick look at Celestia.

"She's fast asleep," he assured her.

"Yes, please," she said gratefully. "How shall we—?" He crossed the room and took Bertrand from her in his free arm, while she scooped up Celestia with exaggerated care. He watched as she tottered back to the chair by the fire, lowering herself into the seat with an almost fearful expression. "I do hope Anne won't be too long," she confessed.

"I suspect she'll take her sweet time," he replied mildly. "Likely stopping to chatter with all and sundry she comes across." Jane's panicked gaze flew to his. "We will manage just fine. Shall I tell you the latest gossip I have gleaned this morn?"

He did not wait for her reply, for he knew full well Jane would feel honor bound to deny any taste for such an activity. To do her justice, he did not think it was something she cared for. Still, he decided to test this.

"Sir James Wycliffe's wooing of Lady Constance Northcott continues as dully as ever. A formal betrothal was largely ignored, as no one could bring themselves to do aught but conceal their yawns and wish the virtuous couple well." Jane sent him a vaguely reproachful look and he smirked at her.

"What say you to Sir James?" he asked suddenly as an unwelcome thought occurred to him. Jane would think the likes of Wycliffe a worthy type, he had no doubt, with his scholastic pursuits. He was also good-looking if you admired classical good looks, he reflected sourly. Wycliffe looked like the hero out of a maudlin ballad.

Jane looked surprised by the question. "He is highly thought of in intellectual circles, I believe," she answered solemnly.

He rolled his eyes. "Not that, Jane," he sighed. "What do you think of his address?"

"His address?"

"His appearance, his manner of speaking, how he presents himself to the world."

Jane hesitated, as though realizing he was leading her toward some kind of trap. "I think—"

"No!" he said, swiftly cutting her off. "I have changed my mind. Do not voice the words that tremble on your lips. They will surely annoy me." Jane blinked. "Let me tell you how you should make reply to please your husband. Sir James is an unmitigated dullard, with scrawny calves and a stooping gait."

Jane screwed up her eyes. "He does not have a stooping gait though," she objected.

Pleased that she had not contested the other two points, he conceded this was true with a murmured, "Perhaps not, but he will get a stooping gait if he continues to study his books to such excess. All scholars do."

She hesitated. "There is some reason you do not like Sir James?" she ventured.

"I? Wherever did you gain an impression like that? I have nothing against him, save that it is tiresome hearing the ladies sigh over the purity of his profile."

At this point, Bertrand seized a firm hold of his gold necklace and gave it a violent tug. Luckily, the chain was a substantial one. "Kindly refrain from that, impudent child," he begged with a pained expression, freeing it from the child's chubby fist.

Bertrand beamed at him gummily. He could see no evidence of teeth, though there might have been a vague suggestion somewhere at the back of his mouth. "In any case," he continued breezily, "you agree about his calves?"

"I have never noticed them, one way or another," she answered with just a hint of asperity. "It is not a habit of mine to—" She broke off her words with a faint exclamation.

"What? Ogle men's legs?"

Jane turned rather pink. "Certainly not!" she spluttered. "I have better things to occupy my thoughts."

"Very well, then let me hear your thoughts on the worthy Lady Constance if you do not consider yourself an authority on men."

"Lady Constance seems to me a very admirable young woman," she answered repressively.

Alisander rolled his eyes. She would not be drawn on this, it seemed. He would have to try a different approach. "The Queen appears to be showing signs of thawing toward Mistress Frances Lessimore of late," he added casually. "Though The Bartree continues as her most constant companion."

Jane stiffened at this, and she looked as though she would speak before stopping herself. *Disappointing.* "I know nothing of the Lessimores," he lied breezily, knowing full well both Mistress Frances's connections at court and the match her parents hoped to barter for her. "Do you?"

"She has but lately come to court," Jane replied, "and has nice manners. I can see why she might please the Queen." There was a faint quiver in her voice.

He snorted. "She's almost as tedious as Lady Constance."

Jane straightened, a mutinous gleam entering her eye. "It seems to me that when you say *dull* or *tedious* that you might just as well use words like *laudable* or *decent*."

He laughed. "I see you are starting to get my measure, wife." She stared at him. "What is it?" he asked curiously. She shook her head. "No, say it," he urged her.

"It is just that—" She looked frustrated. "It is just, I am sure you must feel the self-same way about me, my lord!" At this, two pink spots appeared on both of her cheeks, and she could not look his way, fussily tucking the blanket more firmly about the child in her lap.

Alisander tipped his head to one side, considering his answer. "Perhaps at one time," he admitted softly, "but not for long." Her shoulders took on a rigid look. "It is true. You don't believe me?" He turned to the door Robert had disappeared around. "Very well, I will offer you evidence. Robert!" he called, and after a moment, they heard the old man's shuffling step.

"Milord?" he asked, his grizzled head peeping around the door.

"Come in," Alisander beckoned him. "Robert, you will oblige me by casting your mind back to a conversation we had some weeks ago about the Lady Jane. You will recall, when I told

237

you I was to marry, and you asked me what manner of woman my future wife was."

Robert's rheumy gaze flew to Jane and then back to Alisander. "Aye, milord?"

"You remember how I described her then?" The old man gave a hesitant nod. There was a risk, of course, that Robert might recall some of the more unflattering parts of his description, but Alisander reckoned it was only slight. Even at the time, his old servant had dismissed the majority of his words and viewed the rest of them in the most flattering of lights.

"Kindly relay the gist of it to my viscountess now," he said, gesturing toward Jane. "Or as much of it as you can remember."

Robert screwed up his eyes in the effort of remembrance. "Well, milord, you greatly relieved my mind; I remember that much. You said as how she was a virtuous maid, who kept good time and would never keep others waiting, whether 'twas for an appointed meeting or a kindly word."

Alisander nodded, watching Jane's reaction all the while. She lifted her eyes to the old servant's face and kept them there with such an intent expression that his peace of mind suffered a nasty jolt. *Fuck.* If Robert remembered something negative now, he would surely suffer a setback with her.

He steeled himself as Robert seemed to warm to his theme. "You said as she gave to the poor and said her prayers and was neat as a new pin. Yes, you said she was vastly neat and tidy in her manners," the old servant pronounced emphatically, nodding his head.

Jane's expression turned from baffled to cautiously gratified. She glanced at Alisander uncertainly, as though trying to reconcile such a kindly description as falling from his lips.

238

"Well, thank you, Robert," he started, feeling pleased he had thought to get the old servant's corroboration. "That is—"

Robert turned and started to leave the room before clapping his hand to his forehead. "I clean forgot!" he said, swinging back around again. "There was that business about her eyes being like precious jewels, Master Sander," he added. "I remember that bit most particular, for I've never heard you speak like that about a woman before. Poetical-like."

Alisander froze. Jane gave a faint gasp. Robert nodded at them both, beaming all over his kindly face. "Will that be all, milord?" he asked.

Alisander cleared his throat. "Yes, that will be all, Robert." Gods, he had forgotten he had voiced that foolish thought aloud. He was far too used to saying whatever he felt like saying in front of Robert. Maybe that was a habit he should nip in the bud. Someday it could turn around and cost him dearly.

Alisander shut his eyes briefly before daring to look in Jane's direction. She was bright scarlet by this point, her mouth practically hanging open. *Gods.* Mercifully, Celestia chose this moment to make her presence known. She opened her mouth and let out a pitiful wail, which had Jane springing to attention.

"Oh, Celestia!" she quavered, clearly glad of a means of distraction, and Alisander could not say he blamed her. Glancing down, he found Bertrand mouthing his gold chain, likely enjoying the feel of the links against his erupting gums. So winded was he that Alisander did not murmur a single protest, or even attempt to prize his precious necklace from the revolting infant.

17

Mercifully, as soon as Anne returned, Alisander disappeared from their rooms. Jane had hardly known where to look while he remained. In an attempt to keep her mind off those startling words, she spent the afternoon trailing around after Anne and the babies. Anne had helpfully chattered away the whole time, seemingly oblivious to Jane's strange mood.

Bertrand finally dropped into an exhausted nap around three o'clock as Celestia nursed at Anne's bosom. Jane leaned down over the crib to brush the curling baby hair from Bertrand's face. "He's finally sleeping," she commented softly.

Anne chuckled. "He fought it as long as he could."

Jane straightened up. "I noticed earlier that Celestia no longer wears tight wrappings, Anne. Is that because you bathed her last night?"

Anne's expression wavered. "Well, I 'spose by rights I ought to have bound her back up last night," she said guiltily, "but she's ever so much happier without them, milady. Only look at Bertrand. I never swaddled him in tight cloths and his limbs seem straight enough to me. My own mother never held with it, but well, I know Celestia is not my own child, so perhaps I did wrong."

"Your mother never swaddled you, Anne?"

She shook her head. "The way my mum told it, my older brother, he got terrible sores when she done that with him, on account of its hard to change them, frequent like. When she left them off, they soon healed up. Granny told her his limbs would grow crooked if she didn't bind him, but Mum said that was all wrong. She never swaddled me, and my limbs is all fine. I've only ever loosely wrapped Bertrand, but if you want Celestia swaddled, then I will do it, of course."

Jane hesitated, glancing once more back at Bertrand. "His limbs do seem sturdy," she admitted. "How do you encourage their strength?"

"I always get 'im to kick 'is legs when he's in his bath," Anne said cheerfully, "and to kick 'em hard. That way the muscles get to working. Then afterward, I puts olive oil on the joints to stop 'em squeakin'."

Jane nodded, though she had never heard of children's bones squeaking. "I am sure you know much more about it than I do, Anne, but I do worry Celestia might be rather young to leave them off."

"If you like, I could warm her cloths by the fire and put them back on when she's finished her feed," Anne offered.

Jane bit her lip, then nodded, and when Celestia had had her fill, Anne laid her down and started wrapping her limbs in the constricting cloths. Poor Celestia started crying at once, feebly waving her swaddled limbs in protest. Jane almost joined her. "Oh, she hates it," she said, covering her mouth. Anne looked grim.

"Please, take them back off," Jane uttered, feeling terrible. She honestly did not know what she was doing or what action to take for the best. Even with the linen strips removed, Celestia was inconsolable for at least a half hour, and even woke poor Bertrand at one point with her sobs. Jane was sure that when the baby did drop off back to sleep, it was because she had worn herself out with crying.

Once both children had been comforted and coaxed back to sleep, Jane slunk back dejectedly to Alisander's bedchamber

241

and drifted about the room, feeling like she was already failing Celestia as a mother. She picked up one of Alisander's hair combs and traced the carving up the handle with her finger. Irritably, she told herself she was being foolish, but it made no difference.

She knew what her sister would say. Helen would have said that Anne's mother was an ignorant peasant woman. Despite knowing no more than Jane about rearing children, Helen would not have harbored a single misgiving about what was best for her daughter.

Helen also would not have concerned herself over much about Celestia's welfare, a little voice whispered in her ear. Jane shook her head to dispel the thought. No, that was unfair. Helen would simply have been confident that Mistress Lingard and her lackeys could see to her daughter's needs, that was all.

It was not even as though Jane could consult her own mother. She recalled the short, apathetic letter she had received from her following Jane's news of Helen's death. She had been more interested in the news that Jane had married.

In any case, her mother was hardly a mine of information like Anne's. She and Helen had been raised by someone very similar to Mistress Lingard, though not quite as grand. Jane had no doubt they had been swaddled from neck to foot.

She set the comb down and slumped onto a chair where she let her eyes travel around the opulently decorated room. Alisander de Balon had as extravagant a taste in furnishings as he did in clothing. How bizarre that he had allowed himself to be persuaded into marrying her. Then again, he had apparently likened her eyes to jewels.

Jane straightened up and reached self-consciously for the looking glass. Glimpsing into it did not provide any answers.

Her eyes were simply light blue. He had probably been teasing Robert. It seemed a strange thing for him to do to his servant, but he *was* different with Robert, she reflected. Sort of solicitous and…almost benevolent.

Maybe he had spoken of her in such positive terms because he knew it would please the old man? She considered this a moment. If someone had told her a month ago that Viscount Bardulf would adapt his manner to please *anyone*, she would have doubted the veracity of their words.

He had been flippant and callous of speech the whole time she had known him. She recalled all the times he had made snide remarks about her while she had read aloud for the Queen. A couple of times she had felt like she truly *loathed* him. At least once, she had fantasized about flinging the book at his head.

The idea of him being so considerate toward an old servant was startling. But still, the fact remained, he *was* kindly disposed toward Robert, and he most likely *had* been flagrantly insincere when he listed her virtues. They did not even sound like traits he would admire, she told herself realistically.

She could more easily imagine him mocking her for always being on time and saying her prayers than she could him praising her for it. She stirred uneasily in her chair. She had placed too much importance on a very silly and insubstantial thing. He could not possibly think her eyes looked like precious stones.

Resisting the impulse to take a second look at her reflection, she stood up from her seat and strode about the room. What was she supposed to *do* with herself, cooped up in these rooms? It had been only one day and already she felt restless and discontented. How long did he expect her to confine herself here?

Her eyes strayed over to the curtained bed. She would not *think* about the things he had done to her in that bed the previous night. She could not. Even thinking about the extravagant compliment to her eyes was preferable to that. Turning on her heel, she made for the sitting room, as if pursued by vengeful spirits.

She had no sooner settled herself in front of the fire than Robert appeared at her elbow, bearing a packet of letters addressed to her. "For you, milady," he announced, offering it to her with a bow.

"Thank you, Robert." She took them and was surprised to recognize her mother's wavering handwriting, despite the fact it was now Jane's turn to write. Neither one of them was a keen correspondent, so it seemed strange to receive a second letter from her now.

Once she had untied the string, a bunch of folded papers and two small packages fell out. She realized with a sinking heart that this must be a collective effort from her various maternal relatives. Most of them lived with her mother, so it made sense they would all have sat around the oak table writing their epistles as one. Jane thrust down the impulse to consign the whole lot of them to a deep cupboard, unopened.

Such thoughts were unworthy of her. Her mother's relatives might not be as loathsome as her Cecil ones, but they were just as tiresome in their own way. Having shaken the dirt of Mertford from their shoes, neither she nor Helen had felt the smallest impulse to return there.

Still, ever the dutiful daughter, she had written home once a month, with little expectation of much by way of return. Certainly, she had received very little news over the last few years. When she did hear from them, it was usually a litany of complaints about conflicts with their neighbors and petty quarrels among her various aunts.

Her widowed mother lived in what would have been a vastly pleasant country house if only she had not filled it with all her awful relatives. Jane pulled a face. Still, they must have all been a good deal shocked to have heard first news of Helen's death, and then her own subsequent marriage all within a matter of three weeks.

She picked up the first of the letters and squinted at the inky scrawl. Aunt Maud, if she was not mistaken. Some sort of dried herb seemed to be sticking out of the folds of her letter. Jane did not have the heart to start with Maud's eccentric vagaries, so she set that one aside for later.

Next was Aunt Thomasina's letter. Jane broke the seal and scanned the opening lines impatiently. She could almost *hear* her aunt's unbearably pompous tones. As her mother's eldest sister, she liked to think herself head of Mertford Manor now. This, despite the fact the property was nothing to do with their side of the family. The property had been settled on Jane's mother after her husband's death.

Out of six sisters, only Jane's mother had ever married. The rest of them viewed this as a great act of sacrifice on her behalf, as indeed did Jane's mother. She spoke of her late marriage in long-suffering terms, as though it had been a terrible ordeal she had endured, purely for the sake of putting a roof over her family's heads.

Perhaps it had been, Jane reflected fairly. She could not remember her father, but if he had been anything like Sir Phillip, then he *would* have been hard to put up with. Her aunt's tone grew very stern in the second half of the letter, and Jane collected her nose was out of joint. It seemed she mistakenly

245

thought that permission ought to have been sought from her before Jane's marriage.

This was nonsense, of course. If she had been going to apply to anyone, it would have been to Sir Phillip, but as a matter of fact, the Queen's support trumped both of them. The final paragraph seemed to be some sort of demand as to how much recompense they could expect from her husband, on the occasion of Jane leaving their family for a new one.

Trust Aunt Thomasina to extend the begging bowl, thought Jane, casting aside her letter to pick up a slim, ancient-looking volume that had a piece of paper wrapped about it, inscribed briefly with "For your edification, niece." The spiky writing, if she was not mistaken, looked a good deal like her aunt Gregoria's.

Manifold Instruction on How to Be a Guid Wyfe was the unpromising title of the tome. The pages smelt rather musty, and Jane wondered where on earth her vehemently maiden aunt had obtained such a book. Inside seemed to be a list of exhortations to serve both your husband and the gods with honor. Jane's nose wrinkled at the odor and likewise set that aside, possibly never to look at it again.

Her mother's letter filled her with the usual sense of mingled irritation and guilt that any interaction between them caused. When she had sent the news of Helen's passing, she had included the fact she had been there at the last. Her mother made precious little reference to this and did not seem to derive much comfort from it either.

Where, Jane wondered, were her mother's lamentations over the death of her youngest child? None were to be found within the pages of her letter. Instead, she congratulated Jane on having the sense not to send for her, because "she could not possibly leave her home right now, when such delicate negotiations were taking place between them and their neighbor, Squire Blewitt, over a right of way."

Her aunt Thomasina, she wrote, had been "a tower of strength" in this difficult time, for she had thought of many ingenious ways to deal with the villainous Blewitt. This included reporting him to the sheriff for letting his wife and daughter "flaunt themselves in fur tippets."

Jane's mother included many lines painstakingly detailing that Thomasina believed the squire's womenfolk were wearing weasel fur instead of squirrel or rabbit fur, as they ought to by rights—weasel fur being prohibited to their station.

Jane lowered the letter, feeling her bosom swell with indignation. She had known for many years that her mother was a petty woman, but she had never before realized quite how callous she was, or how indifferent she really was to the fate of her children.

Jane's eyes smarted. Their mother wrote of Helen's death as though it were a minor inconvenience she could not be troubled with. She made no mention of the child at all. Gritting her teeth together, Jane finished the final few paragraphs which were taken up bemoaning the fact that Jane's husband was a "foreigner."

"If you must bring him to pay his respects," her mother concluded, "then for goodness' sake, do not let it be before the feast of St. Diamanda, for at present we have no time to spare for visitors as our efforts are all diverted elsewhere." *Yes, fretting about what the squire's womenfolk were wearing*, Jane thought darkly. Her mother seemed to have forgotten her own origins as the daughter of a mere squire.

247

Jane had just flung her mother's missive to the far side of the table when the door opened, and her husband entered. "My dear, I have returned," he said dramatically. "I find myself at a loose end for a half hour and thought I would check all is harmonious in our little home. But what is all this?" He eyed the scattered surface of the table with interest.

"I received a package from home," Jane admitted after a moment's silence.

"Home?"

"My childhood home," she explained reluctantly, "in Mertfordshire."

"Ah," he said, sitting down opposite her with his usual flourish. "Your mother's people."

"Yes," Jane agreed hollowly.

His eyes traveled over the eclectic collection of items. "Bridal gifts?" he hazarded with a lift of his eyebrows.

Jane gave a mirthless smile. "I think so," she agreed. "Or their approximation of them at least. My mother's family are…somewhat eccentric."

"Yes, I can see that," he said, tilting the book so he could see the title. He smirked. "And who sent this exhortation?"

"My aunt Gregoria."

"But how thoughtful of her. Did she write it herself?"

"She would hardly be qualified, my lord."

He looked amused. "She is, perhaps, a bad wife?"

"She is no wife at all," she corrected him.

"Ah," he said and reached out to flick the strand of herbs extending from Aunt Maud's letter. "And what is this?"

"I neither know nor care," Jane replied, wondering if she looked as sour as she felt.

"That is hardly filial of you, Jane," he said in mild reproach.

"They are from my aunt, not my mother," she responded tartly. "You are heartily welcome to them, if you would like them."

He smirked but reached over and unfolded the page, extracting the stem of dried leaves and tentatively sniffing them. He recoiled at once, dropping the offending item.

"What are they?" Jane asked, mildly curious.

"I have no idea." He picked up Aunt Maud's letter and scanned the contents. "Well, apparently," he said with growing interest, "if they are steeped in water and left to soak for a twelve-hour, they will make an efficacious broth that can then be fed to your unwitting husband, causing his manhood to lose its lusty vigor."

"It does not say that!" Jane choked out, feeling herself turn red. "You are teasing me."

He passed her the first page and Jane gazed at her aunt's matter-of-fact phrasing in fascinated horror. "She—she has always been interested in the study of botany," she said feebly.

"Along with methods of fornication, apparently," he murmured, his eyes traveling over the second page.

"I beg your pardon?" She had surely misheard him, but he seemed too absorbed with the rest of the letter to answer. Jane was almost afraid to ask what it contained. Instead, she glanced down to the bottom of the first page and read: *If he will not be denied, then on no account must you indulge him in any of the following positions, which must be considered lewd and ungodly in the extreme.*

Jane shut her eyes a moment in despair. Aunt Maud could *not* have… With feelings of dread, she dragged her gaze up to find Alisander's steadily upon her and containing a decided gleam. Jane swallowed and he flipped the page to show her a series of woodcut images which made her gasp aloud with horror. Her eyes nearly popped out of her head at the bizarre tangling of limbs depicted thereon.

"I think I'll keep this," he said, even as she made a snatch for it.

"Let me throw it on the fire!" she begged.

"Certainly not! And waste such a valuable resource?"

"Alisander!" She jumped out of her seat and half rounded the table. "Please, give it back!"

"Not a chance," he said, refolding the page and slipping it into the neck of his tunic. "Though you ask so prettily."

"*Please?*" she appealed, taking another step closer, her eyes darting to the unfastened lacings at his neck. Could she attempt to extract the wretched document, herself? No, she realized with frustration. She could never do such a thing. His chest was likely naked under that ridiculous tunic.

He leaned forward. "Not even if you promised me one hundred kisses," he pronounced with relish. To Jane's discomfiture, his gaze dwelt on her mouth the whole time, as though he was imagining it.

Embarrassing heat traveled up her neck. She was going to come over all blotchy again. "There is little chance of that my lord!" she choked out.

"We'll see." He glanced down at the table. "You may commit the pizzlewort to the fire with my blessing."

"I'd be more likely to stick it in your soup!"

He laughed. "Now, don't be cross; I'll give you this back," he said, tapping his breast, "once I have had occasion to study and commit it to memory."

Jane wrestled with the impulse to demand *why* he would waste his time on such a task. She was too afraid of his answer. The amused look on his face told her he was fully aware of the fact. She could *strangle* him!

"Why don't you try it?" he asked softly.

"Strangling you?" she asked in startled tones.

"Is that what you were imagining?" He gave a low laugh.

Why was he always so entertained every time she lost her temper? Honestly, she could stamp her foot by this point, she felt so thwarted. "What else?"

"Taking it back from me," he suggested. "You could just slip your fingers inside the placket…" Jane's eyes widened. "The placket on my tunic, of course," he clarified at Jane's panicked look.

Refusing to acknowledge this indirect reference to the placket on his breeches, Jane directed her gaze instead to the lacings at his throat. She shook her head. "You—you wouldn't let me."

"Oh, I think you'd be surprised at some of the things I would permit you, Jane." His voice was warm again and…husky.

He was so confusing. She took a steadying breath and sat back down. "Well, now at least I know you did not make good on

251

your threat to investigate my childhood. Or else you would surely know that none of my aunts were ever married."

He smirked again. "Oh, your five maiden aunts, you mean?" he asked. "The ones that all reside with your mother at Mertford Manor?" He tipped his head to one side.

"You—you *did* make enquiries?" she asked, aghast.

"Of course. I was merely pretending ignorance. I know all about it."

"All about it?" Jane spluttered.

"Oh yes. I had accounts from several local characters." His eyes rolled upward as though in an effort to recall. "A disgruntled servant had plenty to say about your aunt Gregoria, if memory serves. And there were several accounts of much wrangling over the years concerning a contentious footpath."

"With Squire Blewitt," Jane agreed hollowly. "How is it that—?"

"I have my sources. Did you know that your aunt Maud is a secret drinker?" he asked casually, "and that your aunt Thomasina *is* in fact married. She ran off with an undergroom of her father's when she was but seventeen years old?"

Jane's jaw dropped. "*What?*"

"It's quite true. He abandoned her mid-elopement, so she simply returned home and told no one."

"If she told no one," Jane said slowly, "then how can you have discovered it?"

"It is very rare that an indiscretion leaves no trace at all," he replied with a shrug. "As a matter of fact, your aunt has been blackmailed about it for years by her old maid."

Jane sat back in her seat, quite flabbergasted. Maybe that was why her aunt was always in need of funds?

"But that was not what interested me the most," he admitted, leaning forward onto the table.

Jane's lips trembled to ask what did, but she managed to stop herself. His eyes glinted as though he guessed her struggle. "I fail to believe you found anything more scandalous than a secret elopement," she said instead.

"It was the fascinating story of a young girl not permitted to sit with her elders at table until she issued an apology to her uncle," he said. Jane pressed her lips together when his eyes remained steady and questioning on her. "Did she apologize eventually?" he asked. "My informant thought not, but perhaps he was mistaken in this?"

Jane cast him a skeptical look. "Such a trivial story captured your interest? For my part, I am still reeling about my aunt's clandestine marriage."

"I prefer this story," he said. "To refuse to issue an apology, at such a tender age, speaks of great resolve."

"It spoke of great stubbornness according to my mother. And besides, perhaps the young girl did not deem it such a punishment to take her supper alone. Not when there was such company at table."

He did not smile at this as she thought he would. "And did she? Ever apologize, I mean," he asked.

She paused, letting her eyes drop to the discarded letters on the table. Jane shook her head. "She never did," she admitted quietly, some color stealing into her cheeks at her confession. "And fortunately, six months later, she moved away from Mertford forever."

"Six months?" he repeated quietly. "So long, Jane, to remain steadfast. To a child of thirteen, it must have seemed an eternity."

"You see," she said, glancing up, "I *really* disliked my uncle Humphrey."

He did smile at that, his hand stealing across the table to capture her own. "I think, after all," he said, turning her hand over, "that little Alisander would have liked little Jane."

Jane caught her breath as he stroked his thumb across her palm. "I thought you said little Alisander was not a nice boy."

"Oh, he wasn't."

It was at this moment that the door creaked open, and Robert shuffled in again. By mutual accord, they both moved back, pulling their hands apart in an almost furtive manner. The old servant was bearing a flagon of ale. "Ye're back, milord," he said with surprise. "And early too. Marriage must be making a punctual man of you."

Jane avoided Alisander's gaze, though she could feel it remained on her. She busied herself gathering up her letters into a bundle and retying them up with string. Stupid to feel like they had been interrupted indulging in something they ought not.

She was glad it was not just her who had sprung back so guiltily. In fact, now she came to think of it, Alisander was a good deal more respectful in his behavior in front of Robert. Why was that? As soon as Robert had plunked down the ale and retreated, she spoke the thought aloud. "You are different with Robert than you are with other people, I find."

"Am I?" He sounded bored, his gaze wandering about the room as though she had lost his interest. She felt her instinctive reaction to shrink back into herself, but *something* held her back this time. He did not actually find her dull company. He had told her as much a few times now.

If she was not boring him, then instead, she must be straying into waters he did not wish her to navigate. She had experienced last night how dismissive he could be when she asked about things he did not care to divulge. Then again, he had pried into her own childhood with a shocking want of tact, so why should she tiptoe around his own?

Instead of retreating, she asked boldly, "Has he been your servant for many years?"

He looked faintly surprised by her words. "You expect me to keep track of my servants' years of service?" he asked. "What a novel idea."

Jane paused. "It is of no matter; I can simply ask Robert himself. I am sure he will tell me."

He went still, and an appreciative smile curved his lips. "Ah, Jane, you are growing sadly devious."

"Are you proud? It is doubtless your influence."

"A little," he admitted, "but there are other areas I would *far* rather you followed my example." He gave her a sidelong glance which had her lips trembling to ask *what areas* but then she would be falling into his trap and letting him distract her.

"So…how long?" she persisted.

He rolled his eyes and leaned back in his seat. "In my employ? Oh, it must be some ten years, or thereabouts." *Something* about the way he said that did not sit right with Jane. She examined his words with a frown.

Alisander sighed. "He was the first servant I ever employed," he admitted in the manner of one conceding some great favor.

"He did not know you as a boy, then," she said, feeling strangely disappointed. She had thought for a moment she had discovered some secret.

"Wherever would you form an idea like that? You think because he is an old man with a Lasconian accent, then he must have known me from infancy?" The faint mockery in his voice caught her in a sore spot.

Jane flushed. "No, of course not—" she started before *something* alerted her. She was not sure what. Had his shoulders relaxed infinitesimally? *They had,* she decided, as though he had breathed easier once he had her on her back foot. She had *almost* fallen for his tricks again, she thought indignantly. "Well, I am sure he will corroborate that fact when I get him alone and ask him on the morrow," she said aloud.

Alisander's expression wavered, and his lips quirked up at the corners. "Sneaky Jane," he said softly. "Very well, since you are determined to put me to the blush, it so happens that Robert *did* know me as a child. He was in the employ of my late family, in fact."

She knew it. Jane leaned back in her chair and regarded him thoughtfully. "And as soon as you reached your majority, you sought him out and took him into your own service?"

Alisander gave a short laugh. "Nothing so dramatic, I assure you. Our paths crossed somewhere or other." He waved a hand. "I forget where. No doubt, I was feeling sentimental for the old days." He said the words with such airy carelessness that no one would ever take them for sincere.

"I expect you were," Jane said quietly and was satisfied to see a tiny flicker of emotion pass over his face.

"Jane," he said warningly.

"What? I am not allowed to be curious? Only you?"

That gave him pause. He sighed. "Promise me you won't question Robert in my absence. Talk of the old days…upsets him."

"I should not wish to do that," she said truthfully and hesitated. "Very well, you have my word."

He smiled his most charming smile. "Thank you."

Somehow, Jane thought with dissatisfaction, he always seemed to get his own way. She also did not believe him one bit about just happening to cross paths with Robert somewhere as a grown man. It was, she thought, exactly like her gold ring all over again.

18

Supper that evening was largely uneventful, and Alisander thought Jane's reply decidedly lackluster when he asked how she had spent her afternoon.

"Just how long do you expect me to remain in these rooms, my lord?" she asked, setting down her knife.

Oh, so it was "my lord" again and not "Alisander." "A few days only," he assured her. "The tailor will attend you on the morrow."

"But it will surely take weeks before the new gowns will be ready!" she protested. "There is always an inordinate wait for court clothes."

"Not at all, for I mean to pay an exorbitant amount. My tailor always makes my orders his priority. He will rush it through, never fear. Besides, you are not missing much about the palace. Court has been very dull and stagnant without us this past week, I find." He hesitated. "The King is—er—anticipating a sad event. It has cast quite a pall over proceedings. Several celebratory banquets have been canceled."

Jane looked up at him blankly. "What do you mean, a sad event?"

"His nurse Bathilde is very sick, apparently, and not expected to last the month out." He avoided her eye, only too aware of the stark contrast in Wymer's behavior when it came to the death of his mistress and that of his childhood nurse.

"How sad!" Anne commented artlessly. "Poor King Wymer!"

Ayleth gave a hollow laugh. "He can mourn, then?" she asked waspishly. "This King? When it suits him."

Jane pushed her plate away practically untouched, and Alisander felt irritated. It was damnably crowded at table when they all ate together like this. He had thought he could stand it, for a few days at least, as in the future, he and Jane would take the majority of their meals in the banqueting hall. Now, he wasn't so sure.

If Anne wasn't chirruping away, then Ayleth was sniping at all and sundry. He never had these problems when it had just been Robert and Wat serving him. Oh, and Davis, though Davis generally ate his meals belowstairs. Alisander sipped his wine and gazed around with displeasure.

In one hand, Wat had Bertrand balanced precariously on his knee, and in the other, he brandished a chicken leg. As for Robert, he was not even making a pretense of eating. Instead, he held Celestia in his arms and was crooning an old Lasconian lullaby in her ear.

For once the baby had her eyes wide open and she was gazing up at the old man, her face bearing an almost comical expression of concentration. It had to be a trick of the light, he decided. She was far too young to have actual thoughts.

Alisander cleared his throat. "We have much to discuss, wife," he said breezily, "about your conduct over the next couple of weeks."

"What about my conduct?" Jane asked.

"I have decided you must adopt a new manner around the Queen," he responded crisply. "If you act meekly, she will feel obliged to play the tyrant. It stands to reason."

Jane picked up her ale, an obstinate expression spreading across her face. "I did not know that I *was* acting meekly," she muttered.

259

Alisander sent her a quelling look. "When you left Aphrany, you were out of favor, lowly in order, and despised among her ladies." Jane spluttered but failed to find the words to refute this. "Now you return, an adored bride," he continued, ignoring the disruption. "You will be newly arrayed in gorgeous gowns and precious jewels will hang about your person."

Anne set down her hunk of bread and applauded with gusto. "Thank you, Anne," he said, "I am pleased there is at least one among us who appreciates my vision."

"So, you expect me to act like a spoiled wife, and this apparently will win the Queen over?" Jane asked with open skepticism. "Despite the fact she has made it known to one and all that she prefers the status of her ladies-in-waiting to be unwed?"

"Coo, fancy her bein' so particular," Anne commented, her eyes as big as saucers. Ayleth glared at her across the table, and Anne relented into a chastened silence.

Alisander picked up the bottle of red wine, turning pointedly to his wife. "Shall we take our fruit and cheese into our private chamber?" he suggested, "and finish our discussion there? It is somewhat crowded and noisy in here."

Bertrand backed him up at this point, tipping his head and starting loudly to howl.

"I had better light a fire in your bedchamber, my lord," Wat said, hastily handing the child back to his mother. Anne abandoned her plate with a regretful sigh.

Jane acquiesced to his suggestion readily enough, although, once inside their room, she looked about, a bowl of walnuts in one hand and a bowl of figs in the other. "Your table is covered in trinkets and there is no room for the refreshments," she pointed out. "Shall I set them on the dresser?"

"Just set them down on the bed," he recommended, sitting on the edge of it and removing his shoes. She hesitated a moment before spreading a cloth out in the middle of the bed and placing the dishes on it. Then, she set about following his example, removing her slippers and winding a mantle about her shoulders.

"Cold?" he asked, replacing his tunic with a dressing robe and pouring them both a goblet of wine.

She shook her head. "The fire will soon warm the room."

Wat straightened up from before the fireplace. "Will you be retiring so early, my lord? I only ask," he added hastily, "as I was not certain whether to fetch the water already for your evening wash."

"Fetch it in an hour's time," Alisander suggested, loosely tying the cord about his hips.

"Very well, my lord." Wat shut the door quietly behind him, and Alisander settled back onto the bed.

"Why don't you take off your veil?" he suggested casually. "We may as well make ourselves comfortable."

Jane frowned but sat down before the mirror to unpin her veil. Despite the fact she had not left their rooms, she was still rather formally arrayed. He watched critically as she unpinned the arrangement that had been pinned up at the back but left the braids intact, flipping them over her shoulders.

"Do you never leave it loose?" he asked.

"No, I do not."

"I should like to see it down around your shoulders," he admitted, reaching for the bowl of walnuts. He selected two, placing them in his palm and squeezing them together until he heard the shells crack.

Jane, who had already been reaching for her unflattering sleeping cap, halted. "I thought we were getting comfortable," she said, clearly flummoxed.

"Is it not more comfortable unbound?"

"Certainly not. It would soon become a tangled mess, straggling down my back."

"Who told you that?" He busied himself picking out the walnut halves and discarding the shells. "Your childhood nurse?" He could not hold back the faint taunt in his words, though a combative atmosphere was far from the one he was attempting to cultivate here.

Jane opened her mouth to refute the claim, then shut it again. "As a matter of fact, yes," she answered with dignity.

He could not bite back his grin. "I expect you learned all your lessons by the rote."

She ignored this, but he watched out of the corner of her eye as she reached for her braids and began to unfasten them. He placed two walnut halves on the square of fabric for her and popped the other two into his mouth as Jane slid her fingers through her woven hair to free it from the two tidy ropes.

To his fascination, Jane's pale golden hair had fully taken the impression of the braiding. Instead of lying flat as he had imagined it would, it was a mass of crinkled waves. Seeing the direction of his gaze, she looked a little self-conscious but joined him on the bed nonetheless.

He picked up another two walnuts and cracked them. "Those are for you," he said, nodding to the small pile he had made.

She helped herself to them. "Thank you."

"Your hair looks a little…unruly," he commented, reaching for their wine. "I thought it would be better behaved." She looked at him blankly. "I always imagined it was straight," he explained, passing her a brimming goblet.

"Oh, it is. It was still damp when it was braided," she explained. "This is what happens when that occurs."

He tipped his head to one side. "I rather like the effect." Jane cleared her throat and fussed with her pillows a moment. He wondered if she had swathed herself in her woolen mantle to cover up her delightfully telltale skin. "Did Ayleth dress your hair today?" he asked.

"She did."

"You need to take on a younger maid. Ayleth is old-fashioned, and I don't like the way she scrapes all your hair back."

"You forget, my lord, that I have Marta," she reminded him.

"Marta?"

"The maid I share with Osanna and Patience."

"Ah yes. You will forgive me, but that does not seem a terrible practical arrangement. Surely all three of you require dressing for the same court events."

"We always seemed to manage," Jane replied vaguely.

"When you lived together," he pointed out, "but that has all changed now. If you appreciate the services of this Marta, then mayhap we should poach her from the others," he suggested.

"We are already overrun," Jane said, pulling a face. "Yet you wish us to take on another servant. I do not think we have the room."

"I was going to make enquiries for larger rooms, if you remember."

Jane looked doubtful. "I wish to keep Ayleth with me," she admitted quietly. "At least for now."

"Why? I fail to see her appeal."

She took a deep breath. "I suppose," she said slowly, "because she is the only other person I know who is grieving my sister."

"This comforts you?"

"A little," she admitted. "You see, there are so few of us who mourn her. Even my own mother…" Her words trailed off.

"If Ayleth is a source of comfort to you, then keep her around by all means," he said generously, "but we need to find you another maid for dressing."

"Very well," she said brightly. "When you find us new rooms, then I will take on a new maid." Alisander narrowed his eyes at her, and Jane affected not to notice, making a great show of selecting the fig she wanted out of the bowl.

She settled back again. "The thing with Ayleth," she said apologetically, "is that she has been with my family for over thirty years."

"Yes, but her loyalty has never been yours to command, has it?" He skewered her with a look. "As I understand it, it was first your mother's and then your sister's."

Jane did not look at him but acknowledged the truth of this with a nod. "You think I ought to have brought Beth back with me, instead of Ayleth," she observed with a sigh.

He did not deny it. "Why didn't you?" he asked, reaching himself for the dish of figs.

She tipped her head as though considering her answer. "Initially, I thought that Beth might…might trickle information back to my uncle." Her face flamed. "I suppose that prejudiced me against her, though I now think she will make us an admirable housekeeper."

"It is not so unusual to have a servant with divided loyalties in this day and age," he replied with a shrug.

"You think not?"

"The day of the blindly devoted servant is done." She cast him a disbelieving look. "It is true. Must I give you an example to persuade you?"

"Well, I know you do not mean Robert," she said roundly.

"No, I did not mean Robert," he answered, feeling slightly nettled. "He is a leftover from a previous age. I was alluding to my efficient Wat."

"Wat?" She was startled. "How do you mean? Your servant Watkin is highly obliging."

"Oh, he is that," he agreed, lowering his voice. "He is also in the employ of Lord Vawdrey."

Jane sat up. "He is?" An appalled look dawned on her face as she took in the implications. "You mean…he spies on you?"

265

Alisander nodded. "Oh yes. He has done ever since he entered my service." He reached for two more walnuts and cracked them.

Jane was still staring at him. "Are you quite, quite certain?" she asked in horrified tones.

He nodded. "Quite, quite certain," he answered, though he was not sure why he was telling her. He held out his hand to her with two more walnut halves. She took them from him and ate them absently. "And have you never considered dismissing him?" He shook his head. "Does it not rankle at all?"

"Why should it?"

Jane leaned forward conspiratorially. "That his loyalty is not to you, I mean?" she hissed.

"I do not require loyalty from Wat," he answered simply. "I have Robert for that."

Jane sank back onto her pillows looking thoughtful. Hesitantly, she asked, "Have you never wondered if, at this point in his life, Robert might be happier retired and living quietly in the country with his own family?"

"*I* am his family," he responded bluntly. Too bluntly. *Why the fuck was he telling her this?*

"You are his family?" she repeated. He nodded. "Is that…why you tell him things?" she asked curiously.

"Things?"

"You know…things…" Her words trailed off awkwardly.

Ah, he realized, she meant like telling Robert he meant to marry her. "Things, like I thought your eyes were like jewels?" he asked casually.

Her face reddened at once. "Well…yes," she agreed in strangled tones. "Why did you tell him that?"

Alisander paused in the act of lifting his goblet to his lips. "I get these strange fancies now and again."

Jane swallowed. "So, you did not mean it, then?" she asked in a small voice.

A slow smile spread across his lips. "Why, Jane, do you want me to flatter and make love to you?" he asked. "I would be delighted to do so."

She clutched her goblet so tightly that he was surprised she did not snap the stem. "No," she said, lowering her gaze. "That was not my intent. It just seemed such a bizarre thing for you to have said."

Another woman would have forced a tinkling laugh at this point, but Jane just was not capable of such a thing. For some reason, that realization affected him strangely.

"Topazes," he found himself admitting huskily. "Your eyes look like topazes, Jane, blue ones. I have always thought so."

"Topazes," she repeated in such wonderment that he could not tear his eyes away from her. Her expression was *so…* Words failed him.

He had only seen her face wear that expression once before. *When was that?* It took him a moment to remember. It had been on that occasion when the Queen had singled her out for praise that very first time. He had not realized it, but that look on her face must have remained ever since etched on his brain.

Gods. Had she been so neglected of praise that it affected her always this strongly? And deep down, had he wanted, ever since that day, to see that same look on her face because of *him*? The dawning suspicion became a certainty as his heart beat so loudly that he was sure she would hear it.

You fool, Alisander, he thought in disbelief. He knew he hid a lot from others, but he generally did not hide things from himself! He should tear his gaze away from her face. He ought to say something flippant, maybe bring up her aunt's outrageous letter. That would bring her guard back up and wipe that vulnerable look from her face.

Instead, he whispered her name and, leaning forward, sealed his lips to hers. Jane let him. When he drew back and removed the goblet from her grasp, setting it down on the bedside table, she remained quiet and still. He carefully lifted the linen square, full now of walnut shells, and placed that, too, next to their discarded goblets, then the empty dishes. Turning back to Jane, he asked, "Will you take off your mantle, wife?"

Instead of answering, she simply tugged the garment from her shoulders and began fussily folding it before he closed the distance between them, bundling it up and dropping it over the edge of the bed. "Alisander," she murmured in protest.

"It's too ugly to touch your skin. We'll have the tailor make you something fit for purpose."

"Too ugly?" she repeated, startled, but a sudden impulse gripped him.

"Stay there," he said, practically leaping from the bed and making for his dressing room. When he returned moments later, she was still sat staring.

"What are you—?"

He held up his hand to show her the jeweled choker and the longer matching carcanet. "You see," he said, once more joining her on the bed, "I had these pieces commissioned with you in mind."

She gasped. "Topazes?"

"They are. You permit?"

She nodded and he reached around her neck to fasten first the collar and then the longer necklace. She kept her gaze on his face. "Do they match?" she asked, reaching up to touch one of the large blue stones.

She meant her eyes. He hesitated. Not at this precise moment, but how to explain in a way Jane would not take offense? "All the stones are perfectly matched," he said, deliberately misunderstanding her.

"And do they—do they look as you imagined they would?" she asked tentatively.

The sober-hued gown was all wrong; she wore no shoes, and he had never dreamt that her hair could look thus. "Yes and no," he admitted slowly, wondering why he never told her easy lies. He excelled at lying. He enjoyed the inventiveness too. Somehow, though, he was finding it was more rewarding to tell Jane the truth. "When I say I had you in mind, I did not expect you would ever wear them. I just…took you for my inspiration."

"Oh," she said, sounding a little crestfallen. She lifted her chin. "Did you intend them for one of your lovers, then?"

Alisander was startled. So startled, he once again told the truth. "No. I don't actually do that," he found himself explaining. "Give precious gifts, I mean."

"I suppose that would take more time and effort than you've ever invested in a love affair." Her tone had a definite edge to it.

"Truthfully, I don't think I've had a love affair before," he replied thoughtfully. "I've retained the services of a mistress or two, which must be a different thing, I think. They were paid well, but I never felt remotely inclined to buy them presents."

"Well, thank you for your candor, my lord, but I do not wish to hear all the sordid details," Jane said, reaching behind her neck for the clasp to remove the necklace.

At this, he shoved her back onto her pillows, pinning her beneath him. He let her feel his full weight bearing down on her. No doubt, she felt his arousal too. There was no subtlety about an aroused male lying on top of you. Jane gasped, her eyes flashing up at him.

"Ah, *there* they are," he breathed. "The exact shade."

Jane went still. "You mean," she said in a choked voice, "that my eyes look like topazes when I am annoyed with you." She turned her head aside. "I might have known it was not a compliment," she muttered bitterly.

He gave a short laugh. "I've never given jewels to a woman, apart from you. How is that uncomplimentary? Hmmm?" Grasping her two wrists in one hand above her head, he slid the other slowly down her arm and across her shoulder, lightly caressing her collarbone.

"You *are* becoming agitated, my sweet," he practically purred. Reaching for the choker, he moved it so that one of the cool stones slid across the newly sprung rash. "There, now, does that give you any relief?" Jane panted, glaring up at him. "No?" He ran his hand down to cover her bodice, lightly squeezing her breast. She gave a muffled sound, which should not be as exciting as he found it.

270

"I want to see you naked, Jane," he admitted thickly, "clad just in the jewels. How do you feel about indulging me in this?" Her eyes stared up at him. "*Fuck*, those topazes are not of fine enough quality. Yours blaze with inner fire." Only when her mouth fell open, did he realize he had spoken the thought aloud.

"I—you—"

"Let me remove this unbecoming gown, sweetheart. I'm *begging* you." Jane's eyes searched his face. His sincerity must have shown, he guessed, for she finally gave a nod and the world stopped turning.

"Yes," she sobbed, turning her face away.

He caught her chin, forcing her gaze to his. "Yes?" he repeated. She nodded again. "*Yes, Alisander*," he insisted, though he had no idea why he was pushing it.

"Yes, Alisander," she repeated, and he let go of her wrists, rolling at once off of her. Jane looked for a moment just the tiniest bit disappointed until he began efficiently stripping her clothes off her. "What about you?" she blurted when all her clothes lay in a heap on the floor. She clutched at the necklaces as if they afforded her some modesty.

They didn't. Her gloriously naked body took his breath away. "It feels a little strange with just me naked," she added, and seeing the direction of his gaze, she lowered her hands to self-consciously cover the little patch of gold curls at the juncture of her thighs.

Nothing loath, he shed his robe and breeches with an almost indecent haste. He'd never been so keen in his life, he thought wryly as he turned back to her. Jane's panicked gaze darted from his burgeoning crotch to his face several times before

271

settling with grim determination on his face. He guessed she probably wished he'd kept his braies on.

"You have nothing to fear from me, Jane," he told her as he joined her once more on the bed. Settling carefully beside her, he smoothed the curiously unruly hair from her brow and over her neck and shoulders. "I think I like your hair like this," he murmured, stroking one hand up her smooth back as his eyes wandered greedily over her.

Despite the fact his eager cock was pressed firmly into her soft thighs, his eyes dwelt on her upper body where the jewels lay flush against her heated skin. "Fuck," he whispered. "You are beauteous, Lady Bardulf."

She turned even redder at his words, and he loved it. Reaching out, he slowly adjusted the necklace so that it hung just below her breasts, framing them. Jane shivered. "Does it feel cold?" he murmured solicitously, fondling her breasts all the while.

"A little."

"Look down at the lovely picture you make."

She shook her head. "I'd rather see myself reflected in your eyes." And for some reason the admission made his breath catch.

Reaching for the necklace again, he slid it across her breasts until this time it rested directly against her nipples. "How's that?" he asked.

Jane cleared her throat. "A little cold," she uttered.

"Not uncomfortable?"

"No."

He ran his thumbs over her nipples. Again, she made an interesting noise in her throat. "I have a confession," he said conversationally.

"A confession?" Jane faltered. "Now?"

He nodded. Jane clearly thought speech inappropriate at this time. Naturally, this made him feel all the more talkative. "When I pictured you wearing these topazes… It might have been something like this."

"*Alisander!*" Her scandalized whisper made him shiver.

"I know," he responded gravely.

"Before we were married?"

"Yes," he agreed, "but I never thought I'd actually get my filthy hands on you, not then." He lowered his face to hers and kissed her with slow deliberation, tracing her lips with his tongue and lightly biting her bottom lip. "I have an idea," he said, drawing back but keeping his hand on her hip.

Jane's eyes were on his lips. She blinked a few times to focus on his words. "Idea?"

"Let us have a love affair," he said with relish. "You and I."

The expression on her face was priceless. "A love affair?" she croaked.

He nodded. "Take me for your lover, Jane," he urged huskily.

"But you—I—"

"What?" He smiled lazily at her. "You think I can't be your lover because I am your husband?"

"Well—"

"Let us think of it this way," he suggested. "Lord and Lady Bardulf are a staid married couple of impeccable reputation, but Alisander de Balon and Jane Cecil…now *they* are a different matter altogether."

Jane swallowed convulsively. "They are?" she whispered.

He smiled at her wolfishly. "Oh yes."

"I—I think you'll find that Jane Cecil is also sadly staid," she said shakily.

He shook his head. "You mistake her entirely. Take another look." He turned his head toward the large looking glass on the opposite wall. After a moment, Jane followed suit. She gasped, seeing their combined nudity reflected there. "It's a good thing my imagination was not so vivid," he said thickly, "or I would have been driven wild with wanting you, Jane. And I was already *far* too taken with you."

Jane's head turned sharply back to face him. "With *me*?" There was a wealth of disbelief and longing there.

"You don't believe me?" He gave a short laugh. "When you were gone from court," he confided, "I was bored out of my brain. I can't tell you the disappointment I felt every time I entered the Queen's chambers and found you missing. It got to the point where I would simply turn around and walk back out again."

Jane looked more shocked by this than she had by the sight of his hard cock. She blinked at him. "You—you mean, you missed me?" She could not quite meet his gaze.

He leaned forward. "I mean, that without you, Jane, court was *unbearable* to me."

"*Alisander*," she whispered, and to his utmost shock, she pressed forward, aiming a clumsy kiss to his mouth. So surprised was he that he did not turn his head to catch it, so it landed somewhere to the left of his mouth.

"*Jane*, do that again," he all but begged, rolling onto his back and taking her with him so she lay now on top of him. When she hesitated, he added, "I was *miserable*, my darling, desolated without you."

Her eyes flew wide as she drank in his words, and her lips parted. "Desolated?" she breathed. "Because of…me?"

Gods, her reaction. He nodded. "It was bad enough today," he admitted raspily, "but at least I had the consolation that you were tucked away in my rooms awaiting me." Unable to resist any longer, he let his hands slide from her hips to caress her lovely backside.

She shivered, her arms tightening about his shoulders and, as though unable to do otherwise, lowered her face to his. He was ready this time and made sure to catch her kiss with his lips. To his embarrassment, he could not help a slight reactive buck of his hips.

Jane gave an exclamation and clung tighter to him, as though afraid she'd be dislodged. Fuck, he liked that too. More words, she needed more words, he thought and, for once in his life, struggled to find them. "Rest assured, wife," he wheezed, "if you find it dull to be confined to these rooms, you should walk in my shoes for the rest of the week."

She licked her lips, and he could not help but thrust up again with a stifled moan. He wanted that tongue in his mouth. He was close to begging for it.

"You—you will wish I was there?" she asked, her expression so hopeful, it squeezed his chest and distracted him for a moment from his throbbing cock.

"Yes," he panted. "Always. Always want you there, Jane."

She gasped at his words, a tremor running through her, her gaze riveted to his face. He couldn't stand it any longer, rolling her underneath him. She winced, and he realized the longer necklace had caught in her hair.

"Here, let me take that off."

"You can leave it," she protested, even as he untangled it from her hair.

He frowned. "No, Jane, I can't," he said, flinging the longer chain over the side of the bed. "Not if it's causing you discomfort."

Her hands flew to the choker before he could remove it. "Leave this one, then," she said hurriedly.

"Why?" He hesitated.

"Because"—she looked evasive—"you wanted to see me wear them, did you not?"

He cupped her face, lowering his brow to hers. "Jane, these twin topazes here are the ones I desired most of all. They surpass those poor stones by far."

Jane's breathing hitched. She whimpered. She was in a bad way. Thank gods it wasn't just him.

"Jane, I really need you to kiss me," he admitted throatily, "this time with your tongue. Will you?"

She nodded, and he expelled a noisy breath, lowering his face to hers. This time, Jane wrapped her arms a little too tightly around his neck. Her clumsiness when it came to caresses undid him in all kinds of ways. When she pressed her lips to his, he found it didn't matter anyway, because he could not possibly get close enough and that was before her tongue crept into his mouth and stole all sense and reason from him.

Her kiss went from sweetly tentative to cautiously exploratory. He was half in disbelief that Jane was finally kissing him like this, naked beneath him. He could not get enough of the sweet taste of her. He was moving against her now; he could not help himself. Her belly and hips were delightfully soft and yielding against him, but they were not the spot he craved with increasing urgency.

Open your legs, Jane, was what he ought to say, but by this point, she was kissing him with such abandon that he could not possibly lift his mouth from hers to utter the words. It was only when she parted her legs beneath him that he realized he must have voiced his desire aloud.

"Like this?" she asked raggedly, her breath tickling his cheek.

"Lift your knees." She did so, and Alisander had to catch his breath and squeeze his eyes shut against the sight and feel of her. If he wasn't careful here, he would spend with disgraceful enthusiasm against his wife's stomach.

He cupped her between her legs, stroking a thumb through those intriguing pale curls. "I hope you're as wet as last time, Jane," he whispered. "I'll be *so* disappointed if you're not." She made no reply, apart from a hitch in her breathing.

Deciding on a quick change of position, he sat back on the bed and dragged Jane's thighs over his own, splaying them wide. Jane's eyes widened, but she made no objection to the lewd position. It trembled on his lips to make reference to her aunt's letter, but he had probably pushed her far enough on this second encounter.

"Shhh," he said, though she had not uttered a single word. "Relax, Jane." He traced the intriguing slit between her legs over and over a moment before dipping his thumb inside and pressing it firmly to her pearl.

"*Ohhhhh!*" Jane yelled, jolting violently. She would have shot off the bed if he had not held her in a firm grip. *Was she…? Already?*

He slid two fingers deep and felt her warm sheath clenching and pulsing around him. "Jane," he tutted, rubbing her clitoris with the pad of his thumb as she sobbed and struggled against his plunging fingers. "This is a terrible breach in etiquette, my darling. I had meant to bring you to pleasure myself, and here you are, taking it for yourself, and so *greedily* too."

Her arms fell from his shoulders, and he thought for a minute she would try to deny it. Then he saw the unfocussed look in her eyes which were glazed with desire. It was too bad of him to tease her even at a moment like this, he thought as she whined and arched her back. But he loved it so.

"A-Alisander," she whimpered, her eyes unfocussed and glazed with desire. She scrabbled around with her hands in the bedsheets.

"No, Jane." He frowned. "Hands on me, if you please."

Her hands clapped to his thighs, her fingers kneading and clutching him there as she came apart so completely that he was entranced. Jane was a blubbering mess when she came. He bit his tongue. Gods, how had he known deep down that Jane would be like this?

He stayed where he was, breathing raggedly as he waited for Jane to recover. He dared not even palm his cock which was paining him at this point. He would be lucky if he got it in her before he reached crisis point.

After a few moments, Jane's tearstreaked face blinked up at him. He felt a terrible pang of tenderness overtake him. It was strange to feel conflictingly tender when lust was riding him so hard. What was it about her that affected him so strangely?

"Jane," he whispered, "my sweet dove, are you yet living?" She was so sated, she did not even speak, just nodded, her cheeks very red and her eyes very blue. "I need to—er—come inside now," he said. Fortunately, she was beyond taking exception to his awkward phrasing. She let her legs fall open wider, and suddenly, he was the one unraveling.

"Gods," he muttered, clambering over her. "This may lack finesse." He notched his cock against her damp cleft. There was no "may" about it. He was about to rut her like an uncouth lout. He wanted to set her on her hands and knees, but that was no way to take your virgin bride. Besides, by this point, Jane was limp as a rag, bless her.

He surged forward with a muffled grunt and found himself thrusting home. Jane slapped her hands to his sides, uttering a sound of faint protest. He managed to pause proceedings, his vision wavering before his eyes. "Shall I stop?" he ground out.

Jane considered this. She looked, for a moment, undecided. Then she shook her head. "No."

"Sure?" Again, he was not sure why he was pushing it, but for some reason, he could not do otherwise where she was concerned.

"Quite sure."

279

Always so polite. He caught hold of her behind her knee and spread her wider, then thrust into her with merry abandon. He could not feign indifference or elegance or anything but unbridled enthusiasm at this point. *Jane, Jane, Jane*. Her name pounded through his brain, in time with his thrusts. Gods, he hoped he was not chanting it out loud. He could not be sure.

He just needed to keep hold of the reins until he'd cleared the first fence. Then he could let go and tumble headfirst into oblivion. For the sake of his own pride, he just had to hang on for the tiniest bit longer. Mayhap he could stave off his bliss awhile if he pretended it was anyone other than her spread out beneath him, wet and willing and taking his thrusts?

His mind rebelled at the very idea. It was none other than Jane, and no one else would do. He was sure that no one else's pussy could feel so very *right* stretched around his cock. At this point, he made a tactical error and locked eyes with her. In a trice, it was all over, and he was lost.

He gave a low groan and dropped his brow to hers. Instead of rolling off her, as good manners would dictate, he slumped on top of her like the worst kind of brute. When she failed to call him to order, he remained where he was, catching his breath. He was still in a pleasant trance when the knock sounded on the door.

Alisander's head jerked back. *Fuck*. He had forgotten all about Wat returning with the hot water. Grabbing a handful of bedsheet, he unceremoniously rolled until they both lay cocooned within it with Jane uppermost. They lay still in each other's arms listening to each other's heavy breathing as Wat's footsteps entered the room. There was a thud of the basin, then the sound of steps retreating, and the door closing gently shut.

280

He gave a breathless laugh, running his hand up and down her back. "Well, that was a close-run thing," he observed, and Jane made a choked sound, turning her head to look at him. "I might have to revise the knock and enter rule," he added wryly.

"You don't suppose he will tell Lord Vawdrey about it, do you?" she asked in a wobbly voice.

He pulled back to look at her, a sudden suspicion dawning. "Jane, did you just make a joke?" She shook her head, but he could see the smile she was trying to hide. "You did!"

"A very small one, only," she admitted uneasily.

He snorted and pulled her closer. "You can wash first," he said, tightening his hold of her. "But if you're in no hurry, we could remain like this awhile, I suppose." He felt beholden to at least feign indifference, though he felt strangely content to remain like this, rolled up in a sheet with her.

She gave a noncommittal murmur and settled her head against his chest. "Don't fall asleep," he cautioned with a yawn. "The water will go cold." Jane did not even respond. Most likely she was already dozing. Suddenly, he remembered the topaz choker. Feeling carefully around her neck until he found the clasp, he released it.

He couldn't have that digging into her sensitive skin all night. He flung it over the edge of the bed and heard the dull thud as it hit the rug. Then he let sleep take him.

19

Jane woke in the early hours of the morning to find Alisander gently disentangling himself from her. She lay still and feigned sleep as he crept from the bed and washed in what she felt sure must be stone-cold water. He made next to no sound as he slipped into his dressing room next door and then emerged just as soundlessly to slip from their bedchamber.

She wondered for a moment what he was about, but then rolled over and fell back to sleep. When next she woke, he was sliding back under the covers beside her, pulling her into his arms. "Are you awake?" he whispered softly.

"No," Jane grumbled, and she could feel his lips smile against her brow. It must have been a couple of hours later, at least, that Wat brought in more water for them to wash. This time, Alisander rolled away from her at once, loudly complaining at the earliness of the hour and soundly berating his servant for being mistaken about the time. Wat, now engaged in lighting their fire, responded with great restraint.

Her husband then made a great show of stepping on one of the topaz necklaces and hopping around, clutching his foot, and complaining bitterly about wives who were careless of their jewelry. Jane could not maintain a dignified silence in the face of such provocation. "'Twas you who dropped them on the floor and not I," she said as he heaped them haphazardly onto a dresser.

"Nonsense."

"Besides, they are not mine. You merely 'commissioned them with me in mind,'" she reminded him.

"Of course they're yours." He shrugged. "Did I not make that clear last night?"

"No, I don't believe so." She rolled onto her side to watch him as he took a hurried wash. His second of the morn, she reflected. "If they are for me, then I wonder you did not give them to me as a bridal gift," she pondered aloud, "instead of your own belt and necklace, I mean."

"I did not give them to you for a bridal gift because I wanted to see my own jewels on you," he admitted. "Before you ask, I have no idea why. One gets these inclinations from time to time."

Jane lay awhile considering this. Court had been *unbearable* without her, that was what he had claimed the previous night, and that he *always, always* wanted her with him. She felt her cheeks grow warm. Of course, he was merely being theatrical when he used words like *desolated*, but perhaps, under his peacocking, there *was* a grain of truth and he had missed her.

She swallowed, suddenly realizing how badly she wanted to believe this to be true. *My sweet dove*, that was what he had called her, and her breath grew shallow as she remembered the expression on his face when he had said it. He had looked almost baffled by the words coming out of his own mouth, and his voice had been so gentle, despite the hard press of his flesh against hers.

She had been glad for that tender moment in the aftermath when he had fallen upon her and slaked his lust so vigorously. She pressed her legs together, feeling the lingering soreness there. In a way, it had been gratifying to see him so lost to his own urges, especially after he had wrung such a strong response from her body with his wicked, knowing fingers and his hot mouth. Why should she feel racked by embarrassment when he himself had been so completely abandoned chasing his own pleasure?

On the other hand, there was no mistaking that the final act had been altogether base and lacking in delicacy. Remembering how she had lain with her thighs spread open for his attentions, she felt a slight trepidation. He would have so much more to tease her about after such an encounter. Could she trust him to realize such a thing would be beyond the pale for her?

She just could not be sure of him. He was a terribly teasing creature. The only thing she *could* be certain of was that, astonishingly, in his bed, he did not find her lacking. It was silly to feel so gratified about that, but she could not help it.

If he had looked even faintly bored with her, she would have been *mortified*, but there had been no fear of that. He had groaned loud enough to raise the dead when he had collapsed atop her, and his body had felt like a leaden weight. Strange to say, she had *not* felt particularly awkward about being tangled up with him afterward or falling asleep in his embrace.

"What are you about this morn?" she heard herself ask, immediately wishing she had not sounded so wistful.

He glanced over at her. "You need not envy me," he said with a grin. "I have a tedious meeting with one Alphonse Hubair to suffer through."

Jane frowned. "Is he one of your fellow ambassadors?" He nodded. "What country does he represent?"

He discarded his drying cloth over his shoulder. "Kloberg," he answered shortly.

"Oh. Kloberg is a great ally of the West—with Lascony," she corrected herself. "Are they not?" She would have thought he would have been more enthusiastic about such a meeting.

"So they say," he answered airily, heading for his dressing room. The door shut softly after him. No, he was definitely not interested in discussing his meeting with her, she reflected wryly. She would not feel forlorn about this. Such a thing would be silly.

She had just dragged herself out of bed when he emerged in a short tunic of turquoise with very long tapered sleeves. "Why are you up?" he asked with a frown. "I was going to ask for a bath to be sent in for you."

Jane glanced past him to the looking glass and suffered a nasty jolt. Her hair was an unruly mess and the skin at her décolletage looked blotchy and red. Seeing the direction of her horrified gaze, he laughed and strode across the room to catch her about the waist. "Ah, Jane," he murmured, pressing a kiss to her temple. "Anyone who saw you this morn would know you had been thoroughly mauled."

"I told you what would happen if I left my hair loose!" she retorted, trying to pat it down.

"I like it," he said, turning her toward the mirror so they could see their reflections there. "I like that only I have seen my proper wife in such a state." His hand stroked at her waist and Jane practically sagged against him, feeling weak. Oh gods, why were her legs trembling so? It was almost as if her body was reacting of its own volition.

He looked immaculate as ever, jewels flashing at his fingers and a pearl-encrusted hat set above his waving locks. They presented a strange contrast in appearances.

"I look a mess," Jane murmured, lowering her gaze.

"You look enchanting," he corrected her caressingly. "I am half tempted to disappoint Alphonse and send my apologies."

Jane's head snapped up and she could not hide her panicked reaction. "But if I am to have a bath, what would you do here, my lord?"

"Hmmm, maybe…wash your back," he suggested richly. Jane's response stuck in her throat. "Or someplace else."

"My lord…" she said in strangled tones. His gaze snapped to hers in the mirror, and Jane felt his fingers slide from her waist to clasp her hips in a firm grip.

"You are a temptation, Jane," he said thickly. "I think I should like to keep you tucked in my bedchamber awaiting my pleasure. Mayhap I should chain you to my bed with ropes of topazes. What say you to that?"

Jane's mouth fell open. *What?* For a moment, she felt genuinely alarmed. "Th-that does not sound very practical," she objected breathlessly.

He pressed his mouth to her neck and Jane forgot to breathe. "If you were my pampered mistress, that is what I would do with you, Jane," he said thickly. "Alas, as my lady wife, I could not subject you to such rude treatment."

Jane stiffened. "Is that how you usually conduct yourself with your kept women?"

His smile broadened. "I am not normally so fanciful," he said lightly, wrapping his arms about her middle. "Are you jealous, wife? You have no need to be for you are wife and mistress both, is that not so?"

Jane tried to relax, but the truth was, she felt affronted. "I thought we had done with that nonsense about mistresses," she said sternly.

"And now," he sighed, "you are all prickly and outraged. The strange thing is, I like that too," he said, tightening his arms. "I always have, you know."

In spite of herself, Jane felt herself relax. "I know you like to torment me," she said, trying to sound scolding and failing miserably.

"I do," he admitted softly, still holding her close. "Now turn around and bestow a kiss on me, wife. It would be a great kindness, for I am in a bad way."

"A bad way?" she echoed uncertainly.

He nodded. "In truth, I should like nothing more than to wrap us both in that bedsheet again," he said, nodding over her shoulder toward the bed. "And to stay with you like that all the day long."

Jane caught her breath and turned about in his arms so they were facing. She had a terrible feeling that he could tell how badly his words affected her. Why did she feel so emotional these days? She liked to think of herself as measured and sensible in all things, but she could feel her lips quivering and a flush spreading over her neck. "Very well," she whispered.

Instead of teasing, he bent his neck at once and pressed a hard kiss to her mouth. Jane passed her arms about him, and he startled her by chasing her mouth when she went to pull back. This time he was gentler, sealing his lips to hers and sipping almost sweetly. In spite of herself, Jane relaxed into his kiss and felt herself grow pliant against him, parting her lips for his tongue.

"Ah Jane, how dare you say I torment you," he rasped when he finally drew back. "This tunic is far too short for you to dally with me like that, wife. How am I to listen to Alphonse's prating when you have made me hunger and thirst for you at this indecently early hour?"

Jane could barely meet his eye, but she dwelt on that kiss to an unseemly degree as she soaked in the bathtub once he had departed. Alisander de Balon did not find her dull and worthy. He found her terribly exciting, and the realization made her head spin.

"I said," Ayleth's voice broke in sharply, "are you ready to come out yet?" Jane snapped out of her dreamy state and hastily assented. From Ayleth's tone, Jane guessed she had already repeated the question several times. "You're turning wrinkled from that bathwater, my lady," the servant observed.

Jane stood up and was promptly engulfed in a drying sheet. As Ayleth busied herself laying out clean undergarments, Jane made her way to the looking glass and surreptitiously examined herself. Even after her bath, there were several telling blotches showing where Alisander had mouthed at her sensitive skin. The one at her collarbone had the most unfortunate placement.

Pulling down the sheet, she discovered the worst of them above her left breast. He had *sucked* that mark onto her, she remembered, turning prickly and hot all over. His mouth had seemed ravenous for the taste of her. She had never even dreamt that lovers acted thus. She pressed two fingers to the raised pink skin.

No one would see it and it was nothing to signify, she told herself as she crossed the room to stand before the fire and dry herself.

"I wonder if I might have a word, my lady," Ayleth began grimly, turning from the clothes she had laid out ready on the bed.

288

Jane glanced at her and braced herself. "I will, of course, listen to you, Ayleth, if you have something to say."

"You may think as it's not my place," Ayleth began, and Jane recognized the chastising tone, though she had not heard it in many a year. "The gods know I've tried. I've tried to push the words down, but it won't serve. I need to speak my mind and you, my lady, need to hear it!"

Jane pursed her lips. "Well, I have said I will hear you out, but I can make no promises other than that, Ayleth. Speaking freely can come with consequences, something you will not have reached your age without learning, I am sure."

Two spots of high color appeared in Ayleth's cheeks and her thin lips worked for a moment with emotion. She inclined her head stiffly. "I've served your mother's people since I was but a girl," she started unevenly, "and in fifty years, I've never seen the likes of *this* household!" She clutched her fists at her side. "The way everyone is carrying on here is just not decent!"

Jane lifted her eyebrows but said nothing. Instead, she sat down in a chair and pulled the fresh shift over her head. Ayleth hurried forward to thrust a pair of mustard yellow stockings at her. Jane nodded toward the arm of the chair for she was now wrapping the cloth about her damp hair. "Set them there, please."

Ayleth flung them down. "You must have noticed the state of affairs with that *Robert* as he calls himself!" she began fiercely. "Why, I've never seen such a cozening old rogue! He sits in his stockings of an evening before the fire, drinking the best wines, eating the softest of white bread."

Her hair secured, Jane reached for the stockings, holding her tongue. Ayleth's eyes flashed. Clearly, she found Jane's response lacking. "What's more," she started again indignantly,

289

"he has the largest of the servants' rooms. And his best days clearly behind him! Wat does three times the work and reaps not one-tenth of the privileges."

Jane considered this a moment, in light of what Alisander had imparted the previous evening. "Robert is my husband's oldest and most trusted servant," she stated plainly. "That is why he holds a position of privilege."

"Pah! He is an old rascal, taking rampant liberties on account of his master's partiality for him! And that is not even the worst of it," Ayleth continued. "That Anne should not be encouraged to join in conversation with her betters at table. Lord Bardulf does not so much as make the smallest effort to put her in her place."

Jane stood up and picked up her green silk gown. Ayleth hurried forward to help as she stepped into it and began securing it at the back, her fingers flying over the fastenings as Jane adjusted the neckline to her liking. It just about covered her collarbone, she was relieved to discover.

"He positively encourages her, and so do you!" Ayleth grumbled, tugging on the ribbons. "There is a lamentable lack of decorum all round. That lump Davis is nothing but an uncouth brute, and as for Anne—" She broke off her words with a harsh laugh. "If I did not know better, seeing how you both indulge that brat of hers, I would think it one of his lordship's by-blows." Jane stilled. "That is what people will think, my lady, you'll see," she added venomously. "They'll say as he accepted my lady's bastard, so long as you accepted his!"

Jane gave a short laugh. "You know that is not the case, Ayleth," she said as the older woman started attacking her wrist lacings. "That is a *little* tight."

Ayleth's lips pressed together in a straight line as she loosened the ribbons. "She's got loose morals, that one. Who's to say she

290

won't get ideas? Your sister, my Lady Helen, would have *never* allowed her staff to be so familiar, and neither should you!" She hesitated. "There was more than one pretty maid she had to let go when she was here at court. They drew a gentleman's eye in the wrong direction, if you catch my meaning. Anne's no beauty but she's comely enough."

Jane had to bite her tongue. "Is that the sum of your concerns?" she asked.

"That most certainly is not all!" Ayleth said, brandishing a pair of garters and kneeling at Jane's feet. She tapped one foot and Jane lifted it for her to slip it over her ankle and calf. "Those children should be swaddled neck to toe for the health of their limbs. Why, any fool knows a baby's bones are soft as wax!" She tapped the other foot and Jane complied. "She hasn't even the sense to ask for hooks to be put up for their safekeeping," Ayleth added with deepest disgust.

"Hooks?"

"To hang them from while she is about her work."

Jane could not hide her confusion at this, and Ayleth stood up, plunking her hands on her hips. "'Tis plain to see, you know *nothing* about children, my lady. Both children should be bound to boards each morn. That way they can be set out of harm's way while she does her duties."

"The children *are* her duties," Jane pointed out, but Ayleth ignored this point, rushing on.

"That chamber of Celestia's is a disgrace," she said angrily. "Always in disarray, and small wonder with that whelp of Anne's rolling around and drooling on everything! It's not fitting or right!"

"Nonsense," Jane replied with an edge to her voice. "Celestia is well-fed and content. As for the swaddling cloths, those were removed with my expressed permission. If the child turns out one-tenth as sturdy as Bertrand, then I will be well pleased with her progress."

"I don't say as Anne's not an adequate wet nurse," Ayleth replied after a moment's affronted silence. "But she is *not* a suitable nursemaid for the likes of that baby. She is naught but an ignorant girl at the end of the day, while Celestia is the daughter of a—"

"The honorable Celestia de Balon is the daughter of a viscount," Jane pointed out in a steely voice. "It is *his* name she bears, and mayhap even his title one day." That did give Ayleth pause, and taking advantage of this, Jane continued steadily. "To suggest otherwise is to go expressly against the King's orders, which would be foolhardy indeed." Ayleth's thin face turned scarlet, and Jane let her words sink in.

"As for Anne," she continued steadily, "she is kindly and warm-hearted with good motherly instincts. She is *exactly* the person needed." Deliberately Jane turned and walked over to the dresser, where she sat and, dragging the drying cloth from her head, seized a hair comb.

"If the conditions of our household are disagreeable to you, Ayleth, then you must cast about you for some situation that suits you better," she said, trying not to feel guilty at her words. "If you wish to return to my mother's house, then I can write to her at Mertford. Or, if there is somewhere else you prefer, I am happy to release you from our service."

Ayleth stood frozen for a full minute before joining Jane. She held out her hand. "Give me that comb, my lady," she said stiffly. "You're making a right mess of things."

Jane was under no illusion that she was referring solely to her hair.

She broke her fast, with Robert fussing over her, then spent the rest of the morning in Anne's and the children's company. Celestia was fractious and Anne had to nurse her a good deal. Jane shook a rattle over Bertrand, who happily gurgled back at her.

"Was Bertrand so difficult to settle when he was Celestia's age?" she enquired as Celestia let out another complaining wail.

"Oh, he had his days, believe me! Luckily, I had me mum on hand in the early days."

"She must miss you both, I am sure."

Anne shrugged. "Me brother will have moved into my old room by now. Him and his wife." She pulled a face. "I'm not that fond of Martha, truth be told, and she ain't got much time for me neither!"

"Is that your sister-in-law?"

Anne nodded. "Thinks she's a real beacon of virtue, that one, but if John, that's me brother, hadn't stepped up, then she'd have been in the same predicament as I found meself in!" Anne snorted. "Martha didn't much like me pointing that out, you can be sure! Went running straight to Mum, bidding her to tell me to hold my tongue."

"And what did your mother say?" Jane found herself asking.

"She said, 'My Anne has her faults, but she ain't never told a lie to my knowledge, and if you wanted it kept a secret, Martha Billings, you should have forced Walt's hand before your belly started showing!'" Anne's face split into a broad grin. "She might have guessed Mum's who I get my plain speaking from in the first place!"

Jane hid her answering smile against Bertrand's hair.

Alisander returned at midday, shortly before the tailor arrived. He found Jane in the main chamber, rocking a sleeping Celestia in her arms as Bertrand crawled about the floor. "What a vastly domesticated scene," he commented, closing the door behind him. "But where is everyone?"

"Anne has slipped down to the kitchens," Jane answered promptly. "Wat had some errands to run, and Robert is—er—resting his eyes." Anne had discovered the old man napping in his seat and had not liked to disturb him. Jane had agreed to leave him undisturbed for an hour or so.

Alisander's eyebrows rose. "I see," he said, glancing down at Bertrand, who had made a beeline for his feet and was now pawing at his expensive-looking shoes. To Jane's astonishment, he reached down and hefted the child into his arms, carrying him over to the window, even as he continued his conversation with her.

"I hope you have not forgotten the tailor is visiting with you this afternoon," he said, pointing at the window and directing the child's gaze to the prospect of the castle walls beyond.

"I have not forgotten," she said absently. A knock sounded on the door and Wat's head peered around it.

"Apologies, my lady, I did not realize I would be so long—" He gave a guilty start when he saw his master stood over by the window.

"Ah, Wat," Alisander said smoothly. "I wanted to ask you deliver this missive for me." He shifted Bertrand from one arm to the other and then reached into his tunic to extract a letter.

Wat hurried forward and took it from him. Jane disregarded their conversation around its delivery, focusing instead on Bertrand, who, having grown bored of the view, had now seized hold of one of the drop pearls from Alisander's neck-chain.

The child spent some moments vigorously tugging at it before he started towing it in the direction of his mouth. Jane had just opened her own to warn Alisander of the fact when he calmly reached down and plucked it out of Bertrand's little hand. He provided one of the tassels from his tunic instead before the child could register his displeasure.

Jane's stunned gaze flew to Alisander's face. He directed a swift interrogative glance her way and mouthed *What?* at her. Quickly, she averted her eyes and pretended to be absorbed with Celestia, who was mercifully still asleep.

Alisander turned back to Wat, who was inspecting the letter. "You had better go and deliver it now, Wat," he directed. "We will hold the fort here. No doubt Anne will return at some point when it suits her. Preferably before Monsieur Barbier arrives."

Jane looked up at his dry tone, but his expression was benign enough as Wat slipped from the room. "By the way, you did not mention Ayleth's whereabouts," he added as the door shut after him.

Jane grimaced. "We *had words* this morning, I'm afraid," she admitted. "I think she has retreated to lick her wounds."

"Words?"

Jane shrugged a shoulder, not really wanting to go into it. "Ayleth is offended that we are keeping country manners in our household," she said grudgingly.

"Country manners?" He moved away from the window and dropped down onto the cushioned bench opposite. "I am unfamiliar with the phrase."

"We are not…strictly observing distinctions of rank," she said awkwardly.

"Ah, you mean, such as my returning to find you minding both children alone."

"That among other things," she agreed. "She seems to think people will believe Bertrand is your child," she found herself sharing before she could stop herself. "The way we are 'carrying on.'"

"Dear me!" He looked down at Bertrand and tutted. "He is a bonny child, to be sure, but his beauty is hardly in *my* league. Ayleth must be quite deluded!"

Jane rolled her eyes. "She knows full well that you are not his father. She is just prickly and unhappy with her lot."

He was silent a moment. "Next, she will be suggesting that Anne might catch my roving eye," he said lightly. When Jane gave a guilty start, he smirked knowingly. "I hope you told her that I am too busy worshipping at your feet to spare another woman a glance."

Jane did not know where to look or how to answer. She watched in silence as he set a fidgety Bertrand down on the seat beside him. The child scrunched up his eyes and opened his mouth. At once, Alisander snatched the fancy hat off his head and handed it to him. Bertrand's downturned mouth immediately turned up. He gave a squeal of delight and promptly fastened his gums around the brim. "You do realize," Alisander said suddenly, "that Anne has more than likely sloped off in search of Davis."

"Davis?"

He shot her a look. "It was obvious from the first that he caught her eye. Which is a shame, as I fancy Wat has taken a shine to her, and I imagine Davis a callous type when it comes to women." Seeing Jane's look of astonishment, he added: "Your observation skills, wife, are sadly lacking."

Jane flushed. "You would rather Anne took a liking to Wat?" she said, glancing at the door to make sure it was shut. "Despite his—er—*activities*?"

He looked thoughtful. "You think spies make poor husbands, Jane?" he asked. "Now, why is that?"

"Well," Jane considered, "I suppose I always thought they came to nasty ends. Reaping the rewards of their treachery."

He looked amused. "Poor Wat is most assiduous in his duties, I assure you, and virtuous in all other areas of his life. He supports his old mother and goes to church on Sundays."

"Do you actually know this for a fact," Jane asked, "or is it merely something you amuse yourself imagining due to his sober appearance?"

He laughed. "I never trust appearances," he replied, "and am very conscientious when it comes to employing staff."

She thought about that a moment. "In that case, you must know for a *fact* that Davis is callous when it comes to women," she pressed.

He sighed. "It is the most distressing thing. Your observation skills are terrible, but you do have a certain ruthless logic to your line of thought."

"That's a yes, then," Jane decided with a frown. "Oh dear, we must think of a way to dissuade Anne's admiration."

"You think so? I believe such stratagems seldom work. Indeed, I imagine they would have the opposite effect."

It was plain to see he had little interest in the subject. "Well, in any case," she said briskly, "I appreciate your warning and will take steps where Anne is concerned."

"That was *not* my intent," he interrupted her with a roll of his eyes. "I merely wished to ensure you did not entertain Ayleth's absurdities."

"Oh, well…" Jane's words trailed off. "I handled Ayleth just fine. I think, in her own way, she was trying to look out for me. She was very protective of Helen always."

"Maybe so," he acknowledged, "but if she does not like our *country manners*, then mayhap our household is not the best place for her."

"I relayed as much to her this morn," Jane said quietly, and he seemed to relax at this.

"Good." He tilted his head. "Ah, that sounds like Anne now. Thank goodness. My hat would not have lasted much longer as a diversionary tactic."

Jane frowned, for she had heard nothing, but as she opened her mouth to say so, she heard a door shut and Anne's quick, bustling step in the corridor outside. He must have very keen ears, she reflected, as Anne swept into the room looking a picture of vibrant health.

"Ah, Anne," Alisander drawled. "Your kitchen quest proved fruitless, then?"

"My what?" Anne asked, then glanced down at her empty hands and gave a short laugh. "Oh, that. Well, 'appen I did pick up a pastry, but I ate it on the way back," she admitted guilelessly.

Almost, Jane doubted she had been dallying at all, but then she noticed Anne's flushed cheeks. Oh dear, she thought. A pastry would not have put such a sparkle in Anne's eye.

"They been good?" Anne asked, nodding at Celestia.

"Mostly sleeping," Jane answered as Alisander simultaneously replied, "Awful. This child has all but destroyed my favorite hat."

"Funny-looking sort of hat," Anne said, tugging it out of Bertrand's grasp and passing it doubtfully back to Alisander.

"Well, it is now!" he complained. "I assure you, my dear Anne, that such hats are the *height* of fashion in Kloberg." Anne looked suitably impressed. "Now, if you could clear this room of infants, I would much appreciate it. Your mistress and I are expecting a visit any minute now from the esteemed tailor, Monsieur Barbier."

Anne's eyes widened and she darted forward to scoop up Celestia. "At once, your lordship," she responded promptly. As soon as Anne had whisked the children from the room, Jane turned back to him.

"She was telling the truth," she asserted with confidence, "for there were pastry flakes on her skirts. How is that for observation? And," she added triumphantly, "I happen to know for a fact that Anne's mother says Anne would never willingly tell a lie."

He extended his arm along the back of his seat. "Is that so? Well, if Anne's mother, who neither you nor I have ever met, says so, then it *must* be true," he said mockingly.

She narrowed her eyes at him. "How was your meeting?" she asked.

"Deathly dull."

"Did the ambassador from Kloberg not appreciate your Klobergian hat?"

He smiled reluctantly at her words. "How could he fail to?" He shrugged. "He is a dull-witted fellow, but he has eyes in his head."

Jane snorted. "Are you staying for the tailor's consultation?"

"But of course I am, Jane. You have not the smallest notion how to dress yourself." He forestalled her reply by throwing up his hand. "He has arrived," he said, though Jane had heard no sign of it at this point. Sure enough, moments later, three loud raps were heard.

It was Robert who showed the master tailor in. He looked a little confused and bleary-eyed and Jane guessed the knocking on the door had disturbed his slumber. "Can I fetch any refreshment, my lord?" he quavered.

"Ah no, not for me," the tailor said quickly. He seemed eager to settle to business at once, setting down a bag from which he extracted papers and ink. Alisander looked to Jane, who also declined, and Robert was sent back to the sanctuary of his room, likely to finish his nap.

To Jane's surprise, the tailor's consultation took up most of the afternoon. Alisander treated Monsieur Barbier with the utmost respect, and it seemed they were long acquainted, for he had only to say, "Something along the lines of that cloak you made me that time, in that dusty lavender shade," and Barbier would nod at once in complete understanding and start scribbling notes. Considering how vast his wardrobe was, Jane thought this quite a feat.

She had tried to listen at first when her husband had explained his vision for her, but once he had stressed that all her new clothes were to have either blue or gray undertones, she lost interest. It did not seem terribly exciting after that. "Observe the pale blond of her hair," he had said, and Monsieur Barbier had turned to look at her with the critical eyes of an artist.

"Her skin though," the tailor had ventured uncertainly. "Do you not think such ashy shades would wash her out?"

"No," Alisander cut in firmly. "You must not consider it." When Barbier looked as though to argue, he added, "In social situations, my lady's color grows considerably warmer." Jane felt her skin start to prickle with embarrassment. "You see?" he said as Jane felt her face grow warm.

The tailor nodded in agreement and bent his head over his notebook. Jane sent a resentful look at Alisander, but he was not attending. "All save one dress," he was saying, "which I desire in a bold emerald green. For the neckline"—he appeared to consider, and Jane held her breath—"my lady prefers them high," he concluded. Jane breathed out in relief.

"High?" His tailor frowned. "But—"

"High," Alisander repeated firmly. "And you will adorn both bodice and sleeves with elaborate beading giving the semblance of shapes from nature."

Interest flickered in the tailor's eyes. "Decorative beading?" he repeated thoughtfully. "Generally speaking, in women's attire, such decoration is but tastefully employed, and more discreet than men's."

"Not in this case," Alisander said decisively. "These motifs will be in the bold style I favor. The muted color of the gowns will allow for greater adornment. I want them heavily beaded. You

301

know the sort of thing I like, Barbier, animals and fruits. Maybe, in this case, flowers might be appropriate."

"The motifs should be neither flowers nor fruits," Jane heard herself disagree. "But serpents."

Both men turned their heads sharply to look at her. "Serpents?" Alisander repeated blankly.

"Serpents?" the tailor said in an altogether different tone. He sounded intrigued and she focused on him, affecting not to notice how Alisander was staring at her. "*Serpents,*" the tailor repeated thoughtfully, nodding slowly at first but with increasing enthusiasm. "But yes, we could vary the design, and have them coiled or intertwined differently for each gown. I think my colleague Dunoyer will be very excited to work on this. It is something different. Something unique." Jane noticed he treated her with rather more respect after that; where before, he had looked only to Alisander, now he made sure to include her.

She made a concerted effort to respond to this, gazing at his sketches and nodding, though nothing they depicted made her feel particularly enthusiastic. After the tailor finally departed, Alisander was quiet, retreating more into his thoughts than she was used to. Then again, she had not yet spent sufficient time in his company to anticipate his moods, so she tried not to dwell on it.

It was not until after supper that he seemed to perk back up. Jane had just finished her own wash and been helped out of her dress by a subdued Ayleth when he joined her in the bedchamber and started sloshing water about as he began his ablutions. Ayleth's eyebrows shot up, but she held her tongue as she draped Jane's mantle across her shoulders and picked up her discarded clothes.

"Will you want me to take down your hair, my lady?" she asked punctiliously, though it was clear she was keen to leave the room before Alisander started stripping off.

"No, thank you, Ayleth, that will be all."

Jane remained thoughtful as her maid bowed her head and showed herself out of the room. "Ayleth must have taken her supper in her own room," she said aloud, "for she did not join us at table this eve." She sat on the side of the bed and began removing her hairpins. "Unless she has an acquaintance elsewhere in the palace." Now she came to think of it, that would not be so very strange. After all, she had resided here for almost a year before Helen had been sent away.

Alisander was not attending her. Instead, he was gazing down at his tunic with a look of disgust. "Ugh," he commented, flicking a limp-looking tassel. "I hope Barbier did not notice the state of my tunic. It is no longer fit to be seen in." Jane directed a speaking glance at him. "What?"

"You practically fed Bertrand that tassel to spare your pendant," she pointed out, setting down her hairpins. "I saw you do it."

"But Jane, what else could I do? Only imagine if he had swallowed one of my precious pearls. I could never look at it the same, once it had passed through the dreadful child's digestive system." He shuddered elaborately. "Horrible thought."

"Spare me your dissembling," Jane told him sternly as she took down her hair. "I have seen full well that you are fond of Bertrand."

He turned from the basin and batted his eyelashes at her before he started rubbing his face and neck vigorously with a cloth. "Who? Oh, is that the boy's name?"

"And you prevented him from a hazardous choking fit most efficiently."

"I think you'll find I was preserving my necklace," he said sotto voce.

"In truth"—she took a deep breath—"you are *far* better at handling both of the children than I am." She could not keep a faint note of resentment out of her voice.

He dropped the cloth, reeling back with an expression of horror upon his face. "Why would you malign me like this, Jane? 'Tis naught but a pack of foul lies!"

"I know what you are doing," she said conversationally.

"Oh?" He walked toward her, setting his hands on her shoulders. "And what is that, wife?"

Jane inwardly cursed her tumultuous heartbeat. She had been doing so well, and now he was going to fluster her again. "You are trying to mislead me. To hoodwink me."

"Is that what I'm doing?" He compelled her gently back until she was lying flat on the bed. His voice sounded amused, nothing more.

"Yes, and in the past, you would have succeeded in frustrating me," she admitted breathlessly.

He arched an eyebrow. "But not anymore?" he suggested.

Wordlessly, she shook her head. "I believe I am starting to get your measure now, my lord."

"But I don't want you to change, Jane." His suddenly serious tone caught her off guard.

"Not even in my opinion of you?" She faltered.

304

He cocked his head as though considering this. "I'm not sure," he said, frowning.

"Even if it's for the better?" she persisted.

To her surprise, she thought he looked fleetingly troubled. "I should not want to give you the wrong impression about me," he said evasively.

"You—!" Jane broke off her words in annoyance. "You try to give me the wrong impression all the time, you aggravating creature!"

He had the temerity to laugh at this. "I don't know, Jane, you sound a *little* frustrated right now," he teased. "Let's see what we can do about that, shall we? Hmm?" Jane lay there blinking up at him as he shrugged out of his tunic. "Now, you must promise me you will not take out your wrath on anyone else. That's my role."

"What is?" she asked, feeling quite at sea.

"You must use me as your outlet for stresses and strains," he said firmly. "I want you to. I should like it."

"Use you…?" she repeated blankly. Then a horrible suspicion occurred to her. "Are you trying to get me with child, my lord?" she asked abruptly. The prospect of another baby on the way so soon appalled her.

He blanched. "Gods no! We already have far too many in our household! Every time I so much as open a door an infant tumbles through it!"

"We have two," she corrected him smartly. "And that comment does Anne a grave injustice. She is a very conscientious caretaker; it is not her fault that Bertrand—"

305

"I don't want to talk about Anne or Bertrand," he told her, joining her on the bed, having stripped down to his braies with surprising swiftness. "Though, if we were to catch for another child, it would not be the end of the world, I suppose." He pulled her into his arms. "Anne could deal with it," he continued indifferently. "As you pointed out, she is more than capable of dealing with our monstrous progeny."

Jane spluttered. "Neither Celestia nor Bertrand is remotely monstrous!" she objected unevenly. Nor were they, strictly speaking, their offspring, but she didn't have the breath to add that part, or the inclination really. It was starting to feel like they *did* all belong together somehow. "I had thought—that is, I felt sure you would attend some palace gathering this evening."

"Yes," he agreed. "I had meant to spare you tonight, but I find I've simply changed my mind."

"Spare me?"

"From my lusty embraces so soon after your deflowering," he elaborated.

Jane felt herself blush. "Oh, I see."

"Have you any objection to make?" he asked politely. "If so, there is some event I should in all probability attend." He had slipped his hand between them and rested it on her stomach, waiting for her response.

Jane was not sure what to say. She did not really want him to go, but to admit as much felt a little unseemly. "Is the event an important one?" she heard herself enquire in a strangled voice.

A smile played about his mouth. She felt very aware of the warmth being generated by his hand against her skin. "Oh, some diplomatic gathering," he said airily, propping his head on one hand, his elbow resting on her pillow behind her. "The usual crowd."

"Neither the King nor Queen is in attendance, then?" she asked, her breathing hitching when she felt his thumb stroke her in a light caress.

"No royal presence is scheduled," he confirmed.

"So…it cannot be terribly important, can it?"

The smile came forth at this, curving his lips. "You agree, then? My time would be better spent here?"

"Yes," she said faintly. "I agree."

"*So* glad we are of one accord in this," he said, lowering his voice as his hand slid down and snaked between her thighs. "I would *much* rather dance attendance on you than some stuffy diplomat." Jane's face felt like it was on fire as she let her legs part for him. "Your hair is not all crinkled today," he observed as his fingers worked between her cleft. She felt a rush of wetness there and bit her lip.

For one terrible moment, she thought he was commenting on the hair between her legs. Then she tumbled to his meaning. "Oh no," she mumbled. "My hair was fully dry before it was braided today." A whimper slipped past her lips before she could prevent it. "*Oh!*"

He eased off at once and Jane caught her breath again. "I do apologize. Is that more comfortable for you, my lady?" he enquired politely.

Jane stared at him in bafflement. *What?* "Uh, y-yes, my lord," she answered in confusion.

307

A gleam entered his eye, but he murmured an obliging, "I'm *so* glad. I would be loath to do anything that would discompose you."

Jane's brain scrambled to comprehend exactly what he was playing at, but as he chose at this moment to slide two fingers deep inside her, she did not get very far with her ruminations. Instead, she stifled her gasp and squeezed her eyes shut.

"Have you written back to your family yet?" he asked conversationally, his hand stilling.

Jane's eyes flew wide. "M-my family?" she quavered. Was he not going to kiss her tonight? She felt a little outraged by the oversight.

"To thank them for their marital advice," he clarified. Jane stared at him. Why had he stopped? "Particularly your aunt Maud," he continued lazily. "I had opportunity to further study her letter today. *Most* edifying."

Jane knew she was panting now, but she seemed powerless to grasp control of herself. "Um, my aunt Maud?" she echoed uncomprehendingly.

He nodded. "Your dear aunt that was so kind as to send us the pizzlewort and the illustrated text."

Jane had no sooner made the connection than he added his thumb between her legs, making her gasp. Frustratingly, he did not ply it at the same spot he had before. If she did not know better, she would almost think he was deliberately avoiding it.

"Maybe I should reply and thank her," he debated lazily, "and let her know that I am not the only one suffering with a surfeit of lust. Ah, Jane, if you could only see yourself right now. My poor, needy Jane," he said richly, and he was smiling, actually

308

smiling, *the swine*. Jane let out a whine of frustration. She was aching for him to touch her right.

"Ask me nicely," he suggested, "and maybe I will let you. Unless…" He leaned down and nipped her bottom lip. "You want to take it like you did before, you greedy girl."

Almost without thinking, Jane moved her hips and *slid* against his hand until his thumb was in exactly the right place. She gave a sharp cry of relief, arching her back.

"There? Really?" he asked as if he did not know. He circled it slowly with his thumb. *Too slowly*. Jane panted and struggled against him. It was so close, but not quite there.

"Please, I need—!" She lifted her head off the pillow.

"Show me," he coaxed. "Move your hips again, my dove." Jane felt too mindless with desire to object. Instead, she shifted her hips fitfully. "That's it," he grunted, starting to pump his fingers within her. "*Yes*, Jane," he groaned in encouragement. "Such a nice, tight squeeze. I can't wait to feel it around my cock."

What in heaven was he saying to her? Jane's outraged mind shut down as the pleasure gripped her, and a shower of sparks rained down behind her eyeballs. She let out a moan, which seemed to go on for a disgracefully long time, then sagged back against the mattress, gasping for breath. For the next few moments, all that could be heard was the sound of their mutually ragged breathing.

"Why, Jane," he said reproachfully, withdrawing his hand. "You gave me no warning at all. That's bad form," he tutted, "very bad indeed." Jane just whimpered; she had no idea what he was talking about. "Now, how are you going to make this up to me? I demand satisfaction, madam."

Jane allowed her eyes to flutter open. She beheld him speechlessly for a few heartbeats. "Satisfaction?"

He nodded, gesturing downward. "My cock is about to explode. It will be all over your belly if you don't let me in, like a good girl."

Jane made a muffled sound, then widened her legs. For him. It was a good thing her face was already on fire by this point. "Come in, then," she murmured, eyes downcast.

He gave a gasp of laughter. "Such sweet talk," he teased, but she noticed he did not hesitate to take her up on the offer. Jane braced herself as he slid his fingers between them again, parting her folds to position the bulbous head of his manhood against her slippery cleft before starting the slow push inside. It no longer hurt when he did this, though she could not help but brace herself against his progress, for the unaccustomed fullness was almost uncomfortable in itself.

They both gasped aloud when he finally slid into place, his body resting against hers in the most intimate manner. Even the crisp hair of their most private of places was now intertwined. Jane drew up her knees, savoring the feeling of his weight against the cradle of her hips. His body stilled against her own for a few heartbeats, as though he was letting her adjust, and strange to say, Jane could feel herself opening up to welcome him.

She felt him sink even deeper inside her, his breathing harsh, though he stayed still. There was no question about it. Their joining felt good. His expression wavered for a moment between pleasure and something else Jane could not quite identify. She felt a moment's panic. Was it not as good for him? What was it? What had she done? It was so hard to think when he was stretching and filling her so completely. Despite the thrill of alarm running through her, she could not help but arch her back in wordless appeal. "*Alisander,*" she whispered.

"Oh *fuck,*" he wheezed, shutting his eyes. "I am not going to last. You are not a good girl at all; you're a very bad girl to take your revenge on me like this. How *dare* you?" His shaken words made no sense to Jane, so she gave up struggling to comprehend him and simply let herself focus on how good he felt, biting her lip and pressing her knees into his sides.

His hands grasped her hips hard, and she rocked them against him.

"Jane," he gasped. "You little—" He groaned, pitching forward, and shifted his weight onto his forearms so he loomed directly over her, staring into her face.

Her eyes flew open. "Was that not—?" She had thought he was urging her to move, but it seemed he had been trying to pin her in place. "I thought—?"

"Do it again," he murmured, and when she did, his eyes flashed. "*Fuck.* So good, Jane," he grunted, his eyes glazing over. "Yes, that's it, fuck me. Give me more." She obeyed, and almost cautiously, he started to move against her in tandem. Jane whimpered at the sensation of the slow, pleasurable grind as it started to gain momentum.

She felt so strange, aiding and abetting him in the act. He was not guiding her at all with his hands, and he was staring at her face so intently, she ought to be embarrassed. She was a willing participant this time. Nay, she was giving as good as she got. The realization thrilled her, and directly after it, Jane experienced a moment of clarity. Their laboring bodies, their gasping breath, everything clicked into place. They were working together to reach mutual bliss.

311

Alisander's eyes drifted shut, and his hips started to pound against her own as their rhythm increased. "Fuck—Jane—" he groaned. "I can't— *Gods!*"

It was a lot. It was almost too much. If she was not careful... Her eyes widened. It was going to happen again, she realized, recognizing the frantic shudder running through her. She threw her arms about him, sinking her fingernails into his shoulder blades and wrapping her legs around his back.

"Fuck yesssss," he hissed. She felt his hot breath at her ear. "Now, Jane, you know it's my turn," he admonished her in a raspy voice. "Behave yourself." He sank his teeth into her earlobe and Jane let out a shriek. Everything shook, the bed, where their bodies were joined, the part of him that was embedded so deeply within her that he made her ache.

For one terrible, wonderful moment, she could focus on nothing but the overwhelming pleasure which engulfed her like a wave, stealing her breath and all reason from her. He spoke her name, once through gritted teeth and then again in a sort of awed whisper. Then she was lying limp and shaken, and he was finally kissing her.

"Fuck, that was—no, no, don't cry," he crooned. "Just fantastic, my darling Jane. You were so perfect, just as I always knew you would be. Even more than I ever dreamed you could be."

More nonsense words, she thought dimly, even as she passed her arms around his neck and let him comfort her. "I'm not upset," she managed to sob as he pressed his lips to her eyelids and her cheeks. "Not at all." The tears were simply a sign that she was not intended for such rapture, but how could she possibly begin to explain that?

He pulled back to look down at her face. "I know," he said simply. Which seemed an odd thing to say to a woman who

312

could not stop crying, but so long as he did not think her distraught, she was content to lie still while he tutted and fussed over her. "*Clever* Jane," he murmured, "my beauty, my treasure." For the first time, Jane allowed herself to wonder if he actually meant any of these things. The thought made her heart beat even faster.

Finally, she was calm, and he drew back from her, fetching a cool cloth which he pressed over her face and neck before passing it between her legs. "Shhh, let me make you comfortable," he murmured though Jane had voiced no objection. She felt too worn out for outraged modesty at this point.

She was already drifting to sleep when he joined her again moments later, peppering kisses over her shoulder and settling at her back. "Go to sleep now, Jane," he ordered, wrapping an arm about her waist. A pointless thing to say, she thought with surprise, then promptly realized she had been hanging on until he said it.

20

Alisander was in a good mood the next morning, despite the tiresome need to write his official weekly report. How could he fail to be when Jane was becoming so delightfully abandoned in his bed? She had been shy again that morning, and it had made him want her again with a fierceness that had been a little alarming at such an uncivilized hour.

He had wanted to drag the covers off her and kiss her all over, then tease her mercilessly for good measure. However, she had been tousled and bashful, and he had been forced to content himself with gazing over at her a good deal as he washed and dressed. He had things to do that day, which did not include his wife.

He had pulled himself together again sufficiently to leave their bedchamber, gather his papers, and contemplate his report. In previous times, he would have dashed this off in his quarters, but now since they were crawling with womenfolk and babies, he had to go elsewhere. Also, there was his ridiculously distracting wife. When she was around, he found it hard not to make her his priority. No, he needed to get out of their rooms, or he would end up cornering her in the bedroom, and his duties would be forgotten.

Impulsively, he returned therein, and finding Jane bent over the washbasin in her shift, he turned her about and informed her he was leaving, bestowed a chaste kiss upon her brow, then a not-so-chaste kiss upon her mouth. "Be good today," he told her, "and think of me."

Jane, clearly shaken by such unaccustomed affection first thing in the morning, turned very pink and blurted, "I am always good," while darting her eyes at Ayleth, who she clearly thought he had neglected to notice.

"Yes, you are," he agreed, running a finger down her flushed cheek. Did she really think he had not seen Ayleth laying out her clothes? If the annoying woman had not been there, his embrace would have been a good deal bolder. He would not have turned her around, for one thing. Unable to resist, he dropped another lingering kiss to her lips. "Say you will miss me, wife."

"I—you will be home soon enough, I daresay," Jane choked out in adorable confusion.

"I will," he agreed, "and then I will make you regret this cold leave-taking, madam." He lowered his voice. "I daresay you are not so cool with your lover. It is too bad you make your husband suffer so."

Jane's eyes widened and she stared at him. "You—you are pleased to jest, my lord!" she said in a strangled voice.

He laughed. "Yes, I am," he agreed and slapped her backside before strolling from the room. Her outraged gasp lingered in his ears as he made his way out of the palace. Really, he was in a most remarkably good mood.

Deciding to kill two birds with one stone, he made for the home of a prominent Lasconian merchant, who happened to be one of Wilhelm's premier contacts in Karadok, one Gaston Lemarchier. Lemarchier, plague take him, had been bombarding him with curt requests for a meeting ever since he had returned to the capital.

Approaching Lemarchier's house in Thicket Lane, Alisander paused a moment, allowing the man who had followed him at a discreet distance to observe which door he knocked on.

Lemarchier's manservant, Paulk, seemed surprised to see him but admitted him at once.

"But Monsieur is not expecting you, milord," the servant exclaimed as he took Alisander's cloak and hat. "He is in a meeting right now with one of his associates."

"It is of no matter, Paulk," Alisander informed. "In truth, I am more desirous of a quiet corner than I am of your master's company. I have a report to write. If you can furnish me with a desk and pen and ink, I will be well satisfied."

Paulk led him into a small yet tidy chamber and made haste to procure him writing materials and something to drink. Alisander settled at once to dash off his report with his customary verve. They never took him long once he set his mind to the task, and truth be told, he found some amusement sprinkling court gossip with pertinent facts.

He had just completed a paragraph lamenting the ill health of Wymer's beloved nurse when the door was unceremoniously flung open and Lemarchier stood on the threshold wearing a forbidding frown. "Vicomte!" he growled. "Paulk did not inform me you had arrived. I would have dismissed my visitor at once, had I but known."

"There was no urgency," Alisander assured him, waving his most recent page to and fro so the ink would dry. "I did not want you until I had written my report in any case."

"No urgency?" Lemarchier repeated, coming into the room with his heavy tread and shutting the door behind him. "No urgency? Have you not received my many notes, imploring you to visit?"

Alisander lifted his brows. "But of course I did, my dear Lemarchier. What other business would bring me to this corner of the city?"

316

Lemarchier grunted and crossed to the window, where he squinted down at the busy street. "You were not followed?"

"But of course I was," Alisander answered blandly. "Why would today be different to any other day?"

"Perhaps if you did not dress like such a peacock," the other thundered, gesturing to Alisander's outfit, "you would be more successful in evading Vawdrey's spies!"

"A peacock? No, no, the palette is all wrong for that," Alisander murmured, glancing down fondly at his gorgeous burgundy apparel. "You give me inspiration for my next ensemble, however."

Lemarchier fumed in silence a moment before he started pacing in front of the small fireplace. "His most exalted Majesty demands an explanation for your actions of late. I cannot sufficiently tell you the perturbation they have caused back home!"

Alisander considered this a moment with a faint frown. "Which ones? You will need to be more specific, my friend."

Lemarchier came to an abrupt halt. "You are pleased to jest, even in *this*? I refer, of course, to this ill-considered marriage of yours!"

"Oh, *that*!" Alisander crossed his legs and nodded thoughtfully. "I suppose Wilhelm means to send us a present, but really, His Majesty need not stand on such ceremony. King Wymer has already been so very generous."

"A present!" Lemarchier seemed to choke on his words.

"Some gold plate, perhaps," Alisander mused.

"You—!" Lemarchier struggled a moment to express himself.

317

"Deep breaths," Alisander recommended. "Perhaps a sip of this ale Paulk provided. For my part, I found it rather sour."

Lemarchier remained where he was, nostrils flaring. "By this ill-considered union, you now hold lands in Karadok," he said stiffly. "You have assumed guardianship of one of Wymer's by-blows, no less. In short, your loyalty is now under question at the highest level. To which crown is your allegiance now sworn, Vicomte? That is the question which demands immediate answers!"

Alisander tutted. "You should take a seat, Lemarchier, you are turning quite purple." He smothered a yawn. "In truth, the estate, such as it is, remains in my keeping only for a few years, until the child matures."

"That is not what the document I have seen posits!"

"Is that not the way of things with all lands?" Alisander asked, arching his brow.

"It is not just a question of land!" Lemarchier spluttered. "You would pass the old and *venerated* title of your forefathers down to a—a bastard child of this Argent King?"

"Oh yes," Alisander agreed. "Why not? After all, my own great-great-grandfather only received the title after he agreed to raise the get of old King Edouard, like a cuckoo in his proverbial nest." Lemarchier went off in a coughing fit before dropping down into his seat. "You look stunned, Lemarchier," he commented with a faint smile. "Were you not aware that raising bastards is quite the family tradition in my house?"

Lemarchier wiped his brow. "Nevertheless, the Viscountcy of Bardulf is a Lasconian title," he persisted weakly. "Your behavior, my lord, quite beggars belief."

"Not really," Alisander contradicted him mildly. "In truth, I had not the smallest intention of marrying and 'passing on' my title in any way, so it is of no great matter."

For the first time, Lemarchier seemed to pause. "Then why?" he asked shortly. "Why do such a thing? Why take such a step, and *unsanctioned* at that!"

Alisander sighed. "The simple fact is," he said, holding the other's gaze, "that Lady Jane Cecil found herself in need of a husband, and I could not abide the thought of it being anyone but me."

Silence reigned for all of a minute. "You expect me to report this back as fact?" Lemarchier asked indignantly.

"I can give you no other reason." Alisander shrugged.

The other man scoffed. "Influence, my lord? Money? Lands?" he suggested skeptically.

"By all means, list them as motives if you think Wilhelm will find them more convincing. I just thought I would do you the courtesy of giving you the unvarnished truth."

Lemarchier stared at him, then gave a short laugh. "If you have," he said darkly, "then it would be the first time in your life, Vicomte. Truly it is, as they say, the de Balons speak at all times with a forked tongue."

Alisander widened his eyes. "*Is* that what they say?" he asked softly. "How very interesting."

Lemarchier gulped. "I meant no offence, my lord," he said, crossing his fingers in the old way, to ward off evil. "It is simply well known, that—well—your family has a certain notoriety back in Lascony."

"Ah, I *see*." Alisander nodded slowly. "You refer to that old story, that we are cursed?"

The older man looked discomforted. "Nay, it was not that *you* are cursed—that is—I forget the particulars…" He faltered under Alisander's unblinking gaze.

Alisander smiled. "Ah yes, I recall it now. It is those that cross *us* that are cursed. Such a pretty little tale. Thank you for reminding me. It is good to remember one's heritage. Forgetting the old ways…is never wise."

Lemarchier, he thought, turned rather pale at that. He stayed another hour or so and helped the wretched man finish writing up his official account. The stuffing had been rather knocked out of him by this point, and he accepted Alisander's dictation meek as a lamb.

Alisander did not return to court directly on leaving Thicket Lane. Instead, he visited his favorite jeweler on Goldsmith's Row. He wanted to check on the progress of a sapphire necklace he had ordered the Monday before his marriage and to collect an emerald brooch.

Mr. Haines presented the half-constructed necklace for his inspection, and so pleased was Alisander with its progress that he immediately ordered a matching ring.

"For which finger, my lord?" Mr. Haines enquired politely, quill poised.

"My wife's," Alisander responded promptly. "Her fingers are neither slender nor stout in proportion. Instead, they are a sort of middling sort of size."

Mr. Haines did not look impressed with this estimation. Instead, he turned and summoned his wife and two daughters for corroboration. "Hold up your hands for his lordship to compare," he ordered.

The Haines womenfolk held up their hands obligingly for Alisander's inspection. He scanned them keenly, settling at last on Mistress Haines, much to her satisfaction. "Madam's third finger on her right hand looks to me a match."

He turned to the jeweler. "You permit?" Mr. Haines looked mystified but nodded. Alisander turned back to the jeweler's wife, lifting his own hand to carefully thread his fingers through hers. He closed his eyes a moment, then opened them to find four pairs of eyes watching him avidly.

He fancied both daughters were glad their fingers had not matched, for they looked rather fearful. Fortunately, their mother was made of sterner stuff. "Yes, the third finger is a close match," he concluded, turning her hand over and placing a coin in its palm. "My thanks, madam."

"Of course, milord." She bobbed a curtsey. "I will be sure and remind Adelbert, for I am sure there will be more orders to follow."

Alisander laughed. "You are very astute."

Mr. Haines cleared his throat. "And now, Joan, you will fetch his lordship the emerald brooch."

His purchase brought forth, Alisander unwrapped it from its cloth and inspected the glowing emerald. A slow smile curved his lips as he attempted to view it through Jane's eyes. No doubt she would think the stone overlarge and ostentatious, and that was before you took the large drop pearl and the heavy gold casing into consideration.

"It is perfection," he pronounced, flipping it over to inspect the familiar engraving at the back.

321

Mr. Haines paused, waiting to see if Alisander would immediately pin it to his tunic. When he had first become a customer, the proprietor had been shocked by the fact Viscount Bardulf would wander the streets of Aphrany, decked in precious stones. In vain, he had tried to warn milord that he would be immediately imperiled and at the mercy of wicked thieves. Nowadays, he knew better than to waste his breath.

"I will take it wrapped today."

"Then this, too, is also for your lady wife, milord?" Mistress Haines piped up, a knowing gleam in her eye as her husband slipped the brooch into a pouch and firmly tied the strings.

Had he not known better, Alisander would have thought the unaccustomed warmness that rushed to his cheeks was a blush. "Quite so," he admitted, and the two daughters exchanged significant looks.

Outside the shop, he absently tipped the beggar who had followed him from Thicket Lane and made his way back toward the palace. There was a gathering he ought to attend in the lower gallery, he told himself firmly, for he was strangely tempted to return to his rooms and seek his wife out.

She would certainly be glad to see him, for it did not suit her at all to remain in their quarters. Still, it would not do for him to give *everyone* the impression he was prostrate at her feet these days. No, he decided, he would not look in on her, even briefly. Instead, he would leave Jane to languish until this evening. That, he thought with satisfaction, ought to make her all the keener for his company.

He found he regretted his decision a few times as the afternoon wore on. The Vlandivarian ambassador was new in post and incredibly sincere, a truly hideous combination. After introductions, Alisander retreated to a safe distance to watch his fellow representatives at work.

"I give the fellow six months," murmured Signore Albrici, a seasoned diplomat, halting beside him.

"You are generous," Alisander replied. "I was thinking three."

Albrici's smile broadened as he turned toward him. "How are you, Visconte Bardulf? I hear you are lately married and neglected to invite me. I am mortally offended."

"It was too bad of me, but you know how impulsive I am, my friend."

"Impulsive? But the story I heard was *less* a matter of impulsivity and *more* a matter of cold calculation." He contemplated Alisander coolly for a moment before continuing. "Then again, I might have misunderstood the tale. It was not in my native tongue, you understand." He spread his hands. "Me, I would say you have great self-control, my lord, but what do I know? I am but a poor scholar of human nature."

"You are too modest, my dear Albrici," Alisander tutted.

"Always," the other agreed with a sigh. "It has long been my greatest failing."

"Whoever told you that?"

"My sainted mother, she always remarked upon it."

"Ah, your mother. Now, *I* would have said your biggest weakness was a pretty face."

"Ah yes." Albrici fondled his moustache. "I am something of a connoisseur, it is true. What a pity it is that the ravishing Lady Helen will never again grace Wymer's court," he sighed. "Now *that* was a beautiful woman. Such a shame."

Alisander sent him a swift look. "She has not graced it in over six months now," he said mildly, accepting a goblet of mead from a passing page.

"It is true," Albrici conceded sadly, "there is a sad scarcity of handsome women at this court these days, I find." He shook his head.

"Do you?" Alisander turned to him with a look of surprise. "I had heard quite differently. How strange." He paused to let his words sink in. "I was sure it was you…but perhaps I am mistaken."

Albrici looked ruffled. "But what rumor is this?" he cried, then looked quickly around to gauge if anyone was listening to them.

"Rumor? No, no, you mistake me. It was more of a conversation I overheard concerning how much time you were spending in the company of a certain…widow."

The other man bridled. "But this is a gross falsehood and an impertinence!" He lowered his voice to a hiss. "There is not the smallest question of impropriety! We are—I assure you— cordial acquaintances only!"

Alisander lifted his eyebrows. "There is not the slightest need of assurances where I am concerned, signore. *I* have no connection to that lady's family."

Albrici seemed to recall his surroundings and subsided to a state of twitching impatience. "Always the rumors and speculations in this accursed place!" he grumbled.

"Alas, 'tis true."

"One can hardly even venture out—quite innocently—without others whispering in the corners!"

"It is too bad," Alisander agreed. "Perhaps you, too, ought to marry? It might calm down certain…speculations."

Albrici gave a start. "That lady, she is far from over her mourning period," he said with heavy disapproval.

"Which lady?"

"The widow—" He broke off hastily. "That is, er, I do not know…"

Alisander smiled at him pityingly. "*So* nice to catch up with your news, Albrici," he said, drifting away as the other floundered hopelessly. He walked almost immediately into Lord Vawdrey.

"Ah, Bardulf," the other greeted him serenely. "Fortuitous meeting you here."

"Vawdrey," Alisander returned cautiously. "As you say, always a pleasure."

Oswald Vawdrey's smile broadened as he scrutinized him. "You are having, perhaps, a trying day?"

He pulled himself together. "Not at all. Where did you gain that impression?"

"Oh…nowhere."

Alisander braced himself, but the King's chief advisor seemed in no hurry to get to the point. "There was something you wished to discuss with me?" he ventured.

"Was there?"

"You said our meeting was fortuitous," he reminded him, narrowing his eyes.

"Well, it is always a pleasure to see you, my dear Bardulf," Vawdrey murmured. Alisander almost rolled his eyes. "At least you will not try to force me into a row over mutual trade routes," he added dryly.

"Who has been doing that?" Alisander asked, casting his eye about the room.

"Our friend from Ballamaigne," Vawdrey sighed.

"Ah, I have not conversed with Burkhard today. I am sure you grew progressively vaguer until he reached his boiling point."

Vawdrey laughed. "It is the only way to deal with him, I assure you." His own eyes were passing over the crowd. "But I do not see your friend Hubair here today."

"*My* friend?"

"Lascony and Kloberg are historical allies are they not?"

Alisander snorted. Everyone knew Kloberg was, to all intents and purposes, ruled by Lascony, with its puppet king, King Stefan, barely out of leading strings. "Whereas Karadok and Lascony are historically enemies?"

"Times change." Vawdrey shrugged. "Sadly, sometimes people need reminding of that fact."

"People?"

"Monseiur Hubair seems, at times, more concerned with House Lisle's cause than he does about his own king's."

Alisander tipped his head back. This was so uncharacteristically forthright of Vawdrey; it made him instinctively uneasy. "King Stefan is a mere child," he pointed out, "and likely concerned about precious little."

"He is fifteen," Vawdrey said lightly, "and old enough."

"For what?"

"For plenty of things," the other replied dryly.

"I have not heard that the boy king has done anything notable, if that is what you are asking me," Alisander responded, and Vawdrey's shoulders seemed to relax. "The last time I saw him, Hubair seemed to be in a frenzy over some clandestine betrothal." Vawdrey's enigmatic gaze turned on him. "Not of Stefan's," he clarified, "but some first cousin of his."

"Oh *that*," Vawdrey said with a short laugh. "Tell me, does poor Alphonse still believe it all part of some infernal Karadokian plot?"

"Nothing can convince him otherwise," Alisander answered. "I tried telling him that Wymer would not give a fig if an archduke of some small province in Kloberg is plotting to marry a highborn Karadokian, but really my hands were tied."

"How so?"

"Well," Alisander said with a shrug, "I could hardly point out that Wymer views Kloberg as a nation of pastry-makers, now, could I?"

Oswald Vawdrey's smile flashed out. "I almost pity poor Hubair, trying to express his fears to you."

"No, you don't." He smirked. "Tell me, *is* there a secret betrothal?"

"Oh yes," Vawdrey confirmed. "To the Duchess of Rand's niece, but it'll never come to anything."

Alisander nodded. "It is as I suspected." He glanced at the window again, noting it was getting dark. That was good. It meant he could soon reasonably take his leave without comment.

"You have another meeting, perhaps, planned for this evening?" Vawdrey asked politely.

"Another meeting?"

"Only, you seem to be marking time."

"I? Not at all, I assure you. I am perfectly at my leisure."

Vawdrey smirked. "Perhaps you are simply eager for your supper," he suggested innocently, "or something else to be found back in your rooms." Alisander narrowed his eyes at him. "Tell me, did you meet with any of your wife's family when you were at Kinnerton?" Vawdrey asked. "Only you did not stay there long."

"I met briefly with her uncle," Alisander admitted. "He returned to the capital, I think."

"Oh, indeed, he did," Vawdrey agreed swiftly, making Alisander's ears perk up. "If I might be permitted to make a suggestion, you may want to pay him a second visit when you have the chance." Vawdrey's eyes met his.

"Oh?"

"It is always good to be in accord with your in-laws," he said mildly. "And Sir Phillip seems to have *such* a lot of time on his hands recently. Sadly, it is often the case that those with nothing better to do frequently occupy themselves stirring up trouble."

Alisander paused. "Trouble?" he asked softly.

"He seeks an audience with the King," Vawdrey murmured, barely audibly. "Seeks without success thus far, but an intervention might be timely. Perhaps a kindly word in his ear?"

Alisander swore under his breath. "I had a word. Several actually."

Vawdrey tutted. "Might I suggest a sterner word, or…perhaps something stronger?"

"You might," Alisander said grimly, his mood plummeting. So much for a pleasant night spent dallying with his wife. He would have to venture out of the palace again, and this time, without anyone following him.

21

Over the next few days, Jane turned her thoughts a lot to
puzzling over the enigma of the man she had married. She
found it so hard to make sense of him. The obnoxious, mocking
creature she knew of old did not really fit with this new side to
him that she was seeing.

Of course, he was still a teasing and tormenting creature. He
liked to make his little jabs, but somehow his digs did not really
seem to sting so much now she knew how much he—well—not
liked her precisely. Desired her? The thought alone made Jane
blush, but there was no denying the fact now.

She was sure she would not be indulging such thoughts if she
was not cooped up in these rooms all day. It did not matter how
assiduously she practiced her music and embroidery; her
thoughts would inevitably stray back to this strange man she
had married.

There had only been one night since their marriage was
consummated that he had *not* been all over her once bedtime
was nigh. Jane was not sure of the correct term for marital
relations. It was not something she had ever cared to discuss or
really consider before.

That particular night he had not returned once, and she had lain
awake an age before drifting off to sleep. On waking, hours
later, to find herself still alone, she had been unable to settle
back to sleep. Where was he? Had he not assured her he would
be back directly? He had kissed her thrice in front of Ayleth,
ordered her to think of him, and then he had not returned all the
day long. It was too much!

She had thrown the covers back and left the warm bed to seek him out. Perhaps he had returned, just not to their bed? On first peering into the main room, she had thought it empty before noticing him sat quietly at the desk.

"My dear, you cannot sleep?" he asked without looking up.

Jane was startled, though she could not really say why, not at first. "I awoke and you were gone," she said lamely.

"Well, now you have located me," he countered, meeting her gaze. Something was definitely not quite right, she thought, her breath catching in her throat, for though he smiled, it did not touch his eyes at all.

Then she had noticed his clothes. They were all wrong too, of a dark and sober hue, most unlike anything usually worn by her flamboyant husband. The only black garments he owned were festooned all over with ostentatious devices or silver thread. Whose clothes was he wearing?

As though noting her scrutiny, he stood from the desk and crossed the room to take her into his arms. "I think you have missed me after all," he mused, "if you must come in search of me, wife. Perhaps I should put some of this restlessness of yours to good use? Hmm? What do you say?"

When Jane had simply scanned him with anxious eyes, he had scooped her up in his arms and carried her back into their bedchamber. Once there, he had undressed and washed without any of his usual ceremony, then joined her under the covers, where he had pulled her into his arms and held her very tightly. None of which allayed her sudden unnamed fears.

"Jane," he had murmured against her brow, "you must never think ill of me if you can help it. And if you ever do find yourself disappointed in me..." He hesitated.

331

"What?"

"Then you must be generous and grant me some grace. We cannot all be as blameless as you."

"I am not, nor never have been blameless."

"You are a paragon of virtue compared to me."

"Has something happened?" Jane had steeled herself to ask. "Something that I need to know about?"

"No." His reply had been swift. *Too swift.*

"Did…did someone attempt to rob you again?" she had asked, remembering the fallen thief in the wood, the tale of the stabbing at the tavern. He did not answer for a long moment and Jane felt herself start to grow tense.

"Yes," he said at last, "in a manner of speaking."

"Oh." Jane's thoughts turned over furiously. "And you—you——"

"I am perfectly well," he cut in smoothly, though she had not doubted his own healthy status.

Jane felt herself relax in spite of herself. "That is good."

"Let's sleep now," he had suggested, though he did not release her, and Jane did not think he had sounded even remotely sleepy.

"Very well," she had replied, though she really wanted to ask who the unfortunate person was. Then again, maybe she did not want to know.

It had not stopped her from dwelling on the matter the next morning as she broke her fast. Did he often slip out at night? And if so, was that why he wanted separate bedchambers?

Lowering her piece of toasted bread, she had regarded him frowningly.

Alisander's gaze had lifted from the letter he had been perusing. "My sweet, why are you glowering at me?" he had asked. "You put me out of countenance."

"I doubt that very much."

He tipped his head to one side. "What is it? Tell me, for I'm actually curious."

"I was just wondering…"

"Yes?"

"If you had applied for larger living quarters yet?"

His eyebrows snapped together, and for one instant, she thought he looked annoyed. "How *do* you bear with such a forgetful spouse?" he mused.

The trouble was, Jane no longer believed he was remotely forgetful. Who was this man, she wondered, who she had been bound to by matrimonial bonds? He was not what he presented to the world, she knew that much.

For the rest of the week, he was extremely amorous in his attentions. Ayleth, she noticed, had taken to waiting until he had departed before she entered their bedchamber of a morning. He was not shy when it came to displays of physical affection, even when there was no immediate prospect of bedding her.

He liked touch and he liked proximity, whether it was morning, noon, or evening. Of course, she did not know if this would continue, once she was out of their palace living quarters and mixing once more with her peers. Would he then become the cool and aloof Bardulf once more? The thought was a strangely disquieting one.

No matter how charming and even sweet he could be, deep down she was starting to suspect that, much like the rest of his life, he viewed bed sport as some kind of game, wherein he liked to gain the upper hand. Having said that, it was hard to resent this when he took so much evident pleasure in her arms.

She was not even sure he *had* the upper hand, in truth. Despite her lack of experience, he was palpably eager for her to an almost astonishing degree. Mercifully, for Jane's pride, he seemed to derive as much gratification from her embraces as she took from his. If not for that, she would have found it all much harder to bear.

Midweek, it occurred to her that perhaps it would help if she separated out the traits she knew of old from the more recently discovered side of him. The man who shuddered so elaborately about drooling infants and spent so long at his dressing mirror was Viscount Bardulf.

That meant the man who was so kind and decent a master to Robert, and the man who would unthinkingly comfort a whining child in his arms, was Alisander de Balon. If Viscount Bardulf was the diplomat and courtier who spent his days in the palace halls conversing with courtiers, then it was Alisander de Balon who was her lover at night.

Had he not said himself that Lord and Lady Bardulf were a staid married couple, and it was Jane Cecil and Alisander de Balon who were lovers? They had now been back at court for a week, and she supposed she must be resuming her public life sometime soon. The first of her dresses had been delivered from Monsieur Barbier, but she had not received so much as a word from the Queen, let alone a summons.

That evening she resolved to bring it up with him, as Wat threw more logs on the fire and then withdrew, shutting the door quietly after him. It was around eight o'clock. Anne and the children had already made themselves scarce, and Ayleth had disappeared directly after supper.

Still, when she did lift her voice, it was not to speak of the Queen at all. "Where is Robert this evening?" she found herself asking, realizing she had not seen the old man in a while.

Alisander looked up from the letter he had been reading. He received correspondence of one kind or another on a daily basis, she assumed in his professional capacity. Some of them he left in haphazard piles, others he shoved in a drawer, and the rest, she was sure, disappeared without a trace as soon as he had read them. "Robert?" he repeated airily. "Most likely he is partaking in a cup of wine in his bedchamber. That is his habit of an evening."

Jane nodded. "You are an indulgent master when it comes to him."

His eyebrows shot up. "Well, he is indispensable to me. He is the only one who knows how to adequately care for my many shoes."

She frowned at his dismissive reply. "I counted them the other day," she said accusingly, "and you own fourteen pairs, not two dozen."

"Well," he said, "then clearly 'tis time for me to visit the cordwainer." When she made no reply, he added dryly, "It is really not hard to be kind to someone who does my every bidding, now, is it?"

Jane watched him in silence. "You order the barrel of elderflower wine every month for Robert, do you not? I have noticed neither you nor anyone else cares for it."

He shrugged. "It will grow very boring if you are now determined to ascribe me with every virtue," he drawled.

Seeing this for what it was, a diversionary tactic, Jane ignored him and instead ran through an inventory in her mind. The cake-like loaves of wastel bread which no one else favored. They, too, must be for Robert. It made perfect sense. Ayleth had been quite wrong to accuse him of eating his master's fare. Those things had been specifically purchased with the old man in mind.

Noticing Alisander was watching her out of the corner of his eye, she roused herself to respond. "I will endeavor not to bore you too much, my lord," she said without heat.

His brows snapped down over his eyes. "Don't talk like that," he said shortly. "As if you could bore me."

"You talked like that first," she pointed out. "You said—"

"I know what I said. I was being facetious." A strange expression passed over his face. "I don't think you *could* bore me, Jane," he said. "Even if you tried."

For a moment, she stared. Then she forced herself to rally. "My lord," she said briskly, "you have yawned your way through my every recital for the Queen these past two years!"

"Your recitation is *execrable*," he said with a shudder.

"You see!"

"It does not bore me; it *pains* me. You should not be allowed to read poetry. Your lack of expression when you speak the words and the infuriating way you murder the rhythm—"

"Oh, be quiet!" she interrupted him. "No one else ever complains about my recitation but you!"

He laughed, then looked suddenly thoughtful. "Wait, I have it. Next time we fuck, I shall make you recite 'The Splendor and the Glory' and see if I cannot get you to speak the words with some feeling."

Jane felt her color rise. "I shall do no such thing!" His words had felt like a blow. Part of her wanted to withdraw, to leave the room. The other part of her wanted to tell him how she felt. Tears sprang embarrassingly to her eyes. She took a deep breath. "Please do not use such—such base language, Alisander. At least, not when you speak to me in everyday life." She averted her face. "It makes me feel"—she paused, searching for the right word—"worthless." Her throat closed on the word, and she could not look at him.

Hearing a rustling, she looked up to find him out of his chair and pulling her up out of hers into his arms. "That was not my intention, Jane," he said against her hair, his hand sliding up and down her back in a strangely soothing gesture.

"I know," she answered in a small voice, and he did not speak for several heartbeats, just carried on stroking her back and holding her. It was strangely pleasant to be held by him this way in the dimly lit room. She rather wondered that she should find it so. Even as recently as a month ago, she would never have believed such a thing. Resting her head on his shoulder, she listened to the crackle of the fire and let herself be comforted.

"We both know I like teasing you, Jane," he said softly, "but worthless is the last thing I would ever want you to feel." Jane closed her eyes, and all was quiet for a while. Then he spoke again. "You said 'in everyday life,'" he murmured thoughtfully. "Does that mean colorful language is not so offensive to you elsewhere?"

337

Instead of answering straightaway, she considered. "It did not affect me that way—when you used it as an exclamation," she admitted in muffled tones, "in the bedchamber."

"Well, I am certainly glad to hear that," he said, and she could hear the amusement running through his words. "And I should probably tell you that despite your dreadful recitation, I still vastly prefer your oration above anyone else's."

She tipped her head back at this to look at him. "I don't see how that can be so, in light of how painful you find it."

"Strange, is it not?" he agreed, and oh gods, she could hear in his voice that he was somewhat baffled by it himself. "There is a sort of pleasure in the pain because it is your voice." Jane stared at him, and he shrugged. "Probably not worth dwelling on," he said dismissively. "We all have our little foibles."

"Er, yes," Jane agreed in a stifled voice. His words had left her strangely breathless, as though they were poised on the edge of something. She would almost believe he had made some sort of declaration, or confession to her if it was not for his offhand manner and calm expression.

Could he, in fact, care for her? The thought had occurred to her a few times now. The problem was, he was so flippant and insincere that she would be a fool to take his caressing words as anything more than flummery. Whichever way she looked at it, she was out of her depth to an almost hopeless degree.

"Shall we to bed?" he asked in a lightly conversational tone. Jane could do no more than meekly nod by this point. As though picking up on her temporary weakness, he scooped her up into his arms. "My poor Jane," he murmured as he carried her through to their bedchamber. "So lacking in pursuits that you have nothing better to do with your time than to count my shoes."

338

She could tell he was laughing at her, but she found she did not care. "You should heartily pity me," she said instead and watched his lips twitch.

"Oh, I do. It is outrageous that your husband keeps you cooped up in these rooms, a virtual prisoner." He laid her down on the bed and stood looking down at her, his eyes glinting. "I can see why though," he said. "I'd be tempted to do the same if you were mine."

"I am yours," she answered without thinking, and the spark in his eyes became a blaze.

"Are you, Jane?" he asked, and she hesitated, unsure what she was committing herself to.

He had been playing again, she realized belatedly. He was being Alisander de Balon, her lover right now and not her husband at all. Likely he had been about to make more jokes about tying her to the bed with ropes of jewels, then she had muddied the waters by being a slow-wit. She could kick herself. "I did not—"

"*Are* you, Jane?" he insisted, climbing onto the bed with her, still fully clothed, and hauling her roughly against him. "Are you mine?"

"Yes," she whispered, and he groaned, shutting his eyes a moment. Jane stared. She felt dizzy. Just like that, they were poised back on the cliff edge again. Was it all in her mind, or did he feel the same way? Her poor head felt all of a whirl.

When he opened his eyes, they were calm again, like the sea after a storm, and he breathed shakily out before releasing her and easing his way back off the bed. Jane watched him without comment as he started removing his clothes in an orderly fashion and placing them carefully on a chair. *Enter Viscount Bardulf,* she thought.

"I forgot to tell you," he said conversationally, "but two of your fellow ladies-in-waiting asked after you most particularly today."

"Oh yes?" Jane said cautiously. She should get off the bed herself and start undressing, but instead, she just lay there, watching him playing his part. It was strangely fascinating, and it gave her a sort of horrified thrill to realize that he had subtly changed from Alisander de Balon, whom she *somewhat* trusted, into the Viscount Bardulf, who she heartily detested. At least…she thought she did. Didn't she?

"It is of no use for you to ask me their names," he added in regretful tones, "for they all blend into one, and I cannot distinguish one from another."

A lie, thought Jane. He was actually extremely observant. "I see," she said politely, and he gave her a sharp glance.

"You don't seem very interested, my sweet."

"I daresay I will see them soon enough and find out for myself."

"How fortunate I am to have such an amenable wife," he mused. "I doubt many would be so understanding of my nature."

"Yes, I believe I am starting to familiarize myself with your ways, my lord."

That made him pause. "You are not getting undressed tonight?" he enquired casually as he made his way over to the wash basin, clad only in his braies. Jane admired his physique, which was surprisingly muscular when out of clothes. He looked slenderer when he was dressed somehow. Maybe it was all those fancy fabrics.

Jane shrugged. "I will by and by."

"You are in a strange mood tonight, I find," he said. "I think all this seclusion has taken its toll on you." When she did not reply, he lowered his washcloth to look at her.

"Perhaps," she conceded. "When will that be over, do you suppose?"

He seemed to consider this. "The day after tomorrow, I think. What say you to one more day of exile? People are starting to talk. More and more slip mention of you into conversation, hoping to hear news of you." He looked thoughtful. "In short, Aphrany's court is more than primed for your return."

Jane found herself feeling surprisingly indifferent about it. Perhaps just as well, considering the Queen had clearly not missed her at all. She shrugged again and saw him narrow his eyes. Discarding the drying cloth, he sauntered back toward the bed.

To her surprise, he seized hold of her ankle, half dragging her off the bed. "What are you—?"

Then he sank to his knees, placing her one foot on his shoulder. "No matter what I do, keep this slippered foot here," he said, casting up her skirts and disappearing beneath them.

Jane struggled into a seated position. "A-Alisander! At least let me take off my shoes!" she squeaked as she felt his breath between her legs. This felt highly indecent with her clothes still on and him kneeling at her feet! The way her one leg was raised was frankly scandalizing.

341

"No," answered a muffled voice, and his hand fondled her leg a moment before sliding around to grip her firmly behind the back of her knee, holding her open to him. Then he was licking her there, and she found his tongue could tease and torment without even uttering a word.

Jane turned hot all over. She gazed down at his hand, just below her garter. It felt terribly lewd and decadent to be sat splayed out for him like this, with his face between her legs. *How could he do such a thing?* It was horribly improper. It was... *Oh!* Jane's head fell back.

On the other hand, he *had* done this to her before, so being so shocked was likely foolish. He had enjoyed it; that was what he had said. And she had too. Jane shut her eyes and sank back down onto the bed. She would just have to...take it.

He was slow and thorough, building her pleasure, one minute applying the flat of his tongue, another darting it out like a snake to nudge her most sensitive spot. He would bring her to the brink of completion and then retreat, changing his angle, or the pressure of his tongue, and start the process all over again.

Jane squirmed and wriggled and arched her back to try to get closer still to the source of her torment, but he evaded her with ease, lightly kissing her thighs when she grew more frustrated.

"Alisander!" she sobbed at last, feeling thwarted.

"Yes, Jane?" She was glad he sounded out of breath at least. He wiped his mouth against her thigh and straightened up, standing between her open legs and staring down at her.

Jane blinked up at him. "Last time, you—you let me!" she burst out indignantly.

He laughed and licked his lips. "Last time you were being good," he said lightly, and Jane felt bewilderingly crestfallen.

342

She started to struggle up onto her elbows as he unfastened the strings at his waist. "Sit up," he said almost roughly. The minute she did, his hand fell to her shoulder, caressing her there. "Take out my cock, Jane," he said, his voice silky smooth again. *His what?* Her eyes flew to his.

Jane hesitated. *Was he actually suggesting…?* She gazed dry-mouthed at the unmannerly bulge in his braies. She could either refuse outright, with appropriate horror, or she could do as he asked. Feeling almost in a trance, she reached up to draw down the fabric, revealing the hard evidence of his desire. Freed of the fabric, it practically sprang up and hit her in the face, so swollen was it with arousal.

She glanced up at him and found his eyes glued to her face, rather than his erection. His hand traced up her neck to lightly cup her face. Jane closed her eyes and drew in a shaky breath as he slid his thumb along her jaw. "I want you to kiss me," he said unevenly. "Can you do that, Jane?"

"Kiss you?" Jane repeated, a suspicion dawning. Her gaze traveled from his face to his turgid manhood.

"Yes, there," he whispered hoarsely. Jane swallowed and slowly turned her face to press a light kiss to the swelling flesh there. He made a strangled sound in his throat. "*Fuck.*" She listened expectantly, half fearfully, to see what came next, but to her surprise, all that was forthcoming was his ragged breathing. That kiss certainly seemed to have affected him strongly, she thought, glancing up at his face.

In fact, he seemed to be struggling right now to find words. After a moment, he simply shut his eyes, nostrils flaring. Did he like it that much? she wondered incredulously. Jane had a suspicion that if he could speak right now, he would.

She lowered her gaze again, eyeing that unwieldy part of him that seemed to be straining with all its might toward her. *What a strange-looking thing it was.* How odd to think something so inelegant could lurk between Viscount Bardulf's thighs. The skin had felt surprisingly soft and warm against her lips and not *unpleasant*, precisely. Suddenly, she had an impulse to repeat the kiss that had left him so shaken.

Mustering her courage, she leaned slowly forward, squeezed her eyes shut, and kissed it, this time a little clumsily. Her kiss glanced off it, and she nearly poked her eye out. He let out a gasp, his eyes springing open. "Jane?" he said hoarsely.

"Er—sorry!" she gasped, feeling embarrassed. Closing her eyes had been a mistake. "I thought—"

To her surprise, his hand clamped down on her shoulder, preventing her retreat. "Do you think you could do that again?" he asked politely, though his voice still sounded a little strained.

"Oh." He couldn't have found it so very bad after all. "Well, yes…" she agreed cautiously.

"And maybe use your tongue this time."

"My tongue?" *Oh.* Suddenly, she realized this would be no more than returning the favor of what he did to her. But…she could hardly lap and suck at this ugly, great thing, she thought, her mind reeling. Could she?

Apparently, she could. She did her best, though she was sure she made a very bad job of it. Alisander's hand slid up and down her neck, encouraging her and assuring her he was a grateful recipient, though Jane felt horribly awkward and unsure of herself the entire time.

If she gave herself time to pause and think about it, she just knew she would freeze, so instead, she tried to shut down her thoughts altogether and simply pressed her lips and plied her tongue wherever he guided her. Her face felt so hot, she was sure she would scald his groin.

She could not possibly imagine being as enthusiastic over it as he was. Then, she remembered that she had been the first person to receive these particular ministrations from him, and redoubled her efforts.

Alisander was gratifyingly vocal in his appreciation. He groaned and huffed and panted her name, his fingers gentle in her hair and at her nape. Finally, he caught her chin. "No more," he murmured and bore her back down onto the mattress, aligned their bodies, and drove into her without more ado.

Jane gasped, but then his ardor seemed to quickly ignite her own, and suddenly she was glad he had not let her reach her rapture earlier after all. Had he wanted them to reach it together? she wondered dazedly as their bodies moved in synchronization. If so, how clever of him. The pleasure built and built as he stroked her face, and kissed her mouth, murmuring sweet, sweet words into her ear.

Her laughing tormentor from earlier had all but disappeared. Afterward, he was affectionate, holding her close and settling her comfortably against him. Jane kept her eyes shut, though she could feel him playing with her hair. "Next time, my dove, you could take me in your mouth, if the mood takes you," he suggested.

"In my mouth?" she repeated before she was sure what he was referring to. He made a choked sound that might have been laughter, but she was too tired to take him to task. "You weren't playing fair," she grumbled sleepily. "You kept switching between one and the other, so I could not get my bearings."

"One and the other?" he repeated, a frown in his voice as he ran his fingers through her hair.

"Between Viscount—" She broke off, remembering she had never voiced her theory aloud. "Never mind."

"Tell me."

She shook her head. He would likely laugh, and she would be embarrassed. "No, it is just…a way of thinking I have fallen into recently."

Fortunately, he was too distracted to pursue this. "Your hair, Jane, is the precise color of sunshine," he murmured. "Has anyone ever told you that?"

"No," she admitted, then hesitated. "Helen always used to say she wished her hair was my color," she confided a little awkwardly.

"Hmm. I expect you foolishly wished yours was a warmer shade of gold like hers." She nodded, wondering how he could possibly know that. He pulled a face. "So sadly predictable." She pushed against his chest, and he grinned sleepily, catching her up in his arms and holding her against him. "The way you talk about your sister…" he said slowly.

"Yes?" She tensed. She could not help it. Any talk of Helen made her defensive.

"Makes her sound a good deal more…likable than she appeared at court." She could tell he was choosing his words carefully and appreciated his consideration.

"Yes," she agreed. "For my favorite memories of her are from before we came to court. She was always the best of sisters in those days."

He ran his hand soothingly up and down her back. "It's good you remember her like that."

"Yes," she agreed, relaxing. "It's just…difficult that no one else does. There's nobody I can really talk about her to. It's…strangely painful." As usual, with such talk, her eyes filled with tears. She turned her face into his shoulder.

He did not answer for a moment, just circled his hand across her back. "Well, no one else knew her like you did," he said at last. "Here, she just came across as another ambitious beauty."

Jane nodded. This, she already knew. "Perhaps when Celestia is older…"

"How about Ayleth?" he suggested. "Can you not talk to her?"

"Ayleth was devoted to my sister," Jane replied. "Fiercely devoted, but their relationship…was not that of equals." She struggled a moment to express what she meant. "Ayleth viewed Helen through the eyes of a devotee, almost," she said slowly.

"She will turn your sister's memory into that of some martyred saint?" he suggested with a frown in his voice. "We should probably get rid of her before she can pour any of that nonsense into Celestia's ears."

"I don't think we need to worry about that for a few years."

"Hmm."

"I don't know what to do about Ayleth," she admitted wretchedly. "I think she is desperately unhappy and…and in need of a new cause, almost."

"Well, I don't want that cause to be raising our child in some cult devoted to your departed sister."

Jane had to work hard not to bristle with offense. "She does not really show much interest in the baby, Alisander," she said, lifting her head from his shoulder.

"That's true," he conceded. "I don't think she's the type." He reached up to stroke a thumb over her cheek. "Let us simply keep a watchful eye on the situation, then."

She nodded and lowered her head again with a sigh. Her eyes were drifting shut again. When she heard him speak, she was too tired for the words to register. "What did you say?" She roused herself.

"I said go to sleep now, Jane," he said in an amused voice, but she was already there.

22

The next morning, Alisander finally paid his courtesy visit to the guild of glaziers at their premises on Jarman Street. As their new patron, he had received an open invitation, and he spent a pleasant enough morning being fawned over by Master Arnold and his fellow members.

It was true, they were inclined to be a little stiff and awkward at first, for it was plain that his foreignness was off-putting to them, and his outfit, a pearl-encrusted tunic of burgundy velvet, a little flamboyant for their tastes. Fortunately, he was in high good humor and had a mind to charm them, so they soon relaxed in his presence and warmed up to him.

He received his tour of their headquarters and partook of their bland refreshments with every evidence of pleasure, and soon they were giving him an enthusiastic account of the expansions they desired to make and unfurling many detailed sketches to share with him.

Alisander looked duly impressed, nodded, and even managed a few shrewd suggestions of his own, which went down a storm, until even the most unenthusiastic member of the welcoming party was viewing him with unreserved approval. Promising them he would arrange the necessary meetings at court to obtain the permissions they needed, he bade them farewell and returned to the palace.

To his disquiet, he found his good humor fading with the amount of time he spent away from his wife. He was sorely tempted to return to her at midday, for no good reason at all. Indeed, it would take him out of his way to do such a thing, for he had business at the other end of the castle.

He just about resisted the lure though he knew Jane would be delightfully tense and stewing on her return to palace circulation on the morrow. The opportunity to tease and distract her out of her anxieties was incredibly tempting.

Instead, he was mindful of his duty and wended his steps toward the palace gardens. Once there, he headed down the long path flanked with hawthorn hedges that led to the King's orchards. On a cold day in February, the bare trees would hold little appeal for visitors. Presumably, that was why Hubair had suggested it as a spot for their meeting.

He felt a twinge of irritation when he saw the Klobergian ambassador skulking behind an apple tree in his black-and-yellow-striped tunic. *Ugh.* Listening to Alphonse Hubair prate about conspiracies against Lascony was the *last* thing he felt like doing. And really, did the fellow think that tree concealed him? He resembled nothing so much as a giant bumblebee. "Ah, there you are, Hubair," he greeted him breezily. "Well met."

The other whipped around, for he had not spotted Alisander's approach even though he had not tried to quiet his steps in any way. "Keep your voice down, Bardulf, for heaven's sake!" he hissed. "You never know where Vawdrey's spies may be concealed."

Alisander suppressed a weary sigh. He could already tell that Alphonse was about to be extremely trying. They fell in step together. "Where were you on Tuesday, my friend?" he ventured. "Your absence was…somewhat conspicuous from the gathering in the small gallery."

Hubair looked startled. "Someone remarked upon it?" he asked, sounding faintly anxious.

"Lord Vawdrey himself," Alisander responded rather unkindly. Very few people at court, least of all the foreign ambassadors, did not go in some fear of the King's chief advisor and spymaster.

Hubair paled. "I—er—well." He cleared his throat. "Some other matter had to take precedence that day."

"I see."

"I would hope by now that people are acquainted with my character sufficiently well to know I would not shirk my duty without good reason," he said pompously. Alisander held his tongue. Hubair stole a look at him. "I am surprised *you* had time to attend such a reception, my lord, quite frankly."

"You mean as a newlywed?" Alisander asked innocently.

Hubair turned purple. "Certainly not! I meant with the current political climate being so uncertain!" He glanced about furtively. "I am sure you have been most anxious to assure His Majesty, King Wilhelm, of your continued loyalty to the Lasconian crown. I am somewhat amazed you have not been summoned back home to explain your actions of late," he sniffed.

"Are you?" Alisander asked coolly with lifted brows. "But my loyalties remain quite unchanged, I assure you, my dear Hubair," he replied with perfect truth, for his loyalties had only ever lain with himself.

"That's as may well be," the other responded heavily, shaking his head, "but things look very odd of late. Very odd indeed. The Lasconian ambassador, marrying a—a connection of the King of Karadok and adopting his—" Catching the look in Alisander's eye, he broke off hastily. "I mean, all these

351

imprudent betrothals that have been happening of late," he finished pettishly. "It is all very troubling."

Alisander rolled his eyes. "You refer once more to your archduke and the Duchess of Rand's niece?"

"Shhhhh!" Hubair practically bridled. "No names, if you please, my lord!" He glanced about with exaggerated concern. "To even speak of it out loud is most imprudent!"

"I have heard that entanglement will likely come to naught," Alisander said crushingly. He was tired of humoring Hubair. No one cared about his penniless archduke, least of all Wymer.

Hubair looked terrified. "You have been *speaking* of this?" he gasped. "With another? I told you in the *utmost* confidence, my lord!"

"The other party was fully aware and just as unconvinced by it as I."

Hubair turned stiff with affront. "I see. I see that Kloberg's concerns are not considered sufficiently important to Lascony's official ambassador in Karadok!"

"My dear Hubair, calm yourself."

"I shall certainly write to King Wilhelm with my concerns!" Hubair fumed. "I feel sure I am not alone in my fears and—and my doubts as to your priorities of late, my lord!"

"Well, you must do as you see fit," Alisander drawled. "And I shall continue to do likewise." He had already swept his most elegant bow, clipped Hubair's ear with the swirl of his cape, and was striding off down the avenue before it occurred to him that he never *had* found out what Kloberg's boy-king had been about that had so concerned Oswald Vawdrey.

352

Ah well, he had more important things to think about right now. Namely, what his wife was up to. The irony was that wedding Jane had likely been the one thing he had done in his life *without* an ulterior motive. He had simply wanted her. How ironic that he was now beset on all sides with people thinking he had some nefarious plot afoot.

Looking at it objectively, he supposed it might look somewhat suspicious. What he really ought to have done was humored Hubair, and convinced him that it was Queen Armenal who had persuaded him to take Jane to wife. Then the touchy little man would not have taken such mortal offense.

He ought to have sent such an account to Wilhelm, too, stating as much before the wedding had even taken place. If he did it now, it would look like what it was: an afterthought. The truth was that he had not been thinking straight at all when it came to the prospect of getting Lady Jane Cecil within his clutches. He supposed *imprudent* was the right word after all.

Still, Hubair had annoyed him, which was never wise. It was ridiculous to be put out by criticism of his choice of wife, and doubtless, he was a fool to feel goaded into anger by the likes of Alphonse Hubair, but he simply lacked the patience for it this day. Especially when he was so desperate to return to Jane's side. It seemed like hours since he had quit their bed. Ah well. He would appease Hubair next time.

His steps quickened along with his anticipation as he climbed the stairs to the western wing. It didn't matter how much he told himself to slow down, he found that was the last thing he wanted to do. Finally, he reached their rooms, but no sooner was he inside than Wat sprang into his pathway.

"My lord," Wat said, looking pale but resolute. "Might I be permitted a word with you in private?"

353

Alisander narrowed his eyes at the servant's bleak expression. *Now what?* he wondered. How many more people were going to get in his way when all he wanted to do was enjoy his wife's society? "And I suppose it *must* be now, Wat?" he asked with resignation.

Wat looked a little glassy-eyed, and Alisander was not sure he did not sway on the spot. "If at all possible, my lord," he replied.

"Oh, very well," Alisander sighed. He peered inside the main chamber, half hoping for a glimpse of Jane. He was disappointed in this, for the room was empty for once. "Not a soul in sight." He walked in and beckoned for Wat to follow. "By the way, where *is* my wife?" He was unable to stop himself from asking.

"She had another gown delivered," Wat answered promptly, shutting the door behind them. "And she sent for that maid she shares to help her try it on. She's in your bedchamber."

Alisander was sorely pressed to go and take a look himself, but instead, he turned to the perspiring manservant in front of him. "What was it you wanted to speak to me about?"

Wat swallowed audibly. "My lord, I have a confession to make," he said.

Alisander's heart sank. *Fuck.* Why was everyone being so *annoying* this afternoon!

Five minutes later, he sat in a chair listening to Wat unburdening himself and wondering how to extricate them both from this mess.

"In the beginning, I simply thought of it as serving my country," Wat said hollowly. "You served a foreign king, and I thought it no more than my solemn duty to keep an eye on your

354

comings and goings and report back. But something has changed now," he said wretchedly. "Something's…shifted somehow." He worried his lip a moment.

"Maybe it's the extra mouths around the table. Maybe it's because the household is starting to feel more like a—a *family*," he said, rushing on. "Somehow, I don't feel the same about where my duty lies," he admitted miserably. "Now it feels like I'm doing something low and sneaky. Something to be ashamed of. Something disloyal."

"My dear Wat," Alisander interjected smoothly, "you must not upset yourself. This crisis of conscience is wholly unnecessary. I do not consider you remotely dishonorable." When Wat began shaking his head, he carried on swiftly.

"It is all quite true, I assure you. As to your *loyalty*"—he paused—"I am sure you are loyal to your original master, whose service you entered long before mine. I might add that is entirely what I expected when first I employed you. Indeed," he added significantly, "I considered that to be a point very much in your favor."

Wat had frozen at the mention of his *original employer* and now turned crimson. "My lord, I—I hardly know what to say," he uttered after a moment.

"Why say anything at all? Why can we not simply carry on as we are for the next twenty or thirty years?"

Wat's jaw dropped slightly. "You mean—? You cannot mean—?"

"That your position with me is a safe one?" Alisander shrugged. "Why should I not? You are a discreet, efficient fellow, entirely to be relied upon."

Wat hung his head. "Not entirely, my lord," he said hoarsely.

Alisander tutted. He had tried his best to prevent frank discussion, but it seemed Wat would not be reassured with anything less. "Wat," he said patiently, "try to look at it this way. I have never performed any office in front of you that I would not wish you to report back to Lord Vawdrey and I never will."

Wat started violently at the mention of the King's spymaster. "My lord—" he cried in protest. "I never said—!"

"Now, now, you were the one who insisted on plain speech," Alisander pointed out briskly. "You would not let me skirt politely around the issue, so now you must deal with the consequences."

Wat sank down into a nearby seat looking rather green and shaken. He passed a hand over his brow and gulped. "Yes, my lord."

"I neither desire nor require a confession from you," Alisander continued steadily. "Indeed, I would go to great lengths to prevent such a thing from ever occurring." He shuddered slightly. "It would, I imagine, be a most uncomfortable experience for the both of us."

The ghost of a smile touched Wat's pale lips. "You are generous, my lord."

"It is easy to be generous to someone who makes one's life easier." Wat made a dismissive gesture and opened his mouth as though to disagree. "It is true," Alisander insisted gently. "Quite apart from your endless procession of errands and the masterly way in which you run my household, it is very useful to me that *a certain person*"—he refrained from mentioning Vawdrey's name after Wat's agitated response, but the other man still stiffened—"should have an account of my daily actions so that he may be assured they are entirely blameless."

356

Alisander stood from his seat and walked over to the mantelpiece, whereon he placed a hand and struck a proprietary stance. "I am not a native of this land and it is not reasonable to expect that I should remain here unmonitored. Not in the light of my continued association with a foreign power. Naturally, certain quarters require reassurance that I am not up to anything nefarious. This is not a problem to me. Indeed, I view it almost as a safeguard at this point." Wat remained silent, though from his heavy frown, Alisander deduced he was considering every word furiously.

"You have become uneasy in your conscience, Wat, but let me assure you that you have no need for such scruples. I should not wish you to change a single thing about the way you perform your duties, to *either* of your masters," he finished with a quirk of his lips and saw Wat's color deepen.

"My lord—" he muttered feebly.

"My only stipulation is that you refrain from raising this subject with me ever again," Alisander said, faking a smothered yawn. "For I grow heartily weary of it, and I think we have exhausted it as a topic of conversation for the future."

Wat looked torn. "But my lord, what if—?"

"What if what, Wat?" Alisander asked humorously. The servant did not so much as crack a smile.

"What if I should ever suspect my information on you is incriminating?" he asked, practically wringing his hands.

Alisander gave a twisted smile. "My dear Wat," he drawled, "you may rest assured that if I allowed you to discover it, then it is not *remotely* incriminating." He frowned suddenly as a displeasing thought occurred to him. "Though, I must caution you against becoming reticent with Lord Vaw—" He broke off.

357

"With your *other employer*," he amended swiftly. "He will certainly know if you start withholding information from him and the only result would be him enlisting yet *another* informant which might make my life more difficult."

Wat looked perplexed. "You mean, you genuinely want me to—"

"To continue as you have been, yes," Alisander concluded, nodding.

"I—my lord, I hardly know what to say," Wat admitted.

Alisander spread his hands. "There is not really anything left to say, now, is there?"

Wat cleared his throat. "I suppose not, my lord."

Alisander smiled approvingly. "Carry on, Wat. Carry on."

He gave only the most perfunctory of knocks on the door before walking into their bedchamber. Jane was seated in front of the looking glass while a young woman removed hairpins from her neatly braided hair. It had been arranged most artfully in loops around a plain gold circlet. He guessed this was a new look they were trying out.

Jane met his eyes in the mirror. "Good evening, my lord," she said, clearing her throat. "This is Marta, who has been helping me this afternoon with my new gowns." He spared the girl a glance and a nod before returning his attention to Jane, who was starting to look flustered. "What do you think of this one?" she asked haltingly. "I mean to wear it upon the morrow."

"I can't really see it while you remain seated," he prevaricated. "I like your hair like that though."

Jane stood up and faced him, and he paused to get the full effect. The blue gray of the fabric suited her well, and the cut was unusual enough to draw the eye with its elaborate sleeves and high neckline. Clearly, he took too long scrutinizing, for Jane started to color and turn self-conscious. "I think Monsieur Barbier made rather a nice job of the beading," she said, smoothing down her bodice, which was heavily decorated.

"It is not Barbier, but his associate that does the beading," he corrected her absently. "Come here and let me take a closer look." Jane was so hesitant over her steps that he was forced to close the distance between them himself. He walked around her in a slow inspection, halting behind her and settling his hands at her waist. "Did you guess, wife, that it would affect me this way?" he whispered in her ear. "Seeing my heraldic beast upon your person?" Jane caught her breath.

He half turned and observed that the maid was watching them avidly as she bustled around, tidying things away. "But how could you have known?" he wondered aloud. "When I had no idea myself?" He let his fingertip travel upward as it traced the sinuous serpentine shape which decorated her bodice in a variety of pretty colored glass beads.

Jane shivered and tipped her head back to look at him. "You approve though?" she asked with just the faintest hint of anxiety. "What do you think of my wearing the amethysts you gave me at our wedding?" She touched the jeweled collar at her neck. "I thought they looked pretty with the color of the gown. Do you like the effect?"

"*Like* is not the word. Now be a good girl and dismiss your maid."

Jane looked startled at this abrupt demand. "Dismiss—? But I'm not—"

He turned to the agog servant. "Leda," he said, knowing full well the girl's name was Marta. "You will kindly go away and return in the morning at"—he considered—"ten o'clock."

Jane was quick to object. "That is far too late, Alisander. I like to be up betimes, for the Queen has much—" She broke off, doubtless remembering that the Queen seemed to have been managing just fine without her recently.

"Ten o'clock," he repeated smoothly, filling the awkward gap. "We will undertake your debut as Viscountess Bardulf together, my dear," he said, lifting her hand to his lips and kissing her fingers.

That seemed to silence her, and the smiling maid took the opportunity to curtsey and withdraw. "Now I shall have to call Ayleth back in to help me undress," Jane said with exasperation.

"*I* shall undress you with the greatest pleasure," he assured her glibly, steering her back toward the looking glass. "No, leave that on," he said when she reached for the jeweled collar.

"The amethysts?" She looked back at him quizzically, then seemed to gauge his mood. "*Oh.* Well, but we have not yet had our supper, my lord," she reminded him.

"We can have it in here, just the two of us. Would that not be nice?" he coaxed as he removed the circlet from her hair and began unfastening her laces. "I do not feel up to encountering the likes of Anne or Ayleth over the dinner table. Even Wat is proving tiresome today."

"How so?"

"He's had an attack of conscience. *Most* inconvenient."

"Has he?" Jane looked intrigued. "He and Anne went to see the sights together this afternoon," she confided as he deftly unfastened her wrists. "Ayleth watched the children while they were gone."

"Good grief. Did she? That seems rather obliging and most unlike her."

Jane nodded. "I know, and that is not all. This evening"—she lowered her voice—"I discovered Ayleth in Robert's room, taking her ease."

Alisander froze. "*Where?*"

"Robert's room," she repeated. "I thought she had disappeared again and said as much to Anne. I was quite vexed about it. 'Twas Anne who let me in on the secret. She said that Robert and Ayleth have now become bosom friends after she broke down in tears a couple of evenings ago, and he consoled her." She hesitated. "Apparently, Ayleth told him everything. All about her grief over Helen, and they sort of bonded over mutual loss. I assume Robert is a widower?"

Alisander resumed easing her gown down over her waist and hips until it dropped to her ankles. "Step out," he advised her and, when she did so, whisked it efficiently out of the way, draping it over a chair back. "Yes," he agreed, seeing she was waiting on his answer. "Robert is a widower, but his wife, Jeanne, was nothing like Ayleth." He pulled a face. "No, I can't see it somehow. My faithful Robert, and your dour Ayleth."

Jane, now clad in only a thin shift, wrapped her woolen mantle about her shoulders. "Mayhap she would not *be* so dour if she had a close friend and companion in life," she suggested lightly.

The thought was strangely disquieting to him. "Robert though," he murmured in objection. "No, I cannot believe it, Jane." He stripped off his tunic, replacing it with a loosely tied robe. "You and Anne were likely jumping to conclusions."

Jane lowered herself into a seat by the window. "Maybe Robert thought the same when he heard you were to marry."

He snorted. "Certainly not, for I told him of that myself. Why are you sitting there? Come and sit here on the bed." He removed his shoes and stretched out on the mattress, setting his hands behind his head. "Robert has never shown the slightest interest in women," he asserted, "not since his wife died over a decade ago."

Jane moved across the room to join him. "Well," she said reasonably, "when I knocked on the door and looked in on them, she was sat on his bed beside him, drinking a cup of ale. That *seemed* rather intimate to me, but I suppose it could just be two people who are comfortable with one another."

"Now you merely sound naïve, Jane," he said dampeningly. "That last sentence has convinced me, where your other arguments failed."

She climbed up onto the mattress. "As it happens," she said huffily, "I am not someone given to wild conjecture about other people, and I do not think you are fair to Anne by supposing she is either."

He smirked, catching her about the waist and hauling her on top of him. "Anne is likely the biggest gossip in Aphrany," he asserted as Jane gave a muffled squeak. "Given half the chance, she'll even gossip about herself. Go on," he challenged, "tell me what she said to you upon her return from sightseeing with Wat."

"She said she had a very nice time, if that is what you mean," Jane answered primly.

He rolled her underneath him, and ran his hands up her sides, slipping them under her mantle. "Oh? Is that really all she said?" he enquired, slyly pinching and tickling at her waist.

Jane's face turned increasingly pink as she wriggled in a vain attempt to evade his fingers. "*No*," she gasped. "She told me all about the cathedral, and—*oh!*"

"Do you know," he said conversationally, "how many times I have wanted to do this to you, Jane, over the past few years?"

His fingers stilled and so did Jane. "No," she answered faintly.

He lowered his face to hers. "Every time I saw that demure look on your face."

"Tickle me?" she asked, sounding startled.

"Have you at my mercy," he corrected her, his eyes roaming over her face.

"Wh-why are you looking at me like that?" she asked, swallowing and clearly finding it hard to hold his gaze at such close quarters.

"Because," he answered in a harsh whisper, "now the fateful moment has arrived, I am not so certain who is the victor and who is the quarry..." They stared at one another. Before she could speak, he said in a rush, "I have been thinking about you *all* day." His tone was rough, the confession, unanticipated. He was slightly horrified to hear himself make it.

"You have?" Jane's breath was coming fast.

"I have," he confirmed. "Moreover, I have been sadly remiss in my duties. What have you done to me?" He was fully aware that he should not be talking like this, but in the moment, he felt powerless to stop.

Slowly, Jane's arms extended from her sides in their defensive huddle to slide around his back and pull him closer. Gods, the action undid him. "Naught that you have not done to me," she whispered back, and suddenly they were kissing. It was not polished, and it was not elegant. He shoved his tongue in her mouth, and gloriously, she accepted it with a needy whimper.

When she slid her tongue against his, Alisander groaned aloud. He should stop now. They needed to stop, but Jane was licking into his mouth, and he could not call a halt to it, not if his life depended on it. Instead, he started dragging her mantle from her shoulders and palming and kneading at her soft breasts through her thin shift.

Her little nipples were hard and pink, making him feel crazed with need. Pinching them was not enough, he needed them in his mouth, *right now*. Jane made a noise of displeasure as he lifted his lips from hers, but she shuddered when he mouthed and sucked on her neck before moving down and engulfing her nipples into his greedy mouth.

"*Alisander!*" she gasped, and he braced himself to be reminded that they were waiting on supper—or even that he would mark her pale flesh—but nothing of the sort was forthcoming. Instead, Jane gave a helpless little sob of desire that stabbed him right in the chest.

"Jane." He made a supreme effort and pulled back. "We have to right ourselves—"

The knock on the door startled them both. He was up and off the bed in an instant, adjusting his robe to conceal his blatant disorder. Jane was tugging desperately at the relaxed neckline of her shift to conceal herself.

"One moment!" he called out sternly and stepped up to the door. It was Wat, who hastily averted his gaze when he took in the unruly state of him. "We'll take ours on a tray in here," he told him swiftly and shut the door.

Making back for the bed, he picked up Jane's mantle and wrapped it about her shoulders. "There, now," he tutted, cupping the back of her head and dropping a gentle kiss to her lips. "All is righted." Jane's face was on fire.

"How is it you can hear footsteps from outside of doors?" she grumbled, making her way to the edge of the bed.

"I can't," he answered absently, though she was not really attending, for she was scooting around the bed and sitting herself in a chair by the small table. He retrieved her slippers and brought them to her, kneeling to slip them onto her feet. Her hand fell on his shoulder, and as though unable to resist, he turned his head to kiss her wrist.

Another knock sounded on the door and Wat entered, bearing a tray laden with dishes. Alisander straightened up and moved to the fire, where he threw the last of the logs onto the blaze. Wat, having set down the dishes, withdrew to fetch them more firewood.

In his absence, Robert shuffled in with a jug of wine and two goblets. Alisander eyed him keenly but could see no difference in his trusty servant to indicate the old man was in the throes of some new love affair. Speaking of Ayleth, she, too, made a discreet appearance with a large ewer of steaming water.

Once they had all departed, Alisander sat at the table and cleared his throat. "Well, they all seemed most keen to facilitate our evening," he commented dryly. Jane looked up enquiringly from buttering her bread. "I suspect they'll be making merry without us," he explained.

"You mean Wat and Anne?"

He pulled a face. "Take your pick, Wat and Anne, Robert and Ayleth. It seems we are not the only pair of lovers about the place."

Jane colored faintly. "I am sure they will not be doing anything improper," she said in faint reproach, which just made him grin.

"Jane," he murmured, shaking his head, "you are just making me want to fluster you all over again."

"You scarcely ever cease, my lord," she told him, and he could see she was trying to hide her answering smile.

"No," he agreed. "We do deal rather well together, do we not, Lady Bardulf?" He held his wine aloft, and she clinked her goblet against his.

"We do," she agreed, dropping her gaze. "Do you—do you suppose everyone else will be surprised about that?"

"Everyone else?"

She hesitated. "Our fellow courtiers."

"Ah," he considered. Strange to say, he had not really given the matter much thought.

"Or do you suppose they will not be able to tell?"

He considered her over the top of his goblet. He hoped like hell no one would be able to tell how utterly he was infatuated right now. He would likely be a laughingstock. "I do not know," he said slowly, "but we will soon find out, will we not?"

She looked, he thought, more than a little apprehensive. "Yes," she agreed and took a gulp of wine.

As was his habit lately, a display of nervousness on Jane's behalf brought out his gallant streak. "They will likely see no more nor less than we desire them to see," he said with his most reassuring smile, and he watched her shoulders relax. It was oddly gratifying, soothing this skittish wife of his. He wondered that he should like it so much, whilst simultaneously enjoying being the actual source of her discomfort. It was a puzzle to be sure.

After they had eaten, Alisander took the tray from the room himself. All was quiet without, though when he paused outside Anne and the children's door, he found it ajar. Wat was sat just inside on a low stool, bouncing Bertrand on his knee. Whilst entertaining the boy, he kept up a trickle of comfortable conversation with Anne, who was breastfeeding Celestia.

Once he was assured none of it concerned Wat's extra duties, he left them to it, choosing not to disturb Robert with the empty dishes. By the time he rejoined Jane under the covers, he felt calm and in control of himself once more. "My poor Jane," he murmured against her ear. "You are in a quake about the morrow, but you must not fret. I will not allow anyone to discompose you. Not even the Queen herself."

She gave a small murmur of protest at this, but otherwise lay content in his arms, letting him pet and fuss over her. "If anyone makes my Jane uncomfortable, she must simply pluck at my tunic and I will come to her rescue, yes?"

"Pluck at your tunic?" Jane repeated, sounding slightly annoyed. "I hope I would not do anything so childish!"

"Shhhh, Jane, you must not get agitated, it is not good for you," he tutted. "Your face grows *so* red when you grow vexed."

"Yes, but you like it when I grow hot and blotchy!" Jane pointed out. She was very bad at this game; he did not know why he liked to play it with her so much.

He sighed, slipping his hands between her legs. "I do," he agreed richly as Jane's breathing hitched. "But only *I* am permitted to annoy Jane so deeply. Is that not so?"

She hesitated. "Y-yes."

"A little louder, if you please, Jane. I could hardly hear you."

"Only you," she breathed, pleasing him so much that he touched her exactly as she liked it without prompting. Jane shivered and gasped, closing her eyes against the pleasure even as her legs closed about his hand, holding it in place against her sweet little cunt.

"That's very good Jane, *very* good." It should be amusing how much she responded to commendation, but the fact was that he was far too excited by her wetness to tease much more at this point. He steeled himself to make the effort. "I should have left more candles on," he murmured regretfully against her brow.

"Candles?" she repeated dreamily.

"I was thinking of trying one of your aunt Maud's ungodly positions out, but it hardly seems worth the effort when our bedchamber is so dark." Jane's expression changed so swiftly from blissful to disapproving that he almost laughed. "How about we get you up on your knees, hmmm?" he suggested.

"My knees?" Jane sounded uncertain, so he kissed her brow and helped maneuver her upright. "That's it, now bend forward and rest your elbows against the bed."

"A-Alisander!" she protested, clearly thinking that presenting herself arse-up was undignified. "This can't be right." Still, he noticed with a thrill how obediently she remained as he had arranged her, facing the foot of the bed.

He ran his hands over her pert backside. "Oh, I don't know, it feels pretty right to me," he purred.

"Where is the drawing? Do you have it to hand?" she asked suspiciously as though she would like to consult it, and he had to stifle his laugh.

"I forget where I put it," he lied. "I feel sure we can work it out."

"I don't know…" Jane started but abruptly stopped when dropped his braies and came up flush behind her, rubbing his hard cock against her sex.

"You see," he coaxed, "this would work."

"Um." Jane's voice sounded strained. "Yes, I suppose…" She trailed off. "But—*oh!*" The tip had lodged just right.

Alisander closed his eyes and breathed out, gripping her hips hard and halting his progress. "Yes? No? How do we feel?"

"Well," Jane huffed, trying instinctively to move her hips against him to encourage his entry. *Naughty Jane.* "We—we could try it, I suppose."

"Excellent." He gave a hard buck of his hips and began to slide into her tight, slick channel. He grunted so loud with the relief of it that he almost drowned out her own moan. "Ughh, Jane," he groaned. "What *would* your aunt say?"

"We—we won't tell her," she wheezed, and *oh my gods*, he felt her push back against him. She wanted more. She wanted *harder*. Of course, that meant he had to do just the opposite.

"I shall be very gentle, my dove," he vowed. "I would hate to overwhelm you with the lewdness of this position."

Jane was silent a moment as he tested his own patience with only the shallowest and lightest of dips against the fullness of her backside. This way he would last longer inside her, he consoled himself. He watched Jane clutch and twist the bedsheets beneath her hands.

"Oh," she panted, moving more firmly against him. Almost briskly, one might say.

"Jane," he said warningly, "don't you dare." He narrowed his eyes, feeling her sheath start to flutter and clench around his cock.

"Ohhh," she sobbed softly, her head dropping down. "Oh, I can't—I can't stop!"

"Are you even trying?" he asked silkily as her sweet cunt tightened its grip on him until she had him biting back an urge to moan of his own. He ought to pull out. That would serve her right, but he did not *quite* have that much self-control. His dick would likely fall off in disappointment if he did that, in any case.

"You bad girl," he said in awe as Jane went tense and shuddered all around him. "Oh, you bad, *bad* girl." But he could not keep the note of approval from his voice. He did not sound remotely displeased. Jane sobbed through her release as he rubbed his hand up and down her spine.

All that pleasure, just from having him inside her, he marveled. He was impressed as hell with himself that he had not snapped and spilled deep within her by this point. Once her breathing had evened out and she stopped shuddering, he asked, solicitously, "All better now?"

Jane nodded, a catch in her voice. "Yes."

He tutted. "Really, Jane, I wanted us to peak together."

"I—I'm sorry," she breathed out unevenly.

"Don't be sorry," he said kindly. "But I am going to punish you now."

"Punish me?" Jane's head snapped up. "But—"

"Yes, and in order to make it up to me, we are going to try another of those wicked positions."

Jane made a stifled noise as he pulled out of her and then flipped her over onto her back. She blinked up at him a moment before he seized the backs of her knees and pushed them over her shoulders, pinning them to the mattress.

He had to bite his lip. "*Fuck*, Jane, if you could see yourself..."

"See myself?" she exclaimed. "I can hardly—" She broke off as he nestled the fat tip of his cock between her swollen folds. They were so wet and juicy now; he could not help but groan with pleasure.

"My cock wants to come inside, Jane," he rasped crudely. "Tell him he's welcome."

Jane's expression wavered, her desperate eyes searching his face. She looked thoroughly scandalized, though how she managed it, splayed out so indecently before him, he would never know. He licked his lips. "Say it, Jane," he grunted, watching a milky drop form at his cockhead and leak into her glistening slit.

"He's welcome," she repeated, looking utterly horrified at what she was saying. It should fill him with laughter, rather than lust. In truth, his chest was filled with both. No wonder it was burning. He shoved his way inside her, groaning at the pleasure of her tight, wet welcome.

371

"That's it; take me, wife," he grunted, thrusting deep. Jane's mouth formed a startled *oh*. It wasn't enough. He wanted to hear it. "Oh *fuck*, it's good. It's so good," he groaned. "Tell me it's good for you, Jane," he urged, thrusting against her. Her shoulders were pinned so thoroughly to the mattress that she could really do nothing but take his pummeling strokes.

"Yes, y-yes, it's good," she whimpered, her eyes drifting shut. Suddenly they flew open, and he drowned in their topaz depths as he felt her whole body convulse around him. His own orgasm rolled through him with devastating force.

"*Holy fuck*," he whispered once he could catch his breath. Jane was still softly sobbing as their bodies trembled together. "I'm sorry, my dove," he babbled, collapsing onto his back and pulling her on top of him. He rearranged her limp body over his. His sated cock slipped out of her, even though he didn't really want to leave.

"I'm sorry; don't cry." He brushed light kisses around her face. Releasing the clasp of her choker, he cast it aside and gathered her to him. Jane wept faintly on his chest.

"Oh, my sweet, sweet dove. My angel," he murmured and other such nonsense.

When he found tears on her cheeks, his heart turned over. "Oh Jane, my sweet Jane. Let me. Shhhhh." He didn't even know what he was saying by this point. She wasn't trying to turn away from him or push him away. She lay perfectly willing in his arms, but still, he wanted to comfort her. "Jane, you were *magnificent*. Gods, I've never come like that before. Not ever." He stroked her back. "Tell me you're well."

She turned her head and kissed him, lightly just to the left of his lips. Just a closemouthed kiss, and he felt his heart turn over. "Jane," he whispered. Hesitantly, she lifted her eyes to meet his.

Oh gods, no. Why did he feel like this? His chest felt so full, he could scarce draw breath. "Kiss me," he heard himself beg her. She turned her face toward his and pressed her lips to his. Just a chaste kiss. The chastest, closemouthed kiss, and he felt like his lungs were going to explode. If he didn't catch his breath soon, he was going to black out.

Why the fuck couldn't he catch his breath?

23

Perhaps, not surprisingly, they overslept the next morn. Jane woke only when Wat brought in the washing water and lit the fire. After he had departed, Alisander had pulled her into his arms, and she had fallen back into a deep sleep from which she had not awakened until there was a second knock.

This time, Jane woke with a start and rubbed her eyes blearily as Wat apologetically explained that Marta had arrived to dress her. Jane gasped and threw her legs over the side of the bed. Mercifully, her shift was still intact. "I am not even washed!" she exclaimed as Alisander grumbled and rolled onto his side. "Please ask Marta to grant me a few moments' respite."

Her thoughts scrambled desperately. "Could you bring us more hot water in a second basin, Wat? I'm afraid your master must repair to his dressing room for his ablutions." She turned back to Alisander. "My lord, you must awake!" she urged, shaking his shoulder. "I need you to make yourself scarce."

He opened an eyelid at that. "Make myself scarce?" he repeated. "From my own bedchamber?"

"I cannot wash and dress with you lying here abed!"

"Of course you could, Jane," he disagreed, but sat up and yawned all the same. "Am I to understand you are banishing me from proceedings?"

Jane eyed him nervously. "You are far too distracting," she confessed. "I need to be quiet and calm to ready myself and— and you are quite naked under that sheet, my lord!" she said, wishing she could comment on such a thing without her cheeks turning hot.

"Ah, I *see*. You do not wish this Marta to see what a fine, virile specimen you have in your bed. Well, that is understandable." He nodded. "I will indulge your wish to jealously stand guard over me, wife."

Jane pressed her lips together, willing herself to remain calm. She could see the gleam in his eye already. "You are very accommodating, my lord," she replied in her most dampening voice.

"I am," he agreed. "Fetch me my robe, would you?" He nodded toward the chair in the corner, and Jane made haste to fetch it for him, wincing over the first few steps. There was a deep ache in her thighs from where he had mercilessly stretched them the previous night. Her face turned scarlet at the memory.

Turning back, she masked her discomfort and presented the robe to him. Instead of taking it, he caught her wrist instead, spinning her around and drawing her down to sit into the V of his thighs. "You seem a little stiff this morning, Jane," he commented softly against her ear. "Are you sure you would not like me to give you a nice hard rubdown here to counter the soreness?" He ran his palms firmly over her thighs, almost drawing a sigh from her lips.

"We do not have the time," Jane answered regretfully, instead of lying that her limbs were not remotely stiff, as dignity would dictate. His body felt so nice and warm against her own that she had the oddest impulse to curl into his lap and cry off her return to courtier's duties altogether. What was wrong with her?

"We could make time," he suggested, his lips skimming her neck, his stroking hands becoming a caress of her hips.

She was disgracefully tempted but managed to shake her head with effort. "We told Marta ten o'clock, and I am not her only mistress. It would be most inconsiderate of me to delay her now."

He sighed. "Such a dutiful subject to your Queen," he murmured. "I wish you were half as dutiful toward your husband." Jane's face fell, and he said quickly, "I'm only teasing; don't look like that," and dropped a kiss to her cheek before urging her up to her feet and donning his robe.

She had no idea why her heart had plummeted at his words, but she was left feeling strangely disorientated as he disappeared into his dressing room. Jane washed and Marta dressed her exactly as they had practiced the previous day, with the decorated circlet on her head and her braids arranged so prettily around it. Despite their careful preparations, Jane was sadly distracted the whole while.

Marta added the final touch, an extremely scanty veil, and Jane turned to look at herself in the looking glass. The amethyst necklace sparkled at her throat, casting a pinkish glow over her skin and the blue gray of her gown. She was still not entirely convinced about Alisander's vision. To her mind, she looked somewhat insubstantial and almost…wraithlike.

Her whole life she had been considered a pale shadow of her much more vibrant sister. This look almost seemed to lean into that interpretation. Helen would never have worn such a shade. She would have considered it drab. She would have preferred a velvet of ruby red or a warm amber.

Jane could never think of a gown so sumptuous with its beading and luxurious fabric as drab, but she *did* know it was completely out of step with prevailing tastes. She was going to cut a conspicuous figure as Viscountess Bardulf. Perhaps she should have anticipated as much. "Do you think it looks well?" she asked Marta, biting her lip. The maid did not have the chance to respond, for Alisander emerged at that point from the adjoining room.

He sauntered straight over to her in a dazzling tunic of turquoise and gold. It seemed they were not to match. "What pretty shoulders you have, wife," he said, stopping abruptly before her. Jane blinked. The neckline was high and modest, and her shoulders were the only expanse of skin on view, apart from her neck. Deliberately, he dropped a kiss, first to one exposed shoulder and then the other, making her shiver.

"It was my dress I desired your opinion on, not my shoulders," she said stiffly, feeling horribly conscious of Marta's wide-eyed gaze. She knew for a fact the maid would blab their exchange, down to the smallest detail, to Osanna and Patience.

"Yes, but your shoulders are currently bare and begging for a compliment," he replied nonsensically. "Why is it that you always turn so brittle whenever I pay you a compliment?" he mused. "Is it just me or all admirers you treat so shabbily?"

Jane flushed and darted a glance at the maid. "If I am *brittle*, it is because I do not think your flattery particularly apt, my lord."

"How so?"

"You pay me compliments that do not seem remotely relevant."

"To the situation, you mean?" he asked in puzzlement.

"Relevant to *me*," she corrected him. "My shoulders are not worthy of comment, as well you know. If you paid me a compliment that I could believe for once—"

Alisander rolled his eyes. "Jane, Jane, I really dread to think what manner of compliment you would deem worthy."

She bristled. "I am generally considered very good at organizing matters for the Queen, and—"

He closed his eyes. "She wants me to praise her organization skills, gods above."

The maid giggled, and Jane turned even more stony-faced. "If I am dismissive of your flattery, it is because you told me yourself that seventy percent of your manner is mere affectation."

He smirked. "When did I say that? At Kinnerton?" She nodded. "Sweet of you to hang on my every word," he commented, "but either your memory is at fault or you are willfully misunderstanding me in this instance, Jane. I believe I told you my measure of sincerity is at all times seventy-thirty or thirty-seventy," he reminded her sternly. "In this particular application, I am at least seventy percent sincere."

"I see," Jane replied in clipped tones, though in truth, she was feeling less sure of herself by the minute. "Of course, that still leaves thirty percent to account for."

"Oh, I can account for that easily enough. The measure of insincerity lies in the fact I called your shoulders merely pretty."

Jane made a scoffing sound, resisting the ridiculous impulse to turn and inspect them in the looking glass. She knew full well they were nothing remarkable!

"Will you break your fast now?" he asked. "Or later?"

"I could not possibly eat a morsel."

"Then, by all means, let us make for the Queen's apartments," he suggested blandly, seemingly not noticing how the sentiment made Jane feel quite queasy with nerves.

"I would just like to look in on Celestia before we depart."

"Your maternal impulses do you credit, my dear."

378

After exchanging a few words with Anne and hanging over the sleeping babies for an instant, Jane accepted Alisander's arm, and they made their way down the many flights of steps toward the main wing of the castle.

With each step, Jane's fears seemed to loom ever closer. She had to force her fingers not to dig into her husband's arm. What if the Queen would not even permit her admittance to the presence chamber, let alone the privy chamber? The humiliation would be quite terrible to bear.

"Does the Queen expect me this day?" she asked in a hollow voice.

He shrugged. "I told her I would bring you along when I saw fit and our household could spare you. She knows you have had many adjustments to make."

"And she seemed—receptive to that idea?" Jane asked doubtfully.

"Certainly," he answered blandly, and she realized that Armenal could have expressed no burning enthusiasm to see her.

"Jane, remember what I told you," he warned. "If you act like you have something to be ashamed of then she will react with coolness. She will not be able to resist. Instead, you must be quietly confident and assured in your new estate. You comprehend?"

Jane swallowed. "Yes," she said and took a deep breath. They were now in the main body of the castle and were making their way steadily toward the royal quarters.

"Let us have some conversation now betwixt the two of us. It will help you settle."

379

Jane inclined her head. She could see figures up ahead in full court dress. "Of what shall we speak?"

"Perhaps you should pay me some compliment," he suggested. "It would be good practice for you. You could start with my tunic," he added, "for it is new."

Jane's eyes wandered over the garment, and she winced slightly. It only reached down to his waist and was very tight. She could only suppose the many slits over the chest and sleeves were to allow free movement—that and to give everyone a chance to see the fine undershirt he wore beneath it.

"It's very eye-catching," she ventured, "and short."

Alisander smirked. "I know. My sources in Lascony assure me this is the very latest way of wearing them. You have to admit few men have the thighs to carry off this high cut."

"I would not know, not having seen many men's thighs to make a comparison," she admitted before stealing a look at his profile and reddening. She hesitated before asking in a voice of reluctant curiosity, "What sort of thing do you usually like to hear?" Alisander's smile broadened, and Jane added swiftly, "Never mind, forget I asked."

"You cannot really go wrong with flattery," he told her as if she had not spoken the last sentence. "I am a vain creature at heart and fond of all its forms." Jane's mind turned blank.

"I warn you; I shall not escort you to the Queen's chambers until you have flattered me a little," he said, towing her toward a mullioned window. "I am at perfect liberty to remain here all morning, skulking in the outer corridors, buzzing in your ear like an irritating fly."

Jane gazed out at the gray, unpromising February day. "Do you mean to tell me, my lord, that we will tarry here until I can think of a compliment you deem worthy of you?" He inclined his head.

"We cannot just—" She broke off frustratedly, glancing about. "You are expected by the Queen, are you not?"

"I have already told you my terms for proceeding," he reminded her, stifling a yawn.

"You are *impossible*!"

"I am waiting," he corrected her, inspecting his immaculate fingernails.

Jane heard approaching footsteps. "You—! You have vastly beautiful thighs, my lord," she choked out furiously. "Now can we, please, continue on to the Queen?"

Afterward, it did occur to Jane that he might have been deliberately provoking merely to distract her from her nerves. It was true that she was still in a high dudgeon when they had sailed into the presence chamber. Alisander did not so much as pause for the guards there, as though there could be no question of their welcome therein.

Jane had still been flushed from their exchange in the corridor, no doubt her eyes overbright with annoyance. In truth, she had felt more ready for an argument than to pay her respects to her sovereign. She heard her new title announced and made a deep curtsey beside her husband. Then he escorted her to the side of the room.

The Queen made no inclination from her throne that she was desirous of Jane approaching her, so instead, Jane turned to face the oncoming drifts of courtiers, who were approaching two or three at a time. The first of which were her previous roommates, Osanna and Patience.

"Jane!" they exclaimed in hushed but excitable tones. "We were wondering when you would make an appearance!"

"We did ask your husband," Osanna said, lowering her voice, for Alisander was making desultory conversation now with Lord Wrothby.

"But he was not forthcoming," Patience concluded. "He *does* like to cultivate an air of mystery, does he not?" She sounded faintly resentful of the fact.

"How was the country?" Osanna asked hastily. "And your sweet little baby?"

Jane fought down her instinctively awkward response. "Our child is quite well, I thank you, and Kinnerton will be more inviting in the spring, I am sure."

"We have found a taker for your old room," Patience confided. "You will never guess who." When Jane looked blank, she launched into an account of a falling out between Lucy Melvin and Estrilda Rheinholdt, which had necessitated one of them changing living quarters.

It was a convoluted tale, many of the finer points never being fully explained and consisting of such vagaries as "Lucy maintained that the hair comb was already cracked," and "Of course, strictly speaking, the lock of hair did not really belong to either of them."

Afterward, Jane could not even have said precisely which of the maidens was now residing in her old room, for halfway through the epic retelling she glanced at the Queen and found her staring at her intently. Jane smiled and bobbed a curtsey, then determinedly focused on whatever it was Patience was twittering on about. Or, at least, giving an appearance of it, for by this point, she was hopelessly lost in the narrative.

She had to wait for only three minutes when a discreet cough sounded behind her. Turning, she found the Queen's favorite squire, Piers Winstanley, hovering politely. Really, the boy was getting ridiculously tall. "The Queen would like a word, Lady Bardulf," he said with a pleasant smile. Jane excused herself from Osanna and Patience, who exchanged meaningful glances, and followed Piers back to the dais.

"Ah, there you are, Jane," the Queen said breezily, holding out her jeweled hand. Jane duly curtseyed. "Approach, approach, I hardly think we need stand on ceremony here." She turned to Mistress Bartree. "Magnatrude, perhaps you could look into that little matter we discussed earlier." Magnatrude Bartree looked rather blank at this request but curtscyed all the same and retreated with dignity.

"You are looking well, Jane, I think," the Queen said, looking her up and down critically. "I see the evidence of your husband's hand upon you, but it is subtle. He is clever enough to enhance rather than deter from your essence."

Jane started to color at the mention of "evidence," her hand flying to her bosom where she knew there lingered some telltale signs of Alisander's attentions. *Of course*, she thought, relaxing once her fingers landed on the heavy beading, nothing was on view. The Queen was just referring to her new style of clothing.

"Thank you, Your Majesty," she said, dropping her hand, her composure returned. "Lord Bardulf has proved a most generous spouse."

"That is quite a necklace," the Queen agreed, eyeing the amethysts at her throat. "He has always had a good eye for jewels, that one. You do not find the price you must pay too onerous?"

"The price?"

The Queen gave her a wry look. "I refer, of course, to the keeping of a husband."

"Oh." Jane considered this a moment with a thoughtful frown. "Well, it comes with its own attendant challenges," she admitted, and the Queen's lips twisted into a wry smile.

"Indeed, it does," she agreed, her gaze skittering away to dwell on the far side of the room. "And how are you finding motherhood?" Her words were cool. "The child is well, I trust?"

"She thrives." Jane kept her expression carefully neutral. "Though, I could not be easy leaving her in the country. We have brought her to the palace with us."

The Queen's eyebrows shot up, but she made no comment on this. "Where is your husband anyway? At least he is not one of those that *hovers*. Some of these knights…" She shuddered eloquently. "You can hardly be rid of their hulking, great presences when their wives are in attendance.

"I make no mention of names," she added darkly, "but really, *some* of them are quite insupportable! There is a time and a place, my dear Jane, for husbands; I am sure you agree. At least you will not suffer the indignity of having yours always underfoot."

Jane half turned toward the drifting crowd in the presence chamber. You could hardly miss Alisander, she reflected wryly, not in *that* outfit. She could only suppose the Queen was making a sly dig about him not dancing constant attendance on her like a devoted spouse would. "Quite," she said simply. "He is over yonder talking with Lady Wymarka Kloch."

"Dear Wymarka," the Queen mused. "She is very attractive, is she not?"

384

"Very," Jane agreed automatically, though, in truth, she had always thought that lady's odd manner and huge eyebrows rather off-putting. Alisander had his head bent slightly as he listened to whatever she was regaling him with. Likely some omen or portent, knowing Wymarka. As though becoming aware of their scrutiny, he suddenly lifted his gaze to clash with theirs, and Jane turned hurriedly back.

"I must admit to some curiosity as to how you have been dealing with one another," the Queen said wistfully. "Things have been somewhat dreary here at court. You will have heard no doubt about Bathilde ailing."

"Oh yes," Jane agreed. "Very sad."

"It is sad, I suppose," the Queen mused, "but she is a very old woman, Jane. And one, moreover, who has lived a useful life." Jane gave some murmur of agreement, though in truth, she was distracted seeing Alisander drift away from Lady Wymarka and start heading in their direction.

"The King has spent the past three days at her bedside," Queen Armenal continued. Jane noticed she sounded baffled by his vigil. Seeing Jane's enquiring look, she said, "For some reason, Wymer has always hankered for the closeness a lowborn child shares with its mother. In our country the distinctions are preserved better. But there! We are not in fair Lascony," she sighed, "but barbarous Karadok, more is the pity!"

Jane was somewhat surprised by this outburst. She had never heard the Queen express herself thus before. Was she now to be privy to such talk, purely because she was married to a Lasconian? Jane had never felt in less sympathy with King Wymer, though privately, she did not wonder that he should be attached to his nurse.

Now she came to think of it, would Celestia not always hold a special affection for Anne when she grew older? It seemed perfectly natural that it should be so. "You must have had a nurse yourself, Your Highness," she asked with a frown.

"But yes, I had a nurse," Queen Armenal said dismissively. "My sisters and I shared three. Admirable women, every one of them. I have no idea what became of them though. Doubtless, they carried on with the instruction of many children, until one day they grew too old for such things."

"Bathilde stayed with the King though, did she not? She was an ever-fixed point and constant in his life."

"Yes," the Queen agreed testily, "but that in itself is odd, you will agree!" She turned impulsively toward Alisander, who had come to a quiet stop beside Jane. "Viscount Bardulf, you must bear me out in this matter."

"Dear me," he said, looking between the two of them. "You are having some difference of opinion?"

"You are my countryman, and will doubtless have the same outlook as I," the Queen said, shooting a smug look at Jane. "Tell me, did you have a nurse growing up?"

"I don't remember," he replied, taking both the Queen and Jane aback.

"You do not remember?" the Queen cried. "Exasperating creature!"

Jane narrowed her eyes at him. She found she simply did not believe him.

"That is to say, I remember a young woman who would swing me up into her arms and sing to me," he admitted. "She had

386

long black hair and dark laughing eyes, but she ran off with a groom before I was even in breeches."

The Queen nodded. "Doubtless it was for the best. She sounds most ill-suited for the raising of children. No, Jane and I were discussing quite a different sort of creature. The sensible and solid nurse, with the face of a sheep."

"Ah," he said, enlightenment dawning. "You are speaking of Bathilde. Has she yet shuffled off this mortal coil?"

"Not yet," the Queen answered. "And until she does, Wymer will be quite inconsolable."

"I imagine he will be even more so, once she does," Alisander murmured, shooting a look at Jane.

"What?" The Queen looked considerably taken aback. "Then, you think all this current grief—?"

"Is merely an appetizer to the main course, yes," Alisander finished off swiftly.

Queen Armenal slumped back in her seat, looking appalled. "But this is quite insupportable," she complained.

Alisander cast a speculative look her way. "Your Majesty, why do you not choose to look upon this more as an opportunity than an inconvenience?"

Jane and the Queen both looked at each other and then at him. "How so, my good Bardulf?" the Queen asked cautiously.

"Well, with Bathilde gone, there will be a vast gaping hole in the fabric of the King's existence. As we all know, nature abhors a vacuum." When they continued to look at him blankly, he sighed. "In time, someone else will step forward to fill that gap as confidante and favorite to the King."

The Queen gave a short laugh. "But of course they will," she said contemptuously. "And I think we all know what form they will take, do we not?" Her lip curled. "That of royal bedwarmer."

Jane had to work very hard not to show her unease with the subject, but it did hit rather uncomfortably close to home.

"Not necessarily," Alisander said with a shrug. "The King has never lacked for a bedwarmer, but they have never fulfilled any larger purpose in his life. We all know it was Bathilde to whom he went when he found himself in need of genuine affection and support."

The Queen gave a mirthless smile. "You think I am unaware of the fact? You are wrong. None knew so well the role that Bathilde has filled all these years as I."

"I am sure," Alisander murmured placatingly. "But I could, by far, see him turning toward some other trusted female presence in his life than I could some passing fancy." He paused. "He has always split affection from desire, this Argent King."

Jane noticed the Queen sit up a little straighter. "You think, then…that the King…" She hesitated, then gave a quick shake of her head. "But no! This is nonsense, there *is* no other woman in his life he trusts!"

Alisander tipped his head. "I was thinking of the princess, your pardon, I mean, of course, the *Lady* Una, his royal cousin," he said softly.

Two spots of color appeared in the Queen's cheeks. "*Una?*" she repeated sharply.

Alisander nodded. "But yes. He has grown touchingly fond of her of late, has he not? Since her marriage to that good-looking brute, de Bussell. Does he not now call her 'cousin' and fuss

388

over her visits, as though she were some great dignitary instead of a deposed rival to his throne?"

Jane could see the Queen was rattled by this argument, though she was trying not to show it. There was no denying the truth to his words. King Wymer had more than mellowed in his feeling toward the northern princess. She was now a great favorite in his eyes.

"Pffft!" Armenal said, rallying and waving a hand. "At least *half* of the King's attentiveness is down to his inordinate fondness for de Bussell. He was always strongly prejudiced in his favor. I have sometimes wondered if Sir Armand might not be the very first of Wymer's bastards."

Jane had to smother her gasp. The Queen nodded sagely. "But yes, it would account, would it not, for his bias. It is true, he would have been very young at the time to have sired him, but it is not unheard of. There are certain rumors about Sir Armand's mother, if you poke in the right corners. She was wildly popular at court in her youth and her retreat to the country was both sudden and unexpected." The Queen looked arch. "It was all before my time, of course."

"If so, de Bussell must have inherited his looks from his mother," Alisander pondered aloud, and Jane thought of the tall and dark Sir Armand in contrast to King Wymer, who was fair-haired and blue-eyed and of middling height.

"It is sometimes the way," the Queen said dismissively, resting her chin upon her hand. She was sunk in thoughtful silence for a while. "There is perhaps something in what you say, Lord Bardulf," she conceded at last. "I must think it over, and we will have some further discussion at a later point."

"But of course, my Queen," Alisander agreed airily, as though he had all but forgotten what they had been talking about.

389

It was a dismissal, Jane realized, as the Queen lifted a hand and Magnatrude Bartree hurried forward from her spot. She must have been waiting with bated breath for the summons, Jane thought sourly. Alisander turned to her and presented his arm. She took it and let herself be led away in a leisurely stroll around the grand chamber.

Jane felt strangely troubled by the interaction. It was not that she hadn't seen Alisander enacting similar scenes dozens of times before. She had seen him stir the pot on countless occasions. No, she was not really sure why she felt so uneasy watching him operate his wiles on the Queen at such close quarters.

Perhaps it was because, before now, she had thought him merely an aimless troublemaker, whereas now she suspected his every word and action had some ulterior motive. Was it part of his being a diplomat? she wondered. She stole a sidelong look at him.

"You are quiet, Jane," he murmured, his eyes wandering over the rest of the room as they walked.

"Yes," she admitted. "The Queen was…different with me, somehow." She hesitated, unsure how to explain her feeling. "Before you came along, she was speaking of the Western Isles and how much she misses it."

He snorted. "The Queen likes to sigh over her homeland when it suits her," he said dryly, "but I do not believe she misses it overmuch. There, she was one princess among many. She commands far more respect here as Wymer's Queen Consort than she ever held as Wilhelm's third sister."

Jane digested this for a moment. "Why *did* you suggest…what you suggested to the Queen?"

"And just what was it I suggested?" he asked, raising an eyebrow quizzically.

"Well, that she looks to bridge the gap that will be left in the King's life by Bathilde."

"Is that how you interpreted my words?" he asked, looking faintly surprised.

"It is how anyone would with half a brain," Jane responded irritably. "You even warned her that if she did not, someone else would!"

His lips turned up at one corner. "Tell me, do you think she will heed my warning?" he asked, his eyes snapping to meet hers for the first time.

Jane hesitated to consider this. "Yes," she said grudgingly. "You scared her badly by suggesting the King would grow closer still to the Lady Una."

"I do not know that she was *scared*, precisely." He smirked. "But she certainly did not like the notion."

"You knew exactly how to manipulate her," Jane said accusingly. "I never realized before what a consummate schemer you are."

"Shhhh," he cautioned. "My dear, oblige me by keeping your voice low and sweet or others may also learn my true nature. We should not want that, now, would we?"

Jane found herself scanning the room to make sure they were not observed. "Why are you letting *me* see it now? Because I am your wife?" she asked. Before he could speak, she added awkwardly, "I am still a true subject of this land, Alisander."

He looked amused. "My dear Jane, do you imagine that anything I said was remotely treasonous? I merely suggested to

391

the Queen that she seeks a closer relationship with the King. Wherein lies the fault with that? Should not every wife strive to fulfill such a role in her husband's life?"

"I suppose," Jane replied, frowning. "But I do not think that is why you are urging it."

He inclined his head as though acknowledging the truth of this. "As the ambassador of the Western Isles, it is in my interest to ensure the Queen remains relevant here in Karadok," he said reasonably. "Queen Armenal is not the mother of Wymer's heir. Making every effort to strengthen her position seems a sensible proposition, does it not?"

When Jane remained unconvinced, he sighed. "Would it make you feel any easier in your mind if I told you this suggestion originated with the King's highest advisor himself?"

Jane was startled. "Lord Vawdrey?" she whispered. "He suggested it to you?"

He nodded a glimmer of amusement in his eye. "And if anyone has Karadok's best interests at heart, it is he. You agree?"

Jane nodded slowly. "But the Queen is not at all fond of Earl Vawdrey," she pointed out, "and I am sure he is aware of the fact. Why would he suggest she make herself indispensable to the King?"

Alisander shrugged. "Because," he said, "if Wymer is to have a foreign interest whispering in his ear, Vawdrey would rather it was the devil he knows. This impending 'vacancy' in the King's inner circle puts him in a vulnerable position. Even as we speak, jackals circle, ready to pounce."

Jackals? The image was rather an alarming one. As though noticing her perturbation, Alisander halted before an alcove and led her into it. "And quite besides all that," he concluded,

"Vawdrey is a traditionalist. He believes in the sanctity of marriage."

Jane considered this. "Lord Vawdrey is a most devoted husband, I believe."

"Oh, very much so. No one who has seen him with his countess could ever doubt that fact."

"Hmmm," Jane pondered. Her fears were somewhat allayed, she found, in spite of herself. She liked Fenella Vawdrey very much and only wished the lady spent more time at court. Instead, with two young sons, she attended infrequently these days.

Seeing how intently her husband was regarding her, now they were sheltered from everyone's view, Jane made haste to rouse herself from her thoughts. He was not going to kiss her, was he? Seeing the gleam in his eye, she felt a lurch of alarm. "You will not tell the Queen that your idea originated with Lord Vawdrey?" she asked in an attempt to distract him.

"Gods, no!" He pulled a face. "As you say, she thinks Vawdrey has too much influence at court already. It would simply set her against the idea." He took a step forward, effectively pinning Jane against the recessed wall.

"My lord!" she protested breathlessly.

"Yes, Jane?"

"This is—well—it is highly improper!"

"Is it? How can it be? We are married, are we not?"

"Yes, but—"

"How, then, can there be any impropriety?"

"We are in the Queen's quarters!"

"Does her presence chamber really count?" he scoffed, placing a hand over her breast—her modestly covered breast—but all the same, she could feel his hand there, and it was affecting her ability to breathe. "Any rabble is admitted these days, I find," he said dismissively.

"Rabble that could discover us at any moment!" she pointed out in scandalized tones.

"Then you must keep a lookout, wife, and ensure such a terrible fate does not befall us." Jane tore her panicked gaze from his to stare over his shoulder at the portion of the room she could make out. His face was so close to hers; she could feel his breath on her cheek as he spoke. "You look so pretty, Jane, I cannot stand it. You must take pity on me and let me have a taste of your lips."

Jane's resolve instantly wavered. In truth, he did sound a little tortured. She ventured a quick look at his face to judge his sincerity. It was a mistake. Instantly, his mouth was upon hers, their breath mingling. His lips were firm and insistent, arrogantly sure of their right to take her own, in spite of his beseeching words. Instead of repulsing him, as she ought, Jane melted into him, parting her lips in an invitation he was not slow to take up, and Jane was instantly lost.

When she surfaced moments later, he was holding her firmly upright as she sagged against him. "Jane," he murmured, and she could hear the laughter in his voice. "Your eyes are closed. You are supposed to be keeping a watchful eye."

She whimpered, and he tightened his arms about her. "Shall I say you have been taken faint?" he suggested. "Carry you out of here and back to our chambers and lay you down so I can take care of you properly? Hmmmm?" To her shock, he sounded quite pleased with the idea. Also, she had a very clear notion of what he meant by "take care of her properly." "What do you say, Jane?" he wheedled, kissing her hot neck.

"No, no, you cannot!" she moaned.

"Why can I not?"

"Everyone will stare! Please, Alisander, please!" she begged, realizing her first argument would hold no sway with him. "I could not *bear* it." She made no conscious choice to break out the tears, but her eyes filled with them anyway, and she clutched at him like a supplicant.

He swore softly, cupping her heated cheek. "Jane, you take advantage of my weakness for you," he said sternly. "My idea is a good one. Why can I not?"

She could not even argue, just shook her head as a tear tracked down her cheek and over his fingers. Why did he always inspire such strong feelings in her? It alarmed her, after all the years she had spent privately thinking herself superior to those emotional types, always in the grip of their feelings. She had always prided herself on her privacy and reserve. Yet, here she was, ridiculously swayed by a kiss, her composure quite shaken.

Could it be partly her grief still at work? Helen's death had churned her up something dreadfully, but she did not think it could fully account for the way all her defenses crumpled with just his kiss. "You should not play your games with me," she whispered. "I am not adept in them."

His thumb swiped over her cheek, caressing her there. "Shhh, be calm, wife," he murmured. "I will not do anything you would not like." She relaxed at his words in spite of herself. His grip on her became solicitous, rather than amorous. He sighed against her hair, then turned them about so he was against the wall and looking outward.

"Breathe evenly," he instructed, shifting her weight onto his one arm. "Take this. Wipe your eyes, then blow your nose."

Jane's hand groped for the kerchief he passed her. "Now brace yourself," he murmured. "Lady Gilchrist approaches."

It was strange, Jane reflected, steeling herself at the approach of the perfectly pleasant Lady Gilchrist. A month ago, she would have preferred a tête-à-tête with the lady over Lord Bardulf any day. Now she rather resented her intrusion.

Squaring her shoulders, Jane allowed herself to be shepherded back out of the alcove. "Feeling better now?" he murmured, as though for all the world she had suffered a coughing fit rather than a kissing.

"Er, yes," Jane managed to respond before Lady Gilchrist was upon them. She tugged slightly at his hand which was still at her waist, but he did not remove it.

"I am so glad to happen upon you!" the newcomer exclaimed, her eyes alighting with interest on their clasped hands. "But dear me, does something ail Lady Bardulf?"

"Why, nothing at all," Alisander assured her urbanely. "She has merely been overcome with a sneezing fit."

"Oh, so tiresome!" Lady Gilchrist sympathized. "My cousin used to suffer dreadfully in the summertime."

"How is Sir Neville?" Jane asked, remembering the name of said cousin. "I hear he has been lately indisposed. It seems an age since he was at court. We have all missed his beautiful singing voice." Alisander tensed beside her, and she sent him a quizzical glance.

396

"Oh, poor Neville," Lady Gilchrist sighed. "He has always been sickly, since quite a child." She spent the next ten minutes listing her unfortunate cousin's complaints, along with the fears of his fond mother, her aunt. Jane duly tutted and sympathized, agreeing that, yes, poor health was a terrible affliction.

Lady Gilchrist hesitated a moment before moving away. "I was so sorry to hear about your sister, my dear," she said, pressing Jane's hand.

Jane's breath caught in her throat. She had not received many commiserations on Helen's death. "Thank you," she managed to return, squeezing Alisander's fingers in a deathly grip before she could stop herself.

"I had no idea you were so fond of Neville Wycliffe," he commented blandly, drawing her hand through his arm before leading her toward the center of the room where the largest crowd was gathered.

"Fond?" Jane turned her head. "Nothing of the sort. He has a pleasant voice and nice manners, that is all."

"It is his brother, Sir James, who is considered the more impressive of the two, I believe, though I seem to remember that you thought his legs unimpressive clad in hose."

Jane spluttered. "I? Why, I have never even mentioned them! 'Twas *you* who cast aspersions on his calves, as I recall."

"In any case, stop changing the subject, wife."

"Which subject is it we have strayed from?"

"Whether or not I need to add Sir Neville to the ranks?"

"Ranks, what ranks?" Jane asked in bewilderment.

"Those of your erstwhile suitors, my dear, along with Rodrey Morpington."

Jane gazed at him blankly a moment before looking away. She felt a strange rush of disappointment that he would try to needle her this way. "Why are you being so disagreeable suddenly?" she asked with a slight catch to her voice.

"Because I am jealous, Jane. Is it not obvious?"

"Jealous?" She whipped her head back around to look at him. She had never imagined that he would suffer from such a thing. "Are you still teasing me?" she asked abruptly, pulling on his arm to halt their progress toward the others.

"Right now?" he answered, swinging about to face her. "No."

Now that she examined his face, he did look rather annoyed. "Sir Neville must be a good five years younger than I," she protested.

"What has that to do with anything?" he asked. "He is the boyish sort ladies like to make a pet of and fuss over."

"Well, yes he is," she admitted, "but I have never admired that type."

"No, you would be more likely to admire his brother," he said waspishly. "The honorable Sir James."

Jane's eyes widened. "You *are* jealous, aren't you?" she breathed in astonishment.

"Yes, I am," he said curtly. "And let me tell you, wife, it is a singularly unpleasant experience. It makes me feel *quite* out of sorts and like I want to be revenged on you."

Jane pondered this a moment, her heart sinking. "You mean, by flirting with another lady?" she asked carefully, avoiding his eye.

He reached out and touched her cheek, a strange expression on his face. "No," he said at last. "I mean by dragging you back into that alcove." He darted his eyes in that direction. "And reducing you once more to a pretty little wanton."

Jane shivered slightly. "Can you not wait until we return to our rooms?" she suggested, heat creeping into her face.

"Not really, but I suppose I will have to."

Hearing the murmur of voices, Jane slowly became aware of the fact that heads were turning in their direction. She swallowed. "My lord...?" She faltered.

"I know," he sighed, then muttered something Jane did not quite catch. Afterward, she thought it had been something like, "*Fuck*, I think they will be able to tell after all," but she could not be sure.

The morning passed in a whirl of constant social encounters. Everyone seemed curious to look them over in the light of their recent marriage. Jane received many compliments on her appearance, and several curious ladies asked after the beading at her sleeves and bodice.

"Is it vines, twining about one another?" Constance Northcott had asked doubtfully.

"Silly, it is serpents," Emma Thackeray informed her. Emma was pleased to be in the positon to correct someone else for once.

"I think vines would be nicer," Constance had retorted. "I believe I shall have my next bodice beaded all over with vines."

399

"I have long been considering something similar myself," Emma said airily. "I remarked as much, only last week."

Constance opened her mouth and then closed it again. "Oh, so have I," she said hurriedly. "For simply ages."

Jane resisted the overwhelming urge to look about and see where Alisander had got to. At several points during the morning, he had slipped away from her side and reappeared just as seamlessly without remark. If anyone was asked later, they would doubtless describe him as having been at her side the whole time.

It was quite a feat, considering his ostentatious appearance. He seemed, to Jane, to weave in and out of the crowds with such little apparent effort. Jane kept to the outer chamber, but she would not have been surprised to hear he had slipped between all three of the Queen's rooms at will. Had she never noticed before how skillfully he navigated the palace?

"My dear," he murmured, and Jane gave a start, for she had not noticed he had returned. "Shall we repair to the banqueting chamber for some refreshment?"

She had acquiesced readily enough, but even there, she found her husband frequently vanished from his spot on the bench beside her. He would reappear periodically with another goblet of wine for her, or perhaps a freshly replenished dish, but Jane very much doubted that had been his quest when he originally disappeared.

She would have to keep an eye on him, she decided, and she really did try as the week progressed. The trouble was, he was clearly very practiced at it. Oftentimes, he would take off altogether for some official meeting or other. On at least one of those occasions, he had told her he was meeting with a certain ambassador who she had later seen elsewhere.

He did not even blush when she informed him as much that same evening as they readied themselves for a private supper with Lord and Lady Marchmont. "At the Queen's reception, you say?" he mused, looking up from strapping on his belt. "I *wondered* where he got to. Such a rude fellow. Never sent so much as a word of apology and kept me waiting a good two hours. No manners whatsoever."

Jane had narrowed her eyes at him but held her tongue for Marta was dressing her hair.

"Marta," he said, unfastening his belt. "Could you return in an hour's time?"

Marta lowered her comb and Jane half turned in her seat. "Why need Marta return in an hour?" she asked in growing bewilderment. "As you see, I am already dressed for dinner and either Patience or Osanna may have need of her by then."

"Because I mean to undress you," he replied forthrightly. "And to mess up your hair." He flipped a coin at the girl, who smartly caught it and hurried toward the door.

"I'll be back in an hour, milady," Marta assured her over her shoulder.

Jane's face was bright red by this point. "Must you be so wretchedly provoking all the time?" she fumed as soon as the door closed behind her. "I know full well that you do not have the slightest intention—" He dropped down onto the low seat beside her, pulling her into his arms.

"Jane, my darling, you do not have the first clue," he said and then sealed his lips to hers. It seemed a strange thing to Jane, but if she did not know better, she might even have thought he enjoyed the idea of her stalking his every step. One minute she would think she was being entirely discreet over it, and the next she had a horrible feeling he was fully aware of her scrutiny.

In the aftermath of their passion, she let her mind wander over the conclusions she had drawn thus far. If it was Lord Bardulf who traversed the royal chambers with such consummate skill, then it was surely Alisander de Balon who had just ravished her within an inch of her life.

His one eye flickered open. "Stop huffing, wife, and come closer. I want to take a nap."

"A nap?" Jane went up on one elbow. "Is it possible you have forgotten we have a supper to attend this evening?"

"I have forgotten nothing. We will be fashionably late."

"I have always prided myself on my punctuality," Jane tutted, even as she shuffled closer toward him.

"Of course you have." He yawned, slipping an arm about her shoulders. "I encourage you to lay the blame firmly at my door."

"Oh, I intend to!"

"Is there some reason you are withholding your own embrace?"

Jane glanced up at him. "You mean—?" Hesitantly, she placed her arm about his waist.

"That's better."

Jane lowered her head to his shoulder, her face certainly red again. This felt shockingly intimate. Practically as intimate as the act they had just performed together. Somehow, she had never imagined Lord Bardulf indulging in such things as sleepy embraces with his bedfellows. This surely was Alisander de Balon she was sharing the bed with right now.

24

In all, life at court as a married lady was a vastly different experience to the life Jane had led previously as a single courtier. For one, of course, she was no longer the Queen's favorite. Despite Alisander's optimism about her reclaiming that crown, she was starting to think it would never again be hers.

Strange to say, she did not feel as devastated about that fact as she once would. Instead, she tried to focus on other areas of life at court. Building stronger relationships with her fellow ladies-in-waiting, for one thing.

She still found it so difficult to cultivate friendships, for her reserve was strong. Fortunately, Osanna and Patience, to a slightly lesser extent, seemed to have finally accepted this was her nature and not just her being sadly standoffish.

They would link arms with her and prattle away, even when Jane found herself struggling to respond in a fitting manner to their chatter. This helped her to relax more in their society and even think of a few topics of conversation, which were met with differing measures of success.

She soon found that they were fascinated by any mention of her marriage, however fleeting. Despite showing huge curiosity about the baby, when Jane arranged for them to meet Celestia, they speedily ran out of interest once they had passed her to one another and exclaimed over every tiny feature.

"She does not really look like anyone yet, does she?" Patience had commented, sounding disappointed.

"Not really," Jane concurred. "Though I, too, had dark hair as a baby."

"She must take after you, then," Patience had concluded with a shrug, and Jane had been hugely grateful that neither of them so much as mentioned King Wymer in connection with the child. It strengthened her resolution to be a true friend to them.

"How long before she starts crawling or doing anything of note?" Osanna asked, passing the baby back to Jane.

"I'm not really sure," Jane confessed, "but I should probably return her to her nurse now."

"Yes, do," Osanna agreed cheerfully, "and we can have a nice cozy discussion about Penelope Culmington and the way she has been *carrying on* with Sir Symond Chevenix! And him *practically* betrothed!"

"Ooh yes!" Patience squealed. "Do hurry, Jane. I have much to impart, for I have learned all the latest gossip from Margaret Pryor and, you know, she has *quite* the inside knowledge, for she is from the wretched girl's home county."

It was not until a full three days later, at about three o'clock, that the Queen finally sent for Jane to join her in her inner sanctum. By this point, Jane had all but given up waiting for such a summons. She had been sat with Frances Lessimore, discussing a tapestry project they had agreed to share, when she received the directive from an obliging page.

After excusing herself, Jane made her way into the privy chamber, expecting to find Queen Armenal sat there with a few attendants, but to her surprise, there was no sign of the Queen or her current favorite, Mistress Bartree. Seeing her glance about, Piers Winstanley stepped forward. "The Queen is in her bedchamber, milady. Lord Bardulf is already there. Please walk through and join them; they are expecting you."

The Queen frequently received her closest advisors in her bedchamber. It was considered quite an honor, so Jane was not altogether surprised to hear her husband was attending there. The funny thing was that on entering, she was inordinately pleased to see the bored expression on his handsome face.

He was lolling in a window seat, an open book resting on his knee. When he visibly brightened on her entrance, it gave Jane the strangest sensation of tingling which spread right through her breast. "Your Majesty," she said aloud, ignoring her husband and sinking into a graceful curtsey. The Queen was sat before her looking glass, rifling through her jewelry boxes.

"Ah, Jane," she greeted her. "*There* you are at last. I vow you have been neglecting me. Come and help me choose the right adornment for a quiet supper this evening. The good Bathilde is failing fast now," she said matter-of-factly, "and the King cannot face the banqueting hall."

Jane joined her at once and, after glancing at the Queen's crimson gown, picked out one or two possible pieces at random.

"Not that one, Jane," the Queen said dismissively, waving off a pearl-encrusted brooch. "Pass me the ruby."

Alisander glanced up from his book with a critical frown, and the Queen hesitated. "You think too much red?" she said, holding the ruby to her bosom.

"I would never criticize Her Majesty's choice," he said smoothly, but something about his manner made it quite clear he thought it a mistake.

"Very well, Jane, give me the pearl one," Armenal said irritably. Jane handed over the pearl brooch. Was this really what she had been summoned for? she wondered. It seemed such a trivial matter and surely anyone could have sufficed. Alisander was far better at selecting jewels than she.

"Lord Bardulf and I have been discussing that little matter once more. The one from the other day," the Queen said airily, fiddling with the brooch pin.

"I see," said Jane, though she was a little surprised to be included now in such a discussion. She suspected her presence had been superfluous last time.

"Lord Bardulf believes my way forward an obvious one," the Queen said in somewhat brittle tones. "He thinks it would be in my best interest to consult with *you*, Jane."

"With me?" Jane answered with astonishment. She darted a look at Alisander, who was looking inscrutable as ever. "To what end?"

The Queen gave a short laugh. "Tell her," she instructed him. "Let us see what this wife of yours makes of it."

Alisander sat up, closing his book and setting it on a low table before him. "There is only one way that I can see for the Queen to achieve her aims." He shrugged. "And that is for her to ensure the King falls in love with her."

Queen Armenal paused in the act of surveying herself in her looking glass. She turned from her elegant reflection to regard Jane keenly. "There! What do you think of that, Jane?" she flung at her, and for a moment, Jane thought the Queen was angry, seeing the slight flush on her cheeks.

Then she noted how the Queen's hands kept opening and closing; her usual effortless grace had fled. She seemed agitated. So used was Jane to seeing the Queen of Karadok, all self-assurance and in command of any situation, that it came as quite a shock. It slowly dawned on Jane that the Queen was feeling unsure of herself.

"Why should you not secure the King's love, Your Majesty?" she asked hesitantly. "None is so worthy of it as you." The pearl brooch slipped through the Queen's fingers and fell to the floor. Jane darted forward to retrieve it, handing it back to her.

Recovering swiftly, Armenal pinned it to her bosom and gave a short laugh. "My dear Jane, if I failed to secure Wymer's affections as a tender bride of twenty-two, how in the world would I set about such a thing now, more than a *decade* later?"

Alisander stood up. "I have already told you my thoughts," he said briskly and turned to Jane. "I suggested the Queen consult someone well-practiced in such matters."

His eye dwelt expectantly on Jane, who stood patiently holding the jewelry box. Finally catching his meaning, she started, her eyes growing wide.

"He suggested you might give me some pointers," the Queen said, and Jane was so staggered, she could think of no response. What was he expecting her to do? This was ridiculous! She knew nothing about…about inducing men to fall in love!

"I will leave you to your tutelage, my lady," he said, bowing first to her and then to the Queen before exiting the room.

Of course he *would* exit on such a line after that bow, during which he had held her gaze the whole time. Bowing to her first was a blatant breach of etiquette. As was sauntering from the room after casually implying that he was in love with her. Moreover, that she had somehow *made* him fall in love with her.

Jane's mind was a whirl. It was absurd, she told herself. It was not true; they both knew it. He had said it purely to elevate her position once more with the Queen. Still, her hands trembled the whole time she tidied away Armenal's jewels.

Oh gods. She needed to focus on the situation at hand. Alisander had landed her in a terrible position, regardless of his intention. Doubtless, he thought it a perfect opportunity for her to capitalize upon, but Jane was not the consummate schemer he was, the cunning beast.

She welcomed the indignation into her bosom, for it distracted her from the other disquieting notion he had planted. That he actually cared for her. *Nonsense.* He was merely being provoking, as was his habit, she told herself firmly. *Do not get caught up in some ridiculous idea that he could have spoken in earnest.*

And now she was really up to her ears in trouble. Clearly, the Queen expected her to pass along a whole bag of tricks for ensnaring men's hearts. Something she did not have the first idea about! She could *strangle* him!

"Leave that now, Jane," Queen Armenal said, drifting toward the fireplace. "Come, join me here. I would consult with you." Taking a deep breath, Jane made her way to join the Queen before the fire. "Be seated," she said graciously, and Jane sank into the seat opposite her. For a moment, neither of them spoke. The Queen gazed at her keenly. "Well," she said with a gesture of resignation. "I am all ears. What is it you would have me do?"

Jane cleared her throat and considered the matter. She swallowed down her own bitterness toward King Wymer. "I think, Your Majesty, that the best thing for you to do is show some tender solicitude over the King's bereavement," she said quietly. "Grief can be a terribly overwhelming emotion and you often feel alone, even when surrounded by others. When someone seems to understand how your loss…" She turned away, feeling her eyes well up.

Queen's eyes widened at this advice. "But I have already shown the King great sympathy," she objected. "I even told him of my own fondness for the nurses of my girlhood."

Jane shook her head, remembering the Queen's offhand reminiscences of a few days before. "That was not what I meant," she disagreed quickly. "I am sure your own nurses were good women, but the King—he wants to hear that his own feelings of terrible loss are justified and—and that you understand how his whole life will forever change because this person is no longer a part of it—" She broke off, feeling choked.

The Queen frowned. "I did not feel that way when I heard that one of my old nurses had died," she objected.

"He knows that," Jane answered without thinking. "That is why he feels nothing when you compare your own experience to his." The Queen blinked at this but did not speak. "What you should do, Your Highness," Jane continued, "is acknowledge this fact and stress how *special* his bond was with Bathilde. How superior a woman she was and how—how fortunate they *both* were to have spent so many years in each other's company. That he must now console himself with the fact he eased her passing. That her last breath was spent in the company of her beloved charge, holding his hand, with assurances of his enduring love and affection."

Jane could feel her own eyes grow wet. She could not help but think of how she had eased her own sister's passing and how much that consoled her now.

Queen Armenal looked skeptical. "You do not think such sentiments a little much?" she ventured incredulously.

Jane felt the words like a slap to the face. "No, I do *not*," she retorted.

The Queen sighed at her vehemence. "Perhaps you are right. I am not remotely sentimental. It seems an odd thing to me, that a man capable of waging a brutal war, tearing his whole kingdom apart, resulting in the deaths of hundreds upon hundreds, could snivel into his supper for days over a very old woman passing."

Jane pressed her lips together very tightly. "Doubtless we all have our foibles," she said colorlessly.

"And frankly," Armenal continued with a shrug, "I cannot see how adopting such a stratagem could have secured Lord Bardulf's affections. He, like myself, is not remotely maudlin or prone to sentimentalize his childhood."

Jane felt a spark of irritation flash through her. "Perhaps not, but he does not really have much to sentimentalize, does he? Considering the *horrible* events of his childhood."

The Queen looked startled, her eyes opening very wide. "He *told* you of that?" she said in patent astonishment.

"But of course he did, Your Majesty," Jane answered with more than a hint of impatience. "I am his wife."

"Well, yes, but…" The Queen hesitated. "One would naturally hesitate to speak of such disgrace in one's family history, would one not? Especially," she said, gesturing to Jane, "to one you highly esteem. Lord Bardulf serves the Western Isles most diligently—one assumes in the hope of assuaging his ignominious family history."

Jane regarded her in stunned silence a moment. Clearly, the Queen regarded what happened in a different light than she did. "My understanding is that the crops failed that year, and his

410

older brother was unable to pay the necessary tithe without his people suffering."

The Queen nodded. "It was a sad business to be sure," she said quietly, "but a nobleman's first duty is to his liege, Jane, no one else. My brother, and all the Lasconian court, admired Henri de Balon. He was a perfect flower of youth. When he was cut down in his prime, it was a dreadful thing. My brother's agent in that matter acted swiftly and harshly, but Wilhelm appreciated that if he had not, then he could have had a wide-scale revolt on his hands. This is the ultimate responsibility of kings. It can be a merciless task at times and run contrary to one's own private feeling."

"I understand," replied Jane silkily, "though it must seem unfathomable to outsiders. Such as King Wymer holding Bathilde in such high affection whilst simultaneously having torn his country asunder in a civil war."

The Queen gave a start. "You are right, Jane," she said, nodding her head slowly and transferring her gaze to the fire once again. "I do not extend my husband the same courtesy of understanding that I do my brother." She was silent for a long moment. "So," she said at last, "it was your compassionate nature that earned Lord Bardulf's love?"

Jane struggled with this briefly but could make no answer. Fortunately, the Queen was speaking again, so she did not have to. "I will admit that Lord Bardulf never seemed to me a man who would be susceptible to such things, but there you have it…the inner workings of a man's heart must be a peculiar thing indeed."

"Doubtless," Jane said flatly.

"And now you are cross with me, Jane," the Queen said regretfully. "You think I do not deserve the benefit of your advice and, perhaps, after all, I do not. I am ungrateful." She held out a hand. "Come and tell me you forgive me."

Jane flushed and made haste to clasp the Queen's hand. "Your Majesty, I would never—"

"I have decided," the Queen interrupted her with sudden decision, "that I will adopt your strategy." She declared it graciously, though Jane could tell she was both disappointed and skeptical about everything she had urged. Perhaps the Queen supposed she had the ingredients for some obscure love philter, she thought wryly.

It was a miracle that the Queen was ready when the royal ushers arrived shortly after to escort her to the King's apartments. "I will see you on the morrow, Jane," the Queen said by way of farewell. "You must come to me early," she added impulsively, "as you used to."

Jane's heart sank, though she could not have said precisely why. "Yes, Your Majesty." She dipped a curtsey and beat a hasty retreat.

25

Alisander turned his head sharply, hearing a door open and close. He folded his note and concealed it in his pocket before turning to face the door. To his annoyance, he heard another open and then Jane's unmistakable tones lifted in speech with another. Had she gone to check on Celestia before coming to find him? He stood up and crossed the room to go in search of her.

Sure enough, he found Jane crouched down beside the tub, where Anne was employed in bathing both children. Celestia was gazing up at her, a puzzled expression of concentration on her face while Bertrand splashed about beside her.

"She looks as though she is struggling to make out my face, Anne," Jane said with a trace of anxiety. "I do hope her sight is not failing her."

Anne guffawed. "Lord bless you, milady; they're all like that at first. I used to think Bertrand was practically cross-eyed the way he would squint at me, but he don't do it no more."

Jane nodded, looking relieved. "She is kicking her legs a little too, so that is a good sign, is it not?"

Alisander leaned against the door, his eyes on Jane. She clearly knew he was there but was pretending she had not noticed him. After a few moments, she went to inspect the cloths laid out in front of the fire. "They're nice and warm," she commented, gathering them up and returning to the bath.

Anne looked up. "I'll lift them out, milady. You'll get marks on your silk dress."

Jane glanced down, as if only just remembering her finery. She passed the cloths to Anne before turning impulsively toward Alisander. "Do you suppose they will feel some sort of bond when they are older?" she asked in a low voice. "Sort of like…mock siblings?"

Her question startled him. "Why should they?"

"Well…" She glanced around to watch as Anne lifted Celestia out of the water. "They sleep in the same crib, bathe together in the same tub, and nurse at the same breast," she pointed out matter-of-factly. "Would it be so very surprising if they did?"

"You refer to milk-kinship?" he asked. "I have heard of such a concept, but I don't know that it is one acknowledged in our part of the world."

"What does acknowledgment of such a thing constitute in those parts of the world where it is?" Jane asked curiously.

"Well," he considered, "I believe, much like genuine siblings, they would be expected to retain some measure of attachment to one another and prohibited from ever marrying."

They both turned to consider the two babies lying side by side on the bed. Bertrand, so bonny and bouncing, and Celestia, so delicate and small. "Well, that should not prove any great hardship, surely?" Jane ventured.

Alisander felt that ripple of unease that some folk attributed to someone walking over your future grave. "One would hope not," he said dryly, and resisted the impulse to make a superstitious gesture associated with averting disaster. A swift change of subject seemed in order. "How went it with the Queen?" he asked.

A spasm of displeasure took her features. "You put me in the most awkward position!" she grumbled. "How *could* you?"

414

He laughed. "No, did I really? How so?"

"What did you expect me to tell her?" she demanded. Then, catching Anne's reproachful look, mouthed a silent *Sorry* and tiptoed from the room. He followed swiftly behind her, closing the door after him.

"I merely expected you to advise her to the best of your ability, that is all." Jane swung around and regarded him indignantly. "Keep walking forward," he urged her, ushering her past the door to the main chamber.

"Wha—?"

He turned the latch to open the door to their bedchamber, giving her a little push through it. "By the way, you were right about these quarters."

"How was I right?" Jane asked, wheeling around to face him.

He seized her left arm and started immediately unlacing her sleeve. "There aren't any larger ones to be had. We shall simply have to remain as we are."

Jane narrowed her eyes at him, though she obligingly presented her right arm without prompting. "Did you even make enquiry?" she asked shrewdly.

"No," he admitted. "I have developed a touching faith in your infallibility, it seems."

Jane gasped at his effrontery, and he grinned back at her. He couldn't help it. "And why, pray, am I undressing?" she enquired.

"Why do you think?" He spun her around and started on the laces at her back, angling his head to whisper in her ear, "I am about to be revenged on you, Lady Bardulf."

"Revenged on *me*?" she gasped. "What for, pray?"

"For making me jealous earlier," he answered promptly. "And also distracting me from my duties. I have been thinking of you *far* too much these past few days." It had been far longer than that, but he was not about to admit as much. "People are starting to whisper that I follow in your wake like a devoted lapdog."

"No one says that," Jane scoffed. "And I think you will find *I* am the one owed retribution, my lord! You properly pitched me into difficult waters with the Queen. Moreover, I do not think she was at all satisfied with my advice." She nibbled at her bottom lip.

"Well, that is her lookout," he said callously. "You can scarcely have guided her worse than her own impulses have these past ten years."

"I don't know what you mean! It is the King who has been entirely at fault, not the Queen!" Jane rallied.

Alisander snorted. "Armenal did not make the smallest push to appease or flatter him as a sensible princess would have directly on stepping off the ship that sailed her here. It is not as though Wymer is in any way difficult. On the contrary, he is almost *distressingly* predictable."

He eased the dress down from her shoulders. "In any case," he whispered, kissing her neck as the dress pooled at the floor, "I grow tired of this subject. Step out of your gown."

Jane did so, and he scooped it up, tossing it onto a nearby chair. Then he wrapped his arms around her, drawing her back against his front, and let out a happy sigh.

"I am not sure I was terribly diplomatic," Jane admitted in a small voice, ignoring the fact he was hard against her buttocks. "You see, the Queen rather irritated me at one point and—"

He burst out with surprised laughter. "She irritated you?" He couldn't keep the delight from his voice. "Jane," he said, turning her in his arms and cupping her face between his hands. "Just how is it that you grow more fascinating to me by the day? Can you answer me that?" He frowned, considering. "It is not that way with others."

"It isn't?"

He shook his head. "Not in my experience."

"Oh." She still looked vaguely troubled, so he decided to kiss the frown from her face, first walking her backward until she halted, coming up against their bed. Then he grabbed her about her waist and lifted her onto the mattress. "Shift on or off?" he asked.

She lifted her arms obligingly, and he whipped it up and over her head so she sat naked and blushing before him. "My gods, Jane," he groaned. "Is it any wonder that I cannot think straight these days. Not when I have you in my bed."

"Have you really…been thinking of me? When we are not together, I mean?" she asked with a catch in her voice.

Her words made something twist in his chest. "Yes" was the only reply he was capable of uttering. Then Jane did a strange thing. She put a finger across his lips as though preventing him from saying another word.

Alisander's eyes widened, but he made no objection. Likely she was just not in the mood to be teased, but he found he was happy to fall in with whatever she wanted from him. Once assured he had received her message, she dropped her hand from his mouth to start unfastening his tunic. He watched her, strangely breathless, as she bared his chest, then turned her head and pressed her lips to his shoulder.

Alisander felt his heart sort of swoop in a way that made him turn quite light-headed. He had to back away and divest himself of the rest of his clothes, lest he started staggering under the strain. Once he was naked, he joined her on the bed and they started kissing in—what he could only think of as—an oddly intense fashion.

Instead of brushing light kisses along her jaw as he'd intended, he pressed increasingly hungry kisses along her neck, tracing her pulse there with his tongue. When he kissed her palm, in what should have been a tease, he let her feel his teeth there.

When they got down to brass tacks, they made no sound at all, except his ragged breathing and Jane's bitten-off whimpers and the sound of the bed creaking. He had gritted his jaw at the moment of bliss and swallowed his groan. Jane buried her face in the crook of his neck to muffle her cry of completion.

Was this how normal people fucked? he wondered afterward as he caught his breath. Couples who might not want to alert their household. Of course, Robert was mercifully deaf, and Celestia and Bertrand were mere drooling infants. As for Anne, she was far too sensible to let a thing like the noise of her employers tupping bother her.

The fact was, Jane's bizarre notions of respectability no longer seemed like a challenge to him. If she wanted it this way, he was happy to oblige. Of course, he still had every intention of getting things his own way once in a while, but if she ever initiated, he was more than happy to follow her lead.

When he could bring himself at last to disengage from her, he did so only to rearrange himself behind her and wrap himself about her. Jane was content to let him, catching his hand and pressing it to her breast so he could feel the rise and fall of her steady breathing.

She did not even remind him supper was in an hour or so. He kissed the tip of her ear and let his eyes drift shut. He felt strangely calm and contented. When they ate, they did so in their room, and both were careful to keep their words muted and noncombative for once.

The next morning, he had woken to find her silently watching him. Instead of teasing her, as would once have been his instinctive response, he had rolled atop her, and they had repeated the mostly silent fucking.

It started out lazy and pleasant; he was in no rush and meant to savor the experience. Then it started getting to him, the way she was aiding and abetting him in the endeavor. The way her fingernails sank into his shoulders, the roll of her hips, her muffled whimpers, all of it *undid* him.

In the aftermath, he kissed away her tears and held her gathered very close against him, holding his tongue even when he felt the impulse to call her his dove again. The next thing he knew, Jane's voice was breaking through his reverie. "What did you say?" He frowned. Why was she breaking their unspoken pact of perfect silence? He rolled off her onto his back.

"I said I have to go and help the Queen dress this morning," she sighed.

"Why?" he asked, stretching and smothering a yawn. "Someone else can do it. Come over here and be quiet and still, wife. We still have an hour's respite left us, if I am any judge."

He expected her to argue, or at least demur, but instead of doing either of those things, she scooted closer and wrapped her arm about his waist. "Very well but just for a minute," she conceded.

"Ten minutes," he argued, tightening his arms about her. There was no getting around it, he was cuddling with her. And he liked it.

"Five," she bargained.

"We'll see."

In the end, it was more like twenty before he allowed her to drag herself from the bed. Later, that day, whilst climbing a dusty, abandoned staircase, he forced himself to face a few hard facts. He was getting ridiculously fond of his own wife. He remembered his lapdog comment from the previous day and grimaced. The truth was, he could hardly bear to be away from her side.

He was no longer tormenting her when he whispered her name against the delicate shell of her ear or gently bit her lobe. He was tormenting himself. The thought of getting between Jane's thighs had always excited him, but he had never dreamed that he would derive such strange pleasure in the wake of having her.

He loved being the one to gather her up into his arms and soothe her while she sobbed and whimpered until she was calm again. He tutted and fussed over her like she was something precious, and he got some sort of strange enjoyment out of the way she let him. He had always known his personality was a little out of the usual, but truly, he had never dreamed he had such a side to him.

In the bedchamber, it was annoying how hot he burned for her, almost as though he was in her thrall. In the past, he had enjoyed the role of capricious, indifferent lover, taking a bite

420

here or there, then discarding the succulent fruit as though he'd lost interest. That was how you kept lovers on their toes after all. You made it a game so that you did not lose interest.

There was no way he could ever do that to Jane. For one thing, he found it practically impossible to mask his desire for her. He wouldn't convince her for a second. It was one thing to shake and tremble through your release but quite another to do it when someone briefly touched your face! He shamelessly moaned her name aloud, for fuck's sake.

He chased her lips, even in the aftermath of bliss. Instead of rising from the bed as soon as he could feel his legs again, he lingered, running his hands over her, squeezing her and petting her in a way that was more *tender* than lecherous. Then there was the fact that, quite apart from these practical considerations, the very thought of wounding her made his own chest ache.

He could not even deceive himself that the shameful incident that morning, with the *embracing*, was an isolated incident. It happened every damned time. He sort of looked forward to it in a peculiar way. Like it was his reward at the end of a long day. One time, the previous week, he recalled that he had even done it without having bedded her first!

He had simply reached for her and enfolded her in his arms before Jane's surprised expression had registered with him. He had not even redeemed himself by whispering something annoying or guaranteed to discompose her before releasing her. Instead, he had just kissed her brow. If he was not careful, he reflected, feeling troubled, he would be giving her quite the wrong impression.

After dutifully leaving Jane the previous day closeted with the Queen, he had felt strangely depressed in spirit. It was the prospect of Jane returning to the Queen's feet, he had realized.

421

He was jealous, even of that. He wanted Jane to like *him* better than Armenal, damn it! Was that too much to ask? She was *his* wife after all.

Then the horrible suspicion that Armenal might award Jane some trifle from her jewel box had occurred to him, making his step falter. He remembered Jane's previous rapture on receiving that opal brooch from the Queen. *He* should be the one to put such a look on her face and him alone.

Giving Jane jewelry was his province and right. Not that she had ever reacted in such a gratifying manner to his gifts, he reflected wryly. The emerald brooch had merely stunned her. She had murmured incredulously about its size, as though that detracted rather than enhanced its beauty. He had not had the opportunity to give her the sapphire necklace yet. Perhaps that would do the trick?

He rolled his shoulders, as though to shrug off his cares, and unwound a length of rope which he had left conveniently on a ledge during his previous visit. Using this, he navigated the crumbled steps that had necessitated the staircase's abandonment and made his way to the top where a cache of letters was awaiting him.

He passed only the most cursory of glances over their contents. He could scarcely bring himself to care these days. Usually he liked nothing more than uncovering a good plot. Nowadays, he would far rather uncover Jane. Maybe he should look into dragging Jane to some secluded country retreat for a few days, he pondered.

Not Kinnerton, he told himself with a swift frown. There, she would be distracted by Mistress Beth, who wrote her long enough letters as it was, detailing her every decision and household expense. No, he would investigate finding some small hunting lodge where they would be practically alone together. Mayhap just one discreet servant, or a pair at most, he conceded, if they came with the house.

The important thing would be having the run of the place to themselves. Then, there would be no one else to worry about, and no one else to stumble across them. Jane could be perfectly abandoned with him without fear of discovery. He might not even allow her to fully dress the entire time.

Instead, they could gambol about the place, nymph and satyr, and consummate their passion in rooms with many windows, positively flooded by daylight. Then he could examine her every blush at his leisure.

Yes, he liked that idea, though a cold day in February was perhaps not conducive to his vision. He frowned. Still, even if it pissed down with rain, and they ended up huddled under a pile of blankets, he had a suspicion he would relish every minute with her.

A rustle from below had him retreating behind a dusty column, but it was only a bird, alighting on the arrowslit. It tipped its head to one side and considered Alisander a moment with bright eyes before it was gone again with a rustle of wings.

He breathed out. For a moment there, he thought he must have been followed. The awful thing was it was only instinct that had kept his actions vigilant. His mind had not been on the task at hand at all.

Jane had taken recently to watching him suspiciously when he left her side. He should really have discouraged that as soon as he noticed it. The truth was, though, that he rather liked it. He liked it whenever he had her undivided attention. He sighed.

Alisander was starting to suspect he was an entirely hopeless cause.

26

The Queen had been strangely subdued that morning and sunk in her own thoughts. Magnatrude Bartree had been cold and officious when Jane had first arrived to aid with Her Majesty's dress, but by the end of the morning, she had thawed sufficiently to exchange alarmed glances with Jane.

"Something ails you this morn, Your Highness?" Mistress Bartree had ventured at last in her deep, curiously attractive voice. She would be a handsome woman, Jane thought, if she did not insist on wearing such unflattering headdresses. Those skull caps were so severe.

"No," the Queen had answered swiftly. "I have much to arrange, that is all, and I put my thoughts in order. My dear Magnatrude, you must hurry along to the King's apartments at once and make the enquiry after the good Bathilde. Make it known that the Queen wishes to know if she has passed a peaceful night."

Jane could tell from the lady-in-waiting's reaction that this was not the Queen's usual practice, but she hastened at once to fulfill the directive.

"Jane, you must go in search of Piers and send him to fetch the royal tailor. I want full sets of mourning clothes made up for the King and me, in purest white. Have him bring samples for approval. There can be no delay. The time grows near, you understand?" She sent Jane a frowning glance. "You might want to send for your own tailor also, for I mean to suggest the whole court is plunged into deepest mourning."

Jane blinked. *The whole court?* She was a little shocked. Such things only occurred in Karadok on the death of a monarch.

Perhaps it was different in the Western Isles? Seeing the Queen look at her expectantly, she hurried off to fulfill the request with a prickle of apprehension climbing her spine. She had forgotten that Queen Armenal did not believe in half measures.

By late afternoon, she was feeling something akin to panic at the extravagance of the plans the Queen was making. "Have my pearl coronet brought out of the strong room," the Queen demanded, "for I will wear only pearls when I am dressed for mourning. There must be no gold or any other color in sight, whatsoever."

Jane could see that Mistress Bartree was also much taken aback by proceedings, though perhaps that was because, in the north, purple was the color of mourning and not white. Jane heard her whispering to her own page that he must hie at once to her tailor, for she did not own a single gown of that color.

Then Magnatrude instructed urgently he must make for the home of her dear sister-in-law, the Baroness Kentigern, and beg for the loan of her pearls, though she acknowledged with a worried expression that her brother might not allow it. "You must stress, Unwin, my *dire* need of them," she implored him, then sent him off with a pat to his shoulder.

At three o'clock, a messenger approached from the King. Queen Armenal rose at once. "I will go and join the King at Bathilde's bedside," she said grandly. "Jane, Magnatrude, you may go. I will not impose this duty on you, for I will stay however long is necessary, until the very end."

They both curtseyed deeply, and Jane could see Mistress Bartree was torn between the impulse to vow she would follow her queen into the jaws of death itself, and the need to go beg, borrow, and steal as many white garments as she could procure.

As for Jane, she made her way back to their quarters with a strange sense of dread. She had a terrible feeling her advice to the Queen was going to lead to disaster. On reaching their rooms, she leaned weakly against the door and closed her eyes.

"Why, my lady, whatever's happened?" Ayleth asked, coming out of Anne's room carrying a tray.

Jane regarded her a moment in silence before answering. "Court is about to be plunged in deepest mourning," she admitted hoarsely. "And I did not even wear mourning for my own sister." Her words were choked, and she had to shut her eyes, for fear of disgracing herself.

"Your sister's death was unexpected, my lady," Ayleth said after a heavy pause. "You were too busy fulfilling her dying wishes to pay attention to such things."

Jane's eyes flew open. "Yes," she agreed hoarsely. That was true enough.

"Certainly, no one would have expected you to get married in white!" Ayleth looked shocked at the idea. "No bride would do such an inauspicious thing." Jane smiled at her weakly, and after a moment, the servant returned the gesture. "You honored the Lady Helen in the way she would have wanted," Ayleth said with a nod. "By securing that child's future. You go and sit before the fire, and I will bring you a glass of wine by and by."

The older woman moved purposefully away before Jane could either agree or disagree. With a sigh, Jane took herself into the sitting room and dropped into a seat. Ayleth was right. It was foolish to feel guilty that she had been unable to wear formal mourning clothes for her sister.

Presently, Ayleth brought her a goblet of wine and Robert fussed over the fire, poking it and almost smothering it with too

427

many logs. Hearing barely discernible footsteps in the corridor, Jane's heart gave a great leap, leaving her breathless. "Alisander!" she called out, starting from her chair.

He came into the room. "Are you calling for me?" He took one look at her face and came to her side. "What is it?" he demanded.

She attempted to tell him, but the words were babbled, and her account was confused. After a moment, he passed a solicitous arm about her and started rubbing her back. "So, the Queen…?"

"She said that she is going to take my advice!" Jane wailed.

He frowned. "You make it sound like that is a bad thing."

"Yes! Because she is taking it so far! She says she was up all night thinking about it, and she means to put the whole court into strictest mourning. She has ordered sumptuous suits for herself and the King in full white and—and—"

"It is good you are forewarned of that," he muttered. "I must send at once to Monsieur Barbier—"

"I already have," she interrupted him.

"What? You have?"

She nodded miserably. "I thought I had better." When he looked impressed, she added quickly, "The Queen prompted me to; I did not think of it myself."

"So, we will all be required to wear white?" he said thoughtfully. "A color most becoming to Her Majesty's complexion, though you must be careful not to let it wash you out, my dove. You must wear your new sapphires."

"You have not bought me more jewelry?" she gasped in dismay. "Besides, the Queen said she would not wear any color, even gold."

"Well, *she* may not," he said firmly, "but *we* most assuredly will. I shall wear my rubies. They will look most dramatic against a cotehardie of purest white." He eyed Jane sympathetically. "You are all of a flutter, Jane, your poor thing," he tutted. "It has been too much for you." He towed her toward the door. "Come and lie down with me, wife, and I will soothe your troubled spirits."

"Lie down?" Jane turned her head to look at him suspiciously. His expression was entirely innocent. "Well," she said weakly, "I must admit, I do feel a little shaken."

"Of course you do!" he interrupted her, shaking his head. "And it is not to be wondered at. The Queen has depleted your energy. She has drained you."

"No, no," Jane objected feebly as he steered her through the doorway of their bedroom. "It is just that sometimes…"

"Yes?" he murmured, his hands on her shoulders exerting a gentle pressure until she sat on the bed. Swiftly, he dropped to his knees to unbuckle her shoes.

"Oh, I don't know," she said wretchedly, gazing down at him. "I suppose I worry too much about things."

"You do," he agreed, "and you find it so hard to let go of your worries, don't you, my sweet? Why don't you just let me unwind you, Jane? I'm itching to, you know."

She frowned at him. Why were his eyes gleaming like that? Understanding dawned. "You think *that* would restore my energy?" she blurted in astonishment as he made short work of unfastening her bodice.

He nodded gravely, though his eyes were dancing. "But yes. I will transfer my vital energy into you by way of a secret technique."

"A secret…?" Words failed her. "There is nothing remotely secret about your technique!"

"It will be most invigorating, I promise," he whispered.

Jane spluttered but voiced no objection. "I'm just going to lie here," she warned him. "I'm not going to do anything."

"No husband could ask for more."

Jane snorted. "You are a rogue, Viscount Bardulf. I always suspected as much."

"Shhh, you must not say so," he implored, kissing the back of her neck and peeling off her dress. "Not when I'm trying to worship you with my body."

Jane closed her eyes and chose to humor the man. Afterward, she decided she felt drowsy rather than invigorated, though he had certainly woken her up at one point.

"Jane, Jane," he whispered. "If you only knew how desirable you look like this, so abandoned…" Abandoned? "Your cheeks are poppy red," he murmured with approval, "and your hair is positively…untidy."

Untidy? Her? That couldn't be right. Jane struggled to focus on him.

His lips quirked up at the corners. "You are so delightfully wanton once you give yourself over to desire."

Jane groaned. "Stop provoking me."

"I meant no insult," he murmured, stroking her back. "Indeed, I wholeheartedly approve."

"Abandoned? *Wanton?*" Jane repeated. "Those are not words of approval."

"Believe me, they are in this instance."

Jane became slowly aware of the fact that the hour could be no more advanced than half past four. It was not even a decent time for bed. Gods, she could feel the wetness between her legs. He was leaking out of her. Jane struggled into a seated position, and he roused himself at once, reaching for her shift.

"Allow me," he said as Jane tried to cover her exposed breasts from his view. "Now, if you do that, how am I supposed to get your sleeves over your arms?" he tutted, drawing the shift gently over her head, and Jane relaxed enough to poke her hands through the armholes.

Once her shift was on, he sat regarding her with an expression she might have thought was openly affectionate in anyone else. "Shall I order us a bath, Lady Bardulf?" he suggested, catching hold of her hand and kissing the backs of her fingers.

Us? Really, she should not be so easily shocked by this point. "Yes," Jane responded after the faintest of hesitations and was dazzled by the beauty of his smile.

*

The next morning, the news trickled through the palace in a slow but steady stream. Bathilde had finally passed in the early hours of the morning. The courtiers, while anticipating the King's sadness, were surprised to find all formal palace gatherings summarily canceled, and the entrances to both the King's and Queen's chambers closed off, and their reception rooms left empty and echoing.

431

Only fish was served that night in the banqueting hall, by somber-faced servants. The master of ceremonies made it clear that only hushed voices were to be used in the castle for the next few days, for the King was not just sad, but deeply grieved by Bathilde's death.

And so, things continued. The King and Queen kept to their private chambers, and nothing was seen of them elsewhere in the palace. Monsieur Barbier, the tailor, attended the Bardulfs in their rooms, promising that their mourning outfits would be ready within two short days. He shook his head a good deal over it and said nothing but a death could instigate him to such haste.

Jane thought she had better warn Osanna and Patience of the need for mourning gowns, for surely all the tailors in the capital would soon be employed sewing them once the whole court became aware of the line the royal couple meant to take. She sent her former roommates a note via Wat and received effusive thanks in return written in Patience's untidy scrawl.

It was on the third day that rumors began to circulate that the King had been sequestered the whole time in his wife's rooms. Anne returned from the kitchens full of the news. "They say she is having to console him like a lost child," she announced wide-eyed. Robert and Ayleth exchanged glances while Wat, entering the room, cleared his throat.

"There's a squire outside, my lady," he said apologetically. "The Queen has asked for you to attend her this morning in the King's presence chamber."

"The King's?" Jane asked in surprise. It was only on special state occasions that the Queen would join the King in his larger, more formal rooms.

"I'll help you into your mourning," Ayleth said, quickly coming to her feet. She ended up dressing her hair, too, for Jane did not like to send for Marta, thinking it would be inappropriate to wear an arrangement too fancy, considering the sad occasion.

Alisander did not join them in the bedchamber, and when Jane emerged in her new finery, she was surprised to find he was still seated before the fire. "Come in and let me see you," he called out as she hesitated in the doorway.

Jane straightened her collar of sapphires and came into the room to show him the full effect. He would not pronounce himself satisfied with her appearance until he had twitched her skirts first this way, then that, and tugged at the puffed effect of her full sleeves so they lay right. "That is better," he had murmured before dwelling on the sapphires at her throat. "These look well on you, as I knew they would." He sounded smug. The serpentine design of her bodice he did not mention at all, though he laid his hand against it and traced the undulating shape with his fingertip absently.

"You will not be joining us?" she asked.

He shook his head. "I had to ask Monsieur Barbier to adjust a few things about the fit of my clothes," he said fastidiously. "Besides, there is some small, trifling matter I must take care of this morning."

Jane waited, but nothing more was forthcoming. "Oh," she said, feeling strangely disappointed. "Well, I will see you this afternoon, then, my lord?"

He seemed to debate his answer with himself, then shook his head. "This evening for supper is more likely." Jane nodded, trying not to feel forlorn. She would just have to make do with that.

To her surprise, she found the King's gathering was more official in tone than she had anticipated and comprised of his Privy Council members, rather than his favorites. There were hardly *any* women of the court in attendance at all. In fact, other than the Queen, Mistress Bartree, and herself, she could see no other noblewomen present.

The three of them were decked out head to toe in the white of official mourning, though Jane wore her sapphires and Mistress Bartree wore a fine string of coral beads. Presumably, her sister-in-law, Baroness Kentigern was not willing to part with her own pearls. Either that, or her husband, the baron, had not permitted her to lend them to his sister.

Whichever it was, Jane saw that Magnatrude Bartree relaxed slightly when she saw Jane wore a splash of color at least. As for the Queen, Jane had never seen her in so many pearls. They studded her sleeves and veil, hung in abundance about her throat and wrists, and even dripped from her fingers. No fewer than three large pearl brooches punctuated her bodice.

The King, too, matched his Queen in sumptuous, unrelieved white. His hose, tunic, and even his chaperon hat were purest white, though he wore a gold chain of office about his shoulders. Jane saw the ripple of surprise run through the lords and ministers gathered in the state rooms that morning when they saw the display of full mourning from the royal couple.

The King looked pale and grim as he mounted the dais, the Queen upon his arm. Jane and Mistress Bartree retreated to a respectful distance as discussion started with the King being officially commiserated by Lord Vawdrey on behalf of his council.

Jane found it hard to keep her mind on proceedings that morning. Her thoughts kept wandering as to what business her husband might be about that day. He had not been terribly forthcoming, but then, when was he ever? She roused herself from her ruminations to pay attention when she realized the Queen had started speaking, interrupting Lord Vawdrey's smooth patter.

"But naturally, Bathilde must have five hundred masses sung for her soul," the Queen said solemnly. "As befits her station. The monks must be summoned from the cathedral itself to start them. Then, every ecclesiastical college in the capital must send a delegation to cover in shifts, until they are all read over the next five days before she is laid to rest."

The council members began to stir at this, murmuring in shock and consternation. "Five hundred masses!" bleated Lord Schaeffer, a respected senior counselor. He looked stunned, his head whipping around to survey his fellow lords of the Privy Council. "But—but only a royal sovereign would command such—"

"Silence!" the King roared. "You dare to contradict my Queen?"

"Then, of course, there is the final resting place to be determined," Armenal continued as if no one had interrupted her. She addressed the King solely at this point, ignoring the council members completely. "Has a spot yet been determined, Your Majesty?"

The King shook his head, looking irresolute. "Fitzborough Castle has been suggested," he said in a choked voice, "where I was raised, but—"

"That is quite out of the question," Armenal said briskly. "I cannot *think* who was foolish enough to suggest such a thing."

Jane noticed a section of the council stiffen with affront. She could wager a guess who had suggested it from the expressions on Lord Lowan's and Sir Barrett Covington-Bart's faces.

The King's expression wavered, his eyes moistening. "I confess I was not easy in my mind at the notion." His chin wobbled. "We have never been apart for more than ten days, and then, only in time of war…"

"Of course you have not. Carrying her body so many miles away is quite untenable! Bathilde must be laid close to hand."

The King nodded eagerly. "You suggest—?"

"Kilnacre Abbey, of course," the Queen said coolly. Gasps of shock were heard all about them. Jane's heart raced. *Kilnacre Abbey?* Armenal serenely ignored the stir her words had caused. "Bathilde must be laid to rest where she can await you, as faithful a companion in death as she was in life."

"You mean—?" The King frowned.

"Your Majesty, only royal sovereigns and their consorts are interred at Kilnacre," Lord Schaeffer quavered in horrified tones. "Such a thing is unheard of and would set a most unfortunate precedent."

"That is true, Your Majesties," Lord Vawdrey cut in regretfully. "Even bishops are not permitted a spot in the royal enclosure."

"Indeed!" chimed in Lord Caterby, emboldened by Earl Vawdrey's acknowledgment. "Just where do you suggest we make room for Mistress Bathilde's tomb, Your Highness? Do you suggest that the King's own mother's resting place is disturbed to make room for her?"

Shocked murmurings echoed throughout the chamber, and Jane wondered for a moment if the Queen had not rather overshot the mark. When she had suggested the Queen take Wymer's grief seriously, she had never dreamed that she would take it this far!

Lord Lowan sucked in his cheeks. "You surely do not forget, Your Highness, that your first wife, good Queen Eleanor, already occupies a spot to the left of your own plot." He averted his eyes tactfully at this solecism.

Wymer turned very red and appeared to be on the point of explosion at this reminder of his first wife's resting place. "I am not likely to forget where the mother of my son and heir lies!" he thundered.

"Certainly, we do not forget that fact," Queen Armenal countered coolly. "But I did not mean that any former queens should suffer any indignity in order to make way for Bathilde's tomb." She paused. "My own future plot can be halved, and space given over for it. Both of us, nay, all three of us, including the late Queen Eleanor, may rest in eternity beside the King."

King Wymer's head whipped around, and he beheld his wife speechlessly as the room broke out in an astonished babble of voices. Jane's mouth fell open. She glanced sideways at Magnatrude Bartree, who looked similarly astonished. They stared at one another wordlessly before turning back to face the dais.

The King sprang from his throne and strode to his wife's side, grasping for her hand. "You would do this, Armenal?" he cried. "You would make such a sacrifice for my sake?"

"But of course!" The Queen was entirely calm and matter-of-fact as everyone around them reeled at this unexpected turn of events.

The King quivered in the grip of strong emotion for a moment before turning back to face his Privy Council. "You see this example of noble womanhood before you! Was there ever such a female of such distinction? There is no one like her," he burst out, carrying her hand to his lips and pressing it there passionately. "You have heard the Queen's decree! Bathilde will be interred in five days' time at Kilnacre Abbey."

Jane gasped, as appalled as everyone else, at this total breach in etiquette. She still could not quite believe the Queen's proposal. Such a thing was completely unheard of! Going by the look on everyone else's faces, neither could anyone else.

Only Lord Vawdrey looked as unruffled as ever. "The Queen carries all before her this morn," Jane heard him murmur to Lord Schaeffer, who was still spluttering in horror. "You must not take it so hard, Andrew."

"You think," Lord Schaeffer quavered, "that the King may see reason in time?" He mopped his brow with his kerchief. "The Queen is not Karadok born and bred, so perhaps she cannot grasp how deeply inappropriate such a proposal is, but the King…"

"Hush, my friend," Lord Vawdrey cautioned, and Jane did not catch the rest, for they had swept past her, and he now had a firm grip of Lord Schaeffer's arm and likely his tongue too. Feeling a touch to her arm, Jane turned and Mistress Bartree nodded significantly to the dais.

It seemed King Wymer had taken his fill of everyone present, save for the Queen, for he was leading her determinedly down the steps. Jane and Magnatrude hurried after their retreating white figures, trying to catch up with them. This endeavor proved practically impossible, considering the way the crowds were closing in on them.

Linking arms in rare accord with one another, they fended off the enquiries about their full mourning and pushed their way through by sheer determination. To their mutual dismay, their efforts were in vain. No sooner did they have the door to the Queen's presence chamber in sight than they found it once more barred with guards.

"No admittance to Her Majesty's rooms today, by order of the King," one of the soldiers told them.

Magnatrude glared at him but to no avail. "This is all highly irregular," she fumed.

Privately Jane agreed but could see little point in bandying words with guardsmen. "The Queen will send for us in due course, I am sure," she told her companion.

The older woman looked resigned. "Yes, I suppose that is so," she responded grudgingly. They retreated together and walked toward the courtiers' wing in companionable silence, as both were lost in their own thoughts.

Sadly, Jane's were awash with alarm and dismay. Try as she might, she could not help but think it was her own advice to the Queen that had led to this disaster. What if it should be traced back to her somehow? The Privy Council would doubtless hold her to blame for the Queen's outrageous ideas.

Only once she and Mistress Bartree had parted ways did Jane allow her footsteps to increase with panic. Just as she rushed through the door, she remembered that Alisander was not returning until suppertime and felt her spirits plummet entirely. Then, she thought she caught his accents nearby. Surely, that was him?

A door opened and Robert came shuffling out. "Robert, is your master returned already?"

439

"Just now, milady," he said, gesturing toward the sitting room he had just emerged from. "Can I fetch you anything—?"

"No, thank you, Robert," she assured him, hurrying past him and slamming the door behind her. "This is all your fault!" she blurted immediately on finding Alisander seated at the desk. "Telling me to give the Queen my sincere thoughts! Now she has gone completely overboard, and no one can rein her in!"

Instead of being perplexed at being addressed in such a fashion, Alisander merely looked amused. "Excellent," he replied, sitting back and cracking his knuckles. "You are just in time to help me bulk out my letter to Wilhelm. Now tell me, what has she been doing?" He picked up his pen and held it poised ready to write.

Jane made a noise of frustration in her throat. "She has—she is encouraging the King to indulge his grief to the utmost, without limitation. Moreover, she is helping him plan a most sumptuous and excessive interment for Bathilde."

His pen started moving over the page in its elegant strokes and loops. "What else?"

Jane gazed at him. "You don't understand! Alisander, this is serious! She recommended, in front of the King's council no less, that Bathilde is interred at Kilnacre Abbey! Have you ever heard of such a thing? A *non-royal*?"

"But what a novel idea," he drawled, his pen continuing its course. "Of course, Armenal has always been a woman of singular conviction." He looked thoughtful. "She perhaps lacks the initial spark of creativity, but once she has an idea in her head, you must admit, she runs with it to the furthest extent."

"The Bishop of Hudde will have an apoplexy!"

Alisander shrugged. "If he objects too strenuously, I daresay Wymer will simply replace him with one who is more amenable to his ends."

Jane listened to the scratch of his pen, her mind a whirl. "You—you think so?" She was incredulous. For one horrible moment, it even occurred to her that Alisander might have had some nefarious reason to get rid of the Bishop of Hudde. *Could this have been his intention all along?*

Alisander set down his pen and regarded her critically. "Are you suspecting me of outrageous things again, Jane?" he asked her, narrowing his eyes.

Jane opened her mouth and then closed it again. She recalled that the burial idea was all Queen Armenal's. Her shoulders relaxed a little. "Of course not," she denied, coloring hotly and pressing her hands to her cheeks. "I am a little…disordered, that is all."

He turned fully toward her on his seat. "Come here," he ordered imperiously. It did not even occur to her to deny him. Instead, she walked straight to him, and when he tugged her into his lap, she went willingly.

He set a hand over her bosom. "How fast your heart is racing, wife," he murmured. "Have you been so anxious over this? It is too bad of the Queen. Only I am allowed to make it beat this quickly."

As was her habit when he toyed with her like this, Jane turned instantly tongue-tied. "I—well—that is, yes," she managed to sputter. "But I am the least of Her Majesty's considerations, at this time."

He tutted. "So modest, but you will always be uppermost in my considerations, Jane," he assured her. She grew even more red-cheeked, tucking her chin and attempting to avoid his gaze. "Shall I take care of you now? And soothe that hot little brow?" he suggested.

Jane gazed at him. "Why are you returned so early?" it occurred to her to ask. "I thought you would not return home until suppertime."

He shrugged, avoiding her eye. "It occurred to me, I could write this report here as well as anywhere else. Fortuitously, as it turns out, now you have given me all the news."

"Perhaps you returned so soon because you wished to see me," she hazarded boldly. Surely it could not just be her who was starting to feel this way? When he did not answer at once, Jane felt a sense of dread overtake her. Suddenly, it appeared to her that it was Viscount Bardulf in whose lap she was now sat.

His eyes seemed to have a sardonic gleam to them, and she realized he was about to say something dismissive and maybe even cruel. Jane knew she should brace herself for whatever was about to come her way, but instead she just patiently waited.

Alisander did not disappoint her. He leaned forward. "I collect you are now determined to see me in a positive light, wife," he murmured. "I think you must have fallen in love with me, even if it is only the smallest amount."

The old Jane would have been appalled. Indeed, Jane could feel thoughts shrieking, *Deny it at once before he humiliates you!* in a corner of her mind. Instead, impulsively, Jane reached for his hand. He glanced down in surprise, then back at her face, and Jane knew he must have seen the color slowly climbing up her neck. If he said something cutting now, something very new and tender would shrivel entirely inside of her and die.

It was only the flimsiest and tiniest of shoots in any case. If he killed it now, it would be no great loss, she told herself uneasily as she held her breath. She felt slightly queasy. He was going to crush it, stone dead. *Gods, let it be quick and merciful*, she prayed as she swallowed and bent her neck, waiting for the death blow.

It never fell. Instead, she felt his warm fingers slide over her own, grasping her hand tightly in his own. "Ah, Jane, Jane, what the fuck are you doing to me?" he groaned, pulling her more firmly into his arms. "Don't do this," he warned and then pressed his lips passionately to her neck. "Don't…just…don't," he whispered against her sensitive skin. "We *can't*!"

"I think it's too late for me," she answered, her voice wobbly. "So just save yourself." Oh gods, what was she saying? Was she admitting to…to…?

"It's your fault," he insisted. "It's all your fault. You made me do it. You make me weak." He was pressing open-mouthed kisses along her neck. "We have to stop this," he said shakily. "We have to stop right now."

"Yes, we do," she agreed insincerely, passing her arms about his shoulders and pressing her mouth to his. He wasn't resisting at all. His lips parted over her own, and she knew what he was asking for. Fortunately, prim Jane had fainted into a heap at this point, so bold Jane swept her tongue into Viscount Bardulf's mouth and felt him shudder in her arms.

Closing her eyes tight, Jane kissed him with all the tender lasciviousness he had inspired in her, which was a lot, apparently. She let her hands slide up his neck and into his hair. Her kiss was utterly shameless. It was hot and wet and needy, and Jane's heart felt like it was pounding out of her chest.

She was tugging at his hair and whimpering into his mouth before she came to her senses and drew back. Alisander's arms tightened around her, and she felt herself lifted in his arms.

"No," he groaned as she started to pull back. "No, don't stop, Jane. I've changed my mind. I'll *die* if you stop."

Obligingly, she wrapped her arms back around his neck. "Where are we—?"

"Bedchamber," he said tersely, taking her mouth again. They exited the sitting room and made their way haphazardly down the corridor before Jane found herself pushed up against a wall and thoroughly kissed.

Jane opened an eye. This was *not* the bedchamber. They had not made it that far. In fact, she found it was the bedchamber door she was shoved against. Reaching back, she groped for the door latch, and after a moment, she managed to tip the lever and the door swung inward.

They practically fell inside. "Fuck," Alisander wheezed, slamming it shut behind them with his foot. They collapsed onto the bed, and he started bunching up her skirts.

Jane did not do a damn thing to discourage him. In fact, quite the contrary. In the aftermath, Jane hid her hot face against his chest.

"Oh gods, Jane," he sighed. "You can do that to me again anytime you like."

"I?" She was too out of puff to be really indignant, but she gave it a good shot in any case.

He grinned and passed an arm about her shoulders, lying back with a satisfied smile. "What a little whirlwind you are, Jane," he murmured. "I do so like it when you blow a gale. See how relaxed you are now? Did I not say I would soothe you?"

Jane lifted her head. "*Soothe* me?" she repeated. "You have a very odd notion of how soothing works. Perhaps you have confused the word's meaning with *swiving*."

He gave a burst of laughter. "You are growing so bold of speech of late," he mused. "To think, I used to think you so mealy-mouthed."

"I am still mealy-mouthed."

"No, Jane, no," he corrected her firmly. "A mealy-mouthed woman would never mention her husband swiving her."

"I did not actually—" she started to protest.

"And to think," he sighed, "in my imaginings, your bedchamber etiquette was always so polite. I thought you would climax with a hiccup and a *beg your pardon*," he teased.

Jane gasped. "Alisander!" This was too much. Then a thought occurred to her. "I do not believe you in any case. You said you wanted to see me burst. I didn't know what you meant at first. I do now though."

He nodded, quite unabashed. "You are right, of course. I always knew you would be a sight to behold." He regarded her a moment. "Maybe you're right; maybe I did return early in the hopes you might drag me to bed."

Jane's heart thudded. She lifted her head to look at him. It was so disquieting when he did this and switched on her, especially when she felt vulnerable. This was definitely Viscount Bardulf right now, and he could still discompose her badly when he was like this. "You should be careful," she said faintly, deciding to

445

test him. "Rushing back like that. Lest people start to think you really have fallen victim to my charms."

Instead of denying it, Viscount Bardulf rolled his eyes upward, and he seemed to give her words some serious thought. Jane held her breath, just watching him. "It might be a little too late for caution," he said wryly. "Lord Vawdrey already thinks I am half in love with you," he concluded with a shrug. "He has done so for weeks."

Jane's breath quickened. "Lord Vawdrey? But why would he think such a thing?"

He pursed his lips. "Probably because I rhapsodized about your virtues in front of him one time."

Jane gazed at him. He was being sarcastic, of course. Wasn't he? "And by that," she said lightly, "I suppose you mean you damned me with a lot of faint praise and barbed comments?" *Please deny it*, she thought. Let him have been in earnest for once.

His smile broadened. "We really do know each other very well; you have to admit."

To her horror, Jane felt herself grow choked. She had known, he must have been insulting her, of course. And she had not, even for a moment, entertained the idea that his words could have contained so much as a grain of truth. Why, then, was she struggling now not to cry?

"Jane?" He sounded concerned.

"It is nothing," she choked out. "I am just suddenly rather tired."

446

"You have overdone it," he said reproachfully. "Standing around in that draughty hall all morning, listening to a lot of very dull men pontificating."

Jane pulled the blankets up around her. "I have had a slight headache, that is all."

He frowned. "You have been worrying too much about this business with the Queen. Likely it is the tension of all that frowning that has caused it." He started to reach for her face and Jane flinched back. She could not help it. She felt she could not bear in the moment for her old enemy to touch her. Not right now. Not when…

"Does it hurt that badly?" he asked, leaning over her, a worried look on his face.

To her horror, Jane felt the tears gathering under her eyelids and shut them fast. "Yes."

She heard the bed rustle as he climbed out. "I will have Ayleth fetch you a poultice at once."

Jane listened to the rustle of his robe as he pulled it on before she could muster the courage to sit up. "Alisander?" She could not look him directly in the eye. Instead, she concentrated on the pleating on the blanket in front of her. Still, she could feel his gaze upon her. Mustering her courage, she asked, "Am I your first—that is, am I the first person you have called your dove?"

As soon as she'd asked it, her face flooded with color. *What a stupid question*. He would now eviscerate her for putting herself in such a vulnerable position. He likely called all his women that. Mayhap it made it easier for him when he paid a compliment or threw out an endearment. She steeled herself for his response and faced him.

His expression, however, was not what she had expected. In truth, he looked neither amused nor contemptuous. She was not sure precisely *what* it was in his eyes. It looked almost like fondness. Affection mingled with regret. *Regret. Oh gods*. Jane felt a stab of fear that left her almost dizzy.

"How clever of you to realize," he said lightly. "You are my very own pet dove and quite the novelty to me, so stop looking at me as though I'm about to wring your lovely neck. Instead, I should like to put a pretty collar about it. Would that be so very bad?" When she did not speak, he walked back to the bed and sat on it beside her. "Jane? Do not look like that. You are safe with me."

Safe. Was she? She swallowed and ducked her head. "Like what?" she said with an awkward laugh. "I don't know what you mean." She made as though to turn her back to him, but his hand shot out to catch her arm.

"Jane," he whispered, pulling her back into his arms, and his words were almost a caress. *"Don't*. Do not do that. Let us surprise everyone by being understanding spouses who do not intrude on one another or try to push the other past their point of comfort."

Jane's breath froze in her throat. Was that what she was doing? She felt suddenly mortified. She had embarrassed both of them with that stupid question. It was as she had always thought. She was not sophisticated beneath her court veneer. Not one bit.

"Of course," she said aloud and hoped to gods her voice sounded steadier to his ears than her own. What she really wanted to do, suddenly, was indulge in a good cry. That would release these terrible, overwhelming feelings.

Suddenly it was imperative that he was gone from the room, and she was alone. *Not intrude on one another*. When her body

448

still physically ached from where his had joined with hers? "I will make sure never to encroach on you again," she uttered and forced a smile to her lips.

He frowned slightly at this but released her arm, and Jane huddled down into the bedsheets again. She would plead a headache for the rest of the day if necessary. In the background, he was talking again. Something about fetching Ayleth. *Leave, just leave*. "Yes," she murmured, agreeing with whatever he said.

"I'll leave you to sleep off your bad head, then," he said after a heavy pause.

Recognizing the longed-for word, she peered out of the sheets. "Yes, thank you," she said and meant it. She could not wait for the door to close after him. When he had gone, she buried her head in the pillow and settled into an ugly, jagged weeping that relieved her feelings greatly, though it left her blotched and heavy-eyed.

Ayleth, when she appeared, was sympathetic and tutted and clucked over her swollen, dull eyes. "I never knew you to suffer with bad heads, my lady, neither you nor your sister."

"I will be well presently," Jane assured her and did as she was told, bathing her face in cold water and letting Ayleth help her dress in a loose dressing robe over her shift. It seemed unlikely that she would need to go out and about again today, so she decided to spend the rest of the day quietly.

Alisander reappeared as Ayleth was brushing Jane's hair, only to disappear into his dressing room. When he emerged, Jane pretended not to notice him watching them as Ayleth braided her hair. After a moment, the door softly opened and closed, and he was gone. She was glad he had checked her from

449

embarrassing herself further. Yes, *glad.* She would not make that mistake again.

27

It was the beginning of a trying week for Alisander. Even the elegance of his new mourning outfit, certainly the finest at court, and far nicer than Wymer's, failed to alleviate his displeasure. He had been concerned at first that Jane had taken suddenly ill or that Bathilde's death had somehow sent her back into black despair over her sister.

Then, after a day or so, he faced facts. Jane was neither unwell nor despairing. She was dissatisfied. With him. In vain, he had tried to steer them back onto the desired track. He had thrown out lures, flattery, teasing, and downright needling, only to receive the most lackluster of responses.

His wife was barely engaging with him at all these days, and when she did, it was bland and insincere. All "Yes, husband" and "No, husband" and "Three bags full, husband." After four days of this, Alisander had had enough. It was no good; they could not carry on like this. He was going to have to force the issue.

He glanced at her now as he poured a goblet of foaming ale. "Will you join me in a drink? No?" He knocked back a swig. "How agreeable you are being this afternoon, wife," he heard himself say, even as he willed himself not to say anything cruel. "I have to admit, though, it is almost a *little* dull to find you so passive."

When she gave no reaction to his words, he felt a frisson of alarm in spite of himself. "Are you not feeling well?" he asked, slamming down the jug.

"I?" She looked up from the letter she was reading. It was another dreary letter from Kinnerton and could not possibly be holding her interest. "I am quite well, I assure you."

"Then perhaps you could inject just a modicum of enthusiasm into your conversation?" he suggested dryly. "Who knows? It might add a certain piquancy to the experience."

Nothing. No reaction. He narrowed his eyes. "Are you angry with me, Jane?" That was too direct, of course, but he was tired of tiptoeing around the issue.

"Not at all," she replied levelly. "I am grateful to you."

The strange thing was, she sounded sincere. For some reason that disquieted him most of all. "Grateful?" She nodded. "For what?"

"Oh, for everything, Alisander."

Her use of his name affected him strangely. *When had she last used it?* Not for a while. "So, it's Alisander again, now, is it?" he remarked with a twist of his lips. Jane had the cheek to look mildly surprised by his words.

He ought to call her out. *She* was the one who had caused this upset. He had done nothing amiss, and so he should tell her. Still, something held him back from pushing her too far and shattering her newfound serenity.

He knew, of course, what had caused her sudden coolness; he was just pretending ignorance. Though *why* he was pretending to himself, he could not fathom. He tossed back the last of his honeyed ale, and though it should taste lingeringly sweet, it tasted to him entirely bitter.

He had tried to caution her against mistaking physical intimacy with another kind, and now she was punishing him. It was

452

disappointing but predictable. She was angry and wanted to make him suffer. And she had found a most effective way to do that. He pulled a face and plunked down his cup.

Of course, the best way for him to counter this would be to pretend indifference in return. He *ought* to tell her he was bored of her, to walk right out of this room, to tell her if she did not bolster her ideas, he would take a more interesting lover.

He ought to, but somehow, he knew full well he would not.

"Won't you come and sit by the fire, my lord?" Jane asked. He glanced her way and saw her expression of polite concern. "The fire has not yet taken the chill out of the air, and it is bitter out." A sudden, horrible thought occurred to him. Perhaps, after all, she was not pretending? "Alisander?" she repeated, seeing his sudden stare.

"Jane," he said, pulling himself together, "I want you to stop this. You are not good at playing games, so why bother trying?"

"Games?"

"It is patently obvious what you are doing, and I am not putting up with this anymore, I warn you." When she glanced about the room, looking genuinely bewildered, Alisander felt a moment of panic. Jane was not a good actress. "What is wrong with you?" he demanded, slamming down his goblet. "You are not doing your part at all."

"My part?" she echoed blankly.

Perhaps she thought she could mouth words of wifely solicitude toward him these days, and he would have to make do with that? "Yes, your part," he said testily. "How am I to tease you if you won't act annoyed or flustered or *anything*."

Jane had just opened her mouth to respond when a knock sounded on the door, and Alisander realized her blessed friends must have arrived. With all the palace assembly areas closed, the courtiers had taken of late to hosting their own little gatherings in their more cramped quarters. It was Jane's turn this afternoon.

He rolled his eyes, knowing she expected him to make himself scarce. Quite deliberately, he took a seat. Not even by the flicker of an eyelid did she betray any displeasure at this. It was true, he had business elsewhere, but Lemarchier could wait. He was not in the mood to indulge his official duties when his marital accord lay in tatters at his feet.

Jane folded her letter and cleared her throat as Robert's knock sounded on the door. "Come in!" she called out, and Robert ushered in the young women with a paternal air. Alisander let his eye travel over them with displeasure. Gods, she had the whole gaggle of them, not just the usual two or three! Even that wretched Melvin girl was in attendance. He supposed they must all be starved of entertainment, what with the King having cast such a damper over everything.

Jane stood up, and there were lots of curtseys and greetings and exclamations. With them all dressed in white, they seemed more like a flock of geese than ever. Alisander remained where he was, casting a jaundiced eye over proceedings. Finally, they were all settled, and Jane was handing round cups of ale and urging them to partake of the dishes of nuts and candied fruits.

As his sullenness had evinced no response in his wife, Alisander decided to switch his approach. Leaning forward in his seat, he exerted himself to fully charm the company at large, until he had them all, even the models of propriety like Constance Northcott, sat in the palm of his hand. Jane eased back into her seat with a vacant smile, as if this was all as it should be. Alisander narrowed his eyes at her.

His stories took a slight turn. Now he was regaling them with tales of the Lasconian court and a few choice stories from the Queen's girlhood, which showed her in a decidedly undignified light. He saved the best for last, which was an account of Princess Armenal tripping at her brother's coronation and making a fool of herself.

He fancied Jane tensed for a fraction of a second, but it could have been a trick of the light. "We are all of us clumsy on occasion," she demurred as Patience and Emma giggled disloyally. "Especially in our youth."

"I wasn't," he corrected her swiftly.

Jane did not even bridle. She just sat there politely as the rest of them tittered, her pale eyes so dull they looked nothing like topazes. It was *infuriating*.

"We cannot all be as elegant as you, my lord," Emma Stanhope said gamely.

"Dear me, no," he agreed. "I should not want that. How then would I stand out at this glittering court?"

"I think you would always stand out, Lord Bardulf," Lucy Melvin said. Was it his imagination or was the inflection a little snide? It was so hard to tell. All the Melvins sounded like they had bunged-up nasal passages.

"Indeed," he agreed. "For one such as I, melting into the background is not an option. Some of us draw the eye quite naturally, and others of us"—his eyes flickered over Lucy a moment—"do not." Osanna Spencer lifted her hand to cover her mouth. "You ladies will, no doubt, have observed by now," he continued smoothly, "how poorly this current white garb becomes most men. Alas, it displays, quite shockingly, a scrawny calf or a knocked knee."

"So many of them will not even attempt it," Estrilda cut in. "I have been *quite* shocked! Even Earl Vawdrey has not donned anything but his habitual black!"

Alisander shook his head. "No, no, Lord Vawdrey would never sacrifice his air of mystery. Not after all this time he has spent so carefully cultivating it." Quite unfairly, Alisander was currently nursing a grudge against Oswald, for he blamed him for the fact he and Jane were currently at odds.

It was all that bastard Vawdrey's fault. If he had never been so imprudent as to bring him up in conversation, mayhap this quarrel would never have occurred. Not that it was a quarrel precisely. A quarrel would have been *preferable* to this.

"Oh, but I don't know that we can blame him for that," Margaret Pryor said fairly. "After all, very few men could get away with white hose."

Alisander crossed his ankles as all eyes turned at once to take in the splendor of his legs. "Jane believes my thighs are my best feature," he informed them blandly, though his eyes dwelt only on her reaction. It was disappointingly unruffled. "Though for myself, I do not think they rival my face."

Soon after this, Alisander decided he would think of some excuse and make a hasty exit. After all, what was the use in staying when Jane was being tiresome and refusing to rise to his bait? He stayed out late and did not return until the early hours of the morning when he found her soundly sleeping. He was under no illusion she had tried to wait up for him.

Fleetingly, as he undressed, he recalled that night he had returned from her uncle's town lodgings, and she had surprised

456

him by coming out in search of him. She would not do that now. Eyeing the spill of pale hair on her pillow, he could not resist the impulse to reach out and stroke it. *Am I your first dove?*

Such an indirect way of asking if he cared for her. It occurred to him, suddenly, that he could have just said yes. She might even have been content with that. She might *never* have pushed him for anything deeper. If ever a woman might have settled for so little, it was Jane. She would take any excuse to shy away from emotional displays.

He supposed it came from her keeping them so firmly bottled up for so many years that any attempt to prize the stopper resulted in them overflowing to an alarming degree. Strong feelings left Jane shaken, when she *so* wanted to be calm and collected. Even something as trivial as holding a baby in her arms overwhelmed her. She would grit her teeth and her eyes would fill with tears.

It made something turn over in his chest to think of it. She must, he thought suddenly, have been really brave to ask him that ridiculous question. And it was not as though he could blame her entirely for what had happened. Had he not raised the topic himself, and not in good faith either?

I think you must have fallen in love with me. Why had he said that to her?

Extinguishing the candle, he climbed under the covers and considered this in the dark where it was always easier to breathe. He knew why. He had done it purely to disquiet her, and to frighten her off the subject in the future, he told himself firmly.

Knowing only too well how she shrank from such things, he had cruelly goaded her to see the fear that would spring into her eyes. And when he had seen it, he had been satisfied, for it had assured him that never again would she be so rash as to question his feeling for her.

He knew why full well why he had said that to her. He had known it would send her into a cold panic. And yet…that did not explain the flicker of something else in his breast when he had said the words out loud. It did not explain *the rush* he had felt when Jane had *not* denied it when instead she had reached for his hand.

Alisander gasped, opening his eyes wide. What a stupid bastard he was. He hadn't wanted to frighten her at all. He had wanted to goad Jane into telling him she loved him. He wanted her to say it first. He wanted her to declare it, and then weep over him and give him her bleeding heart for his safekeeping.

He was astonished with himself. It was all very well being a deceitful bastard in his dealings with others, but deceiving himself was quite another thing. What depths of deception did a man's soul have to possess for him to start successfully lying to himself?

He felt winded. Now that he had dragged the feelings out and examined them, he was not even sure *how* long he had been in love with her. He could not remember a time when his feelings had not been…rather *involved* when it came to Jane. Perhaps it went back as far as that first time he had seen her face light up with joy. That time the Queen had praised her, and Jane had *glowed*.

He had wanted her to glow like that for him. And instead— fuck—he had extinguished it. She had been so brave and sweet, and he had made a total mess of it, as he was making a mess of *everything* at the moment. Likely his clumsy words had wounded her. Poor little Jane.

He sought her out under the blankets, dragging her into his arms. *That* was why she had withdrawn from him. Not to punish him, but to preserve herself from further hurt. *Foolish Jane.* Did she not know that *he* was there to guard her now?

Carefully, so as not to disturb her sleep, he curled about her, burying his nose in her hair. She had left it loose, and even in the dark, he could tell it was crinkled from being braided while it was wet. Had she left it loose for him? he wondered. Mayhap he should wake her and find out.

Then again, what if she now meant to bring her politeness to the bedchamber? He could not *stand* it. Not after everything they had shared before. He closed his eyes and considered how best he should have answered that bloody question, instead of trying to push her gently away. Perhaps honestly? he mused. Would that have been worth an attempt?

Yes, Jane, you are the first woman I have simultaneously tormented and soothed. I don't know why. I have never been prompted to act this way by another. I only know that I must be your tormentor, and you my chief delight. Please allow us to continue in this lovely state of affairs, until we both expire of old age and then we can be entombed together under the de Balon family crest.

Was that really too much to ask? He wasn't sure if it was a reasonable request or not, truth be told. Knowing Jane, she would either gaze at him blankly or cry and hold him just that bit too tightly for comfort. Either reaction would be fine, in truth, and preferable to recoiling from him in horror.

The trouble of it was that this was not the only thing he had botched of late. He had made quite a hash of his other, non-husbandly duties also. Neglectful would be the most lenient description of his recent approach.

459

Lemarchier was still not happy with him, which meant neither was Wilhelm. Then, too, there was Hubair, who always took a ridiculous amount of offense. It was possible that Alisander had fumbled his response to the Kloberg situation. Whenever he caught sight of their ambassador lately, Alphonse immediately went haring off in the opposite direction. That was not a good sign.

He sighed and tightened his arms about his sleeping wife. At least when she was asleep she was pliant and warm as ever in his arms. Breathing deeply against her neck, he consigned the rest of them to the devil and relaxed into sleep.

*

Alisander was mindful the next morning of Jane's brittle politeness. He was gentle of manner in his dealings with her, and on receiving a note informing him the King's rooms were to be thrown open that morning, he immediately told her as much. "We had better go forth and find out what's afoot."

She acquiesced readily enough, and once they were both fully arrayed in their mourning attire, they duly made their way in that direction, joining the drifting white clouds of courtiers all moving toward the King's presence chamber.

Any hopes they all may have harbored that the King might be in better spirits were soon dispelled. He started off fairly well, looking subdued but bearing up. Then some fool decided to curry favor by singing the late Bathilde's praises.

Alisander fancied that the entire room tensed as Wymer's lips started trembling beneath his golden whiskers and his blue eyes started to swim. The Queen attempted a valiant rescue, responding in hearty, buoyant tones, but the King was too far gone for that. He reached out a shaky hand to clasp his wife's arm as tears rolled down his cheeks. "She was the best of women!" he sobbed. "Never again will the world see her like!"

"Indeed, she was," Armenal agreed soothingly. "Those of us who knew her could only admire her noble qualities." She paused, then lifted her voice. "Why, she raised a king!" she announced rousingly. Picking up on the cue, the courtiers shouted and cheered. "The Lion of all Karadok!" the Queen proclaimed in a ringing voice.

Wymer's head nodded. "That she did!" he agreed before breaking into noisy sobs.

Before Alisander's fascinated gaze, the Queen rose from her seat and moved to the side of Wymer's throne. "Perhaps—" she ventured uncertainly, but none of them were to discover whatever she was about to suggest, for with an anguished howl, the King seized her roughly about the waist and buried his face against her stomach, where he wept as wholeheartedly and unabashed as a child.

The Queen froze, hesitated a moment, and then reached down to pet his head. Alisander could not make out the words she was murmuring from here, but her demeanor suggested they were nonsense words, the kind used to soothe children. He was surprised Armenal even possessed the vocabulary.

All around them, the nobles were murmuring in consternation, unsure what to do. A good many lords and nobles were clearing their throats and casting longing looks toward the door, unsure if it would be fitting to make an escape from the royal presence before they were officially dismissed.

Lord Vawdrey climbed the steps to the dais. "If everyone could make their way out in an orderly fashion!" he directed firmly, and with varied murmurings, some thankful, others disappointed, the crowds began to head toward the door.

461

Alisander turned to face Jane but found Piers Winstanley now had her undivided attention. At his back, he seemed to have gathered all of the ladies-in-waiting who had managed to array themselves in full mourning garb.

Jane turned to Alisander. "There is a service in the royal chapel this morn," she explained colorlessly. "The Queen's ladies will attend the first mass."

Alisander frowned. "It is cold in the chapel," he pointed out. "Even with many candles lit. You must wear your mantle."

"Will you be joining us, my lord?" Piers asked politely. "You will be most welcome."

"I will not," he answered more swiftly than regretfully. "Alas, I have official business elsewhere which prevents me." He bowed, first to Jane and then toward the rest of them, then turned on his heel and walked straight into Oswald Vawdrey.

"Dear me," tutted Oswald. "This is *most* unlike you, my dear Alisander. Usually you are as sure-footed as a cat."

Alisander narrowed his eyes. "You caused that collision on purpose, Vawdrey," he murmured. "And nothing could convince me otherwise."

Oswald smirked. "As it happens, our meeting is somewhat fortunate despite my crushed toes. I *did* need a word with you about something," he cast around vaguely. "Now, just what *was* it about?" He wrinkled his brow.

"I am sure it will come to mind presently," Alisander retorted, adjusting his ruffled cuffs.

"Perhaps you would accompany me back to my office?" Oswald Vawdrey suggested. "I feel sure the walk there will dislodge the memory."

Alisander eyed him thoughtfully. "Oh, very well," he conceded, just a touch ungraciously. He had a hundred things he *should* be doing, but truth be told, none of them appealed to him remotely either. By this point, his discontent was bleeding into every province of his life.

Vawdrey kept up a stream of desultory conversation until they reached his rooms of office. Once there, he exchanged a few pleasant words with his lackey, Bryce, in the antechamber and then ushered Alisander into his inner sanctum.

Once the door was firmly closed after them, he dropped all pretense of geniality and turned toward Alisander. "Well, now it is just the two of us, perhaps you would oblige me by telling me what the *hells* are you playing at, Bardulf?"

Alisander dropped into a chair and surveyed him cagily. "I don't know," he admitted, "but I feel sure you're about to tell me."

"Do you mean to tell me—?" Vawdrey seemed almost lost for words. He started again. "You are completely *jeopardizing* your position here, Alisander!" he thundered at him. "My gods, I thought I could at *least* depend on you to play your part! Instead, here you are, skipping receptions, turning a deaf ear to intrigue, and practically ignoring the current political climate completely!"

Alisander winced. "I am aware I have not been employing my customary finesse—" he began.

"Finesse?" Vawdrey repeated incredulously. "You've been blundering about with all the delicacy of an escaped bull in the marketplace!"

"Well, I—"

"You've been setting people's backs up, gravely insulting your fellow diplomats, and getting official complaints lodged against you left, right, and center!"

Alisander blinked. "Who the hells has lodged a complaint against me?" he asked incredulously.

"The most grievous one, you mean. The ambassador from Kloberg."

"Hubair! That little fuck! No wonder he's been avoiding me. Still," he added in bewilderment, "what possible reason could he complain about me to the Karadokian authorities?"

"Would you please think straight for one minute?" Oswald begged, sitting on the edge of his desk. "I'm starting to think you've suffered a head injury."

Alisander rubbed his brow. "He didn't complain to you, did he?" he sighed as realization dawned.

"No, he most assuredly did not!"

"He complained to Wilhelm," Alisander groaned, dropping his head into his hands.

"Oh yes, and in the *strongest* of terms too."

"Fuck." Alisander brooded on this a moment. "Even so," he said, lifting his head, "I fail to see why—"

"Perhaps because you have neglected your duties so disgracefully of late, and that you are *completely* oblivious to several plots which I have *not* exactly troubled to conceal from you!"

Alisander had the grace to blush slightly. He tipped back in his seat to contemplate the painted ceiling. It depicted a celestial sky. "Has anyone ever told you, Vawdrey," he commented with a frown, "that there is such a thing as being *too* subtle?"

"Too subtle? Coming from you?" Oswald Vawdrey stared at him. "You usually *love* all the sneaking around. You revel in it!"

Alisander shut his eyes briefly. He hitched one shoulder. "I have not been in the mood lately," he said resentfully.

"Not in the—?"

"Who else complained about me?" he asked sulkily.

"It scarcely matters at this point."

"It was Albrici, wasn't it?" Alisander pulled a face. "You need not answer, for I already know it was."

"Would you *please* focus on the matter at hand, Alisander?" Oswald entreated. "Why is it that *I* am more alarmed at the prospect of you being dragged back to the Western Isles—"

"Lascony," Alisander corrected him.

"—than *you* are!"

"Wait a minute." Alisander sat up. "What did you just say? I cannot possibly return just now. I have…certain responsibilities here."

"Most assuredly, you do," Oswald agreed heavily, though Alisander did not think they were talking about the same responsibilities. "Need I remind you, you have a wife and child here," he added direly.

Oh. It seemed they were talking about the same thing after all. He cleared his throat. "Not to mention I promised my

465

manservant he would never have to set foot in Lascony ever again."

"Well, maybe *he* won't!"

"You don't understand," Alisander said absently. "Where I go, he goes."

"You think I am unfamiliar with the notion of loyalty?" Oswald asked silkily.

"Now don't be offended, Vawdrey." Alisander waved a hand. "Strange to say, I do *not* think that, despite every appearance to the contrary."

Oswald grunted, looking slightly appeased. "You have made things damnably awkward these past few weeks, Alisander," he said with suppressed anger. "I could happily wring your neck right now, so do not tempt me!"

Alisander snorted. "I expect you are sadly out of practice these days."

"*Me* out of practice?" he asked snarkily. "Need I point out that I have had to suppress the information that Sir Phillip Cecil was found at the foot of his staircase with a broken neck for the past three weeks?"

"Well, he was getting on in years, and people *do* miss their footing. Especially when they over-imbibe of an evening, as Sir Phillip was wont to do."

Oswald shook his head. "You could not have dealt with it a little more neatly?"

"The stairs factor was an essential part of the narrative," he explained.

Oswald sighed, pushed off his desk, and walked around it, taking his usual seat. "What, pray, is your excuse for shamefully neglecting your duties of late? And for your arrant lack of tact?" he continued wearily. "I have never known you to lack political sensitivity before. It was the *one* thing about you on which I felt I could always depend."

Looking at Vawdrey's face, Alisander realized that nothing but the truth would do. He released a pent-up breath. "I've been distracted of late. It is Jane," he admitted. "She is not remaining where she should. In the place I put her, I mean. She—well, she keeps—" He broke off. "She is simply not *behaving* as she ought," he concluded lamely.

"Dear me!" Oswald folded his hands on his desk. "Lady Bardulf is not behaving in an appropriately wifely manner?"

"No. She *is*, but that's partly the problem!" Alisander huffed.

Oswald's eyebrows shot up into his dark hair. "Forgive me, but does that not indicate it is *you* who is not acting as he ought?"

"Me?" Alisander was instantly incensed. "I have done naught amiss!"

"You are acting as a husband should?" Vawdrey had the cheek to ask in accents of deepest skepticism.

"I am," he responded a trifle stiffly.

"Really? Might I ask, by your estimation, what such a thing entails?" Vawdrey's tone was smoothly enquiring, but Alisander was not fooled for a minute.

"Well, perhaps my marriage is not being conducted along Vawdrey lines," he responded sarcastically. "No one has tried to nullify our contract so far if that's what you mean, and neither one of us has raised the issue of annulment!"

Oswald's eyes narrowed. "Give it time, my dear Alisander," he muttered. "Give it time."

"And they had better not!" Alisander retorted. "If they know what is good for them."

"If you were to get dragged back to the Wes—to Lascony," Vawdrey corrected himself, swiftly, "then I can assure you, the King would not allow Lady Jane to remain unprotected with such a young daughter in her care. Neither could he permit her to remain married to a foreign subject, disgraced even in his homelands and struck off from official service to his King."

"If I was banished from these shores," Alisander interrupted him forcefully, "then I can assure you that *Lady Bardulf* and *our* child would not be your King's concern under any circumstance. They are *my* concern and *I* alone would provide for them. No one else!"

Vawdrey paused. "By making them share your banishment?" he asked curiously.

"If need be, yes," Alisander admitted, his face flushing slightly. "I may have learned to—to care for a select *few*," he stressed carefully, as more people sprang to mind than he anticipated. Not just Jane, Celestia, and Robert, but gummy little Bertrand, Anne, and *even* Wat. "But that has not changed my fundamental character," he insisted doggedly. "My essence remains selfish, through and through. I would drag all of them into exile with me if needs be." He considered this a moment. "Perhaps you think that is not husbandly behavior. Perhaps *you* think I should be noble, and give them up—"

"Not really," Vawdrey interjected smoothly.

"But you see, I am not noble of nature, and I never have been!" Alisander flung at him as if he had not spoken. "And I have *no intention* of giving up my family now that I have finally found them!"

"Well," said Vawdrey briskly, "those are the first words of sense that have left your mouth in the past month." He steepled his hands before him. "I will admit marriage is no small change to one's status and it can take some longer than others to adjust to the wedded state. However, I will need your assurance, Alisander, that you can fulfill the role of diplomat as well as husband in the future. Otherwise, your continued presence at court is entirely useless to me."

Alisander glared back at him. "As there are *several* ineffectual diplomats littering up the corridors of this and every palace known to man, are you quite sure it is not my role of spy that you are dissatisfied with?" he asked pointedly.

Oswald dropped the pretense. "Well, of course it is, my dear Alisander. Have I not made that entirely clear? You have reported back to your King precisely *one-quarter* of the information I have left for you to discover this past month. Your performance has been quite abysmal. My method of information dissemination has been almost entirely ineffectual without your link in the chain."

Alisander spluttered. "Are you actually scolding me for failing to spy on your court?"

"Yes," answered Oswald forthrightly. "And let me tell you, it is quite outrageous that I am being forced to be this explicit with you," Oswald chided him. "I am *most* disappointed."

Alisander suppressed the impulse to squirm in his seat. "Well, you are not the only one, I daresay," he admitted at last, covering his eyes with his fingers. Jane was disappointed in him too. He felt…downcast. Most unlike his usual self.

Vawdrey eyed him severely. "If you dare fall into a fit of the sullens, Alisander, I shall banish you myself."

That drew a reluctant smile from him. "I know that I need to—to make up some lost ground," he admitted, avoiding Oswald's perceptive eye.

"Do you think, once you have made up this ground," Vawdrey said carefully, "that you will be able to embrace your duties in the spirit that you once did?"

Alisander considered this. "I hope so," he said fervently.

"That is not exactly reassuring," Oswald sighed. "But I suppose I will have to make do with it."

"You will admit," Alisander rallied, "that I have succeeded in getting Armenal to act where the King is concerned at least. She has caught him on her leash. That *was* what you wanted after all."

Oswald's eyes rolled up to the ceiling as he considered this. "I suppose that is true enough," he conceded. "Though her present course of action is causing a lot of fuss and bother among the Privy Council."

"They would all be quite lost without *something* to shake their jowls about."

Oswald Vawdrey tapped a finger against his desk. "I wonder..." he pondered, giving Alisander a long, hard look. Then he seemed to give himself a little shake. "I will admit, I have a certain idea on how I can extricate you from this mess of your own making, Alisander. It is a little...radical, but I believe a situation this dire cannot be solved with anything less extreme. I will be plain; it would involve you putting yourself entirely in my hands."

Alisander eyed him warily. He did not care for the gleam in Oswald Vawdrey's eyes. "What sort of an idea?" he asked grudgingly.

Oswald shook his head regretfully. "No, no, I'm afraid you must be kept in the dark at this stage in order for it to work. Do you trust me?"

"Not for an instant," he responded swiftly.

Oswald smirked. "But you should, my dear Bardulf, at least in this regard. I assure you; I have your best interests at heart."

"Ah, but there remains the question of whether *your* estimation of my best interests would match with my own."

Oswald straightened up. "Very well, I will prove it to you. I personally would list them as follows," he said, beginning to count on his fingers. "One, your remaining in Karadok, two, retaining your official role as ambassador to the Western Isles—"

"Lascony," Alisander corrected him.

"Three, remaining married to one Jane Cecil—"

"That goes without saying," Alisander interrupted with a frown.

"—and four, retaining custodianship of the child Celestia. I list these things in no order, you understand."

Alisander was silent a moment, though he felt thoroughly rattled. "You really think these things are in jeopardy?" he asked. Vawdrey's somber expression persuaded him far more than mere words would have. *Damn it.* Things must be dire indeed if he was at risk of losing *everything.*

"There was an occasion, in the not-too-distant past, when you were kind enough as to do me a good turn, Alisander,"

Vawdrey said quietly. "Do you remember? You were under no obligation, yet you issued me a warning which put me on my guard before an axe could fall upon my neck."

"So dramatic," Alisander murmured. "It was the merest word in your ear." Vawdrey said nothing, just continued to gaze steadily at him. "Oh, very well," he said irritably. "I will do it. Against my better judgment, I will place myself entirely and blindly in your hands, Vawdrey. But I warn you if you should—"

"Excellent," Oswald Vawdrey replied glibly. "You will not regret it. Or if you do," he added conscientiously, "not for too long."

Alisander found himself filled with the greatest of misgivings. *What did that mean?* He was soon to find out.

28

Jane adjusted her stance slightly, for her knees were aching despite the embroidered kneeling mats. They had been praying now for a solid two hours. She watched the King move away from the casket. He looked exhausted; indeed, she was not sure he did not sway slightly on his feet.

Immediately the Queen appeared at his side, patting his shoulder and nodding her head in approval. After one last wistful look at her, back over his shoulder, the King departed. From his expression, Jane guessed the Queen had declined to accompany him.

Jane turned to face front again and tried to concentrate on the words the monks were muttering. Unfortunately, the rhythmic chanting had the effect of making her eyelids grow heavy. A sudden jab to the ribs revived her, and for a moment she thought it was Osanna, who must have noticed she was in danger of drifting off.

Then she realized that someone was pushing in between them. Jane had no sooner turned a look of disapproval on the newcomer than she realized it was none other than Queen Armenal.

"Jane!" the Queen hissed. "I have sent the King back to his rooms. He is most tired. He has not been sleeping well, and this has all been too much for him." To Jane's surprise, she sounded rather pleased with herself. Seeing Jane's expression, the Queen added quickly, "He will sleep much better in his own bed, I daresay. I know I will certainly sleep much better without him in *mine*!"

She leaned in closer. "I make no complaint, you understand. Your instruction proved most invaluable. It is only"—she pulled a face—"sometimes, I feel it is a little too efficacious, you understand?" Jane blinked at her. "It is most gratifying, now the King is mad for love of me," she stated, "but sometimes it is a little much. I hardly have a moment to myself!"

Jane coughed, glancing to the right and left of them. She felt sure the Bishop of Hudde was glaring in their direction. Anyone else but the Queen would have received a severe scolding for all this whispering.

"I will confess," the Queen continued, "to being initially a *little* disappointed with your advice, Jane. It seemed unfathomable to me that such a stratagem should have worked in your own circumstances, let alone mine! Then, I recalled something about Lord Bardulf's background." She looked smug.

Jane tried to hold her tongue but failed the test. "What did you recall?" she could not help but ask.

The Queen smiled. "I remembered that it was not just his traitorous kin he lost in childhood, but his foster family also. Then it made more sense that your compassion and empathy should conquer him so completely. After so many losses, he would of course be susceptible to—"

Jane interrupted her. "Foster family?"

"Yes, the Herveys."

A jarring memory stirred in Jane's mind. "The *Herveys*?" she repeated with horror, thinking of the family who had treated Alisander so poorly as a child.

"Yes." The Queen nodded. "The family of Sir Reginald Hervey suffered so many misfortunes that it soon began to be whispered that they were a family laboring under a dark curse."

Sir Reginald Hervey, that was it, thought Jane. That was the name of the man who had executed Alisander's brother and uncles. Then, in a cruel twist of fate, Alisander had become the ward of the same man, and he and his wife had treated him most cruelly. "What sort of misfortunes?" Jane heard herself ask in a strange voice.

"Oh, he has not told you. I would have thought he would have far rather told you of the Hervey family tragedy than the de Balon one. Still"—she shrugged her shoulders—"such is the mystery of the male mind." Seeing Jane's fixed gaze, the Queen continued in hushed tones. "First, it was the Lady Hervey who met a sorry end. She fell one morning to her death from some walkway which skirted their house. A freak accident apparently. Her fall was broken by water, but then the unfortunate woman drowned before they could recover her."

Jane's breath caught in her throat as she remembered Alisander's words. He had told her that his fondest daydream as a boy involved tampering with the parapet so that one day Lady Hervey would plummet to her death into the moat. *Could it be mere coincidence?*

"Then, only five years later, Sir Reginald's only son and heir met his ill fate. He was stabbed to death after a dispute one night in a tavern and the perpetrator of the outrage never discovered."

Jane closed her fingers around the gold ring she wore on her third finger. The one bearing the de Balon crest. Alisander had told her he stabbed a man in a tavern to retrieve this particular family heirloom. The story sounded remarkably similar. *Another coincidence?*

"Finally, some six months after that, Sir Reginald choked to death on a fishbone one night whilst dining alone." Jane relaxed a little. That one sounded like natural causes at least. "The funny thing was," the Queen continued, whispering, "that both his steward and his cook insisted such a thing was an impossibility, as no fish had been served that night. Yet when they cut into him, what was discovered lodged in his throat?" Jane turned horrified eyes on her. "A fish bone as big as a finger!" the Queen finished triumphantly, then gave a violent start.

They both turned and Jane saw that Piers was standing behind them apologetically. "Your Majesty," he murmured, "the King has sent for you. He asks that you come to him. He cannot sleep."

A spasm of annoyance crossed the Queen's face. "*Already?* He cannot even have seriously tried!"

Piers lowered his gaze. "Yes, Your Highness," he answered gravely.

The Queen turned a look on Jane as if to say, *You see?* then took off in a whirl of exasperation. Jane remained kneeling where she was, her mind a positive spin. She had a horrible suspicion lurking in the back of her mind that she did not really want to examine by the light of day. Could *Alisander* have been the curse of the Hervey family?

But how could that be? He had just been a boy when he was taken into their home. A recently bereaved boy who had suffered from nightmares about the cruel fate of his family. *You would not have liked me, Jane.* That was what he had said.

Would she have? Or rather, did she? Jane hardly knew by this point.

She spent another hour in the chapel until the service was over. Then she walked off the stiffness in her knees by making her way down the long corridor on her way back to their rooms. She had crossed the cobbled bailey and made it almost to the top of the steps leading to the courtiers' quarters when she heard a steady thrumming noise which disconcerted her.

What was that noise? Looking back over her shoulder, she was surprised to see a company of armed guards marching across the courtyard. Why on earth, wondered Jane, would they be coming in this direction? For some reason, her heart started to thud ominously in her chest, and she quickened her pace.

There could be only one reason. They were coming to take someone away into their custody. *But who?* Jane's last fleeting look revealed the soldiers had reached the bottom step. It was at that point she ducked inside the entrance and raced toward their apartment. She could not possibly have said why, but her alarm grew with every stride.

"Ayleth!" she cried as soon as she was inside the door, bolting it fast. "Anne?"

"Whatever is it, my lady?" Ayleth asked, poking her head out of a nearby doorway. Seeing the look on Jane's face, she hurried toward her.

"Soldiers, Ayleth, outside."

"Outside the door?"

Jane hurried past her. "Is your master at home?"

"He's sat at his desk—" Ayleth started, but Jane did not wait to hear the rest. She was already through the door.

"Alisander!" He looked up in surprise and, seeing her expression, stood straight up. "Soldiers!" she blurted.

He gazed back at her blankly. "Soldiers?"

"On their way here, I think! What will we do?"

"You came to warn me?"

She thought for a moment he looked rather gratified. Then a heavy thudding sounded at their door. A baby started to cry, though whether it was Bertrand or Celestia she knew not.

Jane whipped around. "I knew it!" she gasped. "What will we do?"

"If I am exiled, you mean?" he asked and seemed to consider the question. "I suppose…that we would return to the old country and throw ourselves on the mercy of King Wilhelm."

Jane reached out an arm to grab hold of his sleeve. "Should I pack, in case of having to leave in the night? How would we get safe passage there? We have a baby, don't forget, and—"

"I'm teasing," he said, pulling her into his arms. "Don't look so frightened. I would never let anything bad happen to you. Or Celestia," he added thoughtfully. "We won't be exiled. There is not even the slightest possibility of it. I have always promised Robert."

"You are sure?" She clung to him.

He nodded. "But it's nice to know that you would stand by my side. All will be well, Jane," he said soothingly. "Don't look like that."

"Open up, in the King's name!" shouted a stern voice. Now *two* babies were crying. The first must have been Celestia, as the second let out a much louder wail.

478

"Whoever is it? What's to do?" called out Anne's frightened voice as the bangs on the door increased in volume.

"Jane," Alisander said firmly, setting her aside. "I need you to go now into Robert's room and prevent him from coming out and seeing this. I need you to go and do it now."

"But—"

"He can't see them take me like this, Jane. He's seen this once before," he said in such an urgent undertone that she released his sleeve at once and made for the back bedroom, even as she kept her head turned toward him and her eyes fixed on him.

He flicked something off his sleeve and then walked out of the room. "Make way, Ayleth," Jane heard him calmly say. Then there was the sound of bolts being drawn back.

Jane opened the door to Robert's room without knocking and found the old man dozing in his chair. "Oh, milady," he said, rubbing his eyes. "I do apologize—"

"Stay where you are, Robert," Jane urged him, slamming the door behind her and hurrying to his side.

"Milady?" He looked startled but bleary-eyed, and Jane realized he must be half-deaf not to have heard the commotion outside of his room. She pressed her hand down on his shoulder to keep him where he was as she listened to Ayleth angrily scolding the guards.

"What do you think you are *doing*, that's what I should like to know?" Ayleth cried. "Hammering on our door and setting the babes to crying, you nasty brutes!"

"For shame!" Anne added above the clamor. "They was sweetly sleeping too, and now look what you done! Shame on you!"

479

Jane could just about hear the lower buzz of male voices but could not make out their words.

"Have we visitors?" Robert asked in confusion.

"Please remain seated, Robert. They will be gone presently, and your master wished most particularly for you not to be disturbed." The old man remained where he was, though he was clearly perturbed.

Seeing a bottle of wine on the side, Jane hurriedly poured him a cup with hands that shook. "Please drink this and promise me you will stay put until my return."

He nodded. "Right willingly, milady," he said and took the cup from her. Jane hurried out into the hallway and found the rooms empty of occupants.

She ran to the door and let herself out into the corridor where she found Anne and Ayleth stood grimly side by side, watching the soldiers march down the stairs escorting Alisander with them. Celestia and Bertrand were cradled in their arms, still sobbing up a storm.

Jane crossed to the balustrade and watched as the company marched across the courtyard toward the main wing of the palace. *Were they taking him to the dungeons?*

"Come away, my lady." Ayleth's voice was in her ear. "Come away from prying eyes."

Jane turned and was surprised to see the entire corridor was now lined with courtiers who must have emerged from their rooms having heard the commotion. Their expressions were avid with curiosity.

Anne turned toward her tearfully. "Oh, where they takin' him, milady?" she asked.

"I don't know yet," Jane replied, feeling rather numb. "But I will find out, rest assured." She cleared her throat. "Ayleth, we must be very careful not to let Robert be distressed with this news. His master was most insistent. Has Robert told you—?"

"About his son, John?" Ayleth said grimly. "Aye, he's told me, right enough."

His son, thought Jane, the last piece of the puzzle falling into place. Of course, Alisander had told her that his brother's steward, John, had also been hanged, though quite innocent of any treason. John Tunney had used to carve him wooden birds, that was what he had said. *Robert's last name must be Tunney.*

They made their way back inside, and Ayleth hurried into the back room to check on Robert. Jane took Celestia from the beleaguered Anne, and soon they had quieted both children.

"We best keep him busy, my lady," Ayleth whispered when she and Robert appeared presently.

Jane nodded and then cleared her throat. "Does anyone else think it is a little cold in here at present?" she asked aloud.

"I'll light the fire, milady," Robert said, hurrying to the fireplace.

When Wat appeared two hours later looking pale and chastened, Jane took him to one side. "Have you heard anything? About your master?" For a moment, she thought he would deny all knowledge, then he seemed to think the better of it.

"I've asked around, my lady," he admitted unhappily. "The official word is that it's in retaliation for some collapsed betrothal talks."

"Betrothal talks?" Jane repeated in astonishment. "Whose betrothal?" In her own mind, she had been facing up to the fact that Alisander was almost definitely a spy. Such thoughts had fleetingly crossed her mind before, but she had not cared to dwell on them. "He—he was not promised to another lady…?" she began falteringly and dropped like a stone onto a low seat.

"What nonsense are you spouting, Wat?" Ayleth demanded in a hoarse voice from across the room. By tacit agreement, everyone was trying to keep the subject from Robert, who was now doddering about the room lighting candles.

"Well"—Wat took a deep breath—"apparently King Wilhelm of the Western Isles has a niece that has recently married her second cousin," Wat explained in hushed tones. "But going back a few years, there was some talk of her being betrothed to Prince Raedan."

"Prince Raedan," Jane repeated, thinking of the King's son and heir, seldom seen at court, and certainly not yet numbering a man's years.

"Yes, my lady." Wat cleared his throat, sending a fleeting glance at Robert. "Only, you know what royalty's like with their arranged marriages and such like. Apparently, in some quarters it's seen as a deadly insult to Karadok that the Western Isles have allowed this princess of theirs to wed another."

"Surely King Wymer's got better things to be upset over at present?" Ayleth put in crossly. "Is he not supposed to be prostrate with grief?"

"I don't understand," Jane said flatly. "What has any of this to do with my husband?"

"Well, nothing really," Wat said hopelessly. "But it happens sometimes with foreign ambassadors when their country crosses swords with their host country. They bear the brunt of it. Apparently, King Wilhelm clapped *our* ambassador in irons a couple of weeks ago over some spat about an archduke in Kloberg." He scratched his head. "It's all a bit beyond me, in truth."

Anne stood up, plunking her hands on her hips, as Robert disappeared out of the door to fetch something or other. "So, this is just some petty matter what don't even concern 'im?" she said with disgust. "And just for that, the King sent an armed guard to drag him from his hearth and set these poor little mites a-caterwauling? Outrageous! That's what I call it!"

Poor Wat hung his head as though he felt responsible in some way. Then Jane remembered that he was in the employ of Lord Vawdrey. Well, perhaps *that* was why he felt badly about it. Her chest swelled indignantly. "It is *quite* outrageous," Jane agreed. "And so, we shall let everyone know!"

29

Traitor's Tower, the Royal Palace at Aphrany

Alisander turned away from the window and surveyed the rather bare room he now found himself confined in with displeasure. It was raining again, and he should be reveling in the tragic figure he made, shut up, a prisoner, in Karadok's most infamous tower. He *ought* to be thoroughly enjoying himself, playing up the drama to the hilt, but instead, he felt annoyed and uneasy, and it was *all* Jane's fault.

It had been three days, but still, he was haunted by the expression on her face when the guards had been pounding at their door. She had looked so damn frightened and panicked, and she had clutched at him like she was afraid for his life. No doubt she was crying herself to sleep every night and begging for an interview with the Queen that she might petition her on his behalf.

The idea made him feel coldly furious with the world at large. Jane seemed to have no notion that he could very well look after himself—and her, and their child, *and* their servants, and she ought to have more faith in him, damn it! "She has not gone into the country?" he asked with feigned casualness. "How disobedient of her." Oswald Vawdrey glanced up from the chessboard he was studying and made a murmur of agreement. Alisander regarded him irritably. "You delivered my letter, I suppose?"

A look of reproach flitted across Oswald's face. "Of course I did," he replied, sounding faintly injured. "And what's more, I offered a guarded escort for your entire household to take them

484

down to Kinnerton. Your wife, however, is downright refusing to remove to the country. She says that would look as though they were running away, and she refuses to appear in any way ashamed or as though she agreed that you are guilty of any wrongdoing."

Alisander pulled a face. "It sounds," he said acerbically, "as though you have thoroughly succeeded in putting her back up. No doubt you have handled this *all* wrong." He strode across the room and threw himself moodily down into the chair opposite Vawdrey.

"I?" Oswald looked stunned. "You wound me, Alisander. I have been all that is considerate and sympathetic to Lady Bardulf. I even agreed—entirely straight-faced, I might add—that you are an innocent and injured party in this affair. I explained about the delicate nature of foreign relations and how these things must be allowed to simply run their course—"

"And?" Alisander asked pointedly.

"And what?"

"And what response did she make?"

"She gave me very short shrift indeed," lamented Oswald. "She was abrupt in her manner, almost rude I would say."

"*Rude?*" Alisander repeated incredulously, sitting up in his seat. "That does not sound like Jane at all." He shook his head. "Oh, you have made a wretched mess of this, Vawdrey! I might have known I should never have trusted you!"

"Again, you wrong me," Oswald murmured without heat. "My idea was inspired. Both Lascony and Kloberg have reacted entirely as I had anticipated to your imprisonment. Their dark suspicions that your marriage had somehow compromised you have suffered an abrupt reverse. Hubair is now dashing off

485

letters to one and all, bewailing Karadok's tyranny instead of your undependability. Wilhelm is beside himself with fury that we should dare incarcerate his emissary." He reached across and moved his knight. "Your move."

Alisander ignored him. "When I *think* of the effort I made writing that letter!" he seethed. "It would have brought a tear to the eye of even the most cynical of wives. My words were full of a tender, husbandly solicitude." He scowled at Vawdrey. "And thanks to you, it was all in vain!"

"I read it, of course," Oswald murmured. "And in my opinion, you overdid the pathos."

"Nonsense!" Alisander snapped. "What would you know about it?" He tapped his foot against the table leg irritably. "I *implored* her to take the children and all our dependents to the safe haven of Kinnerton, where they will be away from it all. And now what do I find? They are still racketing about court, likely the subject of gossip and conjecture!" His voice cracked a little over the last three words, and he had to make an effort to recover his calm. "She does not enjoy that sort of thing," he said heavily, remembering how distressed she had appeared on returning to court after her sister's death. "It may even make her ill."

Oswald regarded him thoughtfully across the table. "Of course, you know her better than I do," he said slowly, "but it does not seem to me that Lady Bardulf is suffering unduly at present."

Alisander frowned back at him. "What the devil do you mean by that?" He suffered an unpleasant sensation in his gut. Was Jane not missing him at all?

"Well, just that your good lady wife does not appear in imminent danger of sinking into a decline. If anything, she is striding about, her eyes flashing with scorn at anyone who might even imagine her in need of pity."

Alisander looked up. "Like topazes?"

"I beg your pardon?"

He waved a hand. "Don't regard it, pray continue. Tell me what my wife is up to."

"Well," Vawdrey said, "she seems hell-bent on garnering as much support for you as possible and is stirring up a veritable hornet's nest in the process. To be perfectly honest with you, Bardulf, your wife is making things damnably difficult for me at the moment."

Alisander felt a considerable lightening of his mood. "She is?"

"I had been hoping to keep this matter from the King as much as possible. I explained to him it was a mere formality, sticking you in here after the disgraceful treatment of our own ambassador in the Western Isles of late. I had rather thought that his grief-stricken state would aid in this endeavor, but no such luck."

Alisander tipped his head to one side. "You reckoned without his current predilection for the Queen?" he guessed.

Vawdrey cleared his throat. "Quite so. Your wife was swift to inform Her Majesty, and the Queen is outraged that her countryman is currently 'clapped in irons' in Traitor's Tower. She is buzzing in the King's ear about it, and Wymer does not want her to be furious; he wants her to be sympathetic and conciliatory and wholly concerned with soothing his own brow. In short, the King wants me to bring this matter to a swift and satisfactory conclusion. It is almost a pity; I have decided you must remain here until the end of the month."

"Till the end of the month?" Alisander echoed quickly, looking up.

"I think, by then, your loyalty will be considered once more to be pristine and shining forth like a beacon of light."

Alisander's jaw tensed, but he did not disagree with this strategy. "How will you bear it?" he asked instead dryly. "The situation sounds so fraught with difficulties for you. Meanwhile, I am forced to sleep on a bed slung with ropes and to subsist on scraps and thin gruel!"

Oswald glanced speakingly at the tray next to the door which was littered with plates full of crumbs and an empty flask of wine. He made no comment. "I had a most uncomfortable interview with the Bishop of Badsbury yester'een," he continued calmly. "He is also up in arms and demanding your release."

"Old Carsdale?" Alisander said with surprise, thinking of that austere personage. "I have never noticed any partiality for my society on his part. Why, in heaven's name?"

"The glaziers working on Kilnacre Abbey have downed tools in protest at your arrest," Oswald explained wearily. "They are holding the famous east window to ransom in their workshop until your release. Perhaps you are unaware that the eastern window is considered the jewel of Kilnacre? Without it, the pilgrims will surely divert to St. Frode's, and the bishop will lose a good part of his income."

"A bishop pleading my cause, no less," Alisander mused. He placed a hand to his breast. "I might have known my precious guild of glaziers would rush to my defense. How touching."

"You jest but they have caused chaos throughout Aphrany with demonstrations and petitions. Even the King has been forced to acknowledge your surprising popularity at large." At Alisander's skeptical look, he added, "The oriel window in his dressing room was put through by a stone, and we have been unable to get it replaced."

"I hope the wind whistles past Wymer's arse every time he pulls on his chausses," Alisander replied callously.

Oswald Vawdrey laughed. "Your wife is also insisting on her right to visit with you here."

Alisander sobered at once. "Absolutely not."

Oswald Vawdrey did not speak for a moment. "You make things difficult for me, my friend," he sighed.

"On the contrary, I have been a model prisoner."

"Your wife has even visited with mine and set a flea in Fenella's ear."

"Ah, so now we have the truth of it. 'Tis *your* wife that is making things uncomfortable for you, not mine."

"She says keeping Jane from you is cruel, and I am not good at withstanding her," Vawdrey warned him.

"If you permit Jane to come to this filthy place—" Alisander started direly.

"Filthy? No, really, Alisander, that is too much," Oswald chided him. "Royalty has resided in this chamber with less complaint than you give!"

"My wife does not set *foot* in this accursed tower!" Alisander insisted.

"I will do my poor best," Oswald promised. "If we could only make it last another three weeks, I feel sure that even your old friend Lemarchier's heart would soften toward you." Alisander winced. *Another three weeks?* Even the thought of two made him suffer to a ridiculous degree.

"But I do not know how long I can hold out against all their combined forces," Oswald admitted wryly. "It seems like every woman at court is against me. Even my poor Bryce is complaining that the Queen's ladies have taken to following him around telling him he ought to be ashamed of himself. He has been most upset by it. He dislikes the society of women at the best of times."

"My heart bleeds for him," Alisander retorted.

"There was a scuffle in the south bailey two nights ago. That ruffian of yours got into a spat with someone who darkened your name."

"What ruffian?" He frowned. "Davis, do you mean?"

"I think that was his name. Large, uncouth individual."

"Defending the de Balon family name, was he? Stalwart fellow."

"He broke a royal guard's nose," Oswald said coldly.

"Well, I did save his life once," Alisander reminisced. "So, it is likely that he harbors some kindness toward me."

"Not only that," Oswald complained. "But your servant Watkin acts like I have given him the gravest offense."

"Is he threatening to quit your service again?" Alisander asked with a flicker of alarm, "because, if so, you must not let him. I won't have you setting another Betteridge to dog my every step. His predecessor was quite insupportable."

Oswald tutted. "Could we please try and retain some subtlety to our dealings? Without a dash of mystery to proceedings, it all seems so *sordid*," he complained.

Alisander smirked. Without Vawdrey's visits, he realized with surprise, he would have nothing to look forward to at present. He eyed his writing materials with a suppressed sigh. He supposed he really ought to set his mind to official business instead of dwelling on domestic matters.

Mayhap Jane was coping very well at court without him. Maybe she even found things *easier* without him there, getting in her way.

*

It was a mere two days later that a knock on the door heralded the arrival of a visitor. To Alisander's annoyance, it was Sir Symond Chevenix who came first through the door. *Pompous prick.* If it had to be a member of the King's guard, he would have preferred a more seasoned hand like Sir Palmerston du Vrey or perhaps Sir Walter Pomfritt. Practically anyone was preferable to Chevenix, who had an air of self-importance that he was by no means entitled to.

Chevenix was politely addressing someone on the other side of the door. Alisander supposed it was Vawdrey. That bastard's visit was well overdue. He had not seen him all morning. There was a rustling of skirts, and then Jane appeared in the doorway, utterly staggering him.

Alisander stood up so fast, he nearly overturned the table, now spread with writing instruments. He had been halfway through a touching missive to Master Arnold, thanking the guild of glaziers for their unwavering support. The letter lay now abandoned with a spreading ink blot obscuring the last word.

491

"Jane!" he uttered. "What the hells—?"

"I will be just outside in the corridor, my lady," Chevenix said, fixing a stern eye on Alisander. Alisander ignored him. Jane was wearing a fur-lined cape with a matching hat. She was looking, he noticed critically, damnably pretty without a red-rimmed eye in sight. She was also wearing far more jewels than she did usually. They glittered at her fingers, waist, and throat. Had she thought to bribe his way out of prison?

Then something else caught his stunned eye. Was that the emerald green gown peeking out from under her cloak? The one he had ordered from Barbier, specifically, with the idea of her wearing it to celebrate some royal feast and stunning the populace? Instead, Jane had decided to squander its grandeur on a visit to Traitor's Tower.

Alisander was outraged. And that was before he saw she wore the huge emerald brooch, pinned to the middle of her bodice. The one she had seemed so wholly unimpressed with when he had presented it to her. Jane turned back to Chevenix. "I thank you," she said prettily, and the oaf practically preened. Alisander fumed as the door clanged shut and Jane advanced into the room.

"Madam, you did not receive my letters it seems?" he started coolly. "I will have to take the matter up with Lord Vawdrey, who assured me that any note I wrote to my family would be duly delivered."

Jane crossed the room and walked straight up to him. "I did receive them," she said pertly, "and I disregarded both as quite absurd." She stuck her little nose in the air. "Kiss me, please." She tipped her face up, and so stunned was he that he obligingly seized her upper arms and kissed her with unaccustomed roughness before practically shoving her from him.

Jane tottered toward the seat by the window and sank into it, seemingly oblivious to the way he was staring at her. She dragged off her hat, affording him a view of her pale gold hair. "Perhaps you do not feel as though you require sight of me at present," she said thoughtfully. "But you see, I feel quite differently on the matter."

Alisander picked up his overturned chair and set it to rights before he, too, resumed his seat. Quite deliberately, he picked up his quill and scored through the inkblot. If he acted very cool with her, perhaps she would not see the way his heart was practically beating out of his chest. "Oh? And if I might enquire, which part of my company is so vital to you at precisely this moment?" he asked politely. "It has been a mere five days."

"And four nights!" she pointed out.

Alisander blinked. "So," he said, drawing out the word suggestively, "it is my presence in your bedchamber that you miss, is that it, wife?" Predictably, Jane's cheeks bloomed with hectic color. This, of course, was the way to make her back off sharply. She could never abide any teasing on that score.

He threw down his pen and glanced back over his shoulder. "There is a bed to hand, and I should not object to performing my duty if it is so essential to your comfort, wife." He met her eyes, his cool and challenging.

She cleared her throat. "That is good," she said with a swift nod and stood up, unfastening her cloak before discarding it on the chair. It *was* the emerald green gown, and it became her even better than he had dreamed it would.

It was a shock to see her in such vivid color after all the muted mauves and white, just as he had known it would be. He was irritated that the picture she made should be *wasted* in a dreary prison tower when he had imagined a social occasion where she would turn all heads.

"You are no longer in mourning, it seems," he managed to force out as she walked right up to the bed and sat down on the edge of it.

"No," she agreed. "I am not in mourning." She held his gaze, though her cheeks were poppy red.

"That gown is highly unsuitable," he said in a low voice, narrowing his gaze. "As is, this visit."

"I thought you would like it," Jane said, glancing down at her new gown. "Is it not as you envisaged?"

"No," he answered heavily.

"Aren't you going to join me?" She had the nerve to pat the bed beside her.

He huffed. It was all bluster, of course. "Very well." He stood up. "If that's what you want." He strolled over to the bed. "Shall we just toss up your skirts or…?" Instead of responding to his crude words, Jane held up her arms to him, and he knew he was lost.

Fuck it, he thought. He could roll around with her on that sagging mattress for a minute or two without losing his resolve. Besides, that would surely be enough to call her bluff. He sat beside her, dragging her into his arms.

Or rather, Jane pulled him into hers. Her embrace was so enthusiastic that he was the one overborne. He landed on his back and remained there as Jane kissed him as though her sweet life depended upon it. He returned her kisses in the same spirit, expecting her to call a halt at any moment.

494

She did not call a halt. Not even when he ran his hands all over her, groping and grabbing in a most unseemly fashion. "Jane," he said finally, tearing his mouth from hers. "What the fuck are you doing? Are you unaware there is an open grille in that door and soldiers patrol that corridor every quarter hour? One of them will doubtless get a good look at us, if they have not already, and news of it will be *all* over the palace."

"I do not care," she replied breathlessly, her eyes still on his mouth, her arms tightening about his neck. "And neither should you."

"They will say," he persisted ruthlessly, "that you came to service me in a grubby prison cell. It will be a salacious tale bandied about in both guard and throne room."

"Do not regard it, Alisander," she begged. "I promise you, I won't."

He stared at her. "Jane…" He was genuinely shocked.

"I won't give it a thought, I promise," she assured him fervently.

"Jane," he repeated on a groan this time. He spent a good half minute crazily contemplating it before he came back to his senses. "I can't do it, my dove," he replied honestly. "I respect you too much, and besides, I would have to sneak back here in a month's time and murder whoever witnessed it. I'm not speaking in jest when I say this," he added seriously when she made as though to protest. "It could cause some awkwardness. Chevenix's family is fairly well-connected."

Jane lowered her pleading gaze a moment. "What if—what if we hung something across the grille to obscure their view?" she suggested, biting her lip. "We could use my cloak."

He squeezed his eyes shut against the sight, lest his resolve shatter. When he opened them, he felt a little calmer. "If we did that, they would surely break down the door," he explained, "which would be even worse. I could not stand armed men being in the same room with us at such a time." He ran a hand comfortingly up and down her back.

She nodded, but the regretful look in her eye nearly undid his resolve. "I understand," she said, looking so disappointed that he had to kiss her again.

"Jane, my sweet. We have to stop," he was forced to finally protest when she did not.

She eyed him with frustration. "No! If you—" Jane turned very red. "If—"

"What?" he asked, catching his breath. Suddenly, he was desperate to know what she had been going to say.

"If you love me, you would not stop," she said, unable to meet his gaze.

"Jane," he gasped, quite enchanted by her words. "What has come over you? First you attempt to seduce me and now to pry a confession from me." She would not look at him. If they weren't all tangled up in each other, he was pretty sure she would be leaping off the bed right now and banging on the door to be let out. The thought was quite unbearable to him. He rolled over her to prevent her escape, caging her in with his body.

"I do. I do love you," he breathed raspily. Strange to say, it felt like a great weight off his chest to admit it. "I always have, I think. It's the stupidest thing. Now, be a good girl and tell me that you love me."

"N-no." She gulped. "Not until you come back home."

Home? Where on earth was that supposed to be? Alisander regarded her speechlessly, his feelings scattered and confused. He smoothed his thumb over her lips. "But this is quite outrageous," he murmured. "What are you trying to achieve right now? Hmmm?"

"Lord Vawdrey told me that it is all your own fault you are here," she blurted, "and that he will release you as soon as you ask him to."

That bastard, Alisander thought wrathfully. *Trust Vawdrey to throw him to the wolves!* "Well, my dove——" he began patiently.

"And I don't want you to call me that anymore."

"What?" That struck a blow. "Why not?" Jane shook her head, looking obstinate and refusing to answer. "Jane, this is not kind of you," he said severely. "You visit your poor, beleaguered husband under the guise of giving him succor, and instead you cruelly torment him."

"Oh yes," she answered mutinously, "I had forgotten that the role of tormentor was yours alone."

He paused, steeling himself to be stern and speak of duty when all he wanted was to hold her close. "Do you really imagine that I would languish here if it was safe for me to return to your side? Now, we both of us have our part to play. I need to remain here for—oh—at least another two weeks, and you need to journey down to Kinnerton with our household where you can wait this out in peace and comfort, away from prying eyes."

She glared at him. "I am not going into the country, so do not ask me to."

"Why not?" Her downright refusal astonished and outraged him.

"All my friends are here."

"What friends?" he jeered before he could stop himself.

"Oh, you know…Osanna, Patience…" She lifted her hand and pointed a finger at his chest. "You."

Gods. He had to breathe heavily a moment before he could make a reply. "Stop trying to manipulate me, madam," he said thickly. "I know what I am doing, and I will not stir from this tower before the month is out."

Jane lowered her eyes to hide the hurt they revealed. She tried to sit up. Instinctively, his arms closed tight about her. The temptation to just wrap himself around her and never let go had never been so strong. "I am not leaving you here alone," she said, possibly encouraged by his traitorous embrace.

"Not even when I am the one urging it?" he asked through gritted teeth.

She shook her head. "Besides," she added, "I could not possibly leave Robert."

"You would take him with you, of course."

"If you imagine he would journey to some unknown spot in rural Karadok, leaving *you* in the capital, your understanding of his character is a poor one." When he said nothing, she met his eyes. "He loves you."

"Do you imagine you are telling me something I do not know?" he asked irritably.

"Yet, you have not even asked how he fares." Her tone was vaguely accusatory.

"That is because I entrusted him to *your* care."

"Or about the children."

"The same applies to them."

She seemed to be struggling with her response. "It is lucky that I have had able support at this time. Ayleth has been wonderful." She hesitated and said quietly, "I do not ever want to find her at the foot of any stairs, Alisander."

He was so startled by this that he released her and permitted her to sit up. She must have heard about her uncle, he supposed. They sat on the bed side by side; he did not know for how long. He stole a look at her and finally cleared his throat. "Understood," he said and scratched the back of his neck.

"I have written to Beth," Jane said, standing up and retrieving her cloak. "And told her of Sir Phillip's accident. I gave her assurances that her position with us is safe."

Alisander ignored this, coming to her side and wrapping her cloak securely around her, fastening it tight. "Now put on your hat." She did so, and he gazed at her for a long moment. "That hat needs adornment," he said, unable to help himself. "Possibly a plume." Jane rolled her eyes. "I want you to consider what I said," he reiterated, "about Kinnerton."

She took her leave of him in stony silence.

*

Jane did not leave Aphrany. Oswald told him so the next afternoon with great relish. "In fact, her circle of friends is starting to treat your rooms as quite their own," he said, drifting over to the window. "Give it another week, and I dare say the Queen will be among their number, sitting on your seats, eating cheese, and talking political intrigue."

"This is your fault," Alisander said sourly. "Why did you have to tell her I was here of my own volition?"

"I told you I would fold with time," Vawdrey answered serenely. "The pressure was quite intolerable."

Alisander tensed his jaw. "What news from Lascony?" he asked.

"Your friend Lemarchier received a rather stinging missive from my equivalent in Wilhelm's court. It seems they now believe he has been unduly critical of you, painting you in a needlessly negative light. He is being threatened with the possibility of recall." When Alisander said nothing, Oswald turned around. "Do you think that will alarm him?"

"He hates it here," Alisander answered abruptly. "They are merely threatening him with his heart's desire."

"Well, mayhap, you will receive a new and more agreeable liaison in the not-too-distant future," Oswald suggested. Alisander shrugged and Oswald's eyebrows rose. "Even this does not please you, I find."

"Sometimes it is better the devil you know," Alisander grumbled. "At least I am familiar with Lemarchier's methods."

Oswald nodded. "There is something in what you say," he conceded, "but really, Lemarchier does seem to have come to the end of his tether. If he was an agent of mine, I would have cut him loose long ago."

Alisander pushed away his plate of uneaten beef stew. It smelled delicious, steeped as it was in red wine, almonds, and spices. However, he had no appetite since Jane's visit. "How is it with the Queen?" he asked, scrubbing a hand over his face.

"She is still much incensed on your behalf," Oswald assured him. "And makes many cutting comments to me whenever our paths cross."

"I *meant*, how goes her rapprochement with the King?"

"All seems well on that front. Wymer languishes at her feet these days."

"It won't last, you know," Alisander said fatalistically. Vawdrey's smugness was irritating as hell. Alisander had never wanted to smash his composure as much as he did right now.

"Oh, I think it will last," Vawdrey said sanguinely. "For the most part. Why should it not?"

"There are a thousand reasons."

"I choose to be optimistic," the annoying bastard responded. "At least the King is smitten, and it is in the Queen's best interest to make sure he remains that way."

Alisander snorted. "He should not be so damn obvious about it, then. Once she knows she has snared him, she will lose all interest."

"Really?" Vawdrey sat down across from him. "You sound as though you speak from experience, my friend. Is that how it is with you?" He glanced at the chessboard. "Love, in your book, is a game to be played for mastery?"

Alisander glared at him. "I was not talking about me!"

"Something is different about you today," Vawdrey said, tipping his head to one side. "I can't quite put my finger on it."

"I have not bothered to shave," Alisander said sulkily.

"Ah yes, that would be it. Your polished appearance is slipping. It is quite disconcerting."

"Some spymaster you are!" Alisander placed his arms on the table and then laid his head upon them.

"Perhaps you did not sleep well," Oswald hazarded after a moment. "You made some complaint about the bed, I seem to recall." Alisander did not bother to respond. Oswald regarded him in silence.

"How about we put an early end to this confinement?" he suggested at last. "It seems we have achieved our ends after all. Your sternest critics are chastened. Even the King pleaded with me only this morning to show leniency for his sake."

"I told her that I loved her," Alisander mumbled against his forearm. "And she did not reply in kind."

"How very disobliging!" When he made no response, Oswald asked curiously, "How *did* she make reply?"

"She would not," he answered bleakly, "not until I return home, she said."

"My dear Alisander," Oswald replied, not unkindly. "Your next move seems to me almost blindingly obvious."

"How can I?" Alisander demanded. "I don't even know where home is! Besides…" His words trailed off.

"Besides what?" Oswald asked with interest.

"I should likely wait it out." Alisander forced himself to say the words. "Otherwise, this whole ordeal will have been in vain. We should see it through to the end now, however bitter."

"Dear me, you *have* turned over a new leaf! What, might I ask, exactly is it you are waiting for?"

"Some private communication to reach me," Alisander admitted reluctantly. He felt tired and dispirited. Too tired and dispirited for mystery now. "There are certain channels you know nothing about," he said grudgingly, "and I shall not tell you about them, so do not ask. I must wait until I hear via them that Wilhelm gives me his support. There is a vast difference," he said hollowly, "between public statement and private intent. Only when I have received these assurances, will I know it is safe for me to return."

Enlightenment dawned on Oswald's face. "Oh, you mean, one of *these* communications?" he asked, drawing forth three slips of paper from his cuff. "They all say the same thing," he added helpfully. "You will need to decipher them, for they are in a code. If you have forgotten it, I can happily remind you of it."

Alisander raised his head and stared at him. "You *bastard*, Vawdrey!" he said, snatching them from his unresisting fingers. "How long have you had these in your possession? If you tell me it has been *days* that I have been wasting here—!" He ran through the series of letters and numbers, unlocking their meaning and muttering under his breath.

"Right," he said, pushing away from the table. "Have the door unlocked. Fetch the guard, or issue the proclamation, or whatever it is you have to do."

"First you need a shave," Vawdrey said disparagingly, looking him up and down. "And to button up your tunic. I have never seen you looking so slovenly. Such a scrupulous lady is not likely to return your affection, not when you look such a scarecrow. Oh, before I forget"—he reached into his other cuff—"there was another letter."

"Another?" Alisander regarded him suspiciously but reached for it as soon as he saw Jane's scrupulously neat script. Just a glimpse of her handwriting and he felt like his heart had leaped out of his chest.

Mayhap on reaching their rooms, she had repented the fact she had not responded to his avowal of love. Ripping it open, he found it short and to the point.

Lord Bardulf,

I write first and uppermost to reaffirm that I will <u>not</u> be journeying to Kinnerton.

I daresay that you will be released presently, at your own convenience. If you cannot bring yourself to return to our apartments, teeming as they are with dribbling babes and a surfeit of servants, perhaps you could find the time to slink back occasionally to swive your wife?

You could sneak back at dead of night, and no one would even know, save I, that you had visited. I assure you that I will make you welcome, with both open arms and legs.

Your viscountess, Jane

30

Jane still felt a little dizzy with horror whenever she thought of the letter she had written. She tried to thrust it from her mind, but it kept intruding on her thoughts at the oddest of times. Thinking of it at supper, she had gasped and dropped her spoon into her soup, quite drenching her front. Ayleth had clucked disapprovingly but promised to soak her gown directly after supper to remove the stain.

Thinking of it now, Jane clapped hands to her hot cheeks and wondered what on earth had inspired her to such mischief. She would never have had the nerve ordinarily to have written such dreadful sentiments. Indeed, at the time of writing, the only way she could push through was by telling herself that she would never *actually* send it.

It was purely a writing exercise, she had told herself, that she would afterward consign to the fire. Thus reassured, she had lowered her pen once more and let it travel over the page in her neat, practiced hand that she hoped would somehow provoke him to action.

Even thinking of it now, a day later, made her cheeks grow warm and her breath quicken. For she *had* sent it. Knowing full well that in all likelihood a prisoner's letters would be read first by other eyes. Jane paused in the act of running the comb through her hair. She didn't really like to dwell on that aspect.

With a bit of luck, it would have been only Lord Vawdrey who cast a flinty eye over it. He was far too taken with his own wife to dwell overlong on Jane's licentiousness. Moreover, he had been quite kind in his manner with her. Especially when you considered how abrupt and even angry she had been toward him when Alisander had first been taken away.

Fenella, Lady Vawdrey, had been so sweet and understanding and said she quite understood Jane's feelings when she had cried and made a terrible exhibition of herself. It was Fenella who had explained painstakingly that, if anything, Alisander was most likely the closest thing that Lord Vawdrey had approaching the position of friend outside of his family.

Jane considered this now as she drew on a robe over her shift to go and bid good night to the children. In the passageway, she nodded to Davis, who was sat on a stool, a hulking great presence standing guard over the main door. This was a new precaution the household had agreed to without her corroboration.

Not that Jane minded; indeed, she was actually rather touched. He nodded back, and Jane noticed he had a fresh black eye. Really, did the man never stop brawling? Jane was glad it was Watkin who had caught Anne's fancy in the end. He seemed a much more dependable prospect, matrimonially speaking.

She was not surprised, on pushing the door open to Celestia's room, to find Wat stood behind Anne, his arms wrapped firmly about her waist, his chin resting on her shoulder. Jane had a shrewd notion that Anne slipped into Wat's narrow bedchamber for at least a portion of each night recently. She did not really mind this either, not when Celestia was clearly thriving.

Jane knocked lightly now on the door to make them aware of her presence, and Wat sprang away, making for the fireplace, where he started industriously stacking logs. Jane crossed to the crib and looked a moment at the sleeping babies, lightly touching Celestia's cheek and then bidding Anne a quiet good night as she departed.

Next, she knocked on Robert's door and opened it to find the old man dozing in his chair by the fire. Ayleth was knelt over a

506

deep bowl, washing Jane's dress. She raised a finger to her lips and nodded toward Robert. Jane nodded back and mouthed *Good night* before shutting the door softly behind her.

Doing these rounds before bed gave Jane some kind of comfort in the aftermath of the disturbing events of the past week. It seemed to give her an idea of order, which, though largely illusory, helped her sleep at night. She closed the door to her own room, removed her robe, laid it carefully over a chair back, and climbed into bed, folding her hands neatly across her stomach.

She was just thinking about blowing out the candle when she heard a swiftly indrawn breath. "How *dare* you write me that letter, madam," said a familiar voice, filled with so much wrath that Jane gasped and sat up in the bed.

"Alisander!" she squeaked, her heart racing when she found him stood so unexpectedly at the foot of the bed. "When did you—?"

"You knew *exactly* what you were doing, did you not?" he said in a voice that shook slightly as he whipped his tunic up and over his head. "Writing such words in your perfectly angelic hand."

"Yes," Jane admitted boldly, holding his gaze. She saw the answering gleam in his eyes by candlelight.

"Oh? What?" he challenged her, his hands moving to unlace his crotch. "Tell me, then."

"Inflaming you," she admitted, swallowing hard. "Enticing you to my bed."

He breathed out on a hiss. "Now give me that welcome you promised me," he said throatily as he moved toward her.

Jane held his gaze as she drew the covers aside and parted her thighs for him. "Oh, you little—" His appreciative words were cut off as he bunched up her gauzy shift, inserting himself bodily between her legs and seizing hold of the back of one knee to spread her wider for his hungry gaze. "*Gods*, Jane." His voice was hoarse. "Fair warning, I shall give you no quarter. You brought this entirely on yourself."

Jane caught her breath in her throat. How could he look so utterly wild for her? she marveled as he practically *fell* upon her, his mouth hot and devouring. And that was *before* he shifted down the bed. Her chest was already heaving from his punishing kiss. Jane felt a momentary alarm. What if anyone heard them?

She managed to open her mouth to voice her concerns, but then found herself forced to clap a hand over her lips to muffle her cries. He was insatiable. His tongue did not flutter and dart against her there as he usually did. He did not tease at all. Instead, he simply devoured her whole. It was devastating.

Jane had no sooner convulsed against his wicked mouth in terrible, wicked pleasure than he had moved swiftly back up the bed, lifted her knees, and without more ado pushed inside her. "*Oh!*" Jane found herself blinking up at him in astonishment as he immediately stilled, pinning her to the mattress and holding her wrists above her head.

Well, this was new. Jane's eyes fluttered shut. "*There* she is, my good girl," he breathed raggedly against her brow. "I almost feared she had disappeared altogether." Jane remained silent apart from her labored breathing. Her eyes were riveted to his face, but his were roaming all over her heaving bosom. Why was he not moving?

"*Fuck*, Jane," he said wonderingly, releasing her wrists and running an open hand down her neck and over her bosom. "You're so flushed and red." Somehow, the way he said it made it sound like a compliment. "Now tell me you missed me, you wicked girl. Writing me *such* a note, and so disobedient too." Despite his words, his tone was indulgent. "I ought to pull out of you right now, put you over my knee, and spank you soundly."

Jane gasped with dismay. "No, Alisander! I—I did miss you. So much." She passed her arms tightly around him. "I did not mean to make you cross," she blurted, tears starting to her eyes. "I thought—"

"You thought what?"

She bit her lip to stop it from trembling. "I thought you would like it," she quavered.

"Jane," he whispered. "Don't you dare cry. I'm teasing you. I fucking loved it."

"Oh." She gazed at him in mingled relief and confusion.

"Though, I do kind of want to spank you now," he admitted. "And turn your bottom as red as your face."

Jane's gasp of outrage sent him into wheezy laughter. "Don't make me laugh right now," he groaned. "You'll tip me over the edge way too soon."

"I? I have done nothing to—*oh*!" Jane's words were bitten off with a cry as he gave a buck of his hips. She closed her eyes, arching her back.

"Yes, Jane," he groaned. "Take me nice and deep. I cannot get enough of your sweet little cunt."

Her eyes sprang open at his words. How could he say such things, and make it sound almost *laudatory*? She felt her body respond to the admiration in his tone. The crudity of his words almost did not register.

Then, when they did, shockingly, they made her melt even more. He seemed to sink even further into her, and she welcomed this with a cry of mingled relief and pleasure. He picked up his punishing pace, hissing in approval. "That's it, Jane," he purred, "welcome me home, my sweet. Keep those beautiful eyes open for me. I want to see them when I spill in you."

Jane struggled to keep her eyes open as the pleasure streaked through her belly. "Such a good girl," he purred in her ear. "You're so desperate to please, isn't that right, Jane?"

Was it? "Y—yes," she sobbed aloud as he thrust firmly into her.

"This little pussy is so nice and tight. It wants to please me too, doesn't it?"

"Yes," she burst out. She would probably agree to anything at this point. She wanted him to stop talking, whilst simultaneously craning to hear every word that fell from those filthy lips.

"You wouldn't close your eyes now, would you? Not after I had told you not to."

"N-no!"

"That's *good*, Jane. Really good." His words were warm, so warm, and sweeter than honey. They made her feel giddy and way too hot. "Yes, wife," he encouraged her. "That's it, my love, come on. I want to hear you. No one is here but you and me."

Jane gave a stifled cry and collapsed as he drove into her a final time before joining her in sated oblivion. The next thing she knew, she was lying across Alisander's chest, still faintly sobbing as she caught her breath.

"There, there," he murmured as he stroked her tearstained cheeks and between her shoulder blades.

"I'm not upset," she felt beholden to point out.

"I know," he responded. "It's just how pleasure takes you."

Neither of them spoke for a long moment. Then Jane made the effort to lift her head. "For your information, I do not appreciate being *toyed* with in that manner!"

"Don't you?" He sounded mildly surprised. "But you *seemed* so appreciative, Jane."

She narrowed her eyes at him. "*You...*"

"Yes?" There was a definite smile tugging at his lips.

Jane paused, struggling to find the right words. "As a matter of fact, I am not *desperate* to please anyone, just you."

She saw the look of surprised pleasure flicker over his face before he propped himself up on his elbow. "What about...the Queen?" he asked in a casual tone, his eyes glancing away from her own toward the flames flickering in the fireplace.

"What about her?"

He frowned slightly, catching hold of her hand and threading his fingers through hers. "You should strive to please your husband more than your monarch."

She slid a glance at his face. "She's your monarch too."

"Actually, she isn't," he contradicted her. "I'm still officially a subject of her brother's."

"Well, but you are in a foreign land, so I always thought your first loyalty would be to Queen Armenal."

"Then you thought wrong," he answered swiftly.

"I did?"

"My first loyalty is to you, Jane."

She felt strangely winded by this and incapable of reply, at least for the moment, and simply squeezed his fingers.

"Tell me again," he said abruptly.

"Tell you what?"

"That it's only me you want to please."

"You—" Jane glanced away. "Surely your first loyalty is to King Wilhelm?" she hedged.

"King Wilhelm killed my brother." He shrugged. "So, fuck Wilhelm. I feel no loyalty to that bastard whatsoever."

"Alisander!" Jane clutched at him, paling.

He laughed. "There is no one to hear me here but you," he pointed out, running his hand down her side and pulling her tighter into him.

"You should not say such things out loud," she chided him.

"Why?" He caught her gaze. "You, I trust *implicitly*."

Jane gulped. "I am not used to your frankness," she admitted in a wobbly voice. "It is a little unnerving."

He shrugged again. "There are occasions when nothing else will do." He hesitated. "When I called you my dove, Jane, all those times, you *did* know what I was really saying, didn't you?" He lifted their hands, contemplating their intertwined fingers. Jane pressed her lips together and shook her head. He tutted. "But of course you did, or you would not have asked me that question."

Jane's heart quailed, and she made an involuntary movement as though to push away from him. He tightened his arm about her. His other hand came to rest gently against her cheek. "You were so clever, Jane," he said in a marveling voice. "So brave, and I was *such* a coward and I hurt you."

She swallowed and mustered the courage to meet his eyes. The expression there stunned her. "Please ask me again, Jane. Ask me now."

She opened her mouth. "Am I—am I your first dove, Alisander?" she croaked, repeating a question she had loathed herself for ever voicing. She could not *believe* she was saying it again.

"You are my first and only love, Jane," he answered truthfully. "I did not know I was capable of it before you. I did not think I was made that way."

Jane dropped her gaze, clinging to him for dear life. "When did you? I mean—"

"When did I fall in love with you?" he asked, the words making Jane's head reel. He looked evasive. "I'm not sure. It was years ago now." He glanced away, his expression strange.

It dawned on Jane that his face was registering embarrassment, something she had never seen from this shameless creature before. She brought her hand down heavily on his bare chest. "Tell me!" she insisted, trusting her instincts on this.

He grimaced. "Oh very well!" he said grudgingly, reaching above them for a pillow which he pulled down over his face. Not surprisingly, his next few words were muffled.

"What did you say?" Jane demanded, dragging the pillow from his hand.

"I said, I think it was when you danced for the Queen and won her favor." His cheeks were suffused with color.

Jane stared at him. "You—really?" He nodded, not meeting her gaze. "I never really understood what I did so well that day," she admitted honestly, "that I should have secured both your good opinion and the Queen's. I suppose my stars must have been in alignment."

He looked pained. "Jane, don't," he whispered. "I can't stand it."

"What? Why?" He wouldn't answer, would only shake his head. Why did he look like that? Jane could not really make it out. When she opened her mouth to press him further, he promptly rolled on top of her, pinning her beneath him.

"Jane," he said in quite a different voice. "Don't you think I have waited long enough now, my sweet?"

"Waited for what?"

He blew his hair out of his face with an impatient puff of air. "Your declaration, wife. I have been *distressingly* frank with you. *I love you*. I maneuvered the Queen to bring about our marriage—"

"*What?*" The word was a squawk.

"I plotted and schemed to make you mine, and I think the *least* you can do—"

"When did you plot? What scheme?"

"I started baring my soul to you on our wedding night—"

"You did?"

"—and I've scarcely stopped since," he stated firmly. "It was all most strange as I do not usually have loose lips."

"Did you?" Jane was doubtful.

"I told you about my brother, didn't I? I had not spoken of him in…oh, it must be some fifteen years."

Jane thought about this. "That's a long time."

"Yes," he agreed, rolling off her and onto his back. He heaved a great sigh. "I think it was because I wanted you to know my measure, the real me, I mean. To know me and *still* to find me worthy I suppose." He seemed to wince at his own choice of words.

Jane crowded in close to his side. "Worthy?" she repeated.

"Of your love."

She felt winded again. "Alisander…" Her arm crept around his waist.

"You see," he said, covering his eyes with his forearm, "I never really believed that anyone *could* ever love me. Not…the real me. Not that I ever wanted anyone to, except you. But I badly wanted you to…so, I was sort of testing the waters."

"You mean," Jane said carefully, pulling down his arm so she could see his face, "the 'you' that was the curse of the Herveys? The 'you' that reclaimed your family ring?"

Without meeting her eyes, he caught her hand and turned it over to contemplate the simple gold signet ring, his thumb tracing the snake insignia carved there. "Yes, precisely," he muttered. "For some reason, I wanted you to know him, almost from the first. Even though I knew I should keep him in the shadows where he belongs."

Jane tipped her head considering. "I did not actually realize that your steward John was Robert's son until just recently," she admitted. "But I suppose you did lay a breadcrumb trail for me to follow."

"Yes. I wanted you to know me, Jane, and want me anyway." He blew out a breath. "I collect you have heard about your uncle—"

But Jane did not want to talk about her uncle. "I still don't really understand why, though," she puzzled aloud.

"I did it to protect you and Celestia, and what's more I would do it again."

"No, not that," she said hurriedly. "I understand why you did that."

A frown creased his brow. "Then, what are you asking me exactly?"

"Why?" Jane repeated. "Why me?"

"Why what? Why I love you?" She nodded. He was quiet a moment. "I was so bored before you came along, Jane," he admitted. "Bored and, I think now, perhaps a little lonely. And then you became my only and secret delight. I became consumed with you, and then I genuinely fell in love with you, and then you became mine."

Jane gave a murmur of disagreement. "Is that—? I mean, you never seemed—"

He huffed out a breath. "I was in love with you, Jane," he said firmly, snaring her gaze and letting her see he was serious. "I was madly in love with you all along."

"I—you—" Jane flailed about hopelessly and he watched her, a tender smile playing about his lips.

"What's more, it was me who planted the idea of our marriage in Armenal's head in the first place." Seeing she still doubted this, he insisted, "It's true. You know what a tricky bastard I can be."

"Are you in earnest?"

He nodded. "You may be sure; I was very careful to make her think the idea was her own."

"Even then?" she asked incredulously. "You wanted…me?" He nodded and opened his mouth to set about convincing her. "I love you too," Jane interrupted hoarsely.

He caught his breath, then breathed noisily out, then in. "You do?" He stared at her.

"Yes." Jane could feel the unbecoming color stealing into her face and started to tense. Then remembered how much he liked her blotchy. She leaned forward and planted a kiss firmly to his lips. When she would have drawn back, he drew her in closer.

"When did you know?" he asked, his voice husky.

"When did I know I loved you?"

"Yes, I want to know. I *am* very vain, you know. And self-indulgent. I just exaggerate those traits a little."

Jane snorted. "I know. I counted your shoes, remember?"

"Ah, but since then I have ordered another five pairs."

517

Jane smiled and shook her head. "To return to your question," she said, ignoring his nonsense, "it is hard for me to be certain. I noticed, of course, that you kept coming to my rescue all the time, but I could not be certain it was intentional on your behalf. You were such a dissembler," she said accusingly. "At that point, I barely felt I could take a single word that left your mouth at face value."

He gave a twisted smile but said nothing, just continued gazing at her face. "Then once we were married," Jane said slowly, "I began to…to notice things."

"What things?" he asked quickly.

"Just things," Jane said, blushing.

"Like how wild I was for you," he groaned. "I tried so hard, but gods, I could not hide it."

Jane cleared her throat. "In fact, I was not alluding to that at all," she admitted. "For all I knew then, you could have been like that with other women before me."

"I never was," he said swiftly.

She reached up to stroke his chest. "Yes, I know that now, but *then* I did not."

"What did you notice, then?" he asked, frowning down at her. "My beauteous face? My magnificent arse? Wait, 'twas my thighs, wasn't it?"

"Nothing to do with your physical beauty, you vain creature!" she scolded. "I meant, that I noticed how kind you were to Robert, and…and how good you were with the children. When you weren't pretending to be repulsed by them, of course."

He smiled again. "Very observant always, Jane," he murmured, caressing her lower back.

518

"To make sense of you, I started thinking of you in that nonsensical way," she confessed, hiding her face against his chest.

"What way?" he asked, tipping her face up.

"*You* know, Alisander de Balon as opposed to Viscount Bardulf."

"Really? What's the difference?"

"You were Viscount Bardulf in the Queen's presence, but quite often in our bedchamber, you are Alisander de Balon." He snorted. "At first, it used to really disconcert me when you would switch between the two, but then…" Jane's voice turned thoughtful.

"Then what?"

"I realized it was not so clear-cut as all that and anyway… It did not really matter, for I dearly loved them both."

"Jane," he whispered. "Oh my gods, say that again. That was—" He broke off his words to kiss her, gently at first, and then with increasing enthusiasm. "Say it again."

"I love you both."

He drew back instantly. "No," he said, shaking his head. "That won't do. That makes me a little jealous."

"Of yourself?"

He hitched her leg over his hip. "Let's try you on top. We have been neglecting Aunt Maud's instructions."

"I wish you would burn them!" she grumbled even as she allowed him to arrange her over his lap.

He looked instantly guilty. "I know. Which reminds me, I could not burn your letter. If you let me keep that, I promise I will destroy Aunt Maud's," he vowed. "*Gods*, I could not part with your letter, Jane. Not for the contents of all the King's coffers."

"Why should you?" she asked. "It is not treasonous after all."

He gave a startled laugh. "But Jane," he muttered. "What if other eyes should read it, in say a hundred years? What would they think of Lady Bardulf then?"

She felt too light of heart at present to really care. "They will think, my lord, that your wife was a wanton hussy."

He stared at that. "Only for me," he said with a rasp in his voice.

"Only for you," she agreed with a shy smile, then leaned down to kiss him.

Afterward, when Jane was too sated and her limbs too heavy with languor to really care, he rolled her onto her stomach and covered her back with his body, kissing and mouthing her neck, and letting her feel the graze of his teeth there.

"Did you like that, Jane?" he wanted to know. He *had* to know already from the way she had reacted. Still, it was a lot more tiring when she had to do all the work like that. She made a sound of affirmation in her throat. "You will have to wear a high neck tomorrow, my lady," he warned her, rubbing the faint stubble of his chin over her shoulders. Jane moaned against the pillow. "Tell me you will."

"Yes, I will," she promised. Then belatedly, sleepily, she asked, "Why?"

"Because I'm marking your fair skin," he admitted. "Do you want me to stop?"

"No."

"Good," he said with satisfaction. "It's a good thing Wymer means to plague the Queen's every step now," he whispered into her ear. "For I mean to demand *all* your attention these days, wife. I am very demanding."

"Mmmm." Jane was not unduly concerned. "I'm not her favorite anymore anyway."

"No, you're mine," he pronounced with satisfaction. "You always were, but at least now you reciprocate appropriately. Took you long enough."

Jane's eyes fluttered closed. He said something else, but she was not really attending. Instead, Jane was drifting off into beatific sleep.

Of course, he teased her mercilessly the next day in the Queen's presence. Remarking on the height of her neckline and deriding it as excessively modest. Surely, Lady Bardulf was aware the current fashion was for the necklines to extend from one armpit to another? Did he not provide her with enough pin money to clothe herself adequately?

The other ladies present watched them avidly, one moment sympathetic to Jane, and the next minute giggling at her presumed discomfiture. Jane, catching the gleam in his eye, pretended to bridle. "My lord," she objected faintly, pressing her hand lightly to her throat.

"Have I said aught amiss?"

"That word," Jane said reproachfully. When he looked blank, she leaned forward and whispered, "*Armpit*," in a scandalized tone.

For a moment, his expression was still, then she saw he was struggling not to laugh. His shoulders shook, then he bowed his head. When he looked up, he was composed again. "My apologies, madam," he said gravely. "My remarks were in bad taste."

"You are forgiven, my lord," she replied serenely and extended her hand for him to kiss. He was a little more ardent about it than he should have been, and the other ladies abruptly ceased their tittering to stare and whisper among themselves.

Jane heard the Queen address some query to Mistress Bartree, though she did not catch the words. She was too busy gazing at her husband.

"I believe the Bardulfs are sharing a joke, Your Majesty," Magnatrude Bartree replied with loud disapproval.

Alisander smiled at her, and Jane realized she truly no longer cared that she was being supplanted in Armenal's affections. How could she when she was now uppermost in his?

Epilogue

Six Months Later

Alisander had been dog-tired on his return voyage to Karadok. It had been a fool's errand to push on to Aphrany that same night instead of resting, but what could he do? He *was* a fool, and the worst kind, a lovesick fool. He had been away from his wife's arms for a month now and it had been well-nigh intolerable.

On reaching the palace, he found they had all waited up for him. Secretly, Alisander had hoped they would all be abed, but they had kept supper for his return. Jane was showing clear signs of strain when he clapped eyes on her. She had not borne the separation any better than he, it seemed. He folded her close in his arms, tucking her head under his chin for a full minute, but let her maintain her brittle smile and straight spine for now.

She moved away almost at once and was directing which platters should go where and ordering Davis to carry his trunk into the bedroom. She had clearly taken her role as head of the household very seriously. Robert looked anxious as he came forward and scanned Alisander's face, but the old man's soon relaxed into smiles when he saw no shadows lurking there.

Alisander reached across the table and clasped Jane's hand in his over the final course. She made a great show of moving the food on her plate around, but she had scarcely eaten a thing and was a bag of nerves. Her eyes, when they fell on him, were full of fear and doubt. He shot her another reassuring smile and she quickly responded in kind. *Ah, Jane.* She had been terrified he would not return. It made his chest turn over.

523

At the close of the meal, the children were presented for his inspection, and he pronounced that both had certainly grown apace. He cradled Celestia to his chest and peered gingerly into Bertrand's mouth and agreed that, yes, there was definitely a new tooth lurking at the back.

Celestia bore his fatherly regard stoically until she noticed Robert hovering close by and then nothing would do but that Robert should hold her. Robert appeared sheepishly pleased in this role of favorite, and Alisander watched him rock the child, a foolishly fond expression on his face.

"You'd best take her off to bed before she collapses, my lord," Ayleth advised bluntly in an aside, and he thought it excellent advice. Obligingly, once they rose from the table, she helped Jane undress and poured the hot water for her wash.

"*Jane,*" he murmured as soon as Ayleth departed, stepping behind her and wrapping his arms about her waist. "Has all been well?"

"With us? Of course!" She dropped her washcloth and turned in his arms. "Now tell me truly," she said, laying her hands on his face and peering into his eyes. "How went it at King Wilhelm's court? I've been so worried they would not let you return." She bit her lip. "I did not know what I would have done if—" She broke off with a soft sob.

He cupped her face and kissed her until she was both calm and clinging. "They could not have prevented my returning to you," he assured her, "but I did think it would be prudent to couch my return in the most diplomatic terms whilst ruffling the least feathers."

"And did you manage to do that?"

524

He smirked. "So well that we are in danger of having my old estate restored to us." A frown crossed his face. "Remind me to piss Wilhelm off sometime soon."

"Chateau de Balon?" Jane was startled. "I thought it was nothing but a ruin."

He nodded. "It is." He ran his fingers through her hair. "Scarcely anything remains, save one blackened tower. I have neither the funds nor the inclination to restore it."

Jane looked thoughtful. "A chateau would be far too much of an undertaking," she agreed absently, "but a hunting lodge might not." She ducked her head shyly. "You have been promising to take me away to a hunting lodge, have you not, husband?"

He breathed in sharply. "Jane, you would be willing to travel to Lascony with me?" he asked in a slightly disbelieving tone. "'Tis a three-day voyage, do not forget."

"I would travel to the ends of the earth for you, Alisander de Balon," she replied solemnly.

His gaze snapped to hers. What he saw there made his eyes gleam. "You should not say such things, my love," he said unsteadily. "I am selfish enough to take you up on it. You might sing a different tune after a couple of months on foreign shores."

"The Western Isles are only across the channel," she pointed out with the sanguinity of someone who had never set foot in a ship. "And two months out of twelve is not so very long."

"A hunting lodge," he ruminated, scooping her up in his arms. "A bolt-hole for the two of us. That does sound…agreeable." He deposited her on the bed. "We will consider it further. In the meantime, we will tell no one, simply keep it a secret scheme between the two of us."

Jane gave a murmur of agreement, looking pleased at the thought of sharing a secret scheme with him. He started stripping off his clothes at once. "Of course, we must be careful not to speak of it in front of Robert," he said, flinging a stocking over his shoulder. "He never wants to go back there. I seldom speak of home to him."

"Of course," Jane agreed swiftly. "We must never upset Robert with talk of it. And likely such a thing would not be achieved overnight in any case. It would take months to construct and furnish such a place. Not to mention you ingratiating yourself sufficiently with King Wilhelm, so as to assure the land's return."

He made a noise of agreement, though that would not be difficult in truth. "Still," he said, "it would not hurt to dwell on it awhile." He joined her under the covers, huddling close. "Let us…consider the décor."

Jane rested her head against his shoulder. "Topaz blue?" she suggested. "Emerald green?"

"I think hunting trophies are considered more common decoration than jewel tones," he replied.

She turned her head to look at him. "There is nothing common about we de Balons," she pointed out, making him grin.

"We both need to catch up on our sleep," he said sensibly, even as his eyes devoured her. "Once we are both sufficiently rested, then we can reacquaint ourselves—"

Jane whipped her shift up and over her head and he forgot all reason. "Gods, I've missed you, wife," he confessed with a groan and set about kissing her with what little energy he had left to him. It seemed he had reserves that he had heretofore not been aware of.

"I love how you kiss me, Jane," he whispered between caresses. "You're the greatest kisser in all Karadok. All Lascony too," he praised her, meaning every word. "The best I ever had." He smiled against Jane's lips, for he could feel her face getting hot at his compliment. "The best lover too." Jane gave a splutter. "The best wife, the best mother," he continued effusively.

"That's not true. I know that much," Jane interrupted him.

"Well, there's not much you can do for the child right now," he pointed out. "You can't suckle her."

Jane made a stifled noise, and he could practically *hear* her trying to think of a response. Jane was still very bad at paying him compliments and even worse at telling him she loved him. When she did manage to say it, she was stilted and awkward. He fucking loved coaxing those three words out of her.

"I—we—all missed you, Alisander..." She faltered, no doubt realizing this fell short of his giddy heights. "Terribly," she added, looking so sincere that it made his heart thud. "I'm very bad at finding the words," she burst out, frustrated with herself.

He held her very tight. "You are incredible. You can do or say anything with me, and I would love it because I love you." *I love you*; the phrase was practically flowing off his tongue these days. Once he had finally said those words, he had quickly become addicted to saying them.

"I love you too." Her words were muffled, as he had not been able to stop himself from kissing her. Jane moaned into his mouth, startling him. He drew back. "Why, Jane," he murmured, lowering his lashes. "That was meant for a chaste kiss, you wanton creature." He tickled her sides lightly. "You know how shy I am, my love," he said slyly and pressed a kiss beneath her jaw. "You should not take such advantage of me."

She gave a huff of laughter. "No more talking for now," she said and pressed her mouth to his.

He fell back onto the pillows at once. "Stop my mouth, then, if you can." Nothing loath, Jane clambered atop of him and pressed more insistent kisses against his mouth. She often did this now. Jane would rather show her feelings with heated kisses and desperate embraces than words. "I want the words too," he murmured against her mouth once he had the chance. "Give them to me."

"I love you," Jane huffed raggedly. "So much it scares me."

She had done it again, made him feel tender. "Don't be scared. You're safe with me."

She drew back. "That's not—!" She sucked in a breath. "I mean," she said painstakingly. "I'm only scared that if you knew how much, you would not like it! It's a stupid amount, a crazy amount. Sometimes I feel that—" She broke off again and her eyes filled with tears.

"Jane," he whispered. He wondered if someday she would find it easier to talk about these things. He did not mind either way, but maybe she would like to be able to say such things with a more careless air. "Tell me."

"I'm scared that I don't love like normal people do!" She confessed it like it was some terrible sin.

He could not help the smile that curved his lips. "I like it. I like how fiercely emotional you get. It's a nice contrast to your usual calm manner."

She stared at him. "You like it?" He nodded. "Really?"

He pursed his lips as though debating telling her something. "Actually, I really love it," he confessed with a grin. "Like *everything* else about you, Jane de Balon."

She made a choked sound and then flung her arms around him. He squeezed her tightly to his chest.

"Does it worry you that we have not caught for another child?" Jane asked him after a moment.

He tipped his head to one side, considering this. "No."

She glanced up. "Really?"

"I could do without the worry. Childbirth can be dangerous after all," he admitted. Seeing the shadow cross her face, he thought he had better lighten the tone. "Celestia could probably use a sibling to prevent her from becoming a spoiled brat, but she has Bertrand at least."

"You're not worried about having an heir though?" she asked quietly.

"No, for we already have one in Celestia," he said calmly.

"Yes, but…" She was silent a moment, and he thought she was considering how to frame her words. "Do you really not mind? About her not being a de Balon, not by blood I mean?"

"No, I don't mind at all," he answered truthfully. "My great-great-grandfather was not a de Balon either. His father was also a king's bastard."

"What?" Jane gasped. "Of the Lasconian King?" she asked. He nodded. "So, then, if your great-great-grandfather was really of House Lisle," Jane puzzled aloud, "then there is truly not any de Balon blood in *your* veins either?"

He shook his head. "Not quite. You see, it was my ancestress, one Francoise de Balon, who had caught the eye of old King Edouard. She was a most resourceful woman, with cheekbones like razorblades, and a sweet, honeyed tongue.

"When she proved fruitful, her first cousin, Sir Alain de Balon, was persuaded with the viscountcy to marry her and fulfil the role of father. He was—er—not inclined to play the role of husband however, for he had his own lover, whose name was Humphrey. So, you see, it worked out all around."

"Oh." Jane thought a moment. "Is that why you do not mind?"

He shrugged. "Maybe? Does it really seem so strange to you?"

"Yes," she admitted on an outward breath. "Strange and wonderful and unexpected, like everything else about you." She dragged in a breath, and he waited for whatever momentous thing Jane was struggling to bring herself to tell him. "And like everything else," she whispered fiercely, placing her hands on either side of his face, "I love it so much that I can hardly stand it."

"Jane," he groaned and kissed her quivering lips. How strange life was. Strange, wonderful, unexpected, he thought, echoing her words in his head. Aloud, he just said: "I love you, Jane de Balon. More than anything in the world."

"Forever and ever," she agreed in a whisper.

Later, after they had reassured each other of their continued passion, they lay in an exhausted heap. "I meant to be so gentle with you this evening," he said regretfully. "But then you had to be so delicious and have that furious blush I cannot resist."

Tomorrow, he thought, he would drag her behind the screen in the Queen's privy chamber when no one else was looking. Jane would make some token protest, but she would let him have his will in the end, if he coaxed her.

Jane covered his hand with her own. "Tomorrow, I want you to…to be Bardulf again," she said haltingly. "I have been thinking about him a good deal while you have been gone."

"What do you mean?" He was startled.

"Why, that I missed him too."

"Who the hells do you think has been warming your bed all evening?" he asked in amusement.

"Alisander de Balon," she replied promptly. "And I love him too, I really do. But I—sometimes I miss Viscount Bardulf."

"You will see him every day," he assured her, patting her backside, "in the Queen's chambers."

"Yes," she agreed. "But that's not enough. I miss him in my bed too."

He was silent for a long moment, and then he huffed out a laugh, pulling her more firmly into his arms. "Come here, Jane," he ordered, though she was already lying across his chest. "Is it possible, wife, that you are asking me to tease you again?" he asked, his eyes warm. She nodded. "I thought you found Bardulf to be a sad torment."

She nodded slowly. "He is a *wicked*, tormenting creature," she agreed. "And I have grown so fond of him."

He smiled slowly. "Give him a kiss, then."

She passed her arms around his neck and obliged enthusiastically. So enthusiastically that he was soon groaning into her mouth. "Jane," he breathed raggedly, "how am I supposed to be teasing and aloof when you keep seducing me?"

"You can do it if you really put your mind to it," she suggested earnestly, sliding her hands into his hair.

"You also need to do your part, my lady," he said, drawing back at last with a sigh. "I can only be Bardulf if you'll be my innocent, outraged Jane."

She regarded him with a pucker between her brows. "Well, I daresay you will outrage me again upon the morrow," she said hopefully.

"I daresay I will," he agreed, unable to hide his smile.

And sure enough, he did.

THE END

Look out for more books in The Brides of Karadok series coming out in 2025 including Gunnilde's story:

A Most Forgettable Girl

Cheerful Gunnilde Payne is hiding a bruised heart behind her bright smile. When her friend invites her to spend some time away from her provincial home, she jumps at the chance. Distraction is just what she needs to forget the sad disappointment of her childhood sweetheart getting betrothed to another.

All is going well, until Gunnilde overhears herself rudely dismissed by two knights as "nice, plain, and utterly forgettable." Poor Gunnilde is mortified, but as soon as the thoughtless words left his lips, someone starts to notice she has plenty of charm after all.

If you enjoyed this book, please consider leaving me a rating on Goodreads, Amazon, Bookbub or wherever else you leave your reviews. I would be very grateful.

You can find my website at: www.alicecoldbreath.com where you can sign up for my monthly newsletter and find out what I am up to.

Also, please do check out some of my other stories! Many thanks, Alice.

www.ingramcontent.com/pod-product-compliance
Lightning Source LLC
Chambersburg PA
CBHW032257020726
47495CB00001B/139